To Gil
many [...]
bringing the idea to
me in the first place —
and to Margaret.

with love,

Paddy

[the end is now indelibly
imprinted with an image
of Giles reading during
the Soho Chinese festival]

27-5-81

THE GOLDEN VEIL

By the same author

Novels

Lying-in
A Fleshly School
Linsey-Woolsey
Paradise
A Pillar of Cloud

Biography

Gerard Manley Hopkins
A Most Unsettling Person:
Patrick Geddes (1854-1932)

Guidebook:

Poets' London

THE GOLDEN VEIL

A novel based on the life
of
Elizabeth Siddall

by Paddy Kitchen

Hamish Hamilton
London

First Published in Great Britain 1981
by Hamish Hamilton Ltd
Garden House 57-59 Long Acre LONDON WC2E 9JZ

Paddy Kitchen
 The Golden Veil
 1. Title
 823′.914[F]   PR6061.18

ISBN 0-241-10584-6

Printed in Great Britain by
St Edmundsbury Press, Bury St Edmunds, Suffolk

To Doris Ena Kitchen, my mother

Chapter One

Snow falling; white flakes on the grey air like the flecks on spotted muslin. Feather-light crystals layering mud, brick, chimneys and garden until, gradually and silently, everything was covered. The barges in the distance on the river had a rim of white on their folded sails; the cobbled main streets presented a briefly smooth surface soon to be rucked and ridged by the first horse-buses and hansoms to start the evening journey home from the city. In a pocket of London where Bermondsey, Walworth and Southwark met in a network of shops, pubs, houses, tanneries and market gardens, a small girl came out of the terrace-house of a friend and stared.

Objects which had been brown or grey or sooty earlier in the afternoon were now white. The narrow street, called Star Place, which separated her from Number Eight, her home, was as pristine as laundered linen. Mr Searle had taken in the old furniture which usually lay untidily outside his shop, and the huge asylum for deaf and dumb children that blocked the sky at the end of the street was blurred by a curtain of eddying snow.

Lizzy thrust her fists tightly into the ends of her woollen shawl. Playing in a dark back room, she and her friend Violet had had no intimation of the snow. Although cold, she looked at the transformation with the absorbed delight of someone standing in the first warm sunshine of spring. She gave a deep sigh, and caught some snowflakes on the brown woollen lumps of her fists. They were wide, floppy flakes, scattered treasure. She looked upwards, trying to imagine what was taking place above the dense grey and white swirl. Her heart seemed to expand at this magical proof that the whole world could be changed in an afternoon.

A figure loomed before her. Mr Greenacre's bright, fishy eyes gleamed, and she noticed soft splodges of white on his leather jerkin and wiry hair. For a few seconds neither of them spoke, and Lizzy felt that this neighbour, whom she had known all her life, had changed as radically as her surroundings. But he had not been

1

transformed into something exciting and lovely. He had taken on the threatening uncertainty that clung to so many unknown men.

'You'll be wanting a lift, Lizzy,' he said firmly.

She wanted to say, 'No, no, I do not,' but Mr Greenacre had carried her across the mud and puddles in the street ever since she had been old enough to leave the house on her own.

She looked down at her slippered feet, and suddenly she was lifted high and tilted against his shoulder so that — bobbing up and down — she could see the tracks he made in the snow. They were not straight tracks, depositing her in front of the door opposite, but slanted to the corner of the street, past the end of the row of houses and round to where narrow back gardens ran down into a connecting lane. She had time to notice the end of a carpet bag he carried in his other hand, as it bumped backwards and forwards against his leg in time to his walk. It was a dirty bag, with a large stain in the shape of a fiddle.

He walked up the path in a few strides, and slid her gently down onto the doorstep. Then he patted her cheek.

'Safe and sound, Lizzy. Safe and sound.'

She muttered, 'Thank you, Mr Greenacre.' His hand had seemed to linger against her face, as though it were slightly sticky. It reminded her of when her mother made paste with flour and water so that she and Annie could stick treasures into their scrapbook. She lifted the latch, and went into the warm kitchen.

Immediately her mother asked sharply: 'What *have* you been doing? What *have* you been doing?' And a bowl of cold water was poured from the brown jug, and her face wiped with a scrap of flannel. When the flannel was rinsed, the water was pale red.

'I cannot see a wound,' said her mother. 'Does your face hurt?'

'No, mother.' Then, although it did not really follow: 'Mr Greenacre carried me home.'

'Did he touch your face?'

'Just when he said goodbye. Like father does.'

Annie, sitting by the stove sewing and already in a more grownup world than Lizzy by virtue of her extra four years, said: 'I expect he had a cut finger.'

'Hmm,' said her mother.

Lyddy, a year younger than Lizzy, said, 'Perhaps it's blackberries,' remembering how they had walked down to the fields in Camberwell in the autumn to pick blackberries, and how

2

frightened she had been when she realised that all their mouths and fingers were stained a reddish purple.

'Blackberries!' snorted Annie, and Lyddy blushed, not knowing that fruits could only be expected according to their season.

The barrier made of wooden boxes in the corner suddenly broke open as Tump, the toddler girl, pushed hastily away from baby James who had started to cry and to smell simultaneously. Annie automatically put down her sewing and went to deal with the matter. Mrs Siddall told Lizzy that the next time it snowed she was to come home at once.

Lizzy kept silent. She knew there was no point in arguing, in saying she had not known that the whole outside world was turning white. She went to the window, but it was all steamed up, so she started towards the inside door.

'Where are you going, Lizzy?'

'To the parlour.'

'There's no fire. You mustn't get it untidy. Why don't you sit here? The kitchen knives and forks need polishing.'

Lizzy remembered she had polished them just a few days ago. 'I won't be long.' She hesitated for a second in case her mother was finally going to prevent her, then hearing no brusque word, she went quickly from the room, making as little noise with the door as possible.

The air in the dark corridor and dark-panelled parlour was deathly cold. A fire was laid in case her father came home with a friend, but if he was alone it would not be lit, and they would all crowd hugger-mugger into the kitchen. Lizzy went to the window and drew the curtain aside. It was beginning to get dark. The space between the rows of houses was still filled with snowflakes, and the grey air was now tinged with sulphury yellow. The ground was thickly covered, and the prints made by Mr Greenacre were very nearly obliterated.

Tentatively Lizzy touched her cheek with her cold fingers. It felt absolutely smooth and shiny where her mother had scrubbed it. She picked up a thick strand of her long hair in one hand and wound it tightly round the wrist of the other. She thought it looked like a cuff of copper-coloured silk on the dress of a rich lady.

It was the snow Lizzy really remembered — it had gone on falling for five days — and the ride home across Mr Greenacre's shoulder. But her own memories got tangled with the grownups' furtive fire-

3

side reminiscences, and what she learned from them was that she had been taken to a hanging.

Along with many hundreds of other people, the Siddalls had walked through the night to Newgate in order to get a good view of the murderer's death at dawn. The coffee stalls for the five o'clock workers had been opening as the crowds surged up the streets towards the gallows outside the prison, and her father always said he'd never had a more welcome hot drink. But Lizzy could summon up no picture of that bleak, cold morning.

Yet it seemed as if she had always known that the laundress, Hannah Brown, was connected with the snowy day she met Mr Greenacre, and somehow the carpet bag had always been part of the story too. Certainly both Hannah and Mr Greenacre had disappeared from the neighbourhood, and his shop in the next street, from which Annie used to buy spicy Amalgamated Candy, had remained shuttered for years. Something that was said among the grownups made Lizzy aware that unmentionable things had been carried about in the snow by Mr Greenacre, and instinctively she had lumped herself in with these things and remembered the red stickiness her mother had rubbed away so fiercely from her face.

It was a long time later, when she was eleven or twelve, that she learned the full story. Her mother had brought home some butter wrapped in a sheet of paper torn from a journal, and — as they always did — Lizzy carefully flattened the paper for re-use. Clean paper went in one pile, stained or greasy in another. Besides the fragments of dull-looking, close-together printing, there was part of a verse on the paper. Lizzy had always loved the rhymes her mother wrote for them in the scrapbook. She liked the way they had shape and made a pattern on the page, unlike the words in the few books owned by her father. She started to read the grease-marked paper, on which only one of the verses was fully intact:

> Ah, sad and strange as in dark summer dawns
> The earliest pipe of half awaken'd birds
> To dying ears, when unto dying eyes
> The casement slowly grows a glimmering square;
> So sad, so strange, the days that are no more.

The mournful words entranced her, their smooth sound opening up quiet spaces in her mind, and she said: 'May I keep this verse, mother? For the scrapbook?'

4

Her mother glanced at it. 'All grease marked! But if you wish. I'll press the butter out with a hot iron. It's a long time since you opened the old book now that Annie's grown.'

Later that day she removed the butter as much as possible with the flat-iron, and left Lizzy to mix a little dab of paste and find the scrapbook in the corner cupboard in the parlour.

Lizzy looked through the drawings and verses which she and Annie had collected, and re-read the rhymes in her mother's careful copper-plate. Some of these were ones other London children knew, but many were the ones recited by her father in the queer northern voice he could put on. 'Bits of Sheffield' these verses were called, representing a strange and far-off place where the Siddalls had once been rich and where the making of scissors and cutlery approached the realms of art. Her father now mended watches and jewellery, and Lizzy had always gathered that this, though a useful trade, was inferior to that of cutler as once pursued by his father, and his father's father, in Sheffield.

She stuck the verse carefully onto a new page, wondering why neither Tump nor James had become interested in the scrapbook — though when she came to think about it, it was not very surprising. Tump could never settle quietly to anything, and was usually flashing about, her startling red hair making her easy to pick out in a group of noisy children, while James always wanted to be making things so that from the age of five he had insisted on going off each morning to their father's shop to 'help'. And then there was Harry, born three years after James, who they had gradually come to realise would never be much good at doing anything, though he was willing to fetch and carry, and very affectionate. She had once heard a neighbour say that Mrs Siddall had been 'too old' when she bore Harry. Lizzy had gone to the family bible, which had all their names and birthdates on the flyleaf, and worked out that her mother had been forty when Harry was born.

She realised she'd forgotten Lyddy. But then she knew only too well why Lyddy hadn't contributed to the scrapbook. For a year or so, when Annie was growing further and further away from her, Lizzy had clung jealously to anything they still did together, and had refused to turn to Lyddy, so much closer in age, for companionship. The scrapbook had been one of the several things she had refused to share with her. Seeing the book neglected now, and with Annie far away from home in service in Sheffield, she felt a

5

pang of guilt.

Closing the pages, she noticed that the pocket at the back in which she and Annie used to store things before they were pasted in, had some yellowing newspaper cuttings in it which she had never seen before. Curiously, she slid them out and began to read.

All too quickly the hazy memories of Mr Greenacre, which had slipped further and further from her mind until they were only faintly recalled by a day of falling snow, revived. And all the gaps in the story were vividly filled.

It seemed that on the first day of the five-day snowfall, in the year when the newsprint of the longest cutting was still white, Mr Greenacre had killed forty-year-old Hannah Brown, a laundress whom he was due to marry the following week. The crime had taken place in the house where Sarah Gale lived alone with her baby son. It had been some time before the murder was detected. Parts of female bodies were found: legs in an osier bed, a trunk in a field, a head in the river. Gradually they were pieced together to make up one body. When, after a chapel service some time after the snow had melted, Mr Greenacre had suddenly screamed out: 'My God! Hell's on fire!', no one had taken much notice, for he was known to be an occasional epileptic. But at last the disappearance of Hannah Brown, the piecing together of the pickled parts of the body, and the fact that Mr Greenacre had actually called on Hannah's landlady (probably while carrying her head in his carpet bag) to say their wedding was 'indefinitely postponed', came together in the minds of the police and he was arrested and tried for murder, while Sarah was tried and imprisoned as an accomplice. She was given morphia in her cell in Newgate on the morning he was hanged so that she would not hear the abuse of the crowd, but they shouted so loudly that she did hear, and fainted. The actual hanging was an incompetently grisly business. Greenacre danced in the air so long that the executioner jumped on his shoulders to speed things up, until finally the rope broke and they both fell, one dead and one alive, into the trap below. (So many Londoners from the East End, it seemed, had witnessed the event that the word 'greenacre' was later reported to have become dockland slang for a set of bales falling violently out of a sling.)

Lizzy remembered Mr Greenacre's shoulder, and the carpet bag, and his fingers clammy against her cheek. Then, half-running and half-fainting, she rushed blindly through the house to the privy outside, where she was sick.

That night she had The Dream, and the next morning her difficulty with food began.

Some nights The Dream filled the bedroom Lizzy shared with Lyddy like a fluid, shape-changing ghoul in a storybook.

They slept under the rafters, two narrow beds separated by a small window that almost touched the floor. In winter they would wrap any spare, tattered fragments of quilt or cloth around their chilblained feet and ankles, and in summer the moth-filled air that came through the window at night did not take away the heat that had soaked through the roof all day.

They were not companionable room-mates. Lizzy claimed she needed absolute silence before she could sleep, and Lyddy never lay down properly. She used to prop herself up against the rails of the bed, a faint whistling wheeze accompanying each inhalation of breath, and she would fidget at intervals throughout the night.

It was in this uneasy atmopshere, each girl irritably aware of the other, that The Dream, instead of gradually fading after that first, memory-provoked time, took hold. It was coloured red, and its atmosphere was male. In it, Lizzy was always on her own, in a large, but enclosed, space. The shape would slowly advance from the edge towards the centre, towering over her, making her fear not so much violence and noise as smothering and deafness, and she would feel defeated and ugly and totally powerless. Waking, she had a sense of humiliation and then everything seemed sticky and stale.

The first time she lay awake for the rest of the night, listening to Lyddy's difficult breathing and thinking of Hannah Brown. When she went down in the morning, after helping her mother with the ashes and the sweeping, she sat down to breakfast and bit off a mouthful of bread and butter. It seemed to swell and expand inside her mouth until it was as though she had engorged a giant sponge. She could not swallow, nor breathe, and she had to go outside and loosely spit the bread on the grass. There was only a very small amount, soon seized by a pair of sparrows.

Her mother simply thought she was constipated, and gave her a dose on the days when she noticed she was not eating. Tump slyly scooped up any food Lizzy pushed aside. Her father seldom noticed ailments in others, particularly females. Only Harry tried to break off small, choice morsels of his own food and offer them to her. But he was severely reprimanded by their mother.

Every time Lizzy went into the parlour, she was aware of the scrapbook lying in the corner cupboard with the old newspaper cuttings in its back pocket. All the other objects in the room which normally intrigued her, the leather-bound book containing her father's music scores, the china plaque showing the coat of arms of Siddalls past, the dark parchment kept in a drawer whose confusing script was said to grant the freedom of the City of Sheffield to an ancestor, all paled to insignificance beside the account of the murderer with bloody hands who had carried her through the snow.

Then one day she walked into the parlour and her father's violin, instead of being propped as usual so that its strings and frets faced into the room, was leaning against the wall with its plain, gleaming back to her. The simple dark shape of the instrument seemed to numb her mind, and she had difficulty in catching her breath. Then suddenly she felt so weak she had to sit on a stool, hugging her knees, with her spine and head bent right over. A ray of sun pierced a gap in the curtains and reached her hair, making it gleam like precious cloth woven with threads of pale gold and copper as it almost touched the floor.

The violin-shape would not leave her mind. She saw it, bumping backwards and forwards, on the carpet bag. She tried to picture her father lifting his fiddle, tuning it carefully, and playing the sweet tunes he loved to sing, but the instrument remained obstinately by the hearth, its back turned.

The shape was like a figure with no arms or legs or head . . .

Her face was pressed tightly against the side of her hands as they grasped her knees, and she bit one finger hard to stop herself from crying out. She must force herself to go back into the kitchen, back to Harry's games and Tump's tempers and Lyddy's dutiful expression as she did the mending, and receive whatever curt remark her mother had in store. She must not sit here in the room facing the street where a murderer had carried her.

That night The Dream came again. It was bound to, she knew. It was the only time she thought of telling Lyddy about it before she tried to go to sleep. But then she watched her sister preparing for the night — fixing an old bolster against her bedhead to supplement the only pillow they were each allowed — and did not feel assured of understanding. Lyddy so dreaded night time that she became

8

virtually incapable of normal communication just before she started each uncomfortable semi-vigil. Mrs Siddall had, at Lizzy's pleading, taken her to a doctor, but he had been quite adamant that her lungs were in good order — that is, not consumptive. Nervous asthma was not a complaint either he or Mrs Siddall would have considered with sympathy.

This time The Dream, after enticing, mocking, engulfing and terrifying Lizzy, did not finally wake her, as usually happened, but continued. The red presence gradually began to recede and shrink, until at last there was just a violin-shaped stain on a skirting board. Then a bowl of water was brought by a woman, and the stain was lifted up and became limp, like cloth, instead of rigid on wood. It was dipped into the water, gently at first, then briskly, up and down, up and down. It was only after the cloth had been taken away by the woman that Lizzy got near to the bowl. The water inside was stained pale red.

She woke trying to push herself nearer and nearer to the edge of the bed. Its hard frame was sticking into her hip, and she felt she was desperately trying to get herself away from Annie. Then she heard Lyddy's breathing, and for the first time was glad of that plaintive, faint whistle.

Before Annie went to Sheffield, she and Lizzy had always shared a bed. For years this had made Lizzy feel warm and secure — and important, since when Annie came to bed after her, she could ask questions and relate her worries, and be granted the sole attention of the one member of the family who always seemed both kind and competent. Then one morning she had woken up to see Annie standing at the other side of the bed, drawing the blankets up towards the pillow, with an expression of totally uncharacteristic fear in her eyes. She would not answer Lizzy's pleas of 'What's the matter, Annie? What's wrong?', but briefly told her to keep still, and then left the room. Lizzy had been absolutely rigid, her heart thumping in her ribcage.

Then Mrs Siddall had come into the room, her grey hair still down, and without her apron. To Lizzy this was even more unnerving, since their mother always had her hair up and her apron securely tied no matter how early in the morning she went downstairs.

'Get up, Lizzy,' she said sharply. 'And get dressed. Over there — in the corner.'

Lizzy took her neatly folded clothes and went to face the wall. But at one point, ignorance seeming even more disturbing than knowledge, she turned her head quickly to look over her shoulder.

Their bed was stripped. And her mother was holding up the undersheet which was stained with blood in the shape of a lop-sided violin.

A month later it had been arranged through a one-time friend of Mr Siddall that Annie should take up a post as kitchenmaid with a 'good' family in Sheffield. After that morning, Lizzy had been aware of several grave conversations taking place between her mother and Annie.

Nothing at all was said to her about the matter, and instinct prevented her from asking whether Annie was hurt. Her mind connected it with the day they had found blood on her cheek and she had not been hurt.

Some days were better than others as far as eating was concerned, and the summer was best of all, when there was fruit — clean, sweet and fresh — and especially when her mother filled the flowered china bowl with blackcurrants, cherries and strawberries. But in the winter, when vegetables were scarce and fruit unobtainable, and salt meat appeared daily on the table, Lizzy went through agonies. She simply could not eat the meat, and watching her father — and latterly James — smearing it thickly with mustard, made her feel worse. Her mother would have been more strict, making her eat it, had money not been so short. As it was, to have one member of the family who ate no meat, hardly any cheese, and only small helpings of bread and potatoes, was a saving. But she feared that Lizzy would not be robust enough to work in service, and might later be a drain on family resources.

She had however become the most skilful in the family at sewing; any jagged tear was always given to Lizzy to mend. One day Mrs Siddall asked if she would like to try her hand at making a dress for herself. Her old brown one was now too small and would have to be passed on to Lyddy, and her blue one would become her everyday dress. If they could find some strong, cheap material, she could make a new Sunday dress. Mrs Searle next door would help her cut out a pattern.

Lizzy stared at her mother, speechless. She was fourteen years old now, tall and thin, her pale face with pointed chin and heavily-lidded eyes saved from unhealthy delicacy by a scattering of tiny freckles. And her hair, which — unlike Tump's — could in all honesty be given the fashionable label 'auburn', was springy and thick. She was not pretty, but in her quiet way she was beginning to look both dignified and striking.

Mrs Siddall's suggestion gave her a feeling she experienced very, very seldom — one of total happiness. To have a new piece of cloth, not something already worn, and to be able to fashion it for herself. She could not imagine anything more satisfying. Every stitch would be perfect, and the dress would have more style than any ever seen before in Star Place.

Lizzy proceeded carefully. She knew her mother would not allow her to have light-coloured material, nor material that could not easily be washed. She went privately to visit Mrs Searle to make sure that when the time came Mrs Searle's advice on cutting a pattern would achieve the sort of sleeves and collar that Lizzy wanted, and that she would find a way of avoiding the severely-cut type of skirt her mother preferred. After a great deal of thought, she decided the dress should be grey, trimmed with blue. There was a particular shade of grey that was both quite dark, yet soft, and the trimming would be the colour of a velvet cloak she had once seen when her father took them to the zoo.

She never told anyone of her plans for the material, but when she walked back from Elephant and Castle with her mother carrying two brown paper parcels, one of them contained a length of cloth the deep, soft colour of pigeon feathers, and the other some braid and binding the colour of rosemary flowers.

Mrs Searle said, truthfully, that she had never met a girl who picked up the rudiments of dressmaking so quickly, and Mrs Siddall experienced some satisfaction as Lizzy sat hour after hour, executing perfect seams and finishings, never trying to rush, but never getting bored. It meant she should not have too much difficulty in finding work for Lizzy.

When the dress was finished even her father said, 'Lizzy looks quite a lady,' and Harry, who was five, dribbled slightly and wanted to stroke her arm all the time. Lizzy got Mr Searle to give her a jagged piece of cracked mirror, and insisted on putting it up in her bedroom. Lyddy said it was ugly, and that there was no room, but it meant that Lizzy could go upstairs and look at herself in private. She did not particularly like what she saw, but she was absorbed by it, imagining ways of making it look better.

11

One Sunday afternoon when she was wearing the dress and out walking with Violet, they met a neighbour accompanied by a shy boy Lizzy had not seen before. He was the neighbour's nephew setting out for his home in Wandsworth after a visit, and his name was William. It was decided that the girls should accompany him for part of the walk, and that the neighbour should return home to her young family.

William, who was sixteen, had sad brown eyes with thick lashes and he gazed mutely at Lizzy all the time his aunt was speaking. Lizzy, who usually avoided boys because they were rough, looked at his fine dark hair, and at the narrow wrists sticking out of his worn jacket, and thought that he was beautiful. She would have liked to cut him a new jacket, in dark blue cloth, finished with a row of ebony buttons.

Violet tried to conduct a proper grownup and ladylike conversation, but since neither of the others would play their part properly, she soon lapsed into her usual gossipy chatter about the goings-on in their street. Lizzy tried desperately to think of some way of stopping her, and also of discovering the only thing she wanted to know — whether William was coming to visit his aunt again soon — but she failed, remaining completely tongue-tied until they shook hands near Clapham Common where she managed to gasp 'Goodbye'. During the walk back, which seemed very long and dreary, she was nervous that Violet would discover how she felt, and went to elaborate ends to avoid discussing William. Half of Violet's gossip concerned who was 'sweet' on whom, and she would have died rather than be included in it.

Since ironing the butter out of one of Tennyson's verses, Mrs Siddall had kept a look out for any more poetry arriving with the groceries. She did not publicly give approval to time spent on such things, but privately she was rather admiring that Lizzy could get so much out of a few rhyming lines. She even boasted of it — in a restrained, careful way — to one of her husband's friends, and when he called one day with a book of Tennyson's poems especially for Lizzy, she could not refuse the gift.

Lizzy found some of the poems rather obscure, but there were others which she loved. And after her meeting with William *Mariana* in particular seemed to take on a special meaning.

> She only said, 'My life is dreary,
> He cometh not,' she said;

She said, 'I am aweary, aweary,
I would that I were dead!'

She would murmur this over and over to herself, picturing William's thickly-fringed eyes, and feeling exquisitely sad. At first she daydreamed that he would return, and that she would meet him in the street, and they would go for a silent walk to the river, gazing together at the ships and barges and sharing faraway thoughts. But after a while it became more difficult to picture him in her mind, and new pictures formed from the words in the poems. Pictures of bowers and flowers and castles and maiden princesses. And the youths who also entered these pictures, while not entirely unlike William, were not quite like him either. They were something of an improvement.

Out of these pictures she started to write poetry of her own. She did not know where the words came from, and she made no attempt to fashion them carefully, but on some evenings she felt forced to leave the often claustrophobic family circle and go up-stairs to write and write. She had difficulty in getting enough paper, begging James to bring any scraps he could from the shop, and sometimes on cold evenings her mother would come up and order her to stop.

'You can't hide yourself away up here, Lizzy. If it's decent rhyme you're writing you can share it. It's a waste of a candle. You'll catch your death of cold. There's no wonder you can't take nourishment when you freeze your bones up here.' The tirade had many variations.

Lizzy was quite blank in her mind as to whether what she was doing was wrong or not. There were some words she loved to write and she used them again and again. Words such as feather, pale, moon, flowing, white, soul, distant, roses, tresses, dawn. She never used the words red, sunset, laughter, heart, sparkling, tempest, wild or snow.

On warm evenings she would sometimes go out, murmuring that she might call for Violet, and would hurry straight down the street, past the armless and legless cripple who begged the daylight hours away outside the asylum, past the men gathered outside the public house, down a narrow street bordered by a black, windowless, stinking tannery, to a series of lanes that led towards the market gardens. At a point where two lanes converged there was a patch of waste ground, about a quarter of an acre, where elder

13

bushes and high grasses grew undisturbed, and white butterflies touched the flowers of tall mallow plants. Lizzy would slide in among the growth, treading gently, and go to sit in a small area under the bushes, where the grass was thin and green, and the leaves made a roof over her head. Here she would hug her knees, let the silence wrap her round, and feel safe. Then, gradually, she would begin to notice life on a completely different scale from the one she was used to. A spider no bigger than a pinhead would drop on invisible gossamer from the tip of a blade of grass to the ground; a thrush suddenly spurting song would sound as loud as a brass band; two ants dragging a dead beetle across a patch of ground seemed like huntsmen bringing home a dead stag through a long valley. She would watch this world till dusk made the detail dim.

The things she saw on her patch of waste ground never appeared in her poetry. She made no links between that world and the feelings she poured into words. Those words came from her floating mind and from echoes of poems she had read. The elder flowers and insects were quite separate.

Mrs Siddall found that she did not worry about Lizzy too much when she went out in the evening. She had worried about Annie, not because she had thought Annie unreliable, but because with her curves and confidence she could not help but attract men. But Lizzy was not the type: thin, and with a rather disdainful expression, she was the sort people left alone. The next one she'd need to look out for would be Tump. They'd have to start calling her by her proper name, Clara, one day, and she'd be one of those who'd leap from being a girl to a woman within a week, with her combination of cheek and flashiness. Lyddy . . . Lyddy was such a child, though barely a year younger than Lizzy; she'd conceived again before she had enough strength for another child, and the baby'd weighed just under four pounds. If only Lyddy would lie down and go to sleep properly at night, she might put on a bit of flesh and grow stronger.

It had been quite clear in Mrs Siddall's mind for some time that Lizzy would go to work at a dressmaking establishment. When, therefore, she decided the time had come to discuss the practical details surrounding this plan, she was both angry and surprised that her daughter vehemently opposed the idea.

'I'm not going to one of those places,' she protested. 'Stitching seams and seams and seams for hours and hours and hours.' When Lizzy was angry, her normally soft voice did not grow much louder, but it did become very sibilant, so that the s's seemed to merge and hiss like a frightened serpent.

'You sat sewing the seams on that dress you're wearing with never a murmur.'

'But this was for me.'

'What difference does that make?'

Lizzy sighed impatiently. To sew seams to improve her own appearance was a positive action; but to sew them to clothe some anonymous person better off than herself was pointless.

'D' you think,' Mrs Siddall went on, 'you're going to be able to sit around, your head filled with fancy ideas, doing nothing? When I've got one child on my hands who's never going to be fit to earn his living?'

Lizzy felt apprehensive. Of course she knew she would have to work — one day. But she had not faced up to the fact that the day had almost arrived. She still felt so much younger than Annie had seemed when she had gone away.

'There's no suitable work locally,' Mrs Siddall continued, 'you know that. You're not strong enough to go away, like Annie. You have one skill, you'd better use it. Not that it'll be easy to get you fixed with a good establishement. And with your present attitude you'd be lucky to be taken on as a cheap slop worker.'

Unexpectedly Lizzy felt tears come to her eyes, and a painful constriction in her throat. She clenched her teeth together, forbidding herself to cry. She'd once had a friend whose mother was a slop worker, and the two children had taken a message to her in the dark room where she sat sewing cheap shirts, fourteen hours a day, with six other women. Lizzy could still smell the misery and despair in that room.

She tried to substitute a cheerful memory, to block the tears. As often before, she resurrected the day they had gone to the zoo. She remembered the gleaming primrose-yellow ribbons on the bonnet of a lady in front of her as she stood on tiptoe to try to see the wombats.

'I'll work in a milliner's,' she said.

Mrs Siddall had begun to think Lizzy was going to insist on a long and selfish battle. As far as she was concerned, there was precious little difference between a dressmaking and a millinery establishment. The difficulty lay in persuading one of a decent class in either trade to take Lizzy on. If she was successful, their weekly

15

income would be somewhat improved; and there would also be some prospects for the future — provided the girl was industrious.

To Lizzy, millinery was something glamorous and decorative. Rich people had many new hats. Poor people just wore the same bonnets year after year and never trimmed them with primrose ribbons. Dressmaking could, of course, be glamorous, but even the most beautiful dress had yards of monotonous seams, and somehow stitching along contours measured from a stranger's body would be unpleasant as well as boring.

A few days later, she came down in the morning to find her mother wearing her best clothes.

'I'm leaving in half an hour,' said Mrs Siddall, 'to see Cousin Lucy. You're to take charge of everything.'

No further explanation was given, but Lizzy sensed it was to do with her future employment. During the morning, as she peeled and chopped vegetables for soup, washed dirty clothes, and tried to keep Harry amused, Tump was being particularly aggravating. She was barely eleven years old, and what was termed 'knowing'.

'Violet went down to the common with Edward last night,' she announced in a sort of sing-song chant. Then, when Lizzy didn't reply, she added: 'Do you go down to the common with anybody?'

'Tump, be quiet.'

'Well, do you?'

'No.'

'I shall.'

'Of course you won't'

'It's only a bit of old common.'

'Why don't you take Harry for a walk?'

'Oh — let him take himself.' Tump turned her back, and after fidgetting with objects on the dresser, went into the garden.

Harry stared after her. It was difficult to know quite how much he took in of other people's words and tones of voice. But it was apparent that he liked Lizzy, whose voice was soft, best in the family. The others, even Lyddy, were apt to adopt a bracing tone when speaking to him.

He had a narrow face with a sweet expression that only became odd-looking when his mouth sometimes sagged. Lizzy was both flattered by his affection and guilty that she did not often respond to it. Sometimes she loved Harry very much and wanted to protect him, at others she wanted to reject him, finding his 'difference'

16

unacceptable. She had seen grown men who were feeble-minded and had felt repulsion.

Her mother had not returned by the time her father and James were due home from the shop. She asked Lyddy to set the table, persuaded Harry to wash his hands and face, and told Tump she would have no tea at all if she did not bring in the washing and damp it ready for ironing. For a few moments, just as they were all doing as she bid, she had a feeling of acute pleasure. The chores were all done, the kitchen looked welcoming, and she had picked some yellow daisies from the garden and put them in a copper jug on the table. Perhaps that was how the future should be. A home of her own, however modest, where she could organize things as she wished, look after a young husband, and — more dimly in the future — have children. She was apprehensive of her mother returning and of probably being told exactly how and when she was to go out into the world and work. She'd be old enough to marry in two years.

The picturesque domesticity was soon unsettled. Harry started rubbing the soap on to his hair, Tump dropped Lyddy's clean petticoat in the garden and when Mr Siddall and James came home they both demanded to know why her mother hadn't returned, and didn't seem to notice that she had provided them with a perfectly good tea. Lizzy decided that she would certainly not marry until asked to do so by a gentleman of considerable means.

'Do you know why mother has gone to see Cousin Lucy?' she asked her father, when tea was almost finished.

'I've an idea.'

'Is it to do with finding work for me?'

'Your mother'll tell you when she wants to.'

'What do you think I should do, father?'

'Do, Lizzy?' Her father looked at her with some amusement. He had a permanent expression of hauteur combined with humour, and Lizzy did not like to be teased by him. She began to feel uncomfortable. 'That's for your mother to decide.'

'But supposing she decides something I don't want to do?'

'She's the person to judge best what you *can* do. Just as I'm the person to train James.'

Lizzy looked across the table at her brother, small for ten years old, but jauntily trying to ape his father in the way he sat bolt upright away from the back of the chair. Lizzy felt her own body curve and droop.

When Mrs Siddall at last came home she was clearly very tired, though did not say so. She removed her boots, for the soles of her feet were burning with having walked so far, and asked Lizzy to put extra sugar in her tea. Everyone became quiet, waiting for her to speak. To have her out all day, wearing her Sunday dress, on an unspecified mission, made the children uneasy. Lizzy was both afraid and a little self-important.

'You'll have to stand up straighter than that, Lizzy,' said her mother suddenly, 'when you go to see Mrs Tozer. She won't want a girl with sloppy ways.'

'You've fixed her up then, have you?' asked Mr Siddall.

'As far as I can. Mrs Tozer will see her. And if she finds her suitable she'll take her on.'

Lizzy did not like the sound of the name 'Tozer'. It was rough and unfeminine.

'A good class establishment?' Mr Siddall enquired further.

'The largest milliner's in Cranbourn Alley.'

'Cranbourn Alley, eh? The West End.'

'Well it's Cranbourn Street now. They've widened it and put up new buildings. It's quite handsome.'

The West End. Lizzy turned the phrase over in her mind. It spelled fashion, and excitement, and possibility. Not any particularly defined possibility, but something larger and brighter and more luxurious than anything that ever happened to the people who lived and worked in Star Place.

'Is Lizzy leaving home?' asked Tump, her curiosity apparently untinged with dismay.

'Oh — surely not!' Lyddy gave a little gasp, for if Lizzy were going, like Annie, then inexorably it would soon be her turn.

From the corner by the fire, where he was playing with a wooden doll, Harry shouted, 'No! No, no!'

Lizzy looked across at him, suddenly aware that there would never be people outside his family who would care for Harry.

James continued to mend a handle that had broken off one of the saucepans, a task that entailed occasional brief but loud hammerings.

'She'll be a dayworker,' said Mrs Siddall. 'If she's taken on. The hours are eight in the morning till eight at night. They can take their own dinner. And there's free tea and bread and butter in the afternoon.'

Lizzy, who was standing by the outside door, reached out and held tightly onto the latch. Eight in the morning till eight at night, walking three miles either way. It would need to be an elegant and wonderful milliner's to make that bearable. An empire of beauty with customers from the highest families.

'How much will she get?' asked Mr Siddall.

'Seven shillings to start with. If she's satisfactory the first week.'

He looked up at his daughter. 'Well, Lizzy,' he said. 'You'll be earning your keep.'

Lizzy barely nodded. The group in front of her seemed to have become unreal, no longer her family but a circle of strangers. She had become an outsider, and they were all judging her effect on their lives. No one was thinking of her. Her childhood, when inclusion in mealtimes and long domestic afternoons was automatic, was over. Six months ago her mother had lectured her for taking Lyddy to peer into the Vauxhall Gardens. And now suddenly she was to go alone, six days a week, to the West End. The figures in front of her blurred, and she found herself hurrying from the kitchen, up the two steep flights of wooden stairs to her bedroom. There she crouched on the floor by the window, and peered onto the roof of the neighbouring house. A sparrow was chirping loudly on the roof's ridge, busily diverting the attention of prowling cats from its nest in the eaves, where its mate was feeding the fledglings. Lizzy stared at the sparrow, so intent on its task, and for a brief moment envied the intensity of its purpose, the firmness of its voice, and the surety of its actions.

She went to look at herself in the mirror. Violet said that her eyelids made her look haughty. But she could not prevent them half-covering her eyes: that was how they naturally rested. Now she deliberately opened them wide, staring at her irises. The flecks of bright blue, green and grey fascinated her; magnified they would be like the plumage of a beautiful bird.

She stepped back from the mirror. Recently she had grown too tall for her old blue dress — it barely reached her ankles, and her bony shoulders pushed tightly against the thin cloth. Normally she came to bed at the same time as Lyddy, both of them undressing quickly, their backs turned as they put on their nightdresses. Now she began to feel curious about the appearance of her body, about the parts of it which were both intimate yet totally strange.

19

Slowly she began to take off her dress, her petticoat, stays and camisole.

When she was quite unclothed, she went hesitantly to stand in front of the cracked mirror. Her skin was very white, and the hair between her legs was gold like the hair on her head. She knew that already of course, but she had never seen it in a mirror before. She tilted her head back and felt her hair tickle her back. When she raised her arms her ribs stuck out, almost as though they could pierce her skin. Her breasts were wide and firm and shallow. She looked at them and knew she should feel guilty. But she did not. Tentatively she touched one flat, pink nipple.

'Lizzy! Lizzy!' Her mother's almost harsh shout up the stairs made her stiff with fear. If she should see her like this . . . She clutched her petticoat in front of her, put her head round the door and said as loudly as she could: 'I'm coming down. Just a minute.'

'I should think so too.' She heard the footsteps go away from the bottom of the stairs.

The sight of her clothes strewn on the bed horrified her. What had she been thinking of? Supposing her mother had actually come upstairs . . . She dressed as quickly as she could, and straightened her tumbled hair with quick strokes of her brush. Looking again in the mirror it occurred to her that while they might send that girl out to the work of their choice — the girl in the old dress with covered limbs — they could not in any way dictate to the undressed girl with white skin.

Everyone was sitting in the kitchen in the same places as she had left them. She walked over and sat near Harry.

'What do you mean by stalking out of the room like that?'

'I'm sorry, mother.'

'I've walked all over London today to seek advice and introductions on your behalf.'

'Yes . . .' Lizzy's voice petered out.

'What's the matter, Lizzy?'

'Nothing, father. I . . . I just wanted to think about it.'

'Well you'll have to stop thinking and start working,' said Mrs Siddall. 'I'm taking you to see Mrs Tozer tomorrow.'

Lizzy, who had been fiddling with her fingers in her lap, raised her head. As she did so, her chin was pushed forwards and her eyelids drooped. She looked proud in a manner that was touchingly vulnerable in a girl of fifteen, like a quiet figurehead on a

20

defenceless ship going into a storm.

'At what time do we leave?' she asked.

In the fashion league, Cranbourn Street was considered third-rate. It contained several milliners, and provided workmanlike approximations of a high fashion at a reasonable price. Locked between Leicester Square and Covent Garden, it was at the centre of the pursuits and smells of the city. An hotel on the corner exuded odours of French cooking from its restaurant; a grand dome across in Leicester Square housed the biggest globe in the world and provided hourly lectures; and nearby there were an iron foundry, a surgeon, a seal engraver and a lending library. A few minutes walk away, fashionable ladies shopped in Regent Street; and after dark, prostitutes paraded in the Haymarket.

Mrs Tozer was someone whose age and background were impossible to speculate upon. She always wore black, had roan-coloured hair that would not lie flat, and spoke as though she were permanently out of breath. As she herself was the first to say, she was on her feet nearly sixteen hours a day, hurrying between tasks and crises and customers and salesmen. To spend ten minutes with her was to feel quite worn out.

She told Mrs Siddall and Lizzy to go through the shop and wait just inside the workroom while she finished serving a customer. Lizzy picked her way between the polished mahogany stands topped with bonnets of gleaming straw and bright velvet, and followed her mother into the workroom. Here everything was much more dismal and dowdy, with six or seven girls working around a large, scrubbed table, the walls lined with shelves filled with hat boxes, the floor uncovered, and a grey light coming through one small window. One of the girls stopped working and stared at Lizzy with bold, brown eyes, but when an older woman put her head round a screen in the corner and shouted 'Mrs Soames wants wide ribbon' she quickly picked up her sewing.

Lizzy, depressed by what she saw, looked down at the floor where a small piece of peacock blue silk lay on the coarse floor-boards. Her mind fastened on this scrap of material, so bright and rich, and developed it into a full-skirted dress, clothing a fair princess, who waited by a lake of paler blue.

'This way, Mrs Siddall, this way, that's right, behind this screen, now this is Mrs Dunn who will mind the shop for a few minutes. She supervises the girls for me. Teaches them in the early stages. That's right. Now, let's take a look at you, miss. Stand up.'

The space behind the screen was cramped. Mrs Tozer sat behind a table heaped with samples and bills, and she waved Mrs Siddall to the only other chair. Lizzy stood uncomfortably with her back to the screen, making one last attempt to picture the princess by the lake before she gave her whole attention to Mrs Tozer. She discovered that this effort of the imagination gave her strength.

'Now, young lady, your full name.'

'Elizabeth Eleanor Siddall.'

'Age?'

'Fifteen, ma'am.'

'Are you able to arrive here at eight o'clock sharp every morning, and give your full attention to your work until eight o'clock in the evening?'

Lizzy hesitated. Then she was aware that her mother had shifted nervously, and knew that she could not let her down.

'Yes, ma'am. I think so.'

'There's no good thinking about it. It's the doing that matters. You will report on Monday, and Mrs Dunn will test you to see if your work is of sufficient quality. This is a very busy establishment. We have many customers, and they are all important. Every bonnet must be made with care and speed, and under no circumstance will shoddy work ever be allowed to leave the premises.'

Lizzy spoke very little as she and her mother walked home. There was no need to, for Mrs Siddall had a great deal to add to Mrs Tozer's exhortation on the standards that would be expected of her in the future.

In the early evening she fled to her patch of ground and lay under the elders. She didn't want to spend her life in that workroom. She didn't want to spend one day in it. The girl with the brown eyes had looked bold and bossy; she wouldn't be able to hold her own with girls like that. The work looked all right, shaping and blending colours and stuffs, learning the steps from Mrs Dunn, helping to make the bright objects that perched like an exotic flock on the mahogany stands. But not for twelve hours a day. Not to fill her whole life.

The next day all food seemed to swell in her mouth and choke her. She could only get down tea and water. Her father said she was over-excited at the prospect of working in the West End. Her mother called her wayward. Tump grabbed her portion of cheese.

Lyddy said mournfully: 'What will you take to work for your dinner on Monday if you can't swallow?'

'She'll take what she's given,' said Mrs Siddall. But she did especially buy some oranges so that one could be put in Lizzy's basket daily with her bread and cheese.

It was the second week that was the worst. During the first she was absorbing information from Mrs Dunn, and the girls were on their best behaviour. Also she was allowed home early on two occasions. But by the second week she was left on her own a good deal, with specific tasks to complete, and then the chatter of the girls began to alarm her, while the long hours made her so weary she would go to bed almost as soon as she arrived home. It was during this second week that the girl with brown eyes, Ellen, discovered that Lizzy lived in the same direction as her, and insisted they walk home together. Lizzy had not enjoyed her solitary journeys, but they were preferable to Ellen's bold way of looking at young men, and her brassy talk of kisses and walks in the park.

Then on Saturday afternoon there was a particular undercurrent of excitement in the workroom. Ellen and two of the other girls kept whispering and giggling, and when a bonnet was brought in for alteration, Mrs Tozer did not insist that someone stay until midnight if necessary to finish it. 'Monday will be soon enough. We have the Sabbath to observe, and all that precedes it will no doubt have to take its course as usual.'

Normally two of the girls put away their work at half past seven, brought in the bonnets one by one from the shop, and laid them gently on tissue paper in the hat boxes on the shelves. But that Saturday night all the girls except Lizzy joined in this ritual, and as she sat finishing off the seams on a lining, she felt awkward in her isolation. Mrs Tozer paused briefly on one of her never-ending journeys between the shop, workroom and her living quarters to speak to her.

'It's always the same on Saturdays. It's just a bit of fun. Eveyone's welcome to join.'

Lizzy looked up at her, not understanding.

'Finishing that seam are you?'

'Yes, ma'am.'

'You've worked well. I'll say that, Miss Siddall.' She paused. 'Siddall. Siddall. It's a bit of a grand-sounding name for a young thing. Miss Sid. Yes. That's a neat one. We'll call you Miss Sid in the workroom. Though if you've cause to come through to the shop, it'll be Miss Siddall of course. Now, put your work away. There might be a beau for you at the front.'

Lizzy, uncomprehending, folded away the embryo bonnet in a clean piece of linen. The other girls were darting and fussing about her, rushing back into the shop as soon as they had safely shelved another hatbox. Curious, she went to see what they were up to.

The shop seemed full of young men. Four or five of them, quite smartly dressed and carrying top hats, were pretending to help by lifting the bonnets from their stands and handing them — very, very slowly — to the girls. Ellen was smiling and talking and tossing her head at a blushing boy with sprouting yellow eyebrows, and even Mary, the quietest workhand after Lizzy, was talking to a scrawny man with a pock-marked face. Other men walking along the street would pause and peer in, apparently to decide whether it was worth their while to enter the shop. Millinery girls, though Lizzy was not to know it, were considered both fair game and reasonably respectable by the more discriminating young men in need of amorous adventure.

When Ellen saw her, she called: "Come along, Miss Siddall. Come and meet these fine young gentlemen.'

And suddenly Lizzy was aware that all the men were staring at her, and she blushed and hurried back to the workroom. Once she had put on her shawl — drawn over her head and wrapped around her hands to keep them warm — and Mrs Tozer had given the wages due to her with instructions to pass them straight to her mother (it did not occur to Lizzy to do otherwise), she tried to go unobtrusively through the shop and out into the street.

'Stop,' cried Ellen, 'Stop, Miss Siddall. You can't go without me.'

Lizzy looked at her mutely, aware that the pink and yellow young man was staring at her.

'You surely aren't going straight home, on a Saturday?' Ellen continued.

Lizzy nodded.

'Then I must accompany you.'

'No ...'

The young man seized his chance. 'No young lady will walk the streets alone while I am around. I shall be delighted to accompany both you young ladies to your places of residence.'

24

'Thank you,' said Ellen jauntily. 'We are most grateful. Aren't we, Miss Siddall?'

Lizzy did not speak. Ellen always went with her directly over Blackfriars Bridge to the point where their homeward paths diverged. She could not imagine walking all the way to her house in the company of this young man. And in fact, after much delay while Ellen dressed her hair and threw remarks at the other men, they did not walk to Blackfrairs but turned towards Westminster with Ellen claiming that 'A change of view is pleasant in fine weather', although in reality the evening was chilly and very blustery. It soon became apparent to Lizzy that her role was simply to act as a buffer while Ellen decided whether she did, or did not, wish to go to dance in Cremorne Gardens with this young man, and, embarrassed and disquieted, she left them abruptly to cross Westminster Bridge and make her long way home alone.

'Where have you been?' were her mother's first words.

'Coming home.' Lizzy sat, exhausted, in one of the chairs by the kitchen table, and laid her head on her arms. For a moment the warmth in the kitchen, after the sharp night air, made her dizzy. Her mind was filled with a picture of the workroom, with the long hours of stitching and snipping and sticking, with the exaggerated anticipation that preceded the lukewarm tea in the afternoon, with the waves of sleepiness that came over her in the early evening, with the parts of the girls' chatter which she did not fully understand, and above all with the feeling she had that Mrs Tozer regarded her as a good catch. She did not want to be caught for ever, churning out hats for women far richer than she could ever be to wear.

'You've got your money?'

Lizzy sat up slowly. 'Yes.' She felt for the coins and handed them over.

Mrs Siddall's face softened briefly as she counted them. 'You should be proud of this moment, Lizzy. Your first full week's wages. Now. Tell me why you have taken so long.'

Lizzy knew that her mother would object to any report about the young men, and about how Ellen had taken her off in the wrong direction, but she was too tired to think up a plausible alternative. Anyway, none of it was her fault. She couldn't have helped it.

There was only Lyddy with them in the kitchen. The others could be heard singing as Mr Siddall played his fiddle in the parlour. They were beginning the sing-song that was held most Saturdays in their house, attended by two or three of her father's friends, and accompanied with a large pewter jug of beer. It was a jolly tradition — and a safe one: gaiety contained within the home, not the dangerous and uncertain excitement of smart young men handing bonnets to girls they had not met before.

In a low voice she gave her mother a brief account of the Saturday evening procedure at Mrs Tozer's, and how Ellen had taken her out of her way.

'Ellen is the girl who has accompanied you as far as Southwark Street on other nights?'

'Yes.'

'Has she talked to you about young men?'

'A little.'

Mrs Siddall noticed that Lyddy was listening. 'Lydia. Go through to the parlour.'

'But . . .'

'No buts. I know you don't care to sing. But you can listen.'

Unwillingly, Lyddy went. The smoke from the men's pipes made her breathing worse, and she did not care to sing because it always led her to a coughing fit.

'Now, Elizabeth.' Mrs Siddall came to sit at the table too. 'I had hoped to delay this talk. You are young. But the ways of the world force my hand.'

Privately Lizzy breathed a sigh of relief. Her mother sounded stern, but not angry.

'Despite Mrs Tozer being a respectable woman, she cannot move against the times as far as her older girls are concerned. She has to leave their moral destiny to their consciences and to God.'

Mrs Siddall was known, and feared, for her firm grasp of moral values and her ability to express them fluently and forcibly. When one of her lectures was directed solely at Lizzy, she always felt that somehow the words could not really have anything to do with her. Her mother's tone was SO serious, her emphases SO emphatic, that she did not feel any actions of hers could ever warrant such high scrutiny. On the whole, Lizzy could not envisage God taking a very close interest in her. The dreams of castles and beautiful people which made up her ideal world seemed far removed from His high and mighty purpose — though she never properly understood quite what that was all about. The Siddalls went to church fairly regularly on Sunday mornings, but the children were more familiar

26

with Mrs Siddall's notions of right and wrong than with the intricacies of the gospels and the Old Testament.

'If these girls wish to flirt with men they will find plenty of opportunities, as you are discovering. And young men are by their natures always on the look out for . . .' Mrs Siddall paused to search for a suitable phrase, '. . . for girls who "touch", Lizzy. Yes, they like to seek out girls who touch. But these girls have no heed for the consequences. They will not be the girls whom men marry. Men require as wives girls who are untouched. And they require diligent girls, who know the value of money, and can run a regular household. Men are not always able to earn all the money that is necessary in this world. Women must be thrifty and able to go out to work for the sake of the family. Girls who touch are sacrificing their right to create a family. They will have momentary excitement, like moths to a flame, but they will not have the pride and privilege of family life.'

Strains of song crescendoed from the parlour, and Lizzy found herself automatically singing the words in her head.

> Oh, don't deceive me; Oh, never leave me!
> How could you use a poor maiden so?

'So Lizzy, I want you to be very careful to avoid any contact outside the workshop with those girls who touch. And, of course, you must not take up with boys at all. Any boy in future — when you are older — who wishes to take you out, must call on me first. Do you understand?'

'Yes, mother.'

'Now, you will be wanting your supper. Your wage makes a welcome contribution to our expenses. Will you have some soup? There is meat of course. And some milk pudding.'

'I would like some pudding. And I will make tea.'

'No. You stay there. You look tired.' Mrs Siddall turned to go to the pantry. 'Oh . . . and Lizzy?'

'Yes, mother?'

'Let me know as soon as you bleed.' That was all she said, and within seconds she had disappeared into the pantry to get the pudding.

Lizzy remembered the stain on Annie's bed. And the blood in the snowstorm. She wondered, and dreaded, the manner in which she was expected to bleed in the future.

When the pudding was brought, it did not occur to her that she might ask her mother a question on this subject. Nor did Mrs Siddall expect to receive one.

Chapter Two

Within a week, all the girls in the workroom were calling Lizzy 'Sid'. Perhaps by taking up the nickname they hoped she would allow herself to be included more readily in their chatter and jokes, that it would make her seem more ordinary and like themselves. But Lizzy, struggling with the fact that she must avoid, if she possibly could, accompanying Ellen on the walk home, became even more quiet and detached. And her friend Violet had been quite right when she remarked that the drooping eyelids made her look haughty — people did hesitate before teasing or cajoling her.

She soon discovered that the easiest way to avoid Ellen's company was to stay late at the shop. So she would invent small excuses, subterfuges, about wanting to finish certain tasks. Mrs Tozer interpreted this as enthusiasm for her work and — although normally overtime attracted no extra wages — would occasionally slip her an extra shilling. This in turn greatly pleased Mrs Siddall and made her daughter's late working hours seem quite acceptable.

Repetitive tiredness reduced Lizzy's life to a kind of twilight, in which Sunday formed an all-too-brief oasis of rest. It became tacitly understood that she would not attend church, or go on the occasional family Sunday walks, and there were no over-ruling arguments about this, since her wages earned her the right to limited dissent. She would spend those Sunday afternoons lying in a state of lassitude on her bed, images and dreams drifting slowly through her mind, and experiencing bouts of faint nausea. Only occasionally would a sharpness enter her brain, and then she would pick up the Tennyson volume or, briefly, pour her own words onto coarse pieces of sugar paper.

As the year progressed, those words left the realm of young female yearning and responded to something so disgusting and tragic that Lizzy could not bear to read over what she had written. It was a hot summer, the West End struggling to retain its dignity over the smells of sweat and horse manure and rotting waste, while the poor areas, where the canals and river tributaries were open sewers, stank in perpetual degradation. People carried devices to avoid inhaling stench, from expensive pomanders to a single wilting rose, but each morning the oblivious, Turner-yellow sun rose to ferment the evil.

In the cold month of March, when Lizzy had crossed Blackfriars Bridge at night, her exhaustion had been alleviated by the sound of slapping water, the sight of bobbing lights and the tangled masts silhouetted against the indigo sky, and the air, with its intimations of the sea, which she drew deep into her lungs. But on these windless, warm late summer evenings, a rich fetid smell rose from the water like an invisible curtain, and all she could think of was death. She dreaded seeing corpses being carried from houses, and of hearing weeping behind shuttered windows. And night after night her dread was realised, as in the dusk, bowed-headed families would bring out their dead to an awaiting cart. For during that summer thirteen thousand Londoners died of cholera. It reached the children's asylum at the end of Star Place, and each time Lizzy stepped over the threshold into her home she would anxiously, and privately, ascertain that no member of the family was sick.

Trade slumped with the epidemic; her father's shop was poorly patronised, and ladies no longer came up from the suburbs to buy their bonnets for fear of catching the disease. Lizzy became thinner and thinner, until finally her mother took her to the doctor. 'No consumption,' he pronounced, 'but she needs to develop. She will not become fully a woman unless she develops.' Lizzy did not understand what he was talking about, and did not care for the milk he ordered her to drink each morning before she went to work. 'When it's fresh from the cow,' he said, 'without the staleness brought on by this summer weather.' It was so fresh from the dairy at six in the morning that it was still warm. Her mother stood over her while she drank it, and it never quite got to the point that the invisible sponge inside her mouth and throat swelled so much that she could not swallow it.

Then one day a woman came to the shop and ordered three new bonnets in a hurry, and Lizzy was instrumental in getting the work finished on time. In the privacy of her sitting room, Mrs Tozer gave her an extra one-and-sixpence.

'This is sixpence more than usual, Miss Sid,' she declared. 'Sixpence for yourself. You're sixteen now, old enough to have a little of your own.'

Lizzy could not conceive that she could actually spend the sixpence on herself, but at the last moment she kept it back in her pocket and did not hand it over to her mother. For two days she guiltily carried the little silver coin around, and then as she set off home one evening through the cluttered streets of Covent Garden, she found herself listening to the familiar shouts of boys selling off over-ripe fruit to the evening crowds.

'Six a penny,' one shouted. 'Six luv'ly juicy peaches a penny.'

Lizzy stopped.

' 'Ere you are, miss.' The boy held out skinny cupped hands filled with small rosy peaches.

Lizzy drew the cover off her basket and the peaches were tipped in. She handed over the sixpence, and was given five copper pennies.

'Thanks, miss,' said the boy cheerily.

She walked away, and gradually became horrified by the enormity of what she had done. The pennies clinked in her pocket — she would never be able to conceal them from her mother — and it would be unthinkable to return home with peaches in her basket. Nor would she have considered eating them as she walked along the street.

When she reached the river, she paused. The weather was at last beginning to get cooler, and there was a hint of that sharp, smoky tang which meant autumn was on the way. Instead of going straight onto the bridge, she walked down the steps which led to the water where she could look along at the moored barges, one of which was being unloaded by a group of coarse-tongued men. She moved to the side of the steps, behind a jutting support in the river wall, and hoped that the men could not see her. Putting her hand under the cover of her basket, she felt the slightly rough fluff on the peaches and cautiously drew one out.

When she bit into it, it was both sharp and sweet, and the juice ran down her wrist. After she had eaten it, she threw the crinkly stone into the water and reached again into her basket. The peaches were of a size that could be eaten without difficulty in four bites, coming cleanly away from the stone, and in a short time Lizzy had eaten all six. She held out her hand, glistening with juice, and noticed it was shaking. Going to the step above the one where the water lapped, she crouched down and rinsed away the juice, trying

31

not to notice the detritus that floated in small, dense islands on the river's surface.

As she climbed back up the steps, she felt guilty and greedy, but also most pleasantly satiated with the fruit, which had been ripened on stone garden walls by the same sun that had caused the cholera germs to flourish and spread.

Leaning against the balustrade of the bridge was a raggedly-dressed woman, prematurely aged, the lines on her face filled with grime, and sparse grey hair. Her eyes had the same expression as a dead pigeon Lizzy had once found in the street. She took the five pennies from her pocket and held them out to the woman.

'Please take these. I don't want them.'

The woman stared, uncomprehending. Then, briefly, her eyes flickered a response. 'Thank you,' she said in a dull voice. 'Thank you.' Then, as Lizzy walked on, she heard the woman murmur: 'It's too late. But, thank you, all the same.'

After the experience of her first sixpence, Lizzy worked out a more systematic way of using her private money. She kept it in a secret pocket she stitched into the case holding her sewing instruments at the shop, and then when her mother authorized her to buy a new garment for herself, she would get something of slightly better quality than could be bought with the money provided. Her mother then complimented her on her careful eye for a bargain.

One late afternoon Mrs Tozer had some business in the City to attend to, and sooner than leave the shop in the perfectly capable hands of Mrs Dunn, she told everybody they might stop work early. Most of the other girls thought they would go and stroll up Regent Street (ostensibly to look at the shops, but really to eye the young men) while Lizzy privately decided to go home a very long way round — via Vauxhall Gardens. Ever since the day she had walked there with Lyddy, and peered through the railings at the well-dressed women walking with their beaux to the sound of the band, Lizzy had thought of the Gardens as a kind of elysium.

She walked down through Trafalgar Square to St James's Park, skirting the lake to look at the ducks and moorhens, and then across to the top of Vauxhall Bridge Road, where the wheel of a private carriage had become entangled with a hansom cab. The horses were nervous and restive, and a crowd of bystanders clustered in closer as the drivers shouted abuse at one another.

32

When one of the horses lashed out and caught a man's knee with its hoof, Lizzy felt it served them all right.

As she neared the river she slowed her pace, savouring the moment of anticipation before she was able to see the domes and walks of Vauxhall Gardens. On her left as she neared the bridge were the high walls of the penitentiary, sombre against the duck-egg blue sky, while in the distance over the water the thick trees and coloured pavilions looked peaceful and bright in the sun. As she crossed the river, an invisible band started to play and her steps quickened to the beat of a popular march.

There was a place by the railings, alongside a handsome elm tree, where she could tuck herself in unobtrusively and get a good view of the people promenading. She looked at one young woman in a hyacinth silk dress, her fair hair looped under a white bonnet, walking on the arm of a young officer. She sighed. They looked so carefree and perfect, as though they had all the time in the world to stroll in the music-filled air and share one another's company. She tried to picture herself in the gardens, but the only two dresses she had in the world were brown and grey, and her simple bonnet would not take an elaborate trim. She began to feel a bitter envy of the fair young woman, an envy which actually brought a bad taste into her mouth and briefly corroded her pleasure at the beauty of the setting. Then, as the couple passed right in front of her, she saw the officer's face properly for the first time. He had a petulant expression, a very straggly, sandy moustache, and a receding chin. She would not wish to take his arm. There would be no pleasure in walking in the gardens if one's partner were not perfect.

She stood there for a long time, until the light had dimmed from summer gold to grey-violet. The same band still played, the same couples still strolled, but the whole scene was slowly transformed from beautiful to utterly magical for Lizzy by the fact that one by one the lanterns in the trees were lit. Pink, red, blue and amber they glowed under the dense plane trees like fairy moons. She longed to get nearer to them, to walk along the promenade in a fashionable dress with a good-looking partner and . . . be seen. Yes, that was it, she would enjoy being stared at if only she looked just right. She couldn't be dowdy all her life, stitching for other people in a gloomy workshop. It was so unbearably unjust.

She did not attempt to imagine what her contact with her perfect partner would feel like. There was no connection between the band, the lights, the pavilions and gaiety, and those men described by her mother as the ones who sought out girls 'who touched'.

The walk to Southwark soon removed the Gardens from her mind. The dilapidated houses, ragged boys humping packs of goods they had failed to sell, toddlers dressed in nothing but torn shifts as they played in murky gutters, made it impossible to retain thoughts of a world whose inhabitants wore dresses and coats made of clean silk and good cloth, who carried purses lined with money, and had expressions of continuous happiness on their faces.

At the end of September, the merciless summer ended in long rains, followed by October frosts and November fog, and the cholera epidemic ceased. Women once again emerged from the safety of Surrey to refurbish their wardrobes, while watches and little heirloom ornaments were retrieved from the pawnbroker and, in a few instances, taken to Mr Siddall to be put into working order.

It was agreed that on nights when the weather was very bad, Lizzy should accept quiet Mary's invitation to share her cheap room in a lodging house in Covent Garden. She paid Mary a few pennies, and although she hated lying stiffly in a single-bed by this girl who was not family and smelled faintly stale, it was less intolerable than struggling through acrid fog or driving rain, only to get up in the dark the next morning and face exactly the same bleak elements.

During the winter, a thin shell imperceptibly hardened over Lizzy's personality. She realised definitely now that working as a milliner's assistant was never going to give her access to a tolerable world, and her refusal to share in the other girls' relaxed attitudes towards work and men became as much her own wish as it was compliance with her mother's instructions. She did not want to become like them, and for the moment all she could do was work mechanically and save her pennies; and that small store of private money did give her some satisfaction. Above all she began to become objectively critical of her family: noticing how hard her mother tried to be economical, while her father casually shut up shop early when trade was slack and played his fiddle with his friends over a few pints of beer — which he invariably paid for. Not that Lizzy's sympathies were entirely with her mother, for she sensed that Mr Siddall would not have turned quite so readily to male company for relaxation if his wife were a little more convivial. The bickering about money which Lizzy had accepted automatically when she was a child, now seemed unnecessarily destructive, and she could see that the tension it caused had a bad effect on Lyddy's nerves. Indeed, one of the good results of Lizzy's new maturity and detachment was her growing appreciation of Lyddy, who she began to realize was an unusually sweet-tempered girl hampered by her own sensitivity. No decision was ever reached as to what permanent work she might do, but she fell into the habit of helping in a local general store and earned a small wage.

While her outward life was circumspect and fatiguing, Lizzy's inner imagination continued to develop. Sewing and walking are both easily accompanied by daydreaming, and she invented long romantic sagas in her mind. The flash-points were always similar — beautiful people, beautiful settings, both usually vaguely medieval — but the names and the order of the narrative changed each time. The stories were about love and illness and honour, and the protagonists were always exquisitely dressed. The only food that was ever served was fruit and sweetmeats, and there were many bowers of roses and flagons of lilies.

The damson-coloured dress which she designed for herself in the new year was severely plain, but it had a few original details in the cutting that made her look a little like a poor relation of one of the girls in her dreams, and it seemed to set her even further apart from her more gaudy workmates.

Marriage was the solution, the way out, as far as most of the girls were concerned. And, indeed, in February one of them came blushing to work on a Monday with a ring on her finger and announced that she was engaged to marry Ernest who worked at Euston railway terminus. The other girls were practically hysterical with joy. Lizzy experienced a turning in the stomach which had more to do with queasiness than excitement. There was not, she decided, anything at all romantic about a man attached to a noisy, dirty, railway station.

Two more marriages followed in quick succession. Violet — whom she seldom saw now — suddenly married one of the workhands at the local tannery. Lizzy saw the deep disapproval on her mother's face when a neighbour conveyed the news and she connected it with Violet being so young, failing to understand the phrase 'had to' when applied to marriage. Shortly afterwards they received a very formal letter from her sister Annie in Sheffield saying that she was going to marry Charles, an under footman, in three months' time. Everyone seemed quite pleased about that — particularly her father, who said it was time the Siddalls settled back in their homeland. At which Mrs Siddall said sharply that Annie would no longer be a Siddall but a Blackstone.

None of these three marriages gave Lizzy any feeling that the girls concerned had found an enviable solution.

Ellen did not give up trying to entice Lizzy to let herself go and seize some enjoyment. She never actually attacked her attitudes, but would lure her into harmless conversations whose subjects she then deftly changed, and would insist that on some nights at least they walk home together. Lizzy did not mind this too much; she had become used to avoiding dubious subjects by simply refusing to reply, and Ellen would then shrug and talk about her family or the ways of the customers who came to Mrs Tozer's. Sometimes she thought Lizzy was tiresomely stuck-up, but at others she found something appealing in her reserve. It set her apart from the other girls, and occasionally Ellen wondered whether it might not finally prove advantageous to Lizzy's progress in the world. Certainly she was Mrs Tozer's favourite, and Mrs Tozer herself had observed that Lizzy's difference was symbolized in one physical characteristic: her skin. All the other girls had some kind of blemish on their complexions — either spots, or scars, or greasy patches, or sweaty foreheads. But Lizzy's skin was almost unreal, it was so perfect. When she was not too tired its skim-milk whiteness was partly touched with pink, and the faint, tiny freckles on her upper cheeks were like delicate grains of golden sand.

This meant that in the evenings under the soft light of the gaslamps at Mrs Tozer's she sometimes looked more like a perfect wax model than a flesh and blood young girl.

She had gradually become more accustomed to the invasion of the shop by young men on Saturday evenings. On one particular occasion in March, when the lamps were turned low while the girls tidied the bonnets, she looked wistfully out of the workroom window at the strip of sky visible above the buildings. The last remnants of light had almost faded, and the indigo strip was filled with black clouds torn by a high wind. She went into the shop to check a particular instruction about a trimming and did not take any notice of a young man who stood by while Ellen answered her question and

36

then added, 'I'm going straight home tonight, Sid. So come with me.'

'I'm getting ready now,' said Lizzy, and returned to the workroom.

As she had expected, when she wanted to leave, the young man was busy trying to persuade Ellen to go with him. She paused at the doorway, waiting for an opportunity to squeeze by them and make off alone. While she did so she became intrigued by the man's very musical voice, tinged with a slight Irish brogue. Surreptitiously she took a good look at him. He was tall, with intense dark blue eyes, and his manner to Ellen was straightforwardly enthusiastic rather than coarsely sycophantic.

'It would be a pleasure for me, Miss Britten, simply to walk to the river with you and your companion. Then, perhaps, you may feel able to see me on another day. I certainly have no wish to upset your plans for this evening.'

'Sid,' said Ellen. 'This is Mr Allingham. Mr Allingham — Miss Siddall. You've heard what he said, shall we allow him to walk with us?'

'If you wish.' Lizzy had not anticipated that she would reply affirmatively, and realised that she trusted Mr Allingham. And he kept his promise and simply escorted them with courtesy as far as Blackfrairs Bridge where Ellen agreed she would see him again soon.

The following Monday, Lizzy was helping Mrs Tozer attend to a customer in the shop. As she waited while the customer took ten minutes to decide between a peacock or a turquoise trim, Lizzy glanced up at the window as a group of ragged boys hurtled by shouting at one another. They had passed in a flash, and she was left with her gaze fixed on two people standing in the doorway of the shop on the other side of the road. They were looking in her direction, and one of them was Mr Allingham. The other was an exquisite boy of about eighteen wearing a floppy blue cravat. For a second, Lizzy felt she was staring directly into his eyes. She blushed, and returned her attention to the problems surrounding the bonnet.

During the next morning, Mrs Tozer came to the workroom and said: 'Miss Sid, there's a lady in the shop asking to be served by you. It seems she's had a recommendation.'

'For me?'

'For a girl with auburn hair, and you're the only one. Come along.'

Flattered that someone should have found her advice so memorable, Lizzy went through to the shop with a feeling of positive anticipation. A handsome lady, with dark ringlets streaked with grey, and dark eyes deepened with rings of shadow, was looking quizzically at a particularly strident magenta bonnet, while the boy with the blue cravat hovered near her, apparently unable to keep still. Lizzy hesitated.

'Come along, Miss Siddall,' said Mrs Tozer. 'Mrs Deverell wishes to seek your advice.'

'Good morning, Miss Siddall.' Mrs Deverell sounded surprisingly hesitant for such an obviously well-born lady. 'I wonder if you would be so kind as to help me choose a bonnet? Just a simple one you know. For walking out in the mornings.'

'Yes, ma'am.' Lizzy looked carefully at her customer in order to assess her style and needs, while at the same time endeavouring to ignore the presence of the boy.

'This is my son, Walter,' said Mrs Deverell. 'He likes to advise too, but his ideas are apt to be extravagant.' She smiled fondly at him as she said this.

Lizzy gave an awkward nod, but did not look at him.

'I thought perhaps something in a shade of brown,' Mrs Deverell continued. 'To go with this green dress, and also a pale beige one I have at home.'

Lizzy forced herself to concentrate. 'Does that chestnut one please you at all?'

'It looks suitable. Shall we try it? And what would you say about that one with the dark band?'

Satisfied that Lizzy was coping, Mrs Tozer excused herself for a few minutes.

Both bonnets were fetched and tried, and as Lizzy was about to suggest a third, Mrs Deverell said rather embarrassedly: 'My son wants me to put a request to you, Miss Siddall. It is rather unconventional, and I hope you won't take it badly. But you see he is an artist. A painter. And at the moment he is trying to complete a very complex composition — a scene from Shakespeare's *Twelfth Night*. It is a painting he hopes to exhibit next month. But he cannot find a suitable model to sit for the figure of Viola when she is desiguised as a page. It has to be a girl who is both young and beautiful, and very slender. He is sure that if you would agree to model for him, he would be able to finish the painting. Do you think you could possibly consider it?'

Lizzy stared at her. Then she took a quick glance at Walter, and felt quite weak. An artist. That was exactly what he looked like; so dark and romantic, and also delicate, with a pointed chin and slender nose, and full lips that shyly widened into a smile.

'Please say yes,' he said.

'You would of course receive a fee,' added Mrs Deverell.

That really surprised Lizzy. Someone, who as far as she knew had only seen her once through a window, wanted to paint her, and in addition was actually prepared to pay her. She thought it would be one of the most exciting things in the world to see a reproduction of herself through the eyes of an artist.

'It could I am sure be arranged outside your working hours,' said Mrs Deverell.

Lizzy's excitement evaporated. Her mother would never permit her to go to a young man's studio after eight o'clock at night or on a Sunday.

'You would complete the painting,' said Walter quietly, walking around the stand supporting the magenta bonnet, gently touching its brim with his slim fingers. All his movements seemed to spring from a highly-tensed energy, and Lizzy felt an exhilaration simply from being in his presence. He wasn't overbearing and boorish like so many men, but full of charm and quickness that seemed quite unforced. Unlike most men accompanying a wife or relative on a shopping expedition, he did not appear to feel uncomfortable or out of place in a bonnet shop.

'Thank you for asking me,' she replied. 'But I do not have the time.'

Walter's slight body seemed to droop, and he briefly closed his eyes, the long lashes fringing the top of his cheek. 'No free day?' he murmured.

'Just Sunday. And my mother . . .'

'You live at home?' Mrs Deverell interrupted gently.

'Yes.'

'At what time do you finish work in the evening?'

'Eight o'clock.'

'And then you have to make your way home?'

'Yes.'

'How far is that?'

'Three miles.'

'You walk there?'

'Yes, ma'am.'

'Walter, this poor child can't possibly model for you after work. She would die of exhaustion.'

'No, mother. But . . . but . . . Sunday?'

'It is the one day she has with her family. Miss Siddall, forgive me, but how old are you?'

'Sixteen, ma'am.'

'Sixteen. Four years younger than Walter, and already working full hours.' Mrs Deverell sighed. 'Would you like to sit for a picture?'

'Oh yes.' Lizzy's voice was unusually enthusiastic. 'Yes, I should.'

'You see, mother . . .'

'Be quiet, Walter. Miss Siddall, do you think that if I went to see your mother, and explained, she might permit you to sit for my son on perhaps two Sunday afternoons?'

Lizzy was amazed. 'We live past Southwark, ma'am.'

'But would you object if I called on your mother?'

Lizzy tried to gauge the effect of such an event and couldn't. She looked at Walter. 'No, ma'am.'

'Then that is settled. As you see, I spoil my son. But if he feels he needs you to complete his painting, then I trust his judgement. And, if you will forgive a personal comment, you do have a lovely colouring. Now, will you please write down the address of your home for me? I will call there tomorrow. And in the meantime I must complete this pretext of buying a bonnet.'

As if on cue, Mrs Tozer returned to the shop. Mrs Deverell quickly lifted the chestnut bonnet onto her head, allowed Lizzy to adjust it, and said; 'You were quite right in the first place, Miss Siddall. This will serve very well.'

When Lizzy got home she did not know how to explain that Mrs Deverell might call. Partly she was afraid her mother would be angry, but mainly she feared that she herself would be made to look a fool because of course Mrs Deverell would never come. It was all an elaborate whim, developed by Walter and Mr Allingham, and it would have faded by now. Mrs Deverell would never instruct a hansom to bring her all the way to Star Place just to get permission for Lizzy to be in a picture.

But supposing she did come, and her mother had not been forewarned? Mrs Deverell would think she was very rude and inconsiderate. She thought of the steel engravings that illustrated her Tennyson book, the detailed depictions of pale ladies and landscapes done with such intricate skill. To inspire such art must be the highest vocation. And Shakespeare, so it was said, was the most famous writer of all.

When her mother went into the garden to scatter some vegetable scraps, Lizzy followed her. The moon made their few bushes and early flowers look rather like one of the steel engravings — grey, deeply mysterious, yet every contour clear. Lizzy clasped her hands, which were clammy and cold.

'Mother?'

'What are you doing out here? I thought you were off to bed.'

'I want to tell you something.'

'Well I hope it's something good. I don't want any more troubles. Your father comes home from the shop with a face like a wet Monday. And Harry took it into his head to try to feed Mrs Short's baby with garden dirt when she called round today. Nothing's happened at Mrs Tozer's, I hope?'

Lizzy plunged. 'A lady came there today. She is called Mrs Deverell. Her son is an artist. And he wants me to pose for a picture. Mrs Deverell said she would come and call on you for permission tomorrow.'

For a few seconds even Mrs Siddall was at a loss for words. She stared at her tall skinny daughter, whose hair was silvered by the moon. How could anyone want her for a picture? She was neither beautiful nor famous. Yet it seemed unlikely that the so-called lady would be procuring her for more dubious purposes. There wasn't a womanly curve in her body.

'What nonsense are you talking, Lizzy? How did you meet such a person? An artist? Where have you been mixing to meet an artist?'

'Nowhere. He saw me in the shop. From the street. And came back with his mother who bought a bonnet and told me about the painting. It is a scene from Shakespeare. He is painting it for an exhibition.'

'You're talking stuff and nonsense, Lizzy. You are not to go anywhere with this young man, d'you hear me? If you're not home on time every night from now on, I shall expect a note from Mrs

41

Tozer in explanation. Keeping company with that Violet all those years did you no good.'

Lizzy sighed.

'Now, have you understood?'

'Yes, mother.'

Mrs Siddall went indoors, leaving Lizzy gazing down at a clump of moon-grey daffodils. She bent to touch their waxy trumpets and brushed a little sharp-scented pollen onto her finger. As she smelled it, her eyes filled with tears. She thought of Tennyson's dying young girl who only the year before had been Queen of the May.

> All in the wild March-morning I heard the angels call;
> It was when the moon was setting, and the dark was over all;
> The trees began to whisper, and the wind began to roll,
> And in the wild March-morning I heard them call my soul.

But at least that girl *had* once been a queen. *She* wasn't allowed to be anything. Not even in a picture. Her mother would never, never understand that there was a different kind of world, a world where a man could be like Walter Deverell, and the trees could be bedecked with coloured lanterns, and she, Lizzy, Elizabeth Eleanor, need never ever make another bonnet but could wear clothes like the ladies in the engravings, and walk in fields of flowers.

Even if Mrs Deverell called, which she wouldn't, it would be no good. Her mother wouldn't let her go.

She stayed in the garden until she was shaking with cold, then went straight upstairs to bed. When Lyddy asked her what was wrong, she told her the whole story. Normally she never confided, but there was an overwhelming need for her to tell somebody about Walter Deverell.

'Oh Lizzy! How wonderful! And you *could* be in a picture, I know you could."

'She'll never come out all this way. She's a real lady. Not like our usual customers.'

'Then she will, Lizzy. If she's a real lady. She'll keep to her word.'

'But mother will send her away. That's even worse.'

'I'll keep a look out. If a carriage turned up here, I'd see it from the store. And if I do, I'll run home. Mr Brown won't mind.'

'You couldn't stop mother.'

'No . . . I suppose not. But I could listen to what the lady says.'

'Yes . . . Yes, I'd like to know that.'

During the night she had a version of The Dream. But there was no crimson stain, and the hovering presence that threatened her was very shadowy. It was like seeing The Dream through a gauze curtain, with only the moon to illuminate it. In the morning she felt that all her life was being pushed away from her, pushed away in the distance, while she was left simply to fulfil a mechanical routine.

Throughout the next day at Mrs Tozer's, she kept making excuses to go into the shop, just in case Walter Deverell was lingering ouside. But he never was. She dreaded going home to face her mother's sarcastic remarks. But she dare not be late.

As she pulled the kitchen door shut behind her, Mrs Siddall announced: 'That lady was here.'

Lizzy felt as though her inside had melted. So it was true. He did want her. And his mother had bothered to come all this way.

But what had *her* mother said?

'She seems a very considerate lady. Jewish, of course. You can tell from the complexion. But that makes her businesslike. You would be paid a good fee, Lizzy. A shilling an hour. So I have said you may go next Sunday, and the Sunday after, at two o'clock. Mr Deverell will provide the right costume for the picture. And I have ascertained that there will be a suitable place for you to change. Mrs Deverell's husband is in charge of the School of Design at Somerset House, and their son has his studio there.' Mrs Siddall paused. 'You seem to have fallen on your feet, Lizzy.'

Later, up in their bedroom, Lyddy said: 'She stayed for nearly an hour! With the cab waiting. The whole street was peeking out! And she wore the bonnet she said you'd selected for her. She kept saying how clever and pretty you are. And how well you speak. And mother told her about your poems. And how you come up here alone and get cold. And the lady said surely you could have a fire. And mother said yes of course you *could,* but she didn't want to encourage you to be on your own all the time.'

Both girls burst out laughing at this, for there was no grate in the room.

'Then the lady asked about that crest in the parlour, and mother told her all that story about Hope Hall in Sheffield, and how some of the proceeds of the sale should have come to father. And that was why he came to London, to check his rights, and had never gone back in twenty-one years.'

'Oh that old story.'

'Don't you believe it, Lizzy?'

'Is there anything left to believe? The only real connection we have with Sheffield is that Annie's in service and is going to settle and marry there. We've never met any of the relations.'

'But father's ancestors were landowners.'

'And they're buried in the land now, and we live in Star Place in the shadow of an asylum.'

Lyddy gave a little gasp. She was not used to hearing her sister sound so bitter. She tried to turn the conversation back to the subject she found so exciting. 'But you'll be somebody, Lizzy. Now that you're going to be painted.'

Lizzy was about to express doubt; then she remembered that the two Sunday sittings were actually fixed, and that Mrs Deverell had visited this very house wearing a bonnet she'd selected. For the first time for a year the future no longer appeared as a never-ending tunnel of monotony, but contained a possibility of the unimaginable.

Once Lyddy was asleep, her breathing quite calm for once, Lizzy allowed herself the luxury of thinking of Walter Deverell. She could not imagine his face, stationary like a portrait, but her mind recreated the sense of his quick movements, and the feeling he gave of adding vitality to everything that surrounded him. Her walk to work in the morning was not the usual mechanical journey, sleepily oblivious of workers and vagrants in the joyless dawn, but an opportunity to look eagerly across the grey-spired landscape of London to the pearl horizon and to smell the March-fresh wind which blew in from the sea. Invisible barriers had vanished, and she lifted her head and looked with interested curiosity at her reflection in the windows along the Strand.

By Friday, everyone at Mrs Tozer's knew that Lizzy was going to sit for a painting. Ellen had been out with William Allingham, and he had told her how an artist friend had bemoaned his difficulty in finding a slender model, and how he had remembered her companion in the shop, and that just one glimpse through the window had sent Walter Deverell into an ecstasy. At first Lizzy was embarrassed and angry, but when Mrs Tozer took her to one side and told her 'To play her cards carefully, and keep herself to herself like a proper professional beauty,' and Ellen remembered to report the information that Mr Allingham, as well as working for the Irish

Customs, was a poet, she relaxed and did not rebuff the girls when they asked her questions. A painter *and* a poet. That she should have met both in the space of one week!

When she turned off the Strand on Sunday afternoon and walked under the archway that led to Somerset House, she was numb with conflicting fears and excitement. The grand building in front of her seemed even more unreal than the castles of her daydreams, and if Walter had not come walking across the courtyard to meet her, she was sure she would never have dared enter. As it was he shook her hand, said, 'Oh, I am *so* glad you have managed to come,' and gave a little skip as he showed her the way to a side door.

'It's very deserted at the weekend,' he said as they walked down a long corridor. 'But the porter and his wife are behind those doors there, in their quarters, and there are two students in one of the studios sketching a still-life.'

She felt he was anxious that she should not feel awkward being alone in his company.

'William Allingham did ask if he might come along, but I said I'd have to ask your permission first. For next time.'

'He . . . is it so? He is a poet?'

'Yes. Yes, indeed. Did Ellen tell you?'

She nodded.

'Do you like poetry?'

'Yes.'

'Then you must get to know William. He's Irish you know. And his poems are full of magic. Now, here is where you may change. I do hope you will find the clothes comfortable. It is the part where Viola is dressed as a young man, a page, in the court of Duke Orsino. When she is searching for her brother. And Feste, the jester, comes to sing to the Duke. And you, Viola, lean forward, and listen, and watch the Duke's sadness and yearn. Because, as you know, you are in love with him, and he is in love with Olivia.'

Lizzy, who didn't know at all, said nothing, but went into the room, closed the door, and regarded the pile of clothes on the chair. There was a long tunic with double sleeves — tight inner ones, and split, loose outer ones — pale woollen tights, and long pointed leather shoes. They seemed clean, but faintly musty. How could a girl wear such clothes when she was in love with a duke?

When she realised how much her legs were revealed below the

45

tunic, she panicked. Not so much from modesty, as the fact that her knees and calves were quite solid in comparison to the rest of her body. Walter Deverell would take one look at her and send her straight back home. She walked over to the window, her heart thumping, and gripped the sill. The river beyond the trees glinted like pewter. She wished she could drown.

She stayed like that until there was a gentle tap at the door. 'Miss Siddall? Miss Siddall?'

She did not reply.

'Miss Sid?'

The sound of his voice using her nickname made her feel even more dismayed.

'Miss Sid? Are you changed?'

Despairingly she murmured, 'Yes.' And very quietly and carefully he opened the door. She did not turn to face him, and remained by the window.

'That is perfect,' he said. 'Quite perfect.' He took a few steps into the room. 'Please come next door into the studio.'

She still could not look him in the face. 'I feel . . . foolish.'

'No. It's the rest of the world that's foolish, because they aren't dressed for the Illyrian court. Please come and let me show you what to do.'

She followed him into a high studio lit from skylights in the ceiling, and containing a miscellaneous clutter of brushes, jars of colour and chemicals, stacked canvases, old pieces of furniture, treasured objects, flowers long dead, and a heavy easel which seemed to dominate the silent room.

The easel held a large rectangular canvas, in the background of which steps and balustrades and courtiers and trees collided in a mysterious perspective. In the foreground, on a tiled courtyard, boy musicians played to a heavy young man in rich medieval dress who lolled in a seat at the base of a pillar. On either side of him were shadowy sketches of figures. The one of the left, Walter explained, was to be Viola, sitting on the edge of a bench, facing the duke and gazing up at his face. While the figure sitting on a box on the duke's right was the jester, Feste, who was singing the song that was making the duke stare into the middle distance in such a melancholy fashion.

'My friend Gabriel Rossetti has agreed to sit for Feste,' said Walter with a touch of importance.

46

Lizzy scrutinized the face of the duke and decided it would be difficult for anyone to feel besotted by him. But she obediently sat exactly where she was told, arranging her feet and clasping her hands as directed, and found a position for her body which she could hold without too much difficulty. When Walter asked if he could tuck her hair into the back of the tunic so that her profile more resembled that of a boy, she allowed him to do so, laughing as he had difficulty in confining it all.

'This is such fun,' he said. 'You are going to be a natural model.'

When she had been sitting for a few minutes he asked, 'Are you finding it uncomfortable?'

'Not at all,' she replied truthfully.

'Good . . . good.' He continued painting, with quick darting movements of the brush, and said quietly as if to himself, 'It's perfect. You can relax, and yet the pose is still alive.'

She did not fully understand his words, but felt proud. His need of her person to complete his picture gave her a sense of importance she had never experienced before.

Every fifteen minutes he allowed her to break for a few seconds, complimenting her on how still she had kept. 'I've told Allingham not to tell the others about you,' he said. 'They'll all be wanting you.'

She could not really take in what he had said, unable to envisage a host of 'others' all busy with paintings and all in need of someone who looked like her. Indeed she did not fully understand many of the remarks which Walter threw out from time to time, referring as they did to friends and paintings and poetry and theatres, all delivered in an enthusiastic, silver-tongued manner that both eluded and enthralled her. Shyly, she at one point admitted to liking Tennyson, and he seemed overjoyed, reeling off a few half-familiar lines and telling her she had excellent taste.

By late afternoon the light had dimmed, and Deverell mockingly shook his fist at the bulbous dark clouds sliding above the skylights.

'But you'll be tired now, Miss Siddall. So it will be no bad thing to stop.'

'No, Mr Deverell. I can assure you, I am not tired.'

Her prim, definite voice made him smile. 'Well, it would be nice if you would take some tea. The porter's wife will bring some. Would you care for tea?'

She nodded. 'Please.' She did not want to leave him.

When she had changed into her own clothes and returned to the studio, her hair was fastened very softly so that it fell smoothly against her cheek, and then fanned from the nape of her neck out across her shoulders in a copper mantle. She came so quietly through the door that she startled Deverell, and as he jerked his head up to look at her he gave a sharp intake of breath. At first he said nothing, and her expression became apprehensive.

'You remind me of something,' he said. 'Of something written by my friend Gabriel.'

'Is he a poet too, like Mr Allingham?'

'He writes poetry. But he is a painter as well. And the piece I am thinking of is prose. So —' Walter laughed and did one of his dramatic flourishes, '— he is every kind of artist.'

She wondered exactly what prose, written by an artist, was, and how she fitted into it.

'But since you like Tennyson, Miss Siddall, I could perhaps try to interest you in something a little less accomplished, but none the worse for that. We — my circle of friends, that is — have been collaborating on a magazine. The porter here has a whole stock of them, for he's been trying to sell them to the students for us. Would you care to accept one?'

'Why . . .'

'It's not perfect of course. But we mean to show that we can change the course of the arts in this country.'

Lizzy said nothing, and felt quite relieved when a plump woman brought in a tray of tea, including fresh scones and jam. The woman looked critically and then approvingly at Lizzy. 'See you paint her really nice, Mr Walter. She's pretty as a picture to start with.'

'I'll do my best, Mrs Russell. And please, do you think I could have a copy of *The Germ* from Mr Russell for Miss Siddall to take away with her?'

'As many as you like. You couldn't say the call on them was overwhelming, and they're just cluttering up the shelves of the stock cupboard.' She addressed herself to Lizzy. 'And I hope you make head nor tail of it better than I can, dear.'

Walter would have taken Lizzy back to Star Place, but she quietly insisted that Blackfriars Bridge was far enough. They stood there in the dusk, the wind buffeting them so strongly that he took her arm to steady her, leaning towards her so she could hear his words.

'I'm so happy I saw you.'

She smiled, but did not speak.

'You see, our paintings depend on real beauty. Not shoddy make-believe.'

He stared into her face and sighed. Her lids drooped; she found the tenderness in his dark eyes almost too much to bear. Of equal height, they stood there for a moment like brother and sister reunited after a long separation.

Chapter Three

That night Lizzy sneaked a candle up to her bedroom. She had already given a dutiful outline description of the afternoon to her mother, and to Lyddy she now added the information that Walter Deverell was not only handsome, but more kindly and attentive than any man in the whole of London. Lyddy wanted to hear more, much more, but instead Lizzy produced the magazine which instinctively she had concealed from her family — *The Germ* was not, to her mind, a very propitious title to lay down on the kitchen table in front of James, and Tump, and her critical mother and beer-drinking father. She ignored Lyddy's questions about what she was reading, and turned towards the candle, leaving her younger sister to breathe uneasily and watch the huge flickering shadows on the wall.

Lizzy discovered a story entitled *Hand and Soul* by one Dante G. Rossetti, whom she presumed to be the Gabriel Rossetti Walter had referred to, but she found it very heavy going. It was full of Italian names and went on a great deal about painting and the church. By the end of the second page she was drifting towards sleep and gave up trying to read. As she closed the magazine, however, she noticed a poem written by a woman, Ellen Alleyn. Called *An End*, it was about a dead love:

> . . . On the last warm summer day
> He left us; — he would not stay
> For autumn twilight cold and grey.
> Sit we by his grave and sing
> He is gone away.

Lizzy liked that. She read all the poem over again before blowing out the candle.

She fell asleep with the sweetness of the possibility of an incalculable, rather than a proscribed, future lifting her spirit. In some ways the studio had been like a church or cathedral — a tall space devoted to the pursuit of a belief — but pictures and poetry were much more exciting than hymns and prayers.

A week later she approached her second assignment with Walter Deverell without any of her initial fear and shyness. It was a day when early spring sun could be felt warm on the face as well as appear bright to the eye, and seagulls swooped around the scraps on the river, screaming and circling, their wide wings dazzling like new whitewash. She walked towards the Strand with a sense of elation and purpose. Then, when she arrived at Somerset House and, as before, Walter came across the courtyard to greet her, she suddenly remembered it was to be their last meeting. He had asked for only two sittings.

He watched, as she came nearer, the set of her head change from regal to despondent, and was apprehensive. He had meant to tell her straight away that his friend, Gabriel Rossetti, was coming later, and to ask whether she would object. For he had not been able to keep Lizzy's looks a secret, and he had boasted of her to other young painters until Gabriel had insisted on coming to see for himself. And Deverell, like most other people, had no power to thwart Rossetti.

The sitting was well underway, and Lizzy's eyes were becoming sadder and sadder. Still, thought Deverell, perhaps that would add poignance to his picture. He was, after all, depicting the scene where Viola has to hide her love with the words:

> She never told her love,
> But let concealment, like a worm in the bud,
> Feed on her damask cheek. She pined in thought;
> And with a green and yellow melancholy
> She sat like Patience on a monument,
> Smiling at grief.

Lizzy's pose certainly expressed patience, but nothing he said to her would coax a smile.

Then he heard footsteps down the corridor. It was a half an hour before he expected Gabriel, and only a beautiful girl, Deverell reflected, would have made him early. Or the prospect of money.

He spoke nervously, stiffly. 'I think, Miss Siddall, that may be the friend I told you of last week. Gabriel Rossetti. He mentioned there was just a chance he might be passing this way. I hope you won't regard it as an intrusion. But he takes a particular interest in this picture. As you know, he is posing for the jester.'

She felt bereft. Her remaining time with Walter was to be ruined. She would never have him to herself again. She had been sitting there spinning out the seconds, thinking — At least I have another hour and a half . . . At least I have another hour and a quarter . . .

The door opened, and a young man, long-haired and untidy, looked at Lizzy with dark eyes that seemed to see through and beyond her, giving no indication of his feelings.

She remained immobile, like a nervous animal that freezes before darting to escape.

Deverell hastily made introductions and explanations. Rossetti made no apologies for his premature arrival and Lizzy, sensing Deverell's discomfort on her behalf, tried to remain calm.

As the three of them settled into stillness — Lizzy posing, Deverell painting, and Rossetti lolling on an old chaise-longue — Rossetti let out a long sigh.

'Was I right?' asked Deverell.

There was no reply. Rossetti simply made a rhythmic clicking noise with the nails of the thumb and forefinger on his left hand. Without moving her head, Lizzy looked at him covertly. His assurance and air of authority were both fascinating and repellent. And she thought the way he put his feet up in her presence without so much as an apology was extremely rude.

Punctually, after quarter of an hour, Deverell invited her to rest.

'But you were just getting the nose right at last,' said Rossetti.

'Miss Siddall has no difficulty in repeating the pose.'

'What a stickler you are. She didn't look tired. Were you?' He addressed her directly.

She lowered her eyes and for a few seconds did not reply. Then she said, 'No. But in another few minutes I might have been. Mr Deverell is the best judge of that.'

Rossetti burst out laughing — a rich, melodious laugh, but not ridiculing her. 'Girls always defend Walter.'

'Gabriel —' Deverell started to protest, but was immediately interrupted.

'It's perfectly true, my friend, so don't contradict me. For some reason,' his voice sounded teasing, 'they find you irresistable.'

Lizzy felt a blush spread from her neck up into her cheeks. She turned away from the men and stared at a plastercast of some pale goddess, its drapery folds grey with dust.

52

'You will observe, Miss Siddall,' said Rossetti, 'why we are so anxious to find living examples of beauty. To sit for hours in front of a colourless plaster female who has been dead two thousand years, tends to produce art that looks equally dead.'

'You know quite well, Gabriel, that you're not meant to make paintings out of plastercasts. They're for drawing practice.'

'Oh *practise*. Who wants to practise? That's what you and Brown and Hunt go on about all the time. You can't practise living, you can only live. And art IS living.'

'But you have to learn a discipline before you can produce great art,' countered Deverell.

'True. But that learning must be with life. Not in the graveyard of museums. Or worse still,' he waved his foot towards the dusty goddess, 'in reproduction graveyards.'

Lizzy noticed there was a hole in the sole of his shoe. And his black greatcoat, which he had not removed, had the greenish tinge of extreme age.

'An hour of Miss Siddall's time,' said Rossetti, 'is worth all the reproduction statuary in the world.'

'I am quite aware of that,' said Deverell.

Involuntarily Lizzy relaxed. Perhaps he would ask her to sit for him again.

Both men noticed that a vestige of a smile appeared on her face.

Deverell spoke first. 'Indeed, I was going to ask if you would be able to come next Sunday, Miss Siddall. This figure will not be properly finished today, and I want to do as much as possible from life.'

She was about to reply, 'Yes. Yes, if you wish,' when Rossetti said, 'And I shall share the sitting. I would like to draw you, Miss Siddall, for the next issue of our magazine. We have an etching in each issue and I have undertaken to provide the next one.'

There was a silence. Deverell seemed both put out yet admiring as he looked at his friend; Lizzy was mainly relieved that she would be seeing Deverell again, but very apprehensive at Rossetti's intrusion; and Rossetti himself was preparing to leave.

'Three o'clock is it?' he asked. 'The time you begin?'

'It is,' replied Deverell flatly.

'Until next Sunday then,' said Rossetti, leaving the room in a leisurely manner.

When the door was closed, Deverell entreated Lizzy, 'Please say

53

you'll be able to manage another sitting?'

'Yes.' She had decided that if she omitted to mention to her mother there would be a second gentleman present, she would meet with no objection. The money she received had been positively remarked on several times, as had the memory of Mrs Deverell's good manners.

This time she made no comment when she and Walter reached Blackfriars Bridge, and he accompanied her right up to the turning that led to Star Place. They talked about early childhood. Walter had been born in Charlottesville while his father was teaching in America, and Lizzy begged for memories.

'I'm afraid I was only two when we came back to England. My mother often used to talk to me about it, but I really can't remember anything at all.'

Lizzy sighed. 'I wish I'd been born in America.'

'Why?'

'It must be so big and clean.' They were walking past rows of shabby houses, and the smoke from early evening fires hung heavily in the damp air.

'Were you born in Star Place?'

'Yes.'

He took her arm. 'But London is really much more exciting. It's where everything happens. I think living for ever in Virginia would probably be very dull.'

She did not reply.

'You wait and see. I'll get my painting into the Royal Academy exhibition. And Gabriel's going to draw you for *The Germ*.' He hesitated — the magazine had sold very few copies, and there was some doubt as to whether their sponsors would help them print another issue. 'And whatever happens, people are going to want you for their pictures. Though I'm terribly glad it was me who found you first.'

Lizzy giggled. His good spirits were infectious. 'You make me sound like a mislaid parcel.'

Walter was delighted. It was the first time she had joked with him and he liked girls who were jolly and companionable. When his sisters' friends gazed at him mutely and adoringly while their mothers issued pressing invitations to tea, he felt nothing but dismay, while the flirtatiously ribald manners of the models some of his friends employed rather frightened him.

54

'Not mislaid. Gone astray. You shouldn't be having to work all those hours churning out bonnets. It isn't fair. You should have time to explore the world about you, like we do.'

'But you're rich. We're poor.'

Deverell flushed. His family was not rich. He had to give drawing lessons at the Design School to supplement his father's income, and he'd had to beg the fee for Lizzy's sittings from his mother. But he knew that from the point of view of Star Place the Deverells were rich.

'Actually some of our group are really very badly off. But when one of us sells a picture, or gets a windfall, we sort of muck in. Gabriel's always short. But William, his brother, helps him out.'

'He's an older brother?'

'Oh no, younger. But he has a regular job in the excise office.'

'He's not an artist?'

'Well, he writes poetry. But it's not very easy to read. And he writes essays. He contributes quite a lot to our magazine.'

'I suppose it wouldn't be possible for the older Mr Rossetti to have a regular job AND paint?'

Deverell roared with laughter. 'It isn't possible for Gabriel to do *anything* regularly.' He hesitated, and then continued soberly, 'But you can't stop him once he's started. He's more dedicated to art than anyone else I've ever met.'

When she was home, Lizzy had another look at Mr Rossetti's story, *Hand and Soul,* and tried to persevere through its evasive paragraphs. Some phrases and sentences passed pleasingly through her mind, but the Italian names, and the hero's endless struggle with abstract difficulties, were confusing. Then she came to a paragraph which began:

> A woman was present in his room, clad to the hands and feet with a green and grey raiment, fashioned to that time. It seemed that the first thoughts he had ever known were given to him as at first from her eyes, and he knew her hair to be the golden veil through which he beheld his dreams.

Lizzy stopped reading there, and put the journal to one side. She sat on the edge of her bed and repeatedly ran her hands through her hair so that it fanned out from her head. The guttering candle made weird shadows behind her, turning the golden-copper veil into a shifting black cloud.

Just before the candle's wick finally failed, she took up the journal again and looked at its one untitled illustration. On the cover it was simply described as 'An Etching by W. Holman Hunt'. In two sections, it showed a man holding up the arm of a kneeling girl who leant towards some flowers in a pond, and a man lying dead or distraught as nuns with folded hands passed behind him in a procession. The kneeling girl was rather plain. Lizzy hoped that Mr Rossetti would do something more . . . more . . . Here the candle went out.

She shut the journal. She wasn't quite sure HOW she would like Mr Rossetti to present her.

The next time she opened its pages was on the following Sunday morning. The family had gone to church — her mother's confused reaction to her third sitting for Mr Deverell being summed up by the remark: 'I don't see why you shouldn't attend church, Lizzy. If you're not too tired to pose, you shouldn't be too tired to pray. And a good sermon would put you right for the happenings during the rest of the day.' Mr Siddall had said nothing. He had never referred to her modelling, and Lizzy sensed that he thought it a highly dubious acitivity. But she also knew that when there was enough money in the house, her father liked to shut up shop early so that he could be convivial with any of his friends who happened to be similarly idle. Thus far, she had handed over every penny Walter had given her. She settled down to study the journal, uninterrupted and by daylight.

She quickly realized that the etching illustrated the adjacent two long poems — *My Beautiful Lady* and *Of My Lady in Death* – by one Thomas Woolner. Earlier she had been put off by their length, but now she started to read the many verses of the first poem which hymned the perfection of 'my lady' who walked in the country-side with her suitor, admired by the animals and birds, and even the trees and blossoms. Lizzy found it romantic — though not very musical — until near the end when the man finally passionately declared his love:

> Her waist shook to my arm. She bowed her head,
> Silent, with hands clasped and arms straightened:
> (Just then we both heard a church bell)
> O God! It is not right to tell:

But I remember well

*

Each breast swelled with its pleasure, and her whole
Bosom grew heavy with love; the swift roll
  Of new sensations dimmed her eyes . . .

Lizzy slammed the journal shut and buried her head in her knees. She felt herself blushing deeply. Any significance she might have drawn from the poem's abrupt ending at the next verse, and the immediate opening *Of My Lady in Death,* was lost.

She ate no lunch, and set off for the School of Design with a sick feeling in the pit of her stomach. Walter Deverell was the magnet which drew her; but she dreaded seeing Rossetti and of hearing any mention he might make of *The Germ.*

At first she thought Walter was not going to meet her in the courtyard, but he suddenly appeared, running breathlessly towards her and smiling. Immediately she found that she was smiling too.

'Isn't it a *lovely* day?' he declared, taking her hand.

She looked past his black curls to the blue sky above Somerset House, felt the spacious scale of the building around her and the friendly, protective, male hand in her own, and agreed.

'Gabriel would like to do some sketches while you're in your Viola clothes, but he's asked if towards the end of the sitting, after you've changed, you could sit for at least half an hour with your hair down. Would you mind?'

They were nearing the side entrance, and she hesitated. She knew if she went into the building she would have to do as Rossetti asked. But she could not just turn away and leave Walter. And she did not know how to explain why she felt so disturbed.

He sensed something was wrong. 'Don't you like having your hair loose?'

She gave a little sigh, and said coolly, 'I don't mind.'

Gabriel was already in the studio when she entered in her page's costume. 'Hallo, Viola.'

'Good afternoon, Mr Rossetti.'

'You should call me Feste — that's the name of the jester.' He spoke pleasantly, not patronisingly. 'I suppose I ought to put on my costume too, and we could sit together. But mine's a vile pose. I have to cross my legs, fling my arm out, and look as though I'm

57

talking.'

'Which means that he *does* talk,' said Deverell, 'all the time. It makes painting devilishly difficult.'

'I only recite what I can remember of Feste's part.' Rossetti struck the pose on a nearby stool and began:

> Come away, come away, death;
> And in sad cypress let me be laid . . .

Lizzy stared. His normal speaking voice was deep and pleasant, but the way he spoke poetry was magical. She had never heard anything like it. He stopped at the end of a verse and there was a silence.

Then Lizzy said: 'Please — is there any more?'

They did not laugh. Deverell said quietly, 'Miss Siddall likes poetry. She is very fond of Tennyson.'

Rossetti relaxed his pose, put his hand on his knees, and looking up into her face recited quietly:

> Not a flower, not a flower sweet,
> On my black coffin let there be strown;
> Not a friend, not a friend greet
> My poor corpse where my bones shall be thrown;
> A thousand thousand sighs to save,
>> Lay me, O, where
> Sad true lover never find my grave,
>> To weep there!

Lizzy smiled at him, very faintly.

'Don't encourage him too much,' said Deverell. 'He knows he recites well, and he'll go on for ever if you let him.'

Gabriel and Lizzy were still looking into one another's eyes as he spoke. She broke the gaze. She had an odd feeling that she had been looking at someone who was both everything and nothing.

She took up her pose.

Deverell began painting straightaway, but Rossetti fidgetted with his paper, wandered around the studio, and was only just beginning to work when the first fifteen minutes were up. Walter hesitated, and then said firmly: 'It's time for a break.' Rossetti gave a histrionic sigh, and Lizzy said, 'It's all right. I'll go on till the next one.'

When the Viola sitting was over, and she came back wearing her

58

own dress and with her hair down, Rossetti screwed up all his sketches and hurled them into the corner of the studio. Walter looked at her anxiously, afraid she might be nervous or insulted, but she was reminded of Tump's behaviour when something went wrong — how Tump would rip up a piece of untidy sewing, or throw away wild flowers that would not sit right in a jar — and she laughed.

Rossetti glared at her for a moment, and then suddenly he laughed too.

'Sit on the chaise,' he said. 'Lean on the arm with one elbow, and let your hair fall to the front.'

The pose was held without interruption until it was well past time for her to go home, and the clear colour of her hair was beginning to dim in the fading light.

Rossetti remained in the studio when Lizzy and Walter finally set out for Blackfriars Bridge. There was a stiff breeze coming off the river, and she felt chilled and slightly dizzy through lack of food. When they had crossed the bridge, he said: 'You will come next Sunday, won't you?'

'I'm not sure.'

'Why?' He noticed she looked very pale. 'Is something the matter?'

She did not reply.

'Is it Gabriel? Would you rather he wasn't present? I know he's rather . . . overwhelming . . . but he's awfully kind . . . and he's going to do great things. I know that. And he thought you were an absolute stunner!'

His words did not seem to have any effect, and alarmed by her blank passivity he guided her towards a sheltered passageway, half blocked by a pile of building timber. 'Sit here a minute. You look so tired. And the wind makes such a noise in my ears.'

She sat obediently, looking down at the ground.

'Lizzy . . . it's all right, isn't it, if I call you Lizzy? I don't feel right being formal to you.'

She nodded. Usually she hated the sound of the word 'Lizzy' — secretly wanting to be an 'Elizabeth' — but it made a shiver run through her when Walter said it.

'Lizzy . . . tell me. What is the matter?'

She could not find the right words, and for a moment had a desperate feeling that her mind and body were beyond her control.

59

No words to describe her difficulty, and no way to stop her teeth from beginning to chatter.

He bent down and felt her hands. 'Lizzy! You're so cold. We must get you warm.' He squatted down and rubbed her fingers in his palms. She did not flinch away from him, and after a few seconds gripped his hands tightly. 'It's the magazine,' she blurted, 'those poems.'

'Which poems, Lizzy?'

'In your magazine. They are not decent poems.'

He was bewildered. Still holding her hands, he sat beside her on a pile of wood. 'I'm not quite sure which ones you mean.'

'At the beginning. With the picture. I don't want my picture by such poems.'

'It won't be, Lizzy. Gabriel may write something to accompany it. Or it may stand on its own. But Gabriel's poems are always . . . very beautiful.' He was fumbling for words, the problem being that he had never finished reading Woolner's verses, having found them far too long-winded to hold his attention. He tried to envisage what lapse of taste they might contain. It could not have been anything too great. The circumspect William Rossetti — who saw to so many of the practicalities concerning the magazine — would never have permitted that.

In the end he soothed her. He explained that Woolner was primarily a sculptor, not a poet, and that he was a somewhat forthright man, perhaps better suited to strong materials like marble and bronze than to the shades of delicate meaning which poetry should convey. Lizzy became mesmerized by both his touch and the sound of his words. He made the activities of his friends sound so special, so important. Important enough to excuse words or behaviour that in her world would be strictly censored.

When she finally arrived home, all she could really think about was the way he had held her hands. How he had supported her without threatening her, and how much she wanted him to hold them again.

Her mother was furious. Lizzy was late, she was cold, she would be tired for work the next day, and she had brought home no extra money to cover the extra time she had posed.

That last stricture made Lizzy angry. She had sensed when Deverell paid her that he could not offer her any extra money, and that he felt uncomfortable about this. She gratefully drank the tea which Lyddy had made for her, and said to her mother, 'I agreed to stay to help Mr Deverell out. He is anxious to finish his picture. But I did not expect any more money. There is a limit to what he can afford I would imagine.'

'Imagine!' scoffed her mother. 'That's all you do — imagine. It's time you faced up to reality.'

Lizzy stood up and pushed back her chair. Her voice was not raised, but her words were uncontrollably sibilant. 'I work for six days every week making bonnets. Even when I'm sick. I give you all my money.' She had not lied intentionally, but an image of the pocket in her work-case where she hid her extra earnings flashed accusingly into her mind. 'And now I make good money on a Sunday too. Mr Deverell has more posing for me to do. If I stay a bit longer sometimes it is no more than you would expect me to do for Mrs Tozer for nothing. And pictures are much more interesting than bonnets.'

'That's enough from you! You needn't think you can be un-chaperoned with a young man at all hours just because you've got some high-and-mighty ideas about artists being better than what you're accustomed to.'

Lizzy did not reply. She had not the energy or will to try to explain. And if her mother wanted to think that she found Walter Deverell superior to her own family, then let her think it. As far as she was concerned he was superior to the whole world.

She turned to leave the room.

'If you're going up to your room to sulk, you're to see your father first.'

Her stomach tightened with fear at the idea of her father stepping in to the argument. 'He's asked to see me?'

'Not especially. But you're not to think you can come in and out of this house at all hours without bidding people the time of day.'

Lizzy went into the parlour where her father sat in his high wing chair polishing his violin. James and Tump were at the table playing draughts, and Harry was laboriously sorting a box of pebbles according to their sizes. Mrs Siddall often remarked of Harry: 'If only he would apply himself to simple useful tasks the way he does to daft useless ones.' Harry was the only one to smile at her.

'I've come to say goodnight, father. I'm tired, so I will go upstairs.'

'I didn't realise being paid to sit still could be so tiring.' his tone was icy.

Lizzy waited for him to say more, but he continued to polish his fiddle so she shut the door. When she reached her room she was about to collapse on her bed and burst into tears, when she checked herself. She easily *could* weep, but she found she could also suppress her tears. If she cried, then it would be like surrendering to the criticism of her parents; if she stayed calm, then she would be able to think. She sat quietly on the edge of her bed.

She was still in that position when Lyddy came up to bed. No definite plan had formed in her mind, but she had decided she would on no account miss her appointment with Walter the following Sunday. She dared not linger over one particular idea which presented itself, but despatched it to a recess of her memory marked 'forbidden'. This was the notion that by specifically seeking out more posing work, she might be able to afford a cheap room in the house Mary lived in and where she sometimes spent the night. If she kept the money to herself that is.

'I wish they'd show more understanding,' said Lyddy. 'You look so tired.'

'I'm all right.'

'Tell me about the painting.'

Lizzy was not in fact terribly struck by Deverell's representation of her as a page, though she would never have admitted it. She decided to tell Lyddy about Gabriel Rossetti, swearing her to secrecy before she did so.

Lyddy was wide-eyed. 'There,' she said when Lizzy had finished. 'I knew mother and father were wrong.'

'What have they been saying?'

'When you were late. They were sort of hinting to one another. It was horrible. Of course I had to pretend I didn't know what they were talking about. But it was perfectly obvious that even James understood. And Tump certainly did.'

'What did they say?'

'Oh, that it couldn't take all that long just to paint one person. And that artists were unreliable. And that most people looked down on girls who associated with them.'

'They don't know anything about it.'

When Lizzy tried to sleep, it all went round and round in her mind: Mr Rossetti wanting her to have her hair loose, Walter warming her hands, Mr Rossetti reciting, Walter telling her about Woolner . . . and those lines of verse, those wicked, frightening lines. Was it really only this morning that she had read them? At last she slept, and the impact of the events of the day kept The Dream at bay.

In the morning, her mother said, 'Now I hope I made myself clear last night, Lizzy. There are to be no more sittings.'

She did not attempt to argue, and Harry followed her into the garden when she left the house. 'Lizzy?'

'Yes? Quickly — I'll be late.'

'What is an artist?'

She looked at his vacant, kindly face. If it was a struggle for her to make sense of things, what must it be like for him? 'An artist is someone who makes pictures. Who draws pictures of people and houses and trees. And who tries to make them look bright and beautiful.'

Harry smiled. 'Bright and beautiful,' he repeated. 'Artist. Artist. When Dadda said it, I saw a nasty man.'

Lizzy was for once quite glad to reach Mrs Tozer's and immerse herself in the practicalities of bonnet-making. Sunday was still a long way off, and it seemed easier not to think about her mother's interdict. She had not told Ellen about her third sitting for Deverell, and since William Allingham had gone back to Ireland Ellen had not learned about it from him.

During their midday break, Ellen said to her: 'I do miss Mr Allingham. He's a real gentleman. Treats me as though I were somebody.' Lizzy thought about that remark. It could have been said of Walter Deverell. But then, surely, everybody WAS somebody? Why should they be treated otherwise? She felt an unexpected tremor of compassion for Ellen.

'Did you see anyone yesterday?' she asked.

'No. Hadn't the heart to go out.'

Mrs Tozer came striding into the workroom. 'Miss Sid. You know my rules. No callers at the shop. The young gentleman says it is *very* urgent. Two minutes. No longer.'

Ellen brightened up. 'Well, you *are* a dark horse, Lizzy.'

All the girls tried to see through the doorway as Lizzy went into the shop. Walter Deverell was standing sideways to the window, and the light caught his blue eyes and crumpled scarlet silk cravat.

'I'm sorry, Lizzy. I know I shouldn't interrupt you. But I must talk to you. Will you see me after you've finished work?'

'If you wish.'

'I will wait outside. At eight o'clock.'

For the rest of the day Ellen seized every opportunity to probe and tease, impervious to warnings from Mrs Dunn to 'Get on with your work . . . or else.' Lizzy took very little notice. Walter had cut the knot of her worries.

By eight o'clock the lamplighters were just starting on their rounds, and the streets were still softly illuminated by the April sunset which filled half the sky with gold and indigo. Walter was waiting on the pavement, and Lizzy noticed that Mary looked wistfully towards them before making off alone in the direction of her lodging-house.

'Thank you for seeing me,' he said. 'I need your help. We're in a bit of a stew.'

'What has happened?'

'I'll try to explain.' He looked up and down the street. Ellen and two other girls were standing talking a few yards away; they kept eying him and laughing. 'Look — there's a coffee-house on the corner. Shall we go and sit there? You could probably do with some refreshment.'

'Thank you.' Like most dining or coffee houses it was a dingy, utilitarian establishment, but to have any form of nourishment outside her home or Mrs Tozer's was a treat to Lizzy. They sat opposite one another on the high-backed wooden benches that partitioned each table, and ordered coffee and gingerbread. The presence of Deverell, the variation to her normal routine, and the intimate enclosure of the table and benches, made Lizzy feel quite cut off and separate from everyday reality. She waited expectantly to hear what he had to say.

'We owe you an apology, Lizzy. About that poem. I went back and mentioned it to Gabriel. Neither of us had properly studied it before. Everything happened in such a rush. And we both sat down and looked at it. Gabriel was very upset. That you should feel you had been subjected to an error of taste. Of course it was quite un-intentional.'

Lizzy did not know what to say. The embarrassed shame she had felt on reading the verses in question, and this encounter with Walter, with its accompaniment of steaming coffee and sticky gingerbread, were such separate moments of experience.

64

'Anyway,' he continued, 'After we'd talked, Gabriel decided his drawings didn't do you justice. That they lacked sensitivity. So he tore them up, and he refuses to make a rushed etching of something else for the magazine.'

Lizzy felt an involuntary element of disappointment. Despite everything, part of her had wanted to see her image reproduced many times over.

'So I've volunteered to do an etching instead. And I need your help.'

Her disappointment vanished. To be able to help Walter, to contribute in some manner to the enthusiasm he generated whenever he spoke of the work done by himself and his friends, and to be included in something beyond bonnets and watch-repairing and housework, was irresistible.

'Could you possibly come to the studio now? Of course I'll see you right back to your house.'

'Yes,' she said. 'I'll come.'

She knew she would not be able to return home that night.

Chapter Four

The corridors of Somerset House were dark, and the lamps which Deverell lit in the studio made the spaces seem dreamlike and mysterious. There was a note propped on his easel, and he and Lizzy stood and read it together.

> Tupper agrees. Poem will be rarified.
> Here's to the etching. Hunt agrees too.
> D.G.R. (PRB)

'Good,' said Deverell. 'It's all worked out.'

'What does it mean?'

'Well, Gabriel and I hatched a plan that I should make an etching to illustrate a poem we remember Jack Tupper wrote about the scene in *Twelfth Night* when Viola takes messages of love to Olivia from the duke,' he paused to take breath. 'But we thought the poem probably needed a bit of reworking, and weren't sure if Tupper would agree.'

Lizzy looked dubious.

'Oh, it's a perfectly dignified poem. No question of that. Tupper is a very fine person. And it's his brother and father who actually print the magazine.'

'What does PRB mean?'

'Ah! It's a secret really. It's a kind of special society. Of artists who want their work to have all the fine qualities of the early Italians. So it means Pre-Raphaelite Brotherhood. A brotherhood of very special people. Holman Hunt is another member — Gabriel went to consult him about our idea.'

'And you're a member too?' Lizzy was not particularly concerned that she had no idea what Pre-Raphaelite meant. Walter quite frequently used words she did not understand.

'Actually I'm not a full member. I wasn't in right at the beginning, and they've not yet admitted anyone else. Gabriel would like to. But Millais won't.'

'Who is he?'

'Johnny Millais? Oh, he's a genius. He's the best student the Academy Schools have ever had.'

'Is he more of a genius than Mr Rossetti?'

Deverell frowned. 'What a *difficult* question. Millais is the most accomplished painter I know. And Gabriel . . . well, he hasn't painted very much at all by comparison. But . . . he's . . .,' he hesitated, and then said in a rush: 'He's better than all the rest put together in my opinion.'

The light was really too dim for drawing, and Lizzy had to take two poses — as Viola in her page's costume, and as Olivia in her own dress, using a piece of rather grubby gauze as a veil. Deverell promised to be as quick as possible, but it was after ten o'clock when he finished. Lizzy could not conceal her yawns.

'Poor girl. You're worn out.'

She did not deny it.

'I'll go and see if Mr and Mrs Russell are still up, and get you something to eat and drink. And then I'll take you home. We'll manage a cab, I think.' He took some coins from his pocket, giving Lizzy her fee and counting the others.

'Thank you. But I shall spend the night with one of Mrs Tozer's girls. She lives in Covent Garden. I stay with her when the weather is bad.'

'Are you sure that'll be all right?'

She nodded. She would tell her mother she had had to work late . . . and give her a little of Walter's money as proof.

He came back from the Russells with a jug of milk and some bread and cheese. 'I got a frightful ticking off from Mrs Russell for keeping you out so late. But they've let me have the side-door key so I can come and spend the night here, after I've seen you to your room. It's so far to walk home now.'

'Don't you live here?' Lizzy had vaguely imagined the Deverell family were hidden away in one of the wings of Somerset House.

'Oh, no. We were in Chelsea, but last month we moved out to Kew. It's terribly inconvenient — such a long way late at night. But my mother thought it would be nice surroundings for my sisters. And the rent of the house is cheaper. My father has not been very well, and he feels we've got to be careful.' He was beginning to sound despondent, and made an effort to be cheerful. 'Come on — you must eat something. Mrs Russell will never forgive me if you don't.'

Lizzy found that in his company she could swallow food quite easily, and that even the milk did not have its usual slimy feel at the back of her throat. Without premeditation she suddenly said: 'If it is difficult, you must not pay me for sittings.' Immediately, she felt dismay that she had suggested giving up her one opportunity for financial independence, but also pleasure that it was in her power to offer a gift to Walter.

He had been thinking as she sat drinking her milk that she looked more like a child at bedtime than a young woman embarking on a career as an artist's model. Her offer touched him. 'You are very sweet. Very kind and good. But I'm not going to exploit your good nature. You work far harder for your income than I do.'

'I would not like you to be inconvenienced for the lack of a sitter. Because of circumstances.'

'Thank you.' He knelt beside her and took one of her hands. 'Shall we promise to do our best for one another? We will have sittings that do not make you too tired and at times when I can afford to pay you.'

'It need not be the full rate.'

'All right, Lizzy. I will accept that. When necessary.' He bent and kissed the tips of her fingers.

She sat perfectly still. For a few seconds she was entirely happy. She liked the peace of the studio at night-time, with the lamps illuminating only the easel and the dais, and with Walter kneeling by her like a prince in a fairy-tale. She wished they could remain like that for ever. But her head was swimming with fatigue, and even Walter's usual vitality had dimmed. Eventually he fetched his coat, and reluctantly they went out into the street. He left her by the open staircase to a gloomy lodging-house near the fruit market, and a few minutes later Mary — who was a light sleeper — unlocked her door and let Lizzy into a stuffy little room on the second floor.

Since it was not cold, Lizzy made up a rough bed on the floor, and in the early morning, as she breathed in the dust and smell of elderly grime from the rough wooden boards, she was entirely encompassed by The Dream. This time the space resembled the studio, and the ghoul-shapes were the shadows caused by the lamps. Huge and red, they pulsed towards her, blocking the doorway. To avoid them, she curled herself into a tight ball, head in arms, knees drawn up, and clenched her eyes shut. In the pinpricks of white light behind her eyelids she could just make out the shape of Walter's head. When she opened her eyes that shape was imposed on the red monsters. Then it faded, and she waited to be engulfed.

'Lizzy, Lizzy! Wake up. You're having a nightmare.' Mary was bending over her, and the room was full of grey daylight. Nothing was coloured red. Mary's mild, greasy face showed concern. 'Are you all right? You were groaning.'

'Yes. I'm all right.'

'Nothing . . . nothing bad happened last night?' The question was accompanied by a faintly sly expression.

Lizzy knew it was unfair to resent Mary for seeking gossip-information in return for providing a place to sleep, but she did resent her nevertheless. In Mary's experience bad things invariably happened, and Lizzy could never explain to her that Walter Deverell came from a world that was good, a world engaged in the quest for all that was bright and beautiful.

During the morning, while she was endeavouring to ruche and hem a trimming of green velvet which would keep fraying, Lizzy developed a gnawing, grinding pain in the pit of her stomach. By the midday break she could not stand up without holding on to something. At first the other girls accused her of eating exotic foods in the company of Mr Deverell, and Ellen pronounced that she should take a dose of physic to 'rinse her insides out.' Lizzy was in too much pain to respond to these remarks, and finally Mary went to inform Mrs Tozer. She was told to take Lizzy through to the sitting room and make her lie on the sofa.

When Mrs Tozer came in shortly with a cup of tea and a woollen shawl, she found Lizzy on her side, clasping her knees.

Within five minutes a few facts were established, and Lizzy knew that at any time she might expect to start 'to bleed'. She had also been given rudimentary instructions as to what that entailed, and permission to use Mrs Tozer's private store of disposable rags — 'An extravagance I allow my girls.'

Lizzy lay there mutely, sipping the tea and longing for the pain to cease.

Mrs Tozer looked at her, partly critical, partly tolerant. 'You'll be no use today. And you'd better spend the night here. Now — are there any questions you want to ask?'

Able to think only of her discomfort, Lizzy said miserably,

'What is the bleeding for?'

'*For? For?*' Mrs Tozer was not equipped to answer the question from a medical point of view, and unlike some women did not have an evasive philosophical reply readily to hand. She just accepted anything in life that presented itself as a fact and then proceeded to deal with it. 'It isn't *for* anything. It is what happens to all women.'

She was about to leave the room, when she remembered there was a further piece of information she could convey. 'Of course you will understand that it means you have to be very careful. It is a sign that you are old enough to bear children.'

Lizzy tried to assimilate this news. While she was doing so, Mrs Tozer added: 'I noticed you were going off with that young artist last night. You will have to be very much on your guard there. He hasn't touched you, has he?'

Lizzy remembered what her mother had said about girls who touched. 'No.'

'Quite so. Now you have a rest.'

At first Lizzy did not really think about anything. The unfamiliarity of the pain, combined with the unfamiliarity of Mrs Tozer's sitting-room — crammed with furniture, and cluttered with plants, ornaments, pictures and hangings — forced her into a limbo where she felt cut off from all her past life. She lay there with apparently no other function than to wait. But when the bleeding had begun, what then?

Late in the evening she discovered that it brought only intermittent relief from the pain. Before leaving her for the night, still on the sofa but covered now by a blanket, Mrs Tozer poured a few drops from a bottle into a cup of water. 'Drink this, Miss Sid. It'll bring you relief.'

She did as she was told.

After two or three minutes the pain began to fade, and images from the past returned to her mind. She remembered her patch of wasteground, and the red and black butterflies that clustered on the nettle plants in summer. And she recalled good afternoons at home, when the sun had shone into the kitchen and her mother had baked bread and told them stories of her childhood. She remembered the day she and Violet had walked with the boy named William, and she realised that his eyelashes had been thick like Walter's, and that what had cut her off from Violet was their different reactions to boys. Violet had wanted to be with them, to pursue them and be pursued — fighting, teasing, pushing, chasing. Lizzy had wanted to watch, to watch for the occasional beautiful characteristic such as silky hair or a gentle mouth.

Walter Deverell had held her hands.

His mouth had touched her fingers.

Did this make her a girl 'who touched'?

And why was it that it had happened on the day before she started to bleed?

Her sleep was unlike any she had ever had before, floating high on adventurous dreams that did not threaten her, and bringing her into morning with a sense of hope. The pain had gone, and she felt almost as though a long journey had been successfully completed.

Mrs Tozer asked her how she had slept.

'Very, very well.'

'That's the drops. Like magic they are. But only if used sparingly.'

The only reference the other girls made to the previous day was Ellen's, 'It's a shame it takes you like that. I'm lucky, never feel it. But Mrs T's a good sort when it comes down to it,' and Lizzy felt that she had entered something in which they all shared. But some part of her deeply resented that sharing: she did not want to be like them, though she could now tolerate their jokes and attitudes, and even enjoy a sense of companionship through work.

During the long stretches of the afternoon, she was pinning and stitching and fixing in a state of semi-consciousness which was quite familiar to all the girls. And through the enclosed world of silk and cotton and straw filtered a voice that penetrated to her marrow. It was her mother's. Mrs Siddall stood at the doorway into the shop deep in conversation with Mrs Tozer.

They walked through the workroom to Mrs Tozer's quarters, neither of them glancing at Lizzy. Then ten minutes later she was called.

Her mother sat on the edge of an armchair, decorously holding a small glass of cordial. She did not look Lizzy in the eye.

'Your mother has been worried, Lizzy. But I have explained to her why you have not been home.'

Lizzy waited. The previous night could be explained, but how about Monday?

Mrs Tozer continued. 'And we have agreed that since it seems to have taken you badly this first time, you'd better not try walking

71

home of an evening. For the rest of this week you can either sleep here or with Mary.'

Lizzy could not believe it. Suddenly the week opened out into a long stretch of freedom.

'I'm sorry she has been a trouble, Mrs Tozer. Not able to do her work.' Mrs Siddall still did not look at her daughter.

'It can't be helped. These things take different people different ways. Working with so many girls I've learned to take the rough with the smooth.'

'You've been most kind, I'm sure. Now Lizzy, I shall expect you home on Saturday evening without fail. And you are to work extra hard to make up for lost time.'

Lizzy was puzzled; her mother had warned that this illness would overtake her, and yet now seemed to imply that its advent and effect were her own fault. 'Yes, mother.'

'You're extremely lucky that Mrs Tozer is so understanding.'

'Needs must, Mrs Siddall. Now — if you're ready, I could show you the way out the back. Miss Sid, if you'll just stay here we'll settle arrangements for the rest of the week.'

'Yes, Mrs Tozer.'

When Mrs Tozer returned, she looked somewhat stern. 'Since your mother seemed a little flummoxed by your "starting", Miss Sid, I did not reveal to her the discrepancy in your whereabouts on Monday night. I shall assume you were already feeling unwell. But I repeat what I said yesterday, you will have to be very much on your guard. Do you understand?'

'Yes, ma'am.'

'Good. Now, I expect you would prefer to go with Mary. You are used to that?'

'Yes.'

'Then you have a word with her when you get back to the workroom. And see you get that bonnet finished before you go. You'll have to make up some extra time.'

'Yes, ma'am.'

Lizzy left the room, and Mrs Tozer poured some cordial (a term she applied to all forms of alcohol) into a glass for herself. Having reinforced her warning to Lizzy, she felt she had done her duty. She had not particularly wanted her sleeping on the sofa again, since she liked to spend an hour in her sitting room before going to bed, reading a romance and frequently replenishing her glass.

As she had the extra money from Walter, Lizzy decided she would ask Mary if it might be possible for her to take a separate room in the lodging house for three nights. Mary agreed to come with her to find out, and after work they approached the taciturn landlady — who looked Lizzy up and down, inspecting her for moral and medical defects. She was offered a small, bare room on the ground floor, and payment was taken in advance.

'Will you come up with me for a while?' asked Mary. 'We could talk. I've got a little bread and cheese.'

'I think I'd rather stay here. Thank you.' Lizzy knew Mary was disappointed, that she was shy and lonely and would like someone to provide a little warmth and friendship. 'I'm still . . . tired.'

'I understand.' Mary left her, and climbed the stairs to the room that was both an improvement on the slum-dwelling where she had spent her childhood, and too miserably isolated a space to call home.

Lizzy closed the door and stood in the middle of her room and threw out her arms. For the first time in her life she was to spend a night alone in a room which she could lock against all comers. She took a deep breath and subsided on to the bed. A sudden sense of independence made her feel giddy.

The room had a washstand with a china bowl and jug; water was fetched from the pump in the yard. She would be able to wash and undress and brush her hair in total privacy. It felt like luxury. First, though, she would go back into the streets. Her freedom had made her hungry, and she had a little money left.

Normally when she walked out on her own, people took little notice of her. She wore simple clothes, usually looked downwards, and never did anything to attract attention. But that evening her unaccustomed independence made her look curiously about her. To her consternation, people — men — looked back. She almost returned to her room without buying anything, but her desire for a piece of the sticky gingerbread from the coffee house prevailed.

She woke early to the noise of porters' trolleys clanking over the cobbles outside. The shapes of the unfamiliar jug and basin against the flaking wall reminded her where she was. Thursday, Thursday morning already. Somehow she had to contact Walter, for she had never told him she would not be able to sit for him on Sunday. She considered how to do this, and decided that the best way would be to write him a note and deliver it to the Design School. She remembered the note Gabriel Rossetti had left on the easel, and this reassured her that he would not object to a letter that was informal and short. The gingerbread she had brought back to her room had been wrapped in a piece of white paper, and she flattened this out and found the pencil she kept in her purse.

Dear Mr Deverell,

> I may not come out on Sunday. I am free
> today and Friday.
> > L.S. (from Mrs Tozers)

At seven o'clock she left the lodging-house and walked to Somerset House, her daring ebbing somewhat as she crossed the courtyard and then pulled the heavy bell-handle on the side-door. She waited a long time, unsure whether to ring again. But at last there were footsteps, and Mrs Russell, still smoothing her hair, opened the door.

'Yes?' She did not sound too friendly. Then she saw who it was. 'Goodness me, young woman. Whatever are you doing here at this hour?'

'I'm sorry. But I have to start work soon at the bonnet shop. And I need to tell Mr Deverell I won't be free on Sunday.' She brought out her note, and handed it over with the writing facing upwards. 'Please, could you possibly give this to him?'

Mrs Russell scanned the message. 'Ah well, of course, if that is all. I will see that he gets it.'

'Thank you.' Lizzy hesitated, and then could not resist saying, 'Do you think you will see him today?'

'Yes, my dear. He has his drawing class.'

Lizzy smiled. Then there was just a chance . . . just a chance that he might respond to her note by the time she finished work.

But when the long, and uneventful, day was over, there was no sign of Walter Deverell outside the shop. Lizzy looked covertly up and down the street, but still could not see him. She hesitated, uncertain what to do. If she went straight back to her room, and he turned up a few minutes later, she would miss him altogether.

'Are you coming now?' Mary was at her side.

She improvised. 'Soon. I just want to get a little air. Shall I come up to your room for a while when I come in?'

'I'll walk with you, if you like.'

There wasn't any answer to that, so Mary dutifully accompanied

Lizzy as she looped around the adjacent streets, returning three times to one or other end of Cranbourn Street, but never catching a glimpse of Walter Deverell. Finally they went to Mary's room, where Mary offered to share a hunk of stale bread and hard cheese. But Lizzy claimed not to be hungry, knowing she would never be able to swallow, as disappointment was clamping at her throat, and the faint bedroom-smell offended her nostrils.

She did not enjoy her second night on her own. Listening to Mary talking about the unlikelihood of ever finding a respectable young man to free her from the drudgery of bonnet-making had been dispiriting. Suddenly independence did not amount to much if all it meant was solitary evenings in shabby rooms with no promise of anything better for the following day. By the next morning she had convinced herself that Walter did not want to see her any more, and that it had all been a kind of joke — the praising of her looks and the odd, intent way Mr Rossetti had asked her to sit with her hair down. His drawings had all been destroyed, and probably by now Walter too had decided she did not inspire good pictures. As she sat at the worktable with the other girls, she felt sentenced to insignificance. Stitch, stitch, stitch, snip; stitch, stitch . . . Another well-made but ordinary bonnet would soon find its way to the head of somebody's smug and ordinary wife.

During the afternoon Ellen, who was serving in the shop, came into the workroom and surreptitiously handed a well-folded note to Lizzy while pretending to enquire about the completion of the bonnet. Her last whispered words were: 'You lucky devil.' Lizzy was left clutching the note and not knowing what to do. No one had noticed its passing — Mrs Dunn was behind the screen, and Mrs Tozer in her quarters. But she was terrified that if she opened it someone might see, and she would end up having it taken from her at least until the end of the working day. Visits to the privy were only really allowed during breaks, but she had been told that girls in her condition might overlook this rule. Quietly she left the room and made her way to the backyard.

Leaning against the door, which had no lock, of the windowless shed, she unfolded the note. A tile was missing from the roof, letting in much-needed air and light, and also, on occasions, rain, wind and snow.

Dear Lizzy,

I did not receive your note until this morning.
I will wait for you outside the shop at 8 this
evening.
                    Yours sincerely,
                    W.D.

She hardly dared read the note through a second time. She refolded it, and reached up under her dress to the top of her corset, where she tucked the folded paper next to her breast.

When they met, Deverell's mood seemed strange. He appeared to be very pleased to see her, grateful for her note, but also distraught. After they had reached the quietness of the studio he told her what was wrong.

'I was unable to come here yesterday because my father is ill. I had to stay with my mother to see the doctor.'

'Walter' — it was the first time she had used his first name out loud — 'I am sorry. Is he better?'

'A little. But he won't be able to come to work for some time.'

'Will you still come here?'

'For the moment I will take extra classes. And give instructions from my father to another teacher who will do his duties for him.'

She tried not to let the relief that Walter was not going to be banished to Kew overcome her sympathy concerning his father.

'But I'm afraid, Lizzy, I won't be able to stay here very long tonight. I promised my mother I would not be home too late.'

'I understand.'

'But I saw Gabriel earlier, and he said he would like to see you.'

She stiffened, looked at him with an element of reprimand.

'You needn't if you don't want to. We could leave early. But he wants to talk to you about posing in a general way — so many of our friends know about you now and would like to employ you.'

'But Mr Rossetti destroyed his drawings of me.'

'Yes, because they didn't do you justice. I'm afraid mine don't either, but I'm not such a perfectionist. I did the Viola etching in rather a rush, and just handed the plate over to the printer.'

Lizzy, not fully comprehending, said nothing.

'Since you're not free on Sunday, I'll have to finish the painting without another sitting. But that should be all right. Only they have to be sent in next week.'

'Sent . . . in?'

'Well, taken in, really. Gabriel and I were planning to send our paintings in for the Academy exhibition, but we've decided not to. It's tiresome to submit to a jury of old fuddy-duddies. So we're going to hang them in the Free Exhibition. That's open to everybody.'

'Can anyone go and see it?'

'Of course.'

'Where will it be?'

'The Portland Gallery. In Regent Street.'

Regent Street! Her picture would be on show in Regent Street . . .

'I'll take you along there. To the opening. Would you like that?'

'Oh — yes. But . . .'

'But . . .?'

'When will it be?'

'Yes, of course. You might not be free.' He searched through some papers spread untidily on the table. 'Here we are. Next Saturday. Next Saturday afternoon from three until six.'

Tears of resentment stung the back of Lizzy's eyes. 'I . . .' She found she could not speak.

'You're supposed to be at work then, aren't you?'

She nodded.

'I tell you what. We'll have a word with Gabriel. And if he agrees we can fix you up with some sittings, couldn't you ask for Saturday afternoon off?'

Lizzy recalled the way Mrs Tozer had once said to her, 'Play your cards carefully, and keep yourself to yourself like a proper professional beauty.'

'I believe that if there were to be fairly regular professional sittings, Mrs Tozer would not mind if I went to the exhibition.' She sounded much more resolute than she felt, but she sensed that if she let this chance slip by, if she failed to 'play her cards carefully', the fragile goal of independence would sink completely in a sea of complications.

'In that case, we must certainly see what we can do.'

When Gabriel arrived, Walter explained the situation to him briefly, before departing for Kew.

Lizzy sat on the edge of the chaise-longue, very nervous at being alone with Mr Rossetti.

'I am sorry those verses of Woolner's upset you. Particularly as

77

you had taken the trouble to read our magazine.' Rossetti was standing by the fireplace, quite a long way from her.

She stared at her lap, and murmured, 'It does not matter.' The long ensuing silence made her feel even more awkward, and she stammered, 'I — I did like the poem by Ellen Alleyn.'

He walked quickly over and sat at the other end of the chaise. 'You really are a remarkable girl. Ellen Alleyn is my sister. Her real name is Christina. Christina Rossetti.'

'Your sister?' Lizzy was very surprised — and pleased. 'How old is she?'

'Nineteen. She's my younger sister. Maria is the oldest, she's twenty-three. And William and I come in between.'

'Do you all write poetry?'

'Yes. But Christina and I do it best.'

She smiled. He reminded her of Tump again.

'Well — we do. There's no point in being falsely modest. I must show you some more of Christina's verses. You are — perhaps — just a little like her. Calm. Reserved.'

She longed to tell him that she wrote poetry too, or at least tried to; but she did not dare.

'Perhaps one day you will meet her.' A slight flicker of doubt crossed his face as he said this. 'Now, d'you think you could get your Mrs Tozer to agree to let you go whenever one of us needs you? Holman Hunt wants to meet you, and so does Johnny Millais, and they've both got particular paintings in mind. And, of course, I want to use you whenever I can.'

Lizzy took a deep breath. It would have been easier just to say 'Yes', but she knew she must be cautious. 'I don't think Mrs Tozer would like me to go just any time. But if it was always the same time. Like a particular afternoon . . .' Gabriel nodded. 'You see my mother expects me to take my regular wage home.'

'Parents always do, don't they?'

He spoke to her so directly, on terms of such equality, that she was surprised.

'I mean,' he went on, 'they bring you into this world that is full of wonderful things like poetry and history and painting, and then wonder why you don't want to work in an office or a hatshop all day.'

'Oh,' she said, 'I do agree.'

He was delighted by her warmth. 'In fact I'm being unfair to my

78

parents — my father especially. They encourage me to paint. But they do so *approve* of William's regular job.' He scrutinised her carefully. 'Your parents probably need your wage though?'

'Yes . . . but . . .'

'But?'

She felt deeply guilty and very excited as she voiced her thoughts. 'Well . . . father has a shop. He mends jewellery and watches. But he likes to close early. And James, my young brother, helps him. And Lyddy, who's next to me, works at a store, and earns a little now. My mother is very careful. Then there's Tump and Harry.'

'They are young children?'

'Yes.'

'And you think it would really be possible for them all to survive without you?'

'Without *all* of my wages.' She felt ashamed as she said it.

'So you could be a little independent?'

She nodded.

'Do any of them like poetry?'

'No. Just songs. Parlour songs.'

He did not speak for quite a long time. Then he said: 'Which would be your best afternoon for regular posing?'

The names of the days flashed through her head. In her mind they all had colours and shapes. Perhaps Wednesday, because it was such a solid rectangle of dark indigo, stuck in the middle of the week, and seemed to drag more than any other day.

'Wednesday?'

'You ask your Mrs Tozer about it, and I'll fix things up with the others. Now — would you like to come for a walk by the river?'

It was half-past nine, and she was tired, but she said 'Yes.' Any chance to experience more of this new world was irresistible.

As they walked, Gabriel talked. He talked of poetry, the power of words, the magical sliding and shifting of meaning between one language and another. He had spent the afternoon translating a poem from medieval Italian into English. Suddenly the idea of 'foreignness' took on another aspect for Lizzy. Until then, a foreigner had been someone who looked and sounded different. But Gabriel, although unconventional, did not look particularly un-English, and his voice was as precise as a preacher's Yet he had this foreign landscape of words inside his head, words that to her would be meaningless and which to him held the same beauty as

79

Tennyson's.

'Are you from Italy?' she asked.

'Indirectly. My father is, and so is my mother's father.'

'And you have been there?'

'Oh no.' He seemed indifferent to the idea. 'I don't need to. My father never really left. He always speaks Italian, and Italians visit our house all the time.'

This conjured up in Lizzy's mind a large hallway and drawing room, panelled and lit by chandeliers, with dark-haired visitors in bright clothes thronging about and speaking in excitable voices. Yet Gabriel's clothes were so shabby, it did not look as though he lived in a grand house.

'Oh!' he suddenly cried, 'Look!'

Crouching in the semi-darkness by a boat drawn up on the strand was a ginger cat, busily tearing at the remains of a raw fish. Gabriel did not try to approach it, but squatted down at a distance, saying softly, 'There's a clever cat. Did you steal it from a fish-monger? Or catch it like an angler? There's a handsome one.'

Lizzy was amazed to see a grown and educated man speak to a stray cat as though it were a person. She was used to her mother throwing stones to frighten cats away from their garden, insisting they were 'dirty, flea-ridden creatures.' She noticed that the cat looked at Gabriel with curious, unafraid eyes.

When finally he left Lizzy at the lodging-house, and she let herself into her room, she realised she was very hungry indeed. Unlike Walter Deverell, Gabriel Rossetti had never once offered to get her some refreshment, and it was too late for her to go out alone. As she undressed, she carefully took Walter's note from her corset, unfolded it and re-read it several times. The words began to dance before her eyes, and she brought the paper up to her mouth and kissed it three times softly. He had touched it. He had shaped those letters. He had written to her. He had written 'Dear Lizzy.'

She lay in bed wondering if she dare ask Mrs Tozer about Wednesday afternoons before she had received confirmation that she would definitely be employed to pose. Yet if she did not ask, and then was suddenly expected by Mr Rossetti to be free, it would be very awkward. She remembered how Walter revered him, describing him as 'better than all the rest put together', and decided she must seize her chance.

80

Chapter Five

'You are thoroughly irresponsible!' Mrs Siddall had her hands on her hips and faced the open kitchen door. The sound of her words floated into the garden where the mint and lemon balm thrust their fragrant shoots through the earth and into the May sunshine, and the yellow daisies called leopards' bane were bright against the wooden gate. As a child, Lizzy had imagined a time when leopards stalked the streets of London, and the flowers were a necessary precaution for all households. Now she wiped the pots from Sunday dinner, and pressed her lips in an obstinate line.

'I obtained a good position for you, the best position of any girl round here. And you throw it away!'

Lizzy waited. No more words followed, so she said quietly, 'I have only arranged to have Wednesday afternoons free. Mrs Tozer was perfectly agreeable.' This was true.

'And Saturday? How about Saturday? You know it is often one of the busiest times.'

Mrs Tozer had not, in fact, been *quite* so agreeable about that. 'Only this once, Miss Sid. If you're going to have your picture painted every Wednesday, I can't afford to let you off every Saturday to see it hung up in some public place. But just this once. Since it's the first time.'

Lizzy thought that if Mrs Tozer could be sympathetic about her longing to go to the Free Exhibition, then her own mother certainly ought to be.

'If you'd worked hard, you had a secure future with Mrs Tozer.'

'But I'm not leaving her. I'm just — '

'Don't argue! You know perfectly well you've got your head set on getting mixed up with that artist bunch. It'll lead you nowhere. You won't find a husband that way, my girl.'

'I'm not — '

'Then you should be. You're seventeen this month. And you're a woman now. I don't want any trouble on my hands.'

'Mother, I'm only trying — '

'I don't want to hear any excuses. You've always been self-willed. It's no example to your younger sisters.'

'I've never done anything that either Lyddy or Tump — '

'Tump! The airs and graces Madam Clara puts on she certainly doesn't get from me. Your father's right. He said no good would come of being paid just to rest on your backside.'

Lizzy stared at her mother. All the closeness of her childhood — the regular domestic discipline, the occasional demonstrations of affection — seemed to have been nullified by the hard, angry face of the woman who was almost shouting at her. That woman no longer appeared to be her mother. She had become her enemy.

She carefully wiped the last of the pots and put them away. Without saying anything, she left the kitchen and went upstairs to her room. Her breath was coming in quick, short gasps. Her mother's voice pierced up the stairs.

'We don't want any irregularities in this family!'

It was a statement which on the surface made little sense to Lizzy, but whose meaning reached her instinctively. For a long time she sat on the edge of her bed, trying to control her breathing and to suppress the waves of bitterness that made angry words stream through her head like wasps. When she felt calmer, she made a vow: this was the first and last time she was going to be treated like a common tart by her own family.

In the late afternoon she went downstairs. It was warm, and her father, together with James and Tump, was sitting outside the front door talking to passers-by. Lyddy was helping her mother to do some mending in the kitchen, and Harry was fidgetting idly by the back door. Lizzy took a good look at each of the groups, fixing them in her mind. Lyddy tried to catch her eye, but no one spoke to her.

She went up to Harry. 'Would you like to come for a walk?'

His gentle, bony face lost its vague expression, and became eager — over eager. 'Yes Lizzy, yes Lizzy, yes Lizzy,' he chanted. Then he rushed into the yard shouting, 'WALK!'

Lizzy felt both pain and exasperation as she watched him. Her mother said, 'You always over-excite him.' She did not reply.

As they walked down the street, she said to Harry, 'I'm going to show you somewhere special.' He smiled, but she felt he had not understood her words.

82

The top of his head did not yet reach her shoulder, and she looked down at the floppy, straw-coloured hair, and the old brown smock which for once he had buttoned correctly. As they walked up by the tannery, the stench heavy in the warm air, she said, 'Harry, will you remember this walk? Remember which way to come?'

Unexpectedly lucid, he replied, 'By the black houses. Into the smell.'

'Yes. Then straight on.'

The buildings petered out, and the lane led through vegetable gardens to Lizzy's waste patch. 'Here,' she said, 'Through the bushes.'

She had to get almost on her hands and knees to push through the hazel and elder, and Harry followed very closely, anxious to keep up. When Tump was made to take him out, she often deliberately tried to lose him by hurrying ahead and taking unexpected turns. He had dreams of being stranded.

'There.' Lizzy stood up in the clearing. The tall grasses brushed against her skirt, and the bushes and saplings made a close circle, open only to the blue sky. 'You can come here whenever you like. And be quite quiet.'

Harry looked about him, and suddenly flung himself down on the grass, face upwards. 'Sky, sky,' he said. 'Sky.'

Lizzy smiled, and lay down beside him. And she too, for a moment, experienced a world which was simply sky.

When they left, Harry said, 'Take me soon. Again.'

Her throat burned. 'You're going to have to find it by yourself, Harry.'

He looked up at her, suddenly forlorn and uncomprehending.

She told only Lyddy of her plan, after they had gone to bed and were lying on top of the covers in the stuffy attic room. 'I'm sorry,' she concluded. 'I'm afraid when they find out I'm not coming back there'll be a scene. And they'll question you. But you must deny that you know anything about it.'

'Oh Lizzy. Must you go? I'm sure mother will calm down.'

'No . . . no. I'd have to be different — to please her. And I can't be.'

Lyddy looked fondly at her. When Lizzy wasn't being too reserved or haughty, she loved her very much. And at night-time, in her cream gown with her hair brushed until it crackled, she was the

83

most beautiful girl Lyddy had ever seen. If she was to go, then the one thing that made her feel a little different from the other girls in the street would have gone too. Through Lizzy, she felt she had indirect contact with a wider world.

'Please. You will see me. Somehow?'

Lizzy thought for a while. 'Yes. We will arrange something. I can always get a message to you at the shop. And you know where Mrs Tozer is.'

'You will be there?'

'Of course I will. That's the only way I can keep myself.'

'Supposing they . . . the artists . . . want you to pose more . . .?'

'It would never be that much.'

But in the morning when Lizzy packed a bundle of her belongings into an old shawl, and by subterfuge carried it out of the house without her mother noticing, she did not envisage, as she walked towards Cranbourn Street, that she would be at Mrs Tozer's for the rest of her life.

Lizzy sat on the creaking iron bed, her bundle beside her. Mary's landlady, Mrs Foley, had given her the same room as last time, extracting a week's rent in advance. This had used up nearly all the money she had been saving in her workbox.

And so now she was free. But there was nowhere to heat water to make tea; no cup or bowl or bread or milk. Just the four flaking walls and her own uninterrupted feelings.

She stood up and untied her bundle.

At exactly the same time the following evening, Tuesday, she again sat on the bed. Her few belongings were now laid out, and there were some cherries in a screw of paper on the washstand, but nothing had happened to deflect her attention from the loneliness of her freedom. There had been no word from either Deverell or Rossetti. She had permission to take the following afternoon off, but no promise of a sitting. All day she had longed for Ellen to bring a secret message through from the shop, telling her when she would be required. And all day she had dreaded that her mother would suddenly appear, angrily demanding to know why she had not been home.

She went to sleep that night having decided that she must take a message round to the Design School first thing in the morning. But when morning came, she had not the courage to put herself forward in such a manner.

'Now then, Miss Sid,' said Mrs Tozer breezily when she arrived with Mary at the shop, 'it's today you're doing your studio work, isn't it?'

The grandeur of that phrase 'studio work'! Lizzy murmured 'Yes,' and tried to keep the sense of panic that gnawed at her stomach under control. She avoided talking to the other girls as they settled to work and they were too used to her uncommunicative moods to try to break through her reserve.

At two o'clock, she put away her work, donned her bonnet, said a quiet 'Good afternoon,' to Mrs Dunn, and left the workroom. Her feet moved quite briskly through the shop and into the street, but she did not feel any sense of control over her movements. She had no idea where she was going to go. It was like sleepwalking on very thin ice: any second she would wake up and find herself drowning.

> 'In robe and crown the king stepped down,
> To meet and greet her on her way;'

declaimed Rossetti, stepping forward from the next doorway.

> ' "It is no wonder," said the lords,
> "She is more beautiful than the day." '

Lizzy gasped so sharply, she almost lost her breath.

'We did say Wednesday, didn't we?' said Rossetti, taken aback.

'Yes.' The word was squeezed out, soft and sibilant.

'Well, that's what I thought. Now, let me tell you my plan.'

Almost before he had finished talking, he started to walk towards Leicester Square, and Lizzy fell into step beside him, the centre of her new world suddenly restored. The fact that she did not particularly like Mr Rossetti, and that he was wearing a summer jacket so shabby one might have hesitated to give it to a beggar, counted for nothing. Her 'studio work' was not a chimera after all.

As they cut up through Soho, he explained that he was taking her to his studio in Newman Street. He had started work on an ambitious new canvas, and he wanted her to pose for one of the main figures. It was only when he led the way up narrow stairs to the studio on the first floor that she began to feel apprehensive. It was a very shabby house; a placard announced that a 'Dancing Academy' had its premises on the ground floor, and she could hear an out-of-tune piano and the pounding of not very delicate feet.

'Frightful racket,' said Gabriel, unlocking the door.

It was not at all like the studio at the Design School. The room was small, dirty, and darkly panelled. The bare window did let in quite a lot of light, but the pieces of broken furniture and dusty hangings might have been better left in shadow. In one corner there were a lot of empty bottles. Gabriel saw that Lizzy eyed them apprehensively.

'Don't worry,' he said, 'I'm not a boozer. Brown says I ought to paint them. Bottles. He says once you can paint a bottle you can paint pretty well anything. Boring old bottles, I call 'em,' His voice was resonant and steady, but he kept looking at Lizzy as though he could hardly believe she was there, and did not quite know what to do with her. They stood, feet apart, on the bare floor, half looking at one another and half staring around the room. Simultaneously they both looked into the mirror on the wall opposite the window. It was the one ornate piece of furniture in the room: a great curving gilt frame, all scallops and scrolls. The mirror itself was dirty and the silvering was damaged, but their images were clear enough, each staring at the other's reflection.

'Stay there,' murmured Rossetti. 'Stay just like that.' He moved the large, and virtually bare, canvas that was propped against the one good chair to a corner, and sat down with a board and some paper across his knees. Then he started to draw. His pencil made an urgent, continuous, scrabbling sound, like a small animal desperately trying to escape from a box. He kept looking at Lizzy and then at her reflection, at her and then the reflection, until she began to feel she was split in two.

Her head was swimming, both with the long pose and the things which had not been settled. How long was he employing her for that day, and was she going to be taken to the opening of the Free Exhibition on Saturday, and — above all — when would Walter be needing her again? Rossetti had casually mentioned that Walter's father was still very ill, but nothing more. Everything felt temporary and unplanned, as she stood in that dirty little room. It wasn't like posing properly in her Viola costume.

Suddenly he pulled the paper from the board and took a new sheet. She realized he was going to start all over again.

'Please . . .' she said faintly.

'Sorry. I was forgetting. I don't know how Deverell works with those clockwork breaks of his. Go on then — walk about — stretch

86

your legs.'

She went over to the window, conscious he was staring at her all the time. Fighting her shyness and fear, she asked, 'Do you think Mr Deverell will be able to see me on Saturday?'

'Saturday?' he said casually, and then went silent.

She looked out of the window on to a derelict backyard. Tears were starting in her eyes, and she felt she had come to the end of everything. She hated this room, she was frightened, and the broken sheds and rusty implements below were an appropriate image of what the world seemed to offer her.

'Oh of course,' he continued, 'it's the exhibition. You're coming with us, aren't you?'

She turned swiftly, her face pink, the unshed tears shining across her widened eyes. 'I still may come?'

'Of course. Why ever not?'

At last, after what seemed like many hours of posing — it was in fact nearly three — he said, 'I'd better be getting home. I promised William and Christina we'd read poems together after tea.' Then he looked at her, suddenly unsure. 'And you? Where will you go now?'

'To my room.'

'Room?'

'I have left home.'

He was concerned. 'Why?'

'Because . . .' She could not explain. 'It seemed easier . . . more convenient.'

'You're not in that gloomy old lodging house I dropped you at the other night?'

She nodded.

He sighed deeply, comparing his lot with hers. It made him uncomfortable that he could not invite her back to tea to meet his family. But although the Rossetti household was a very modest one, his mother and sisters could not be expected to receive a girl who earned money by posing and went to artists' studios unaccompanied.

As he paid Lizzy, he said, 'We must find a way to do things better.'

She did not wonder what he meant, anxious only that Saturday's plans should be made. Hesitantly, she asked, 'What time does the exhibition open on Saturday?'

'Three o'clock. Deverell and I will be at your lodgings a quarter

87

of an hour before that.'

That piece of information was enough for Lizzy to build her whole future on, and she felt no resentment as she made her way back to Covent Garden alone. Even the fact that Rossetti had paid her only enough to cover a two-hour sitting did not perturb her. Her whole imagination was fixed on Saturday: on what she should wear, on what an exhibition of paintings might be like, and on what Walter would do and say.

At two o'clock on Saturday she left Mrs Tozer's and hurried to her room. In the centre of her bed was her summer bonnet, transformed by the addition of a band of white satin and velvet lilies. She had made these from scraps, working until the early hours of the morning and using up the candle that was supposed to last all week.

She changed into her best dress, a deep olive green, and carefully arranged her hair to loop smoothly round under the bonnet. There was no mirror in her room, and she could see only a very faint reflection of herself in the glass of the window as she tied the pale ribbons under her chin. She hoped the effect was both tasteful and striking.

When she went outside, Deverell and Rossetti were already coming down the street. She was shocked to see how tired and pale Walter looked, and forgot to be nervous about her own appearance as they greeted one another.

'I am sorry not to have seen you this week. But I could not leave Kew.'

'Your father?'

'He is still not well. Not at all well.' He stared blankly at the ground for a moment, and then abruptly shook his head. 'But I am free today. And so are you.'

'Yes.'

Their eyes met, and he suddenly smiled. 'We will enjoy ourselves.'

Gabriel stood a few feet away watching them. The expression of pleasure on his face faded and was briefly replaced by one of desolation, like a poor man observing a feast.

But Deverell turned to him and made a remark, and soon Gabriel was exclaiming in an astonished, emphatic way: 'How did you *know,* Miss Siddall? How could she have known, Walter?'

'Known what?'

'Lilies, dumb friend, lilies! How could she have known to wear them?'

Walter stepped back and saw the bonnet properly for the first time. 'Cunning, aren't they?'

'Cunning is *not* the word. They're positively prophetic.'

Lizzy was beginning to feel more and more uncomfortable. She reached up nervously to touch the flowers, as if to ensure they were still mere scraps of cloth.

'Or did you tell Miss Siddall about my painting?'

'No,' said Walter. 'I haven't told her about any —' He broke off. 'Oh, I *see*. I see what you mean.'

'Well I don't.' Lizzy was surprised by her own firmness.

Both men laughed. 'Come on,' said Rossetti, 'you're going to see my painting now. In the exhibition. And you'll find it contains a lily like the ones you're wearing.'

They set off, Lizzy a little disappointed that her bonnet had not elicited a more orthodox complimentary response, but filled with happiness to be walking with Deverell once again.

There was already a large crowd at the exhibition. Some people were smart and fashionable, others rather unconventional, some shabby, and a few were positively eccentric. Lizzy felt overawed, and kept very close to Walter. However she soon discovered that little was expected of her. Her companions burrowed through the crowd, glancing at paintings and exchanging rapid comments which she did not understand. Each time she tried to take a proper look at a painting, they darted off again. It was in any case impossible to stand back to see a picture properly, because everywhere people stood right in front of them, talking, talking, talking. She did not think she had ever seen so many people with so much to say. Then suddenly they were right up in front of her painting. There she was, leaning forward with what she thought was a rather silly expression on her face; and there were her knees and calves. That was the worst part. They were so big. Nearly as big as Rossetti's knees and calves in his jester tights.

She turned away. And when she looked again she could not see either Walter or Gabriel. For a second a feeling of panic overcame her — what if someone should speak to her? But she made herself walk slowly towards an empty space in the corner of the gallery, and realised that no one was going to accost her. She could even look at a painting properly for the first time.

The one in front of her was very strange. A girl, wearing a white shift, was hunched nervously on a bed, while another figure, also clad in a white shift, held out . . . a lily. A white lily, the same as the ones on the bonnet. The figure with the lily — she thought it was a young man — had bare feet, and seemed to be standing on a pale flame. Just below his feet, in the bottom left-hand corner, were the initials 'DGR' and the date 'March 1850'. She looked again at the girl, so pinched and pale, and noticed for the first time the halo disc behind her hair. Of course, a bible subject. But it was so unlike any bible picture she had seen. The girl looked so real. Yet she must be the Virgin Mary, and the young man must presumably be the Angel Gabriel. How did it go? 'Hail, thou that art highly favoured . . .' How odd, to think of Mr Rossetti painting the Virgin Mary. Could he possibly have made this pale, translucent painting in that dirty little room?

'What do you think?'

She started, not realising that Gabriel was standing just behind her.

'Do you think I've managed the lily all right?'

'Oh . . . Yes. I . . .'

'Yes?'

'I wonder . . . I know it must be . . . Mary . . . but the girl?'

'Who sat for me? Christina mostly. My sister. It's her head, anyway.'

'That is your sister? The one who writes poetry?'

'Yes.'

Lizzy stared and stared at the face. There was something about it that made her feel very strange. The expression in the girl's eyes as she looked at the proffered lily was so fearful.

Two men came up and glanced at the painting.

'Bit wishy-washy, what?' said one, in a booming voice.

'I'll say,' said the other, sounding very bored.

They did not bother to give a second look, but strode away.

Lizzy saw the colour drain from Gabriel's face. He said nothing, but touched her elbow, and walked out of the gallery, beckoning to Deverell on the way. Once they were on the pavement he offered no explanation, but just said, 'We'll go to Newman Street.'

Lizzy was surprised Walter asked no questions, but simply fell in with the change of plan. For herself she was deeply disappointed at being plucked from the crowd of onlookers, only to go to that dingy little studio. She could not imagine why anyone should want to leave such an exalted gathering. The blunt comments they had overheard meant little to her. When Mrs Tozer did not like a piece of work, she thumped her fist on the table and said, 'This is a grotesque, ill-made, *misbegotten* malfection, which no woman should be asked to place on her head.' Unlike Rossetti, Lizzy had not been conditioned to expect praise.

There was a bakery in Newman Street, and Walter bought three sugar buns which they ate sitting on the broken chairs in the studio. Lizzy tried to think of something to say that would break the awkward silence which Rossetti's mood seemed to impose.

Very tentatively she asked, 'Are your plans for the magazine all finished?'

Rossetti let out a histrionic groan, and she was embarrassed and confused, not knowing where to look. Suddenly she could eat no more of the sweet bun. Deverell tried to lighten the atmosphere, but he was in too low spirits generally to be very successful. 'It's money,' he explained. 'We're not sure if we'll be able to meet the printer's bill.'

'But the magazine is ready?' She wanted to see the etchings for which she had posed.

'Yes. When we can settle the bill.'

A door banged below, and there were loud footsteps on the stairs.

'Brown!' exclaimed Rossetti.

One hand opened the door as the other knocked, and a vigorous-looking man, with a wide brow and inquiring blue eyes, stood at the threshold. 'Why are you sitting here?' he asked. 'We were supposed to meet at the Portland Gallery.'

Gabriel went and clasped his shoulder. 'Sorry, my friend. It became . . . intolerable.'

'But —'

'No post mortems. I am going to introduce you to the most stunning model in London. Miss Siddall, this is our good friend Ford Madox Brown. Bruno, this is Lizzy, Miss Elizabeth Siddall.'

A hand was held out to her eagerly, and Mr Brown's clasp felt both friendly and gentlemanly. He said, 'How are you?' as though he meant it, and the silence and gloom which had preceded his arrival vanished. At first he spoke about the exhibition, of particular paintings he had seen, and then he turned to Lizzy,

91

asking her about her work and her family. She had never before met an educated person who took such a concerned and detailed interest in her background. At one point Rossetti became bored with all the talk of bonnet-making and relatives, and said, 'Miss Siddall likes poetry, you know.' This seemed particularly to engage Brown's attention, and when he had established that she possessed a volume of Tennyson's poems, he asked, 'Did you then go to school?'

'Oh no. We had lessons from our mother. She taught us all to read and write. Except Harry.'

'Your younger brother?'

'Yes. He . . . cannot learn like ordinary people.'

Brown nodded. 'You know, that's perhaps the most precious gift a parent can give. The ability to read and write.'

'There were plenty in our street who never learned. And mother could be very strict.' She had a particularly vivid memory of one very hot afternoon when she had to stay in the kitchen perfecting a page of pothooks and hangers before being allowed out to play.

'If only all mothers could do the same.'

She noticed that Gabriel and Walter exchanged glances when Brown said this.

'Have you anything to show me, Gabriel?' Brown asked, looking around the studio for evidence of new work. 'Oh, I say,' he had seen Lizzy's half-eaten bun, 'that looks inviting.'

'Are you going to finish it?' Rossetti enquired, and when she shook her head he handed the bun to Brown.

It vanished in two mouthfuls, and Lizzy was surprised that someone who seemed so polite and gentlemanly could be quite so urgently hungry.

Rossetti took some drawings from an old tin chest, and laid them out on the floor under the window. Deverell and Brown stood over them, while Lizzy hung back, glimpsing what she could from the side. Each drawing showed a couple, man and woman, facing an identical couple. In one, the outline of the ornate mirror was recognizable, so that one pair was clearly a reflection of the other, but in the rest of the drawings there was no mirror and the couples gazed at each other in disbelief and horror. In all cases their clothing was indistinct — draped and gathered in a vaguely medieval fashion — but the faces were clear: the woman was Lizzy, and the man Rossetti.

Lizzy had a shock, seeing herself depicted in varying stances at

92

the side of Gabriel. It was as though they were characters in a story which he knew and she did not. But her face, as he had drawn it, was fair in every instance, giving an impression of both mystery and beauty.

'The double-ganger legend,' Brown was saying. 'It could make a very powerful painting. And well-suited to your style. You must develop it, Gabriel, work it up into a really finished picture. No giving up half way.'

'What's your opinion?' Rossetti asked Deverell — who now looked frightened as well as fatigued. 'I can see you have strong feelings about it.'

'You know the meaning of the legend?' said Deverell quietly.

'Yes.'

'Then why did you use your own face? And Lizzy's?'

'They were the ones that were available.'

Walter said no more, but Lizzy could see he was distressed. 'What is the legend?' she asked quietly.

Rossetti just gave a sad smile, and Deverell shook his head as though it was too difficult for him to speak. But Brown looked openly at Lizzy and then at the drawings and said gently, like a teacher talking to a favourite pupil, 'It's a puzzling one. Though simple too. Just that if ever someone meets their double — a person who looks just like them — then it's supposed to be an omen of death. What makes Rossetti's interpretation so strong is the idea of having two people.'

Lizzy looked at the drawings and felt a shiver of excitement. It was like an eerie ghost story — herself and Mr Rossetti meeting death together. But that kind of demise did not disturb her; the kind, that is, which could be put into pictures. The deaths that haunted her came from cholera, or poverty, or — dimly yet most potently — murder. She gave a little laugh.

The laugh upset Deverell even more. In a few minutes he insisted on taking her back to her lodgings.

It was a warm evening, and she was delighted to be alone with him. She forgot completely about the drawings, and asked him a question about Madox Brown. 'He seems so kind. Fancy asking me all about my family. Is he a famous artist?'

'He's a very good one. The most hard-working I know. Gabriel admires him a lot. And he's very interested in families. Ordinary families. He doesn't like things that are too smart or high-falutin'.

93

And . . . well, he's got a special reason to talk to someone like yourself. Not many people know, but he is secretly married to a girl of about your age. She comes from the country, and he is teaching her to read and write, and generally conduct herself. So that she may take her place as his wife.'

Lizzy was astounded. 'He is married to a girl of my age who cannot read and write? And he seems quite old.'

'He is nearly thirty, I believe. He was married before, and has a daughter, but his wife died.'

Lizzy thought of the kindly, searching expression in Mr Brown's eyes. 'How sad he must have been. But he has found someone else . . .'

'Emma. He has high hopes for her.'

Lizzy did not say anything for a while. The fact that someone like Mr Brown could be married to a girl as young, and more ignorant than herself, was of peculiar interest.

Their route led them past the Portland Gallery, and Walter asked her if she knew exactly what it was that had made Gabriel leave in such a hurry. She said no, but also told him of the overheard remarks made by the two men.

'So that was it.'

'But he couldn't have left just because of that.'

Deverell was indignant. 'Yes he could. What right have they to criticize a genius?'

Lizzy had no way of knowing quite how a claim to genius was established, or what kind of behaviour it permitted. But she did know that her mother could not abide people unable to take criticism in a manly way; and since she was feeling very resentful towards her mother, she looked upon Rossetti's weakness with indulgence. Contrarily, although at the beginning of the week she had dreaded her mother coming to investigate her disappearance from home, she by now interpreted her non-arrival as a lack of concern.

'I wish I didn't have to go back to Kew,' sighed Deverell as they drew near Covent Garden. 'I don't know when I shall be able to come up again.'

'Is your father very ill?'

'I think so. The doctor doesn't really seem to know what the matter is. Keeps prescribing different things, then says it will pass in a few days. But all the time he seems to be getting weaker.'

'So you are unable to do any painting?'

'I've rigged up a sort of makeshift easel in the garden shed, and go there when I can. But it isn't very satisfactory.'

'I wish I could do something to help you.'

'I wish you lived nearby. My sisters are no good for posing. They talk all the time. And they're not very pretty.' He gave her a smile. 'Come and have some coffee and gingerbread before I leave you. And I will talk only of pleasant things.'

He kept his promise, making her laugh, and telling about escapades he had had while still at school. For a while his face lost its troubled look, and any passer-by glancing in to the coffee shop would have thought they were the most happy and light-hearted of young couples.

But then he had to take her to her door, and once again she realised her future had dropped away. No meetings with Walter to look forward to; no sitting arranged for Wednesday; no little deposit of money to safeguard her needs. Just the room and the bonnet-shop.

'I so hope you will soon be back at the Design School.'

'So do I, Lizzy. I miss our sittings very much.' He took both her hands in his, and looked up at the gaunt old lodging house. 'Don't you get lonely here?'

She nodded.

'Oh, Lizzy. I'm sorry. It can't be any fun for you.'

'I . . . don't mind.' She sounded very bleak.

'Did you partly leave home so that it would be easier to do sittings?'

'Well . . .'

'And now I've let you down.'

'It doesn't matter. You haven't.' Her hands had lain passively in his, but now she pressed his fingers to reassure him and looked up into his eyes.

Her hair was still in a smooth curve, her bonnet straight, and her skin smooth and clean. 'Lizzy, we don't deserve you.' He drew her to him so that he could brush each of her cheeks with his lips. 'You're like a lovely flower. All smooth and fragrant.'

Chapter Six

The kiss changed things for Lizzy. It made Deverell's absence more bearable, and the manner in which it had been bestowed — openly and with tenderness — gave her a sense of security. No matter how wearisome her days were, she could relive again and again those few seconds when her being had been absorbed by his embrace.

She made no attempt to define what she wanted of Walter in the future, but when she sat for Rossetti — who turned up regularly on Wednesdays to collect her — she shyly dropped remarks that might lead him to talk of Madox Brown. In that way she hoped to find out more about Brown's young wife. But Gabriel seemed to prefer to talk about his friend's pictures, and Emma remained a tantalizingly vague figure in Lizzy's mind.

On the fourth Wednesday after the exhibition Gabriel came to collect her, but had not enough money to pay for a sitting.

'I'm sorry,' he explained, 'but William wouldn't oblige.'

Lizzy had by then met William, and felt a little uneasy about the painstaking, balding twenty-year-old, who apparently had to be both his brother's keeper and his slave. She was also now alert to the fact that artists quite frequently did not have any money. When Brown had finished her sugar bun, his hunger, she now realised, was something quite customary. So she was in a dilemma. Should she swallow her pride and go back into Mrs Tozer's for an afternoon's paid work, or sit for Rossetti for nothing?

'I've asked Holman Hunt if he'll drop round to Newman Street. He wants to use you, and will probably fix something for Sunday.' Rossetti waited for her reaction, his impatience apparent.

'You mentioned some time ago I might work for Mr Hunt.' She tried to imply that an earlier introduction might have prevented this financially fruitless afternoon.

'Yes. I wanted to keep you to myself.' He looked away as he spoke.

His statement annoyed her, and she said, 'Well, I suppose I shall have to come and meet Mr Hunt.' To herself she added, 'If I am to pay my rent.'

They walked a long way in silence, and then Rossetti suddenly announced, 'One day you will live in beautiful rooms furnished with silks and tapestries.'

She gave a cool, disbelieving little laugh.

'You will,' he insisted. 'One day.'

Before William Holman Hunt arrived, Gabriel made no attempt to do any painting or drawing, but paced up and down while he told Lizzy of the cruel reception Hunt's picture had received in the Royal Academy exhibition. 'Both he and Johnny Millais have been dreadfully pilloried.'

'Why?'

'Because the critics cannot face reality. They cannot accept that religious figures were made of flesh and blood. Johnny painted Jesus as a boy in his father's shop. And it *looks* like a real carpenter's shop — which indeed it is. It was freezing cold and draughty when Johnny worked there — he even caught a chill.' He strode towards the bookshelf. 'Just you listen to what Mr Charles Dickens, that great champion of ordinary people, has to say about the painting in his new Journal.' He rummaged angrily among an untidy pile of books and papers until he found a copy of *Household Words*, and putting on a pompous voice he read: ' "In the foreground of that carpenter's shop is a hideous, wry-necked, blubbering red-haired boy in a night-gown who appears to have received a poke in the hand from the stick of another boy with whom he has been playing in an adjacent gutter, and to be holding it up for the contemplation of a kneeling woman, so horrible in her ugliness that (supposing it were possible for any human creature to exist for a moment with that dislocated throat) she would stand out from the rest of the company as a monster in the vilest cabaret in France, or the lowest gin shop in England." '

At this point, Lizzy could not stop herself from laughing. It seemed so peculiar that anyone could get quite so worked up over a painting.

Rossetti cheerfully threw the journal across the room. 'It IS ludicrous, you're quite right. But I can't stand artists who are not generous to their fellows.'

'My father likes to read Mr Dickens' stories.'

'Yes — we all like to read his stories. He should stick to his stories. But they've got it in for us PRBs. They don't like what we're trying to do.' He sighed. 'And to think that this time last year we all thought we were on the road to fame.'

Lizzy did not say anything. She found the chasm between ambitious aspiration and material achievement in the lives of Rossetti and his friends rather bewildering.

When Holman Hunt arrived, she did not immediately take to him as she had to Madox Brown. He was friendly towards her, but his unusual violet eyes, set above a pugnacious little nose and disconcertingly sensual mouth, made her feel uncomfortable. However, he invited her to sit for him the following Sunday, and she was relieved that he casually confirmed the matter of fees. She was not so pleased when she learned that again she was to model for a girl dressed in boy's clothes — Julia in *The Two Gentlemen of Verona*.

Rossetti guessed at her dissatisfaction. 'Miss Siddall deserves finer feathers. But I suppose Silvia is already cast?'

'Yes. Miss Miller has agreed to model for Silvia.'

Teasingly, Rossetti sang:

'Who is Silvia? What is she,
That all our swains commend her?'

and Holman Hunt looked acutely embarrassed.

After he had left, Lizzy enquired, 'Who is Miss Miller?'

'She's Mad's latest find. Very pretty . . . jolly . . . but not astonishing and rare. Not like you.' He looked at her intently, and continued quietly, 'Stay like that, looking down at your hands. I will draw now. You don't mind?'

She shook her head. Staring at her fingers, one of them as rough as a nutmeg grater from sewing, she breathed deeply until the blush his compliment had caused had drained from her face. Then, hearing the familiar delicate scratch of the pencil on cartridge paper, and knowing that Gabriel was fully concentrating on her pose, a sense of importance buoyed her spirits.

'Why do you sometimes call Mr Hunt "Mad"?' she asked, just before she left the studio.

'Because he is. Do you know, when we shared rooms two years ago, he used to hold conversations with the Devil. He gets days when he's very fearful and depressed. He's got a notion in his head that he must go off to the Holy Land to paint if he's ever to achieve

98

anything.'

Whatever vague image of Hunt's likely surroundings this information prompted in Lizzy's mind was quite destroyed by the actuality. His studio was by the river in Cheyne Walk, and there was nothing melancholy or spiritual about the atmosphere there the following Sunday afternoon. Hunt was accompanied by a slender, handsome young man with a limp, who was introduced to Lizzy as 'My friend and fellow-artist Frederic Stephens.' On a table there was one empty, and one half-empty, bottle of wine, together with the remnants of some bread and cold beef. Lizzy was invited to take a glass of wine and admire the view of the river before she changed into her costume. She refused the wine, but stepped on to the balcony to see the red-sailed barges through the late summer trees.

'I think Miss Siddall is quite right not to partake,' said Stephens. 'I always fall asleep when I pose after wine.'

'And Mr Rossetti talks while he poses,' she said, which made the others laugh. Emboldened she asked Stephens, 'For whom do you pose?'

'William here. And old Brown — you've met him?'

'Yes.'

'I'm going to be Christ for him. *He* says I've got a saviour-like face.'

Hunt snorted at this, and Lizzy was somewhat shocked. Though it was true — Mr Stephens's face was rather holy-looking.

'And I was Ariel for Johnny,' he went on. 'That was agonising. I had to stand for hours like this.' Awkwardly he put one foot in front of the other and, bending slightly forward, cupped his hands over his ears. 'I thought I'd never be able to straighten my back again.'

'Johnny's searching for an Ophelia now,' said Hunt, looking speculatively at Lizzy. 'I shall introduce you to him. Gabriel and Walter have been hiding you away for too long.'

She had by then heard many references to John Millais and was quite anxious to meet him — not least because, despite Charles Dickens, he seemed to be the most successful of the group. 'Do you think I might be suitable?'

'Yes. But . . .' Hunt was smiling.

'But . . .?'

'Well, it's the drowning scene. And Johnny's a great stickler for realism.'

99

Lizzy looked rather wildly towards the river and Hunt laughed. 'It's all right. It wouldn't be out of doors. He'd fix something up in the studio.' He poured the rest of the wine into his and Stephen's glasses, and Lizzy began to get nervous that the sitting would never begin.

'Where is my costume?' she asked. The landlady, who had let her in, had already shown her the room where she might change. Hunt immediately fetched it, and began to position his easel.

When the sitting was over, he expressed pleasure. 'You keep so still, and yet you don't "freeze". Please — will you stay and take some coffee with us?'

She agreed, and they sat at the balcony window talking and drinking mugs of coffee from a well-used brown pot. Lizzy found herself unexpectedly at ease, discovering that both men were Londoners from homes not so tremendously better off than her own. Stephen's father was an official at the Tower of London, and he offered to tell her stories of the headless ghosts of famous people who had been beheaded there.

Lizzy shuddered. 'No, thank you.' She remembered Mr Greenacre — beheading was not so very different from hanging.

They had not time to respond to her refusal, for there were people speaking loudly down below. 'That sounds like Woolner,' said Stephens, 'and Jack Tupper.'

'Let's play a joke.' Hunt's eyes were very bright.

'What?' asked Stephens eagerly.

'I know! We'll pretend Miss Siddall is my wife.' He looked to Lizzy for permission, but she was much too stunned either to acquiesce or object. Not only was it a preposterous suggestion, but she had heard the dreaded name 'Woolner', author of that offending poem.

There was a clatter of footsteps on the wooden stairs, and Jack Tupper and Thomas Woolner burst into the room, each carrying a bottle of wine. They both began raucous greetings, and then stopped abruptly when they saw Lizzy. She remained by the window, embarrassed and angry, while Hunt and Stephens went into the centre of the room.

'So sorry,' said Jack Tupper, 'Didn't mean to —'

'You're the first to know,' said Stephens. 'Hunt's pulled a fast one on us all.'

'What do you mean?' asked Woolner. Lizzy noticed that his

100

voice was deeper, more resonant than the others, and he seemed to tower over the rather delicate Stephens.

'Allow me to present . . .' said Hunt, and then could go no further without laughing.

'Mrs William Holman Hunt,' completed Stephens.

There was utter silence. Lizzy looked down at her lap, not knowing what to do, and then felt her temper rising. She stood up and stared across at Woolner, who stared back, his eyes very dark under thick fair hair.

'Oh . . . I say,' said Tupper. 'Mrs Hunt . . . you are the most wonderful, unexpected, surprise. We are very honoured.' He gave a little bow, and came towards her with his hand outstretched.

In the seconds it took for Tupper to say these few words, Lizzy experienced the most curious mixture of feelings. When she had got to her feet, she had done so with the intention of hotly denying that she was Hunt's wife, and of dashing out of the house. But the expression on Woolner's face, and the tone of Tupper's voice, halted her. They looked awed — not just surprised, but awed. If, she felt, she chose to act for a few minutes the role of Mr Hunt's wife, she would be found acceptable. She was not tempted to enter the joke, but she realised that she might have done so without humiliation.

'No,' she said, 'I am not Mrs Hunt. They are playing a trick. My name is Elizabeth Siddall.'

'Oh,' said Woolner, apparently not at all put out, 'You're the girl Rossetti's been raving about.' Then he lunged towards Stephens and Hunt, making wild mock punches — an activity which involved much squealing and shouting.

Jack, however, continued to hold his hand out to her. 'Well, I'm still jolly pleased to meet you. Though Hunt is a dreadful hoaxer.'

Lizzy reluctantly accepted his handshake, and then with dignity gathered up her shawl and bonnet and announced that she was leaving. The three engaged in horseplay were nonplussed, but Tupper walked to the door and opened it for her. 'I'm sorry,' he said. 'I fear you may have been offended.'

Lizzy bowed her head but said nothing, and went quickly from the room. She walked back past Chelsea Hospital, through the new streets of grand houses that were springing up in Belgravia. In some of these she could look down inside the basement kitchens, their windows open to let the cooking heat escape into the warm

101

evening, and see groups of servants working or having their tea. For a moment she wondered if that were not a better life: to have a bed, company, and regular food all under one roof. But then her customary distaste at the idea of being 'in service' to a family rich enough to delegate all menial tasks returned, and she walked firmly on towards St James's Park. She went very slowly by the perimeter of the lake, watching particularly the ducklings that bobbed importantly up and down, and thinking randomly of Harry, and Walter, and Mrs Tozer, and Rossetti, and her mother, and the dreadful Hunt who had ruined what might have been a good day. When a rakish-looking man suddenly broke through her thoughts with a 'Let me walk you home, miss?', she felt like bursting into tears. Life seemed to consist of not being able to see the people you liked, and having people you detested imposing themselves on you. But she kept her composure and covered the rest of the distance back to Covent Garden at a smart pace.

Once in her room, she took off her dress in order to preserve it, and sat on the bed with the fourth and final number of *The Germ* on her lap. Rossetti had given her a copy, and she treasured it not for Walter's rather awkward depiction of herself as both Viola and Olivia, but for a poem called *A Modern Idyl* which, although unsigned, she knew from Rossetti that Walter had written. It was quite a long poem, about a child cousin playing in her father's garden, and Lizzy found it both comforting and charming. She murmured some of the lines to herself, like a benediction.

> The sunlight smote the grey and mossy wall
> Where, 'mid the leaves, the peaches one and all,
> Most like twin cherubim entranced above,
> Leaned their soft cheeks together, pressed in love.
>
> *
>
> Fair pearl, the pride of all our family:
> Girt with the plenitude of joys so strong,
> Fashion and custom dull can do no wrong:
> Nestling your young face thus on Nature's knee.

She made a vow that the next time she saw Rossetti, she would pluck up courage and ask him if he could possibly tell her when she might expect to sit for Walter again.

This did not prove as embarrassing as she had feared, for at their next sitting Gabriel was full of indignity about what he termed

Holman Hunt's 'disgraceful hoax'. Evidently when he had been told about it by Woolner, he had immediately written a note to Hunt ordering him to apologise to Jack Tupper, and took it upon himself to apologise to Lizzy.

'I really am most frightfully sorry. I never intended that your working for Hunt should involve this kind of prank. If you don't wish to return for another sitting, he would quite understand. Though of course he very much hopes that you will forgive him and help him complete the painting.'

Lizzy quickly decided that with such an apology Hunt's sitting fees could not be overlooked. 'I will, but . . .'

'Yes?'

'I would rather Mr Woolner and Mr Tupper were not likely to be present.'

'Of course not. I understand completely. In fact, I had planned that I might be there next Sunday, if you agreed to return, just to supervise that everything was in order.'

'Thank you.' Rather to her surprise, Lizzy realised that she would feel more comfortable if she knew that Rossetti was going to be there. Encouraged by his kindness, she said, 'Is it likely, do you think, that Mr Deverell will be painting again soon at the Design School?'

'Poor Deverell,' Rossetti sighed. 'I really don't know. His father is apparently very sick. And he's not too well himself. He stays out at Kew to help with the household, and tries to earn a bit of tin by giving drawing lessons to the local young ladies. But he's pretty miserable. He has to do his own work in a garden shed that leaks. We go to see him when we can, but it's such a long way to walk, and the fares are a problem. I try to remember to write to him, to cheer him up. Tell you what — why don't you drop him a line? I know that'd please him. Tell him I'm behaving like a gentleman, even if Hunt isn't.'

Lizzy suddenly smiled. 'Yes,' she said, 'I will.'

The smile soaked up all Gabriel's attention. He gazed at her face, glimpsing how happy she was capable of being. Then he wrote down Deverell's address for her, not looking at the letters as he formed then. And later, after she had gone, he drafted an obscure poem which he sent to William for his opinion. It began:

She knew it not, — most perfect pain

103

To learn; and this she knew not. Strife
For me, calm hers, as from the first.

Lizzy wrote her letter to Walter the next evening. She had asked
Mrs Tozer if she might purchase a sheet of good writing paper, an
envelope, and a stamp from her, and had carried these items
carefully back to her room. It was the first time she had ever
prepared a letter for posting in a royal mail box, and as she
sharpened her pencil with the knife she used for her small items of
food, she felt rather important. At first it was difficult to find
enough words to make real sentences, but then as she thought more
of Walter and less of the impression her letter might make, the
words came tumbling forth and she had soon filled up both sides of
the paper. She ended by saying:

> I am grateful always that you found me capable of
> working for artists. I hope you will not think me
> impertinent if I say that you are the kindest to work for. I
> hope I will be able to pose for you again when your
> father is well. Mr Rossetti is very kind and regular. I like
> the Design School better though.
> I am,
>
> Yours truly,
> Lizzy
> (Siddall)
> P.S. I like to read 'A Modern Idyl'.

When she came to copy the address from the slip of paper
Rossetti had given her, she found his writing difficult to decipher.
She puzzled over the name of the house for some time, and then
decided to copy Gabriel's letters exactly, trusting they would make
sense to the postman.

After work the following Saturday, the doorway of Mrs Tozer's
had its regular quota of male hopefuls. Lizzy was by now quite
practised at deflecting any advances they might make, and it was
becoming tacitly assumed by some of the girls in the shop that she
was unofficially affianced to the bohemian-looking gentleman
who collected her every Wednesday. She did not know of this
rumour — and would have scotched it soundly — but enjoyed the
indefinable air of respect with which she tended to be treated. As
she walked briskly by the young men, and looked appreciatively up
at the remaining blue of the September sky before it filled with

darkness, she felt a tug at her sleeve.

'Lizzy!'

She looked down. 'Why — Lyddy!' The lift the fine evening had given to her spirits combined with delight at seeing her sister. She kissed her warmly — something which she had not done for years.

'Oh Lizzy!' There were tears in Lyddy's eyes. 'Why have you not been home?'

Lizzy's joy ebbed. She had realised for some time that the weeks since she had left Star Place were stretching into months, and that she ought to contact her family. But the longer she left it, the easier it became not to worry, and she still felt that if her mother had really cared she would have come after her.

She gave Lyddy's arm a squeeze. 'Come on,' she said. 'I've just got my wages. We will go to the coffee-house on the corner. They make lovely gingerbread.'

Once they were settled on one of the wooden benches, Lizzy asked if their parents had sent Lyddy to see her.

'No. It was my decision. You don't mind?'

'Lyddy — I'm ever so glad. Tell me all the news.'

'Well . . . there isn't any really. And I'm afraid I came because they would keep talking against you. Said you didn't care about the family. That kind of thing. Because you'd never visited. So I said I would come and see how you are.'

'You're a good girl. And I'm sorry. I know I've left it too long. It just seemed . . .' She looked at Lyddy's tired, kindly face. 'No — it doesn't matter.'

'Just seemed . . .?'

'Well, not worth coming just to quarrel with mother. I wanted to see you of course. And Harry. But I've been posing on Sundays. And Wednesday afternoons. . .'

'It's a long way to walk. If you're not sure of your welcome.'

Lizzy nodded. 'Yes, I'm sorry, Lyddy.'

'It's all right. Especially now I've seen you. And you're at the bonnet shop, and posing on Wednesdays and Sundays. Just like you planned.'

'I suppose mother and father thought I'd be doing unworthy things.'

Lyddy did not reply to that, but said, 'Please Lizzy. Would you come home tonight? To please me?'

105

'Tonight?'

'Well, if you're posing tomorrow, there won't really be any other time. We could go home now, and then you could stay tomorrow until it's time to leave for your sitting.'

Lizzy thought about it. The idea of sleeping in the attic room again, listening to Lyddy's breathing and emerging from oppressive dreams, dispirited her more than she would have anticipated. She realised she had become used to the independence of her own cheerless room, and was reluctant to return to her parents even for just one night. She knew she was being selfish to Lyddy, but nevertheless felt unable to turn up at Star Place, expecting to stay overnight, as though nothing had really changed.

'I don't think I'll come for the night, Lyddy. Try to understand.' She could see Lyddy was on the verge of tears. 'But I will come tomorrow morning. As early as I can. Until it's time to go to Mr Hunt's.'

'Can I tell them you're coming?'

'Yes. It's a promise.'

She walked back with Lyddy as far as the south side of the river, and stood watching her disappear into the semi-darkness. The moon cast some light, and the air was soft. She hoped their mother would not be waiting to castigate her sister. She knew it was unfair that she had found the strength to strike out on her own, while Lyddy was unlikely ever to become independent.

When she turned into Star Place at eight o'clock the next morning, she felt very strange. Church bells had accompanied her walk, and the comparative peace of Sunday made it seem as if she were returning from real life to a land that had been asleep — where nothing had happened since she'd gone away.

But minor things had happened. There was a new coat of whitewash on the kitchen walls, and an unexpected crop of red poppies had seeded themselves in the garden. Her father and James had become totally immersed in the separateness of the male world, uninterested in the reappearance of a female renegade. She felt like a visitor, not someone who belonged. Only her mother's critical glances, and Harry's hysterical welcome, were totally familiar.

She had decided she would leave before dinner, and spent the morning sitting in the kitchen with Lyddy and her mother. Tump flounced through on her way to play with friends, and Harry wandered aimlessly in and out of the garden. As she answered her mother's questions — which really took the form of barely-concealed accusations — Lizzy wondered what the point of her visit could possibly be. She tried to keep calm for Lyddy's sake, but hearing her own voice translate the unpredictable experiences of her meeting with Rossetti, Deverell, Brown and Hunt, into safe, acceptable little statements made her feel resentful and pent-up. It was no good her mother wanting her to get on in life, and holding out nothing better than becoming a supervisor in a bonnet-shop or marrying a railway porter or a footman.

When the time came for her to leave, she did so with relief. Stepping out towards Chelsea, even the prospect of Holman Hunt's excitable behaviour seemed preferable to the stifling atmosphere at home.

Only Rossetti and Hunt were present at the sitting, and Lizzy enjoyed it. Both men worked hard — Hunt at his easel, and Rossetti moving his stool from time to time to draw her from different angles. She liked it like this, the needs of all three of them enmeshed positively, with no outside hindrances. Then, while she was changing in the next room, she heard very light footsteps on the stairs, and when she returned to the studio there was a girl, younger than herself, standing by the window, her amazing mantle of bright red hair almost aflame. Lizzy stood in the shadow by the door, like the moon temporarily eclipsed by the sun.

'Miss Siddall,' said Hunt, 'May I introduce my Silvia. Annie Miller.'

The girl bounced forward, her breasts bobbing in a tight, cheap dress, her fleshy lips in a broad grin. 'Hallo Lizzy. Pleased to meet you.'

Lizzy extended her hand. 'Good afternoon.'

It had already been agreed that she would stay for coffee, so she had ample opportunity to observe the effect of Annie Miller on Rossetti and Hunt. Hunt was clearly besotted by her — responding to her vulgar quips and giggles with hearty laughter and many little touches of her hair and upper arm. But it was Rossetti's behaviour that most discomfited her. Although she never felt completely at ease with him, she had grown to rely on his chivalry. He had never once spoken a coarse word to her, nor attempted any improper physical gesture. And she positively enjoyed the way he talked about his poetry and painting, even though she understood only a fraction of what he said. But with Annie Miller he became just like

107

the admirers who waited outside Mrs Tozer's on Saturday nights — except that his attemps at flirting were not so adept.

Lizzy sat apart from the three of them, incredulous and cool. She declined Gabriel's offer to see her home, inventing the pretext that she might call on one of Mrs Tozer's girls who lived nearby. As she went down the stairs she heard Annie's throaty, noisy laugh, and the words, 'Oh my! What a duchess!'

Once again she faced the walk back to Covent Garden from Cheyne Walk with her head teeming with doubts. She had been paid, certainly, and not openly insulted. But if a girl of Annie Miller's type was included in the PRB circle as readily as she herself had been, then the conduct of that circle must be questioned. She would not allow herself to admit it, but it appeared that her mother might have been right after all.

A boy was selling some of the early crop of apples from a large basket on a street corner, and she bought some to take back to her room. As she walked down the long stone corridor at the lodging-house, the landlady called to her and gave her a letter.

'The postman brought this for you, Miss Siddall.'

'Thank you, Mrs Foley.' Her heart was racing as she took the cream envelope, with its careful script and bold 'Kew' postmark.

'Not bad news, I trust?' Mrs Foley's tenants usually received letters only when a relative had died or they had not paid their debts.

'I think not.' Lizzy was not prepared to explain further, and with another 'Thank you' continued down the corridor.

Her impulse was to tear the letter open the second she was inside her room. But she forced herself to be methodical. The apples were placed on the washstand, her bonnet hung from a nail in the wall, and her dress taken off and draped over the back of the chair. Then she sat on the edge of the bed with the letter, pausing for a second to sniff the sharp scent of the apples spreading into the room.

For the rest of her life she would connect the smell of early Worcesters with Walter Deverell. Carefully, she broke the seal and drew out a thick sheet of cream paper.

Dear Lizzy,

How kind of you to write to me. For I know how hard you work. But how like yourself to do so. I am glad that Gabriel is looking after you. He is such an excellent

108

fellow. Life here in Kew is very dull, but my poor father cannot help being ill. A new doctor is coming to see him tomorrow. Perhaps he may be more effective than the others. He has a reputation for working miracles. I am pleased you like my poem. I wrote it about my little cousin, who is so graceful and charming. Just as you must have been when you were a child. Take care of yourself Lizzy, dear. I hope I will be able to see you soon.

Your faithful friend,
Walter Deverell

She read the letter over again and again. And before she went to sleep that night, she said to herself, 'I'm sure that Annie Miller doesn't receive letters like mine.'

A statement which was corroborated three days later when Rossetti informed her that Annie could neither read nor write. They were in his studio, and he was making a very half-hearted attempt to block in a figure on his big canvas. Lizzy had noticed that each time he tried to work on the painting he became irritable and sluggish, whereas when he made individual sketches of her he was full of energy and enthusiasm. He had asked her what she made of Annie, and she replied noncommittally that she had not been in her company long enough to form an opinion.

'She's a spirited young thing,' said Rossetti. 'Dragged up in complete poverty. Put out to work in a public house when she was twelve. Of course she can't read or write. But Mad wants to have her taught. Thinks he can make something of her.'

Lizzy sniffed. To her mind Annie was a type unlikely to be changed through learning her alphabet.

'And there's an opportunity coming up when you could get to know her better,' Rossetti continued. 'We're planning a spell in the country. Hunt wants a real rural background for his painting, and I want to start a fresh one. This monster's dying on me.' He jabbed a brush at the canvas. 'I'm going to start the painting that will really launch me. The subject's going to be Beatrice meeting Dante in the Garden of Eden. Of course I want you to model for Beatrice. And Hunt will need you for Julia. So you will come, won't you?' He delivered the invitation in a throwaway manner, but waited most intently for her reply.

'To the country?'

'Yes. We've chosen Knole Park. It's very beautiful. And we've been recommended respectable lodgings in Sevenoaks. Could you not at least take a whole weekend off?'

'Miss Miller is going, you say?'

'Oh yes. Mad will want her there.'

'No,' said Lizzy primly. 'I could not manage to be out of London.'

Gabriel looked at her suspiciously. 'It's Annie, isn't it? You don't like her?'

'I am not accustomed to people of her sort.'

'It's not her fault,' he said defensively, 'that she was born in a slum.'

'I have known very poor girls who were not the least bit vulgar.'

He did not reply to that, but noisily put the canvas against the wall and pulled out some of his double-ganger drawings. After staring at them a long time, he said, 'I would look after you, you know. And while we're both away there won't be any sittings for you.'

'One weekend is not so long.'

'Oh, Hunt and I are planning to stay a couple of weeks.'

Lizzy just shrugged, but inside she was deeply angry that Rossetti could consider that she would acquiesce to staying away not just with two gentlemen, but also with that odious common girl whom any observer of their party would immediately identify as a hussy. Why, if they had been in lodgings, she would presumably have had to share a room with her. It was unthinkable.

Rossetti knew she was upset, and when it was time for her to leave, said 'I'm sorry, Lizzy. I didn't mean to offend you.'

'I would appreciate notice of your arrangements. Will you have left for the country by next Wednesday?'

'We haven't fixed actual dates yet. But — no, not as soon as that.'

'Will you be requiring me?'

'Yes, Lizzy. Yes.' He spoke to her reflection in the mirror, staring at it hungrily in a way he could not do directly to her face. 'Oh — and I almost forgot. Deverell will be in town tomorrow to see to some business for his father. He would like to meet you after work. Will that be convenient?'

This time it was Lizzy's turn to say, 'Yes, Mr Rossetti. Yes.'

110

Chapter Seven

Several times that autumn Walter came to meet her when she finished work. If it was fine, they would walk along the main streets looking into shop windows before returning to Cranbourn Street for a hot drink and gingerbread; and if it was wet, they would spend all their time on one of the hard wooden benches of the coffee-house, looked upon quite benevolently by the caustic manageress.

Deverell did not speak much of his family troubles, and Lizzy avoided referring to her financial worries caused by irregular sittings. Instead, they lapsed into a kind of fantasy conversation, full of 'when I begin to sell my paintings' and 'when I have left the shop and have plenty of leisure', and furnished with exquisite clothes, fine buildings, heroic poetry, and exotic journeys. Deverell's imagination was fertile, and Lizzy had no difficulty in entering his dreams. He did not depict this future as exclusive to themselves — Rossetti, Brown and others were frequently mentioned — but Lizzy was quite content just so long as she was included, and neither Annie Miller nor any of the other girls who sometimes posed for the PRBs were mentioned.

Once Walter came to see her with the news that some of Rossetti's belongings at Newman Street had been seized. The dancing-school proprietor had done a flit without paying the rent, and Gabriel was being held liable as a sub-tenant. Fortunately, due to his own irregular hours, he had actually observed the proprietor's midnight getaway, and had taken the precaution of immediately removing his most precious books and drawings. Indeed he had gone into hiding with these for a few days in case they were found and seized. His mother and sisters had been greatly put out by the affair, and William had either refused, or been unable, to help. But now it seemed that an aunt had come to his rescue, and had given him enough money to retrieve his furniture — particularly the ornate mirror he so cherished.

'How about Mr Rossetti's father?' enquired Lizzy.

'Oh, he's . . . well, either above or beyond such matters. He spends all his time on his occult Dante studies, you know — that's why Gabriel's other name is Dante. His work is very obscure and mysterious, and not at all lucrative. And he can't speak English properly so he wouldn't be able to deal with bailiffs.'

'So Gabriel will have nowhere to paint?' Lizzy could see her earnings becoming even more spasmodic.

'Not immediately. But . . .' They had been strolling up Regent Street, the lights from the shops and street lamps slightly blurred behind the remnants of a fog that had muffled London for two days, and they stopped in front of a grandiloquent display of oriental silk carpets.

'But?' asked Lizzy, looking past him to what seemed like acres of soft turquoise and gold, with statuesque motifs of birds and dragons and peonies.

'Don't depend on it, but I think Gabriel and I may be in a position to take a studio together in the new year.'

She did not allow herself to be immediately joyous. 'In central London?'

'Oh yes. No more exile in Kew. We think my father has taken a turn for the better, but he has decided not to return to the Design School. So my mother's promised to try to help me out with the rent of a place of my own. And Gabriel's aunt will probably do likewise for him.'

Lizzy noted the 'try to' and 'will probably', but nevertheless permitted herself a deepfelt, 'That would be really so very nice.'

'It will, Lizzy, won't it? It'll be a start. If Gabriel and I are together, we'll make paintings that will show the world. And you'll sit for us. And between us we'll soon be able to live in beautiful places and make beautiful things for the rest of our lives.' He seized hold of her hand. 'I'm so glad I've told you. At first I thought I'd keep it a secret until we'd actually got somewhere. But now we can both spend Christmas looking forward to it. Oh — I feel so happy I could run!' He looked ahead along the pavement, which was not so very crowded. 'I say — why don't we?'

Lizzy giggled. 'Yes! Why not?'

Clutching hands, they dodged between the other pedestrians, Lizzy's small steps very quick and nimble, and Walter's red cravat working loose and streaming out behind them. For a few moments Lizzy felt as though they could go on running like that for ever — or

112

at least until they reached their paradise. But by Oxford Circus they were both breathless, and collapsed against a stout marble pillar, laughing.

Walter arranged to see her once more before Christmas. It was to be on her half-day, Wednesday, which immediately preceded Christmas Eve, and when the time came she was most surprised to find him accompanied by his mother.

Mrs Deverell greeted her warmly, and suggested they might go to a well-known restaurant in Leicester Square. Lizzy was taken aback. She had never been to a proper restaurant before, and became suddenly self-conscious of her home-made dress and woollen shawl.

'Will these clothes . . .?' she began.

'My dear, your dress is a good deal better cut than many we shall see there, and you are certainly more spick and span than my son.'

They both looked at Walter, whose dark hair was over-long, and brown velvet coat shabby, and both forgot to criticize as he smiled at them and lowered his long eyelashes.

'You're incorrigible,' said his mother. 'You know, Lizzy — may I call you Lizzy? — we tease him at home with a song from *The School for Scandal*.'

'Mother! Don't you dare.'

'How does it go?' Lizzy asked.

Leaning close to her ear, Mrs Deverell sang one line very softly, 'Here's to the charmer whose dimples were prize . . .', at which Walter tugged her away, and insisted they go immediately to the restaurant.

It was a popular rather than an exclusive establishment, specializing in grilled meats, and Lizzy did not feel overawed. She was able to eat two lamb chops without difficulty, and privately decided that meat which one met for the first time well-cooked on the dining-table was much more palatable than meat which one collected from the butcher's in a scrap of bloody paper and helped to prepare for the oven. Mrs Deverell asked her several friendly questions about her circumstances and then, as they finished the meal off with a sweet pudding, she looked at her with some concern.

'I feel I owe you an apology, Lizzy.'

The statement so surprised Lizzy that at first she did not say anything. She just looked at Mrs Deverell, then at Walter, seeking elucidation.

'I'm afraid I don't understand,' she said at last.

'Your present position. Living on your own, away from your family. And being partly dependent now on the whims and irregular finances of these young artists. If I hadn't indulged Walter, hadn't approached you in the first place, you might be better off.'

Lizzy was amazed. 'But Mrs Deverell, it was the best thing that ever happened to me in all my life.' Involuntarily she glanced at Walter.

Mrs Deverell nodded slowly. Tears were smarting behind her eyes. 'I just pray it will work out well for you.'

'Now that father's getting better . . .' began Walter.

'Yes,' said his mother gently. 'Now we hope that father is getting better.'

When she and Walter said goodbye to Lizzy, Mrs Deverell slipped an envelope into her hand. It contained a card with 'Christmas wishes from Dorothy Deverell' written on it and two crown pieces.

The next day, Christmas Eve, was an extremely busy one at Mrs Tozer's. Ladies tended to put off ordering new bonnets until the last minute when, realising they would have nothing smart to wear to church or impress their relations, they hurried to the shop in the confident knowledge that Mrs Tozer would fulfil their demands. There was no question of the girls complaining. They would stay until midnight if they had to, since only then would they receive their wages and Christmas box. With the newfangled Boxing Day falling on a Saturday, they then had the mixed blessing of a three-day unpaid holiday.

Lizzy had visited Star Place once more since Lyddy came to see her, and it had been agreed that she would spend Christmas at home. Mrs Siddall had made a reference to her Christmas box, and Lizzy realised how much of her mother's resentment was because she had never sent money home after she moved into lodgings. But if she were to feed and clothe herself, and pay the rent regularly, how could she?

However, for the past month she had eaten even more sparingly than usual, done extra tasks for Mrs Tozer, had sittings with Hunt and Rossetti, and managed to save a total of twenty shillings to take to her mother, to which she had added Mrs Deverell's two crowns — a total of thirty shillings in all. When, at nine o'clock, the last

114

bonnet was packed in its box and given to one of the girls to deliver to the customer's house, and Mrs Dunn had handed round glasses of cordial and mince-pies, Mrs Tozer came bustling into the workroom and gave half-crowns, crowns, or half-sovereigns to the girls, according to their performance and seniority. Lizzy fingered her half-sovereign lovingly. But she slipped it into the little velvet purse she had sewn for her mother.

'Huh!' exclaimed Mrs Siddall when the purse was handed to her. 'Whoever heard of a velvet purse in Star Place?'

All the Siddall family were gathered in their front room at half an hour before midnight to welcome in Christmas Day. Lizzy had arrived at eleven o'clock, tired and cold, and at first had wondered if she would be able to keep her eyes open until midnight. But Lyddy made her toast and hot chocolate, and Harry insisted on demonstrating a peculiar wooden cup he had whittled for her, and Tump — grown suddenly ladylike — demanded her opinion of a shawl she had made, so she was restored by a sense of inclusion and welcome. And when her mother took out the contents of the velvet purse, Lizzy could see that even her father was satisfied.

James, who at twelve seemed more like an undersized man than a growing boy, said solemnly, 'We will find that very handy over Christmas, Lizzy.'

Tump fingered the empty purse and looked at the stitching 'It's beautiful, Lizzy.' Still holding the purse, Tump looked urgently at her mother. But Mrs Siddall paid no attention, though Lizzy longed for her just to unbend and say, 'Oh, all right, Miss Clara, you may have it since I'll never use it.' So she brought out her other gifts, all made by candlelight in her unheated room: a pipe-case for her father, mittens for Lyddy, threaded beads for Tump, a scarf for James, and a handkerchief for Harry embroidered with flowers and birds.

'Well,' pronounced Mr Siddall, who had been sharing the earlier part of the evening with two quart pots of beer, 'I can see you still think of us, Lizzy.'

She didn't reply. Making the presents was easy — she enjoyed that. Understanding each and all of their recipients was much more difficult. But at least they all seemed pleased, and as midnight approached Mr Siddall took the bottle of maderia that stood by the fire. 'I think Lizzy, you are old enough to join your mother and me now.'

'Oh — may I? May I too?' exclaimed Tump.

'Clara!' said Mrs Siddall. 'Be quiet.'

Tump subsided, and accepted the glass of lemonade Lyddy had ready for her.

When midnight came they all drank a toast 'To Christmas, may it be happy and peaceful for all,' and then Mr Siddall brought out his violin and they sang 'God rest you merry, gentlemen' — not very musically, for Harry was completely tone deaf and Mrs Siddall was the only one with a really strong, true voice. When they had finished, Lizzy, unaccustomedly mellowed by the madeira, said, 'Let's just sing one more,' and Mr Siddall refilled their glasses and played 'The holly and the ivy'. The tune was a difficult one, and he played fast, so by the final chorus all the children were laughing at the disarray of their singing.

'Don't be disrespectful,' said Mrs Siddall, not too severely.

'I don't suppose even Jesus could always sing in tune,' said Tump, and before her mother could expostulate, Mr Siddall laughed out loud.

'Please go to bed, mother,' said Lyddy. 'I'll clear the glasses and plates away.'

'And I'll help you,' said Lizzy.

When the two girls were alone in the kitchen, Lyddy said wistfully, 'I wish it was always like this.'

'I wish it was always even better.'

'I like it when we're just all together and in a good temper. But I expect you miss . . . your friends.'

Walter was never really out of Lizzy's mind, and the second glass of madeira had the effect of merging her thoughts of him with her feeling for Lyddy and relief that the evening had gone so well. She opened the kitchen door and looked up at the stars. 'No. Not just this minute. Because everything's soon going to be so wonderful.'

Lyddy, sober and loving, said, 'I am glad.' And because there was only one meaning she could find for her sister's statement, she assumed that one day Lizzy would marry Walter Deverell.

Early in the new year Deverell and Rossetti took three rooms on the first floor of a house in Red Lion Square near Holborn. Various relatives helped out with the rent on the understanding that with such privacy and space, saleable pictures would be bound to result, and Lizzy was one of their first visitors. She took to the place immediately. Although bare and rather dusty, the main room was

116

a great improvement on Newman Street, and it was not far from Mrs Tozer and her lodgings. She could therefore call in any evening after work if Walter needed her — or indeed Rossetti, for she did not discriminate against him as far as posing was concerned. They both paid her a little when they could, and always shared their supper, so she did not complain. To see Walter regularly was enough; and, although she did not realise it, the companionship that developed between the three of them was very comforting.

Apart from one weekly visit home, Walter slept at Red Lion Square, and Rossetti soon joined him when his family moved to a house in Mornington Crescent which was not particularly to his liking. The idea was that his mother and sisters would run a day school there for the daughters of tradespeople, and Gabriel found their ineffectual planning, plus his father's unhappiness at being uprooted from their old home, depressing. His aunt had given him sufficient money to keep him for a couple of months, and he would produce something wonderful to sell at the Free Exhibition in the spring. Yet the painting of Beatrice meeting Dante in the Garden of Eden had not even been started — he had found Knole Park wet and uninspiring — and Lizzy overhead from a conversation between him and Brown that the painting he had exhibited at the last Free Exhibition had not yet been sold.

But he was working. Pinned to the board on his easel was the beginning of a glowing watercolour. She gathered from Walter that it was to be called *Beatrice, meeting Dante at a marriage feast, denies him her salutation,* and while she had posed for all the female figures in the wedding procession, her actual features were recognizable only in the face of Beatrice, who regarded the intent gaze of Dante with hauteur.

Once, when she was alone with Walter, he told her the story of Dante's idealised love for Beatrice, and explained how much the poetry it had inspired meant to Gabriel. 'He talks of doing a whole series of Dante and Beatrice paintings, and he always says that you're the only person who could possibly model for Beatrice.'

This pleased Lizzy. That Dante had worshipped Beatrice from afar, and had found his spiritual salvation through her, seemed most poetic. It reminded her of Tennyson. She smiled at Walter and asked if he had decided yet what work he was going to prepare for the Free Exhibition.

A shadow crossed his face. 'Not yet. I shall know by next week.'

117

The following Monday he had set up a large canvas, but made no attempt to tell her what its subject was to be. He just asked her to take a certain pose, and began to block in one of the figures. But he worked dispiritedly, and during a break she asked him if anything was troubling him.

'Not really. Nothing new.'

'Your family?'

'Yes. I keep feeling I ought to give up painting. Get a steady job like William.'

Intuitively she said, 'Your mother would not want you to do that.'

'No. You're quite right. She wants me to be an artist.'

'Anyway . . . you told me what happened when Gabriel went for a post last year.'

This made Walter laugh. For before Rossetti's aunt came to his rescue, and stung by critical remarks from William and his father, Gabriel had announced loudly to all and sundry that he was going to seek a post and contribute to the family income. The job he had selected was, of all things, that of a railway telegraph operator. He had presented himself for interview at Nine Elms Station in Battersea, and been shown what he would have to do. He had listened carefully to all the technical explanations, but concluded politely that he would never master either the telegraphic device or its code. And in any case, as he told his friends afterwards, the 'clock, click, click' noise which the device emitted made him laugh. So he returned home and had never mentioned the idea of taking a job since.

One Sunday afternoon Lizzy went to the studio and found Madox Brown deep in conversation with Gabriel and Walter. It seemed that an influential literary figure had invited all the PRB circle to a party, and Brown was wondering whether or not to take Emma.

'She is beginning to get fractious at being left out of my social life.'

Lizzy sat quietly in a corner while the discussion continued, apparently absorbed in her own thoughts. But after Brown had left, it having been agreed that he should take Emma, she suddenly asked Gabriel, 'Is your sister who writes poetry going to the party?'

He was most surprised by the question. 'Christina? No. She does not care to go out very much. And she has been rather depressed lately.'

'Why do you ask, Lizzy?' said Walter.

'Because I should like to go to such a party. And I should like to meet Miss Rossetti. *And* Mrs Brown.'

They both stared at her. And she felt horrified by what she had said.

Then the two men exchanged glances and looked embarrassed.

Rossetti began to prevaricate. 'I should think it will be a dull evening. Not like the jolly times we have here. Where we're all friends.'

But Walter interrupted. 'My parents and sisters have been invited, and my father is urging my mother to go. My sisters hate artistic circles, so I will ask my mother if she will chaperone you, Lizzy.'

A great hollow of fear formed inside her head and stomach, and she could find nothing to say. She managed a tepid smile.

'You're sure you really want to go?' asked Gabriel searchingly.

His slightly ironical tone of voice restored her powers of speech. 'Yes,' she said, with the trace of a quiet hiss. 'Quite sure.'

For two nights she lay awake wondering how she could extricate herself from the situation. It was the way the three men had discussed Emma that had made her speak out so impulsively. They had mentioned her youth, her rural ways, her lack of conversation, and then somewhat patronisingly had decided that she would benefit from the party. Admittedly all Brown's comments had been made in an affectionate voice, but Lizzy still felt it was a peculiar way to speak of a wife. And she also felt that since she did not suffer from rural ways, and could adequately hold her own in a conversation, she was entitled to some social recognition. The hours spent in the studio were amicable and warm, making the hours at Mrs Tozer's seem by contrast increasingly drab; but Lizzy wanted to experience a wider, more conventional, society — she still remembered the curtailment of their visit to the Free Exhibition with regret.

Yet to push herself forward in that way was unspeakable. Nevertheless, a kindly note from Mrs Deverell was transmitted via Walter saying that she would be delighted if Lizzy would go with them to the party, and she knew it would be even more rude if she now refused. Walter seemed genuinely delighted — 'It will be much more fun with you there' — but Gabriel acted rather grudgingly,

119

and began to say that he might not go.

Lizzy's nights continued to be largely sleepless, but this was because she was making a new dress. To have one suitable both for the party and general wear later was a problem, and in the end she chose a heavy black silk material, and made it up in one of her own high-necked, flowing styles. The party was on the Saturday, and she asked permision to stop work at four so that she might prepare for it. When Mrs Tozer learned that she was to be collected by carriage, and accompanied by both Mrs Deverell and Walter, she was most impressed. 'Quite a step up in the world, Miss Sid.' Which, indeed, it almost literally was, Lizzy thought, when the time came for Walter to hand her up into the high, gleaming vehicle. As she swayed gently to the unfamiliar movement of the springs, while the horse stepped out briskly along the Charing Cross Road, she glanced at the pedestrians hurrying through the damp evening, and wished that time could, if not stand still, at least slow down. She had always longed to ride in a carriage, and the presence of Walter together with the friendly conversation of his mother, made the experience in every way delightful. It even enabled her to put aside her fears about the party as they bowled out of Camden Town and along the country road to Hampstead.

The disembarkation from the coach, and ushering into the large, well-lit house of Mr George Westbury Jones, were accomplished without difficulty. There were greetings and introductions, retirement with Mrs Deverell to remove wrappers, and then the entrance to the actual party accompanied by Walter and their host. Almost the first person they encountered was John Millais, who greeted the Deverells affectionately and, on being introduced to Lizzy, said 'I have been wondering for a long time when I was to have this privilege.' He reminded her of an enthusiastic new curate who had once called at Star Place, with his pink cheeks and wide-awake blue eyes, and she privately decided that she would feel quite secure should he ever invite her to sit for him.

A middle-aged couple, friends of Mrs Deverell, looked at Lizzy with piercing curiosity as they were introduced to her, and she wondered what would happen if she satisfied their inquisitiveness by saying, 'I'm a bonnet-maker who poses for artists.' Instead, since the conversation centred solely on the weather, she made her contribution to the general satisfaction that neither snow nor ice had made it difficult to travel out in Hampstead. 'I have noticed there is often a mild spell in February' — which was true, for poverty made her something of a connoisseur of weather.

Following Mrs Deverell, she accepted one glass of mulled wine and two little sweetmeats, and felt it was only fitting that their flavours should be quite new to her in common with almost every other aspect of the evening. It was she who first saw Madox Brown, and was flattered when, on catching her eye, he came striding across the room and introduced Emma to them.

Lizzy's first reaction was that Mrs Brown's simple woollen dress was most unsuitable for a party. But Emma's manner, like that of her husband, was so straightforward, Lizzy forgot to be super-cilious. While Brown spoke to the Deverells about the North London Drawing School where he gave classes, Emma turned to Lizzy and said in a pleasant, lilting voice, 'Isn't it lovely here? It's so *warm*. And so many lamps and candles.' Lizzy agreed, and soon Emma was telling her about the rooms where she and her husband lived which, while overlooking Hampstead Heath which was very pretty, were so dreadfully cold and cramped. Lizzy did not tell Emma about her lodging house — she wanted to forget about such things for the evening — but she talked in a general way about winter conditions in London, and felt that it would be unusually easy to make friends with Emma Brown.

She noticed that William Rossetti had come into the room, and Brown soon called him to come and join them. William did so, but she thought he seemed discomposed when he saw her, and he cer-tainly greeted both her and Emma very coolly. He soon made excuses to leave them, and Brown remarked, 'William's turning very grand now that he's become an art critic.'

'Is that so?' enquired Mrs Deverell.

'Oh yes. He's going to write regularly for *The Spectator*.'

'How very nice.'

Walter, who had taken refills of mulled wine each time they were offered, remarked, 'I hope the readers will understand him. Sometimes his sentences are more like thorn thickets than state-ments.'

'Walter,' Brown reprimanded, 'that's scarcely generous. He always tries so hard to champion all our paintings. Though,' he added, 'I sometimes feel William is eight years older than I, rather than the other way round. He is becoming positively venerable.' He looked around. 'And where is Gabriel? Surely he is coming

121

tonight?'

Deverell hesitated. 'I think he had decided not to.'

'How very odd. I would have though Gabriel was the last person to miss a party.' As he spoke, Brown looked from Walter to Lizzy, and seemed to draw his own conclusion.

When the guests had been circulating and talking for nearly an hour, Mr Westbury Jones announced that there would be a short recital. Chairs were set out in the neighbouring room, and they would be privileged to hear both some new poems and some new songs. Lizzy had not heard of any of the three young men who then proceeded to offer their wares, and so much had been happening that she found it impossible to concentrate very hard on their out-pourings. But just being in an elegantly-furnished room, sitting on a little gilt chair, and listening to real poets and a musician in the company of ladies and gentlemen, was more than enough.

They had to leave shortly after the recital, since it was a long drive back to Kew. Their host shook her hand most warmly and said, 'I hope we will see a great deal more of you, Miss Siddall, you are an ornament to any gathering.'

When their carriage reached Tottenham Court Road, Walter said, 'I wish we didn't have to drop you off, Lizzy.'

'Yes,' added Mrs Deverell. 'It must be lonely, returning to your room.'

Lizzy considered for a few seconds. 'It would have been much more lonely to spend the whole evening there. Now I've got all the things that happened at the party to think about. I can't ever thank you properly for inviting me to come with you.'

Mrs Deverell patted her arm. 'It was the least we could do.'

When they stopped outside the lodging house, Walter jumped out and handed Lizzy down. 'I'll come to the studio tomorrow,' he said. 'Will you be there at three?'

As usual she was punctual, and arrived only a few minutes after Walter. He was lighting the fire, trying to create a little comfort in the rather bleak room.

'Draw up a chair, Lizzy. Let's warm our feet.' The flames burned yellow and blue through the paper and kindling, and then gradually licked their way into the coals, turning a glowing orange. 'Mother's given us some muffins. We can toast them later.'

'She is kind.'

'She likes people to be happy. I just wish things were easier for

122

her.'

'There is still uncertainty about your father?'

'I'm afraid so. Grandfather has made us a loan. But we don't know when he'll be able to work again. And my sisters always seem to need new dresses. And there's my career . . .'

'What is your big painting going to be? Can you tell me about it?'

He became very withdrawn, gazing into the fire with a troubled expression. 'I feel so guilty about it, Lizzy. Yet I feel compelled to do it.'

'What do you mean?'

'It's called *The Doctor's Last Visit*.'

She thought about this for some time. 'You mean . . . it's connected with your father?'

'The idea came to me after that last doctor had been to see him. And I don't seem able to shake it off. I see it all so clearly in my mind.'

'Then perhaps you must do it.'

'But it seems almost . . . criminal. Tempting fate.'

'Well,' she said uncertainly, but realising how impermanent the studio might be, and how necessary it was for him to sell his work, 'the important thing is to finish something really fine. And I suppose you must trust the ideas that come to you.' As she spoke, she was remembering how she sometimes cut material without a pattern, instinctively knowing how to achieve the right result.

'Yes, Lizzy. You're so sensible. And I'll set to in just a minute. But first, I must say something to you.'

She waited.

'My mother spoke to me after we had left you last night. She's worried — this is a little awkward — that you should not be misled.'

'Misled?'

'About intentions. She knows how much I like you. But with everything so uncertain I mustn't begin to think too much about the future. And she is concerned I might be taking you too much for granted.'

Lizzy sat very still. Part of her welcomed the frankness of his speech, but another part found it foreboding.

'Have I offended you Lizzy?'

'No. No, not at all.'

'You look . . . so distant.'

'I was only thinking.'

123

'What were you thinking?'

'Of how the future . . . isn't really there.'

'You mean the future we've talked about? On our walks, and the night we ran in Regent Street?'

'Yes.'

'It must be, Lizzy. One day. If we work hard.'

'But I don't do anything. Just sew bonnets.'

'Mother said you looked like a princess in your dress last night. She said you must have made it yourself because it was so lovely. No one else used that line. That must be a little like painting.'

She felt a quiet satisfaction.

Suddenly he burst out: 'Is it awful at Mrs Tozer's? Doing all that work, day after day? And not living in a proper home?'

She realised she could endure things which he could not. 'It would be awful if it went on for ever. But Mrs Tozer is fair. Most employers aren't.'

He looked away, acknowledging that she had experience of the world in a way that he had not.

'Lizzy . . . ?'

'Yes?'

'You're the first girl I've ever really talked to.'

She knew it ought to be enough for her that he had said this. But it wasn't.

'Thank you,' she said politely.

He stood up and began to position his easel.

Throughout the following month Walter worked night and day on his canvas. Lizzy posed whenever she could — as the grief-stricken wife and the two bewildered daughters of the dying patient — despite having a heavy cold. For some time she had had her own bottle of 'drops' from the pharmacy to ease her monthly pains, and she took to using them also for the neuralgia that accompanied the cold. They made the long hours of the day pass more bearably, and a dose last thing at night brought deep sleep.

She guessed from Walter's manner, as well as the evidence of her eyes, that the painting was not going well. The composition looked clumsy, and the faces refused to take on their rightful expressions.

Then, one evening, Walter was not at the studio, and Gabriel sat by the fire writing poetry. Lizzy looked out on to the square below with a sense of foreboding. It was late March, and there was just enough light for her to make out the obelisk in the middle of the square, and the low-branching trees. A gardener had been setting plants in the flowerbeds, and in a few weeks the black earth and black branches would be covered with flowers and leaves.

'Where is Walter?'

'He was called home suddenly.'

'His father is worse?'

'I'm afraid so.' He looked down at what he had been writing.

'I had better leave.'

'No, Lizzy, stay. I cannot draw tonight. But sit with me for a while.'

She took the other chair, and listened to Gabriel scratch out words and click his fingernails, while she gazed at Walter's abandoned canvas and thought how pointless the pleasures of spring were going to be if he had to stay in Kew.

'I'm trying to write a sonnet about hope,' Rossetti suddenly announced. 'But it's a dreadful failure.'

'Hope?' Her voice was thin.

'Despair seems to suit the prevailing mood rather better.'

'Hope,' she repeated quietly. 'It's a strange word.'

'Is it?'

'My father's ancestors were called Hope. He came to London to make a claim on a share of the proceeds of Hope Hall in Derbyshire when it was sold. But he never got anything. And he never went back to Sheffield. Anyway, that's how the story goes. Hope in vain, if you ask me.'

Rossetti looked at her speculatively. 'You mean your ancestors were landowners?'

'So father says. We've got a crest at home that's supposed to be the family coat of arms.'

'Really? What more do you know about the Hopes?'

'Nothing much. Just that the Siddalls and the Hopes intermarried. And that up to my grandfather's time Siddall had only one 'l'. But it was so often misspelt, it was decided to use two.'

'But that is the older version, with one "l"?'

'Yes. I think it goes back a long time.'

'Then you must spell it like that, Lizzy.'

'Why?'

'It's more poetic if it's older. And it looks more unusual.'

'I think I prefer two. After all, you have two s's and two t's.'

He laughed. 'But I'm a foreigner. You claim your English

inheritance.'

'What difference does it make?'

'People respect old families.'

'You mean you will now respect me more just because I've told you Siddals have existed for centuries?'

'No, Lizzy. Not me. But some people might.'

She remembered his brother's behaviour at the party. 'William?' she asked quietly.

'Conventional people.' He looked impatient. 'Oh, damn it. Yes, William.'

'He objects to me?'

'I've been asking Christina if she will come here one day and meet you. But I think he has said something to put her off.'

'William doesn't think I'm good enough to meet your sister.' It was a statement, not a question.

'William doesn't know the difference between gold and brass.'

Before she went to sleep that night, Lizzy tried to think about her ancestors. Perhaps it was better to have a real family line, anchored in property and marriages, than just to have sprung from nowhere in Star Place. Yet even if she had been an orphan, abandoned in a doorway, with no stories of Hopes and Siddals, she did not see why that should have made her inferior. She was the same, no matter who her great-great-grandparents had been. And if she was good enough for Dorothy Deverell and Mr Westbury Jones, she was certainly good enough for Christina Rossetti.

She went to the studio the following evening to see if there was news of Walter, and found him on his own in a state of despair.

'It's no good, Lizzy. He's dying.' He went and slumped on the window seat, his forehead pressed against the cold glass. Without thinking, she put her arms round his shoulders, and tried to comfort him.

'Perhaps there is still something. . . '

'No, there isn't. Even the doctor admits it. It's just a matter of time. A few days.'

'Please don't distress yourself too much.'

He turned and held her, tightly like Harry used to when he was very small. And as she had done for Harry, she stroked his hair.

'I can't help it, Lizzy. I hate myself so much. Because what I'm most upset about . . . is that I'll have to leave here. Leave the studio. And go back to Kew. Give drawing lessons. Try to keep the family

126

together.' He was on the verge of weeping. 'I'm so selfish.'

And so am I, she thought. For I am thinking only of that too. Not of Mrs Deverell who has been so kind, or of poor Mr Deverell. She looked back into the room at Walter's unfinished painting. The head that lay on the pillow was the only one without features.

'I'm twenty-three,' said Walter. 'I ought to be man enough to shoulder the responsibility.'

'I wish I could help you.'

'Oh Lizzy. I so wish you could too.' He lifted her hand from his shoulder, and held it between his. Then he kissed it — first on the palm, then on the back. 'This is what matters to me. You coming in to our lives and making our paintings real. And Red Lion Square. It's been so perfect. You, and Gabriel, and me.'

Yes, she thought. Gabriel matters as much to you as I do.

'Let's pretend,' he said, 'just for the rest of the evening, that it's going to stay the same.'

Mr Deverell died three days later, and Walter did not return to Red Lion Square. Lizzy helped Gabriel pack up their things, as he could not afford to stay on alone. Madox Brown had a small studio near Rossetti's old one in Newman Street, and he decided to move in there for the time being. Brown did not use it very much, preferring to work at home in Hampstead, and Gabriel explained to Lizzy that she would be able to come round every evening, just as she had at Red Lion Square.

The prospect filled her with gloom. Rossetti's intensity, his sporadic fits of almost demonic drawing, and the long lackadaisical hours when he talked and talked, were no substitute for Walter's company. Yet what else could she do? Even Rossetti was preferable to the company of Mary at the lodging house. And she needed some contrast to the deadening hours spent bonnet-making.

As spring advanced, she became depressed and lethargic. It was almost as much as she could do to get up and arrive at Mrs Tozer's by eight o'clock each morning, and by midday she was ready to curl up in a corner and sleep. Mrs Tozer questioned her once about the general state of her health, and suggested that she was not eating enough. This was true, for whereas suppers at Red Lion Square had been simple but adequate, being supervised by Deverell, suppers at Brown's studio were frequently non-existent. Rossetti sometimes brought her elaborate pastries or chocolates, but more often than

127

not there was just coffee.

The Free Exhibition came and went, and Rossetti had nothing to send in. Walter had made a desperate bid at continuity by submitting a canvas he had done the previous year in the garden shed at Kew; it was called *The Banishment of Hamlet*. Brown and Hunt and Rossetti all talked about it, but did not offer to take Lizzy to see it. The Royal Academy exhibition opened, and Brown and Hunt and Millais were said by *The Times* to have 'an absolute contempt for perspective and the known laws of light and shade' together with 'an aversion to beauty in every shape.'

Then suddenly everything changed in a most bewildering way just because a critic called John Ruskin wrote two letters to *The Times* in defence of the PRB painters. Lizzy found it hard to understand how pictures that had been unsaleable one minute suddenly became valuable because of the publication of two letters in a newspaper. After all, William was a critic, and his praise of his friends' paintings in *The Spectator* had apparently not had any good effect at all. But there it was, and Hunt sold his scene from *The Two Gentlemen of Verona* for £150. He employed Lizzy to sit for another painting, and she privately revered the name of Ruskin, both because his one criticism of Hunt's painting had been 'the commonness of feature' and 'unfortunate type chosen for the face of Silvia', and because he proved how comparatively uninfluential William was.

One evening she went to see Rossetti, and found that Millais had called with the express purpose of talking to her.

'I believe you have heard about my Ophelia painting, Miss Siddall. I have been working on the outdoor background for some weeks now, and will soon be ready to start the figure. There is no one I would rather have pose as Ophelia than you, but I am afraid it will entail difficulty. The model will have to lie fully-clothed in a tub of water — though my mother has worked out a way to keep the water warm. And I will need to employ her all day, probably for about a month. I understand that you may not find that possible.' He then went on to name the weekly fee he was prepared to pay, which was far in excess of anything Lizzy had previously earned. She quickly worked out that if he employed her for a month, she would have enough to live on for three or four weeks after that. And the prospect of two months without bonnet-making was irresistible — even if Mrs Tozer would not take her back.

128

'That will be possible,' she said quietly.

Gabriel, who had been hovering by the window, said loudly, 'That's settled then.' She thought he seemed put out.

Before he left the studio, Millais said casually, 'Ruskin's been round to see me several times now. He wanted to take me to Switzerland, but I told him I don't need mountains and rushing torrents for inspiration. I found everything I needed for Ophelia's river on the banks of the Ewell.'

After he had gone, Gabriel said dourly, 'Johnny always falls on his feet.' Then he brightened. 'Well, Lizzy. There's one thing. You'll be the centre of attraction at the Royal Academy next year.'

Chapter Eight

The dress of heavy silver lace was still soaking wet when she put it on at the beginning of each session but the first. It hung coldly down her body like fish scales, and made her teeth chatter and her skin stand up in goose-pimples. Millais's mother lit a fire in the room where she changed, but nothing could alleviate the unpleasantness of that sodden gown.

Lizzy did not, however, complain. From the moment she had first seen the exquisite detail of the riverbank which Millais had already painted — the willow tree, the briar rose, the teasel — she wanted to be part of that picture. Gabriel had read her the scene in *Hamlet* where mad Ophelia recites sad rhymes, and also Gertrude's description of her drowning, and Millais's setting made it all seem so tragic and real. She lay in the bath, with the warm water soaking through the cold fabric until it reach her skin, and wondered what it might be like to drown. Her hair was spread out in the water, her hands slightly lifted, and in order that she might keep the pose for a long time there were concealed cushions in the water under her head and shoulders.

Afterwards, Johnny's mother gave her towels and then a hot drink and a meal while her hair dried by the fire. He usually went on working in the studio, and Mrs Millais was full of praise for his diligence and genius. It was very different from Gabriel's working surroundings.

On the day of Lizzy's last sitting, Mrs Millais had to go out. But she explained she had left instructions with the maid about a meal and thanked Lizzy for being such a patient model. The lamps under the bathtub were lit, and the water should just be reaching a reasonable temperature.

Lizzy half listened to these remarks, and made brief conventional replies, but she felt too miserable to respond with any enthusiasm. She clambered into the tub, the intricate antique dress flopping heavily into the water, and lay back and waited while

130

Johnny arranged her hair. Gradually the warm water seeped through to her body, and he, as usual, became utterly absorbed in his work.

Walter had come to the West End the day before, and had made no attempt to see her. In fact it seemed as though he had deliberately avoided her. She had gone to Rossetti's studio as previously arranged after her sitting with Millais, to discover that Walter had left just ten minutes earlier.

'Did you not say that I was coming?'

'Yes. But he had to get home.'

'He wouldn't wait just ten minutes. . .?'

'He couldn't, Lizzy. He was only here for half an hour. It was quite unexpected. He had been to see his father's lawyer.'

Tears had sprung to her eyes, and she had stood by the window fighting them back, while an almost unbearable ache gripped the sides of her throat.

Gabriel had not said anything while she regained control of herself. He just kept glancing at her, waiting. Then he had asked her to pose with her head bowed, her hands folded. 'Like a dove,' he had said.

She did not feel like a dove, meek and contented. She felt frightened and unhappy, like one of the London pigeons that were always being harried from pillar to post.

It had been an enormous relief to leave the bonnet shop to begin with, but now she was beginning to realise that her future was more uncertain than it had ever been before. Mrs Tozer had briskly regarded their parting as final since she could not afford to have girls who came and went as they pleased, and for a week Lizzy had been buoyed up by her freedom from the weary hours of sewing. Millais paid her daily and treated her as though she were a real professional. But when she went to sit for Rossetti after her sessions with Millais, he did not give her any money at all, and once he even borrowed from her to buy some food. And now that Walter had apparently chosen to forget their friendship, there would be only Rossetti, impecunious and unsystematic, to turn to once the Ophelia painting was finished.

After Mr Westbury Jones's party she had hoped she would see more of Emma Brown. But she gathered from Gabriel that Emma was expecting a baby and did not go out very much, and although he sometimes went to the Browns' Hampstead home, no one ever

131

suggested that she might go too. And there remained the sour fact that while Mrs Deverell had accepted her, she had still not been introduced to Gabriel's parents and sisters. And now it seemed that even the Deverells had no time for her. Surely Walter could have stayed for just a little longer, just to greet her?

Keeping a still pose had become as natural to her as breathing, and while she examined all these unhappy thoughts her expression never changed, her hands never quivered. But then suddenly her attention became centred on her body because her left foot, which for some time had been simply numb, got cramp. She concentrated on not moving, not showing signs of pain, and very gradually the cramp passed. The water in the bath, she realised, had become quite cold.

She looked up at the skylight and judged that the sitting should have ended some time ago. Usually Mrs Millais knocked on the door and reminded Johnny of the hour. The fuel in the lamps must have run out. She was about to say something, but changed her mind. What did it matter? Johnny apparently wanted to continue, and she had nothing to stop for. If the cold seeped further and further into her bones, and her skin turned blue, it would not concern anyone but herself, and she was quite indifferent.

She had reached a state almost of trance, neither fully conscious nor yet unconscious, when suddenly her whole body convulsed in a fit of shivering.

Johnny, struggling to perfect the relaxed curve of the fingers of her left hand, jerked backward in surprise.

'Lizzy . . . what — ?'

Then he saw that she was trying to sit up, and was shaking so much that she could not hold the sides of the bath. He hurried to her, and lifted her out of the tub and carried her to the rug by the fire. The water that ran from her and soaked into his clothing was stone-cold. He looked at the lamps under the bath, and then at the time. It was an hour and a half after they were supposed to finish.

'Oh Lizzy — why ever didn't you speak up?' He left her by the fire, and went to fetch towels and her own clothes. 'Shall I send the maid to help you dress? Can you stand?'

She nodded, her teeth still chattering. 'I . . . I'll . . . be all right.'

'I'll go and get you a hot drink.'

Slowly she managed to undo the lace dress, and wrapped herself in the towels. She stayed for a while on the rug, hugging her knees, feeling the warmth from the fire on her face. Ideally she would just have liked to keel over on her side and sleep. But she knew she must rub herself dry and dress before Millais returned. He brought her hot milk laced with brandy.

'The maid said she knocked. Did you hear her?'

Lizzy shook her head.

'Nor I. But why did you not speak out?'

She tried to think what the right answer was. But in truth, she did not really know. The nearest she could get was, 'It seemed a pity to interrupt you when you were working so hard.'

'But you could have made yourself really ill. Didn't you feel that?'

She could not say to him that it did not matter. Warm or frozen, well or ill, it made no difference.

He went out and found a cab to take her to her lodgings.

Lizzy could not get to sleep that night. The brandy had warmed her temporarily, but once its effect had worn off she started to shiver again uncontrollably. She had her old shawl wrapped around her as she lay shaking under the bedclothes, but it made no difference at all. With difficulty she got up and poured a cup of water from her jug and mixed some of her 'drops' into it. She did not bother to measure the dose with any care. She clambered back into bed, and drifted into a feverish doze.

In the morning she became convinced she was dying. Her head ached so much it felt it would split apart, and her limbs were stiff and sore. But worse were the pains that ripped through her chest every time she tried to take a proper breath. She lay longing for everything to stop.

Some time during the day there was a quiet, repeated knocking at her door. It would cease for a while, and then start again. Lizzy heard it as though it were at the end of a long corridor. She made no attempt to respond to it. Then there was the sharper noise of the handle turning, and Mary came into the room.

Lizzy did not properly hear the debate which took place between Mary and Mrs Foley, their landlady. The upshot of it was, however, that Lizzy was ordered to leave her room immediately. Mrs Foley did not allow sick people on her premises — hers had been the only uninfected lodging house in the area during the cholera outbreak, and she could not fall down on her standards.

133

Lizzy's purse was found, her things packed, and she was half-carried out into the street and put into a cab. Mary was in tears, insisting to Lizzy that she would accompany her if only she would say where she was going.

'No,' whispered Lizzy. 'I shall be all right.'

'But where will you go?'

'Star Place.' There was no other choice.

The old cab horse jogged along, and she jolted against the hard leather seat wishing that she might not survive the journey.

The next few days and nights blurred. She remembered thinking that she must certainly be going to die because a doctor was there — an authoritative young man whose precise accents seemed to reverberate back and forth across the attic bedroom. He attended her more than once and asked many questions. Sometimes, in his black coat with his sleeked-back hair, he became confused in her mind with the doctor in Walter's painting.

Then a morning came when the cold on her face bore relation to the wintry clouds outside, and the warmth of her body under the covers felt natural, not feverish. But only Lyddy seemed glad that she was better. Her mother came upstairs to inform her grimly that Mr Siddall would speak with her that evening, and when she asked if Harry or Tump would come to talk to her, she was told that they had better things to do.

The light had faded by the time her father came, and he brought a candle which he raised high when he first entered the room. She looked up at the flame, and the dramatic shadows on his face, and waited.

'The doctor's bill,' he announced, 'is seven guineas. He has advised us that we should send it to Mr Millais. What do you have to say to that, miss?'

Lizzy was dumbfounded. She could not understand how the doctor came to mention Millais's name.

'Well, come on, speak up. Your mother tells me you are recovered today.'

She took a deep breath. 'Who is the doctor, father?'

'Dr Macfarlane. I had heard of his reputation. Your mother seemed to think you were in some danger. Though your recovery has been speedy.'

'Why should Dr Macfarlane mention Mr Millais?'

'Why? Why? Because of all you told him, of course. Babbling on,

134

so I gather, about the cold bath. Lying in the cold bath. My daughter — in a bath — for an *artist.*'

'I talked to him about the painting?'

'Your mother thought you would never stop.'

Lizzy tried to piece the various bits of information together. 'The doctor thinks my illness was caused by the bath becoming cold?'

'Of course. Lying like some half-wit.'

'It was not Mr Millais's fault. He forgot the time. His mother usually reminds him. I should have spoken to him.'

'You should not have been there at all. He will receive the bill. And that is the end of it. No more artists.'

'Father . . .'

'*No more artists!* To think I had a moment of fear that you might have been in the bath . . . improperly clothed.'

'I was Ophelia, father. She drowned because of the weight of her dress in the water.'

'Playacting! You will provide me with Mr Millais's address to-morrow.'

He picked up the candle and left the room, treading heavily down the narrow stairs. Lizzy could not recall another occasion when he had been up to her room, even when she was ill as a child. She had recently seen a painting in a gallery window of a vixen and her cubs cornered in a copse by a pack of hounds. She felt rather like that vixen now. But she had no cubs to consider — just herself.

Half an hour later Lyddy brought her supper upstairs, and Lizzy thought she looked so apprehensive and tired that it was almost too unfair to include her in her quickly-made plan. But she had no choice. She explained to Lyddy that she was going to write a letter to Mr Rossetti, and asked her to get an envelope and a stamp and post it. And should, by good luck, their father ask her to post the envelope containing the bill to Mr Millais, then she should hold that back and see it did not go until the next collection.

'But Lizzy, I've never sent a letter. I don't know . . .'

'Lyddy! Listen.' She tried not to be impatient, though tiredness was by now overcoming her, and the frustrations of events were turning it into temper. She explained that Mr Brown at the store would have an envelope and a stamp, and she would give Lyddy the money to pay for them and also the address to copy out. Now all there was to do was to write the letter. The only paper in their room was her volume of Tennyson. Regretfully she tore out the flyleaf and asked Lyddy to get her pencil from her bundle.

8, Star Place.

Dear Mr Rossetti,
I had to come home because I was ill. I did not realise
what happened. A doctor came and now there is a bill
which my father will send to Mr Millais because I
mentioned the bath when I was ill. I did not know what I
was saying.

   I have had to leave Mrs Foley. My father is angry and
I am worried about resuming my work. I do not wish to
upset Mr Millais — please will you explain matters to
him. Please could you write saying there is work for me
— a business kind of letter. It is the only way out for me.
I will work to pay off the bill somehow.

Yours sincerely,
Lizzy (Siddall)

It was easier to remain in bed while she waited for a reply — if
there was to be a reply. She still felt weak, and although in happier
circumstances it would have been more comfortable in the warm
kitchen, at least in the attic she was private and could slip in and out
of the cold, daytime dreams that haunted her mind. The following
day, when Lyddy posted the letter, passed, and most of the one
after. It was the time of evening when her father and James were
coming home, their men's tea ready on the stove, and Harry was
hankering after bread and jam and Tump after amusement. Noises
and voices drifted upstairs, emphasizing her isolation.

Then unaccustomed, urgent sounds interrupted the normal
routine. Horses hooves, a reverberent knocking at the front door,
footsteps, a voice of quality. She could not make out the words, but
it was definitely a lady's voice — the sort of voice that used to excite
the girls at Mrs Tozer's, for they preferred real ladies to their more
usual clients who strained so desperately to sound refined.

Lizzy held her breath, trying in vain to hear what was being said,
and then expelled a great sigh when the unmistakable voice of
Rossetti followed that of the lady. Hearing it in her parents' home
was inexpressibly strange, as though two forces which were mag-
netically opposed had come together.

The talking went on for so long that she began to fear the visitors
would leave without communicating directly to her. Then at last

136

she heard Lyddy coming up the stairs.

'Oh, Lizzy, Mr Rossetti's downstairs! And Miss Leigh Smith. They're going to take you. Father's agreed.'

'Take me . . .?'

'Miss Leigh Smith has somewhere for you to stay. And Mr Rossetti has been explaining to father all the work there will be for you when you are quite well. They've come in Miss Leigh Smith's carriage. I've never seen anything so beautiful!'

Lizzy thought quickly. She remembered hearing Gabriel and Walter talking once about a Barbara Leigh Smith. It had been something to do with her generosity, and Gabriel had referred to her as 'a jolly sort of fellow' which had sounded rather odd.

'Father has agreed?'

'Oh yes. I think he's quite overcome. Miss Leigh Smith is such an impressive lady. Have you been in her carriage before?'

Lizzy shook her head.

'And Mr Rossetti is talking away to him. Telling him how respected you are.'

'Has father mentioned the doctor's bill?'

'Oh Mr Rossetti has brought payment for that. From Mr Millais.'

It was as though the hounds had suddenly turned, leaving the vixen free to seek a safer lair.

'Will you dress, Lizzy? Or Miss Leigh Smith says you could just wrap up tightly in rugs, if you don't feel up to dressing. She says they've got warm rugs in the carriage.'

'No, I'll dress.'

When she was ready, she went down to the parlour leaning on Lyddy's arm. Her legs felt distant and unreliable.

'Miss Siddall,' said the tall, plump young woman standing by the fire, 'I do hope we haven't made you come down too soon. But I promise you the ride will be smooth, and my friends the Howitts will take care of you.'

'Thank you,' said Lizzy, trying to sound as though the plan came as no particular surprise and wondering who the Howitts were.

Gabriel, who had been sitting in the window with her father, stood up when she came in to the room. They exchanged complicit glances.

'How are you, Miss Siddall?'

'Nearly recovered, thank you.'

'We were all so distressed.'

'Elizabeth has only herself to blame,' said Mr Siddall. 'She has a tongue in her head.'

'Do you have your luggage?' asked Gabriel.

'I'll fetch it,' said Lyddy quickly. And then quietly to Lizzy, as she helped her on to a chair, 'Will you take everything?'

'Yes.' She felt quite outside all that was taking place, and so the sight of Gabriel talking to her father, and the authoritative young lady questioning Tump, did not seem quite so bizarre as it might have done. Lyddy brought down her two bundles of belongings, and Gabriel and her father supported her out to the street and into the carriage.

Many of the inhabitants of Star Place had gathered to stare at the polished coachwork, the spirited bay horse, and the sturdy coachman. Lizzy looked out at her mother, who was standing on the doorstep, and thought she detected an expression of controlled pride on her face. Only Harry turned his back on the coach's departure, disappointed that Lizzy had not come home for good.

As they turned out of Star Place, Gabriel began to laugh — a deep chortle that resounded in the enclosed space.

'You see,' he said, 'it worked. We've got you, Lizzy.'

'Be quiet, Gabriel. Miss Siddall's far from well. Now, my dear, let me explain. First of all, I am Barbara Leigh Smith, and I like all my friends to call me Barbara.'

They had reached the West End by the time Lizzy knew what was to happen to her, for Gabriel would keep interrupting Barbara's explanations with lengthy and excited comments. They were on their way to Hampstead, where a Mrs Mary Howitt lived with her two daughters in a delightful country cottage which had a studio in the garden. Mr Howitt had just gone away to Australia to prospect for gold, and had offered Gabriel the unlimited use of the studio until his return. While she was recovering, Lizzy would stay in the cottage but then, when she was well, the studio could be fixed up as her own private apartment. She would be bound to like the elder daughter, Anna, who was a very sensitive and talented artist, and Mrs Howitt was the best person in the world to look after an invalid. She was also a writer, and could translate from both Swedish and Danish.

Lizzy felt quite overwhelmed by all this information. Then at one point she ventured to say, 'I do hope Mr Millais was not too put

138

out,' and Rossetti looked briefly displeased.

'He's lucky to get away with just a bill. It won't happen again. You won't sit for him again.'

'That,' said Barbara firmly, 'will be for Lizzy to decide. Particularly when she's seen the painting.'

'Have you seen it?' Lizzy asked.

'Yes. Gabriel used me as his envoy, and I thought the least I could do was ask to see the masterpiece that's caused all the trouble.'

'Did you like it?'

'It's beautiful. Pathetic and beautiful. Seeing you lying there, I just had to come to your rescue.'

Gabriel looked put out. 'Johnny will go too far. Realism isn't the be-all and end-all.'

Lizzy's first impression of the Howitts' home was of clutter and comfort. It was apparent that the practice of painting, writing and reading was of supreme importance to them from the number of sketchbooks, pencils, dictionaries, journals, illustrated volumes and novels that rested on the warm polished surfaces of the sitting-room furniture. There was nothing sombre or heavy about the cottage, and the bedroom Lizzy was taken to was decorated in shades of pink and fawn.

Mrs Howitt, small, grey-haired and motherly, helped her put away her things and brought her warm water.

'Once you're in bed, Anna will come and see how you are. She's around your age. My younger daughter, Emily, is longing to meet you, but you're not to let her plague you. You need rest, I'm sure.'

'I don't know what to say, Mrs Howitt. This is all so . . . unbelievable.'

'You're not to say anything. When I received Barbara's message this morning that someone all those wonderful painters admire so much was in need of help, that was enough.'

Since the studio tended to get damp, Mrs Howitt decided to wait until the spring before fitting it out for Lizzy, and in the meantime she was to live as one of the family. Both she and her daughters were missing Mr Howitt, and Lizzy in some measure provided them with a distraction.

It was her first experience of civilised life. The Howitts were not rich, but they took certain things for granted: two servents, varied menus, leisurely walks, new ideas. Mrs Howitt encouraged her to spend time looking at their books and journals, and when one day she discovered Lizzy writing verse, she expressed real pleasure. Tentatively, realising that Mrs Howitt was not going to demand to see what she had written, Lizzy told her how she had written poetry when she was younger and had more time. Shortly after this, Anna asked if she would like to try doing some sketching, and Lizzy shyly sat in front of a spray of leaves in a vase and tried to copy the outlines on paper. To her surprise she found it quite easy to produce at least a recognizable image, and Anna said she must draw for half an hour each day since she obviously had talent. Lizzy agreed, provided Anna promised not to show her sketches to anyone.

There were quite often visitors at the house — not for formal occasions, but to talk about publishing projects, exhibitions, reviews, and to seek news of Mr Howitt. Lizzy was ashamed of her ignorance, and used to sit quietly taking everything in and trying to piece it all together to make sense. When she first came to the house people were still talking about the Great Exhibition, and then suddenly ghost stories took everyone's attention, and tales were related that had been dredged from old books and the more sensational magazines. Lizzy rather enjoyed these sessions, and once almost plucked up courage to announce that she had once known a murderer. When she got to bed, however, she was glad she had not spoken. To revive memories of Mr Greenacre, and his blood-stained bag carried across the snow, in these pleasant surroundings would be like tempting the devil. The only person who did not enjoy ghost stories was Barbara Leigh Smith, who said she found no entertainment in talk of death.

Lizzy mentioned this remark to Gabriel, who loved ghost stories, when she was alone with him one afternoon. He gave her one of his most intense, brooding stares, and finally said, 'That is because her mother died when she was only seven.'

'But she has a rich father.'

'Yes. But he's blind. And she loved her mother most especially.'

Gabriel used to come to the cottage two or three times a week, and usually spent some of the time alone with Lizzy making preliminary sketches for paintings. He told her there was no need to think of professional modelling for the moment; like the garden studio, it could wait for the spring.

Lizzy found her new life so comfortable, so interesting and yet untaxing, that she was more than willing to leave all practical matters until the spring. She often thought privately of Walter

Deverell, but she knew from various remarks made by visitors that he was still in Kew struggling to make money to keep his family together, and that there was no hope of seeing him. Her feelings of loss and sympathy found expression in her verses, and the fact that it was considered quite normal for her to sit in the window-seat overlooking the garden writing poetry in a little red book for half the morning, was more than enough for the time being.

Chapter Nine

On sunny days the studio was beautiful. The jasmine, whose sprays touched the french windows on to the garden, made delicate shadows on the white walls, and the old velvet cushions on the chairs were a warm golden shade. On wet days everything looked more drab, and the damp patches became darker, but even then, with plenty of wood for the fire, it was comfortable. An iron spiral staircase led out of the studio up to a small bedroom, and here Lizzy made her den. For the first time in her life she had somewhere to put everything, and her Tennyson was set alongside other volumes of poetry which Mrs Howitt had given her, while her own writings and drawings were kept secretly in a drawer of the table.

The plan was that Gabriel came during the daytime to use the studio, and that she had her main meal with the Howitts but was otherwise as independent as she wished. The only trouble was that Gabriel often did not start work until it was nearly time for her to cross the garden for dinner, and he seemed unable to paint unless she was posing. Also he preferred to continue until nearly midnight, which she thought the Howitts might consider improper. But all Mrs Howitt said was, 'A studio with good natural light is wasted on Gabriel, he gets all his marvellous mysterious effects from working by lamp and candle.' When he stayed until late he would say, 'Oh well, I'll knock up old Bruno and use his sofa, it's too far to walk to Mornington Crescent. I only hope the baby doesn't cry all night,' and wander off into the dark after giving Lizzy one of his expressionless, dark stares.

Once, when she needed new boots, she asked him whether Hunt or Millais might have work for her, since he gave her only occasional small fees. He had not replied for a long, long time, and then had simply said, 'I would rather you did not.'

She fell into the habit of rising late, and spent the mornings in a cocoon of idleness. One day, she had just come down and was sweeping the hearth, when there was a tap at the window and she looked up to see a young woman carrying a baby. Cautiously she went to open the door, and then realised it was Emma Brown.

'Mrs Brown?'

'Miss Siddall, good morning. I hope I haven't come at an inconvenient time?' The polite, conventional words were pleasantly tinged with a country burr.

'No . . . please. Please come in.' At this point the baby made a gurgling sound, and Lizzy automatically put a hand out in order to draw back the shawl to look more closely at its face. 'Oh — what a beautiful baby!'

Emma beamed. 'Isn't she? Her name is Catherine.'

Lizzy made Emma comfortable, and lit a small fire which burned palely alongside the square of bright sunlight on the wall.

'I've only just learned you're living here,' Emma said. 'I heard you stayed with the Howitts when you were ill, but I didn't know you had moved here.' She looked around with open curiosity.

Lizzy hesitated. It seemed strange that Gabriel should have gone so often from the studio to spend the night at the Browns, yet never have mentioned her presence in it.

Emma continued. 'We knew Mr Howitt had lent his studio to Gabriel, of course.' She was looking inquisitively across at the easel, and the series of Dante and Beatrice drawings pinned to the wall. 'You are fully recovered now?'

'Oh . . . yes.'

'Only Gabriel's been telling everyone you aren't fit enough to pose for them. Holman Hunt's been wanting to get hold of you for weeks now.'

Lizzy said nothing.

'Gabriel was simply furious with Millais, wasn't he? But my husband tells me that it is the most beautiful painting.'

Lizzy enquired after Mr Brown and his work, and learned that he was desperately trying to finish two paintings and despairing of completing either.

'What we shall do for money by the end of the week,' said Emma, 'I don't know. We've sold everything of value that we own.' She did not sound too despairing, and Lizzy could tell she counted on her husband to surmount the difficulty. 'Don't you get bored here by yourself?'

'No. I like it. I have been reading such a lot. And . . .'

'What?'

143

'Anna persuaded me to start drawing regularly.'

'Can you do it? I tried, but I'm a complete dunce. Will you show me what you have done?'

'If you wish.' She went up to her room and fetched the sketchbook, which was now almost full.

Emma gave Catherine to her to nurse, and looked slowly through the pages. 'Why, you are clever. These are quite lifelike. Oh . . . look! That's Barbara Leigh Smith, isn't it?'

Lizzy smiled. 'You recognize her! She and Anna were sitting in the garden one day. They didn't know I was drawing them.'

'You ought to show it to her.'

'No. Only Anna knows about my sketching. Please, you won't tell anyone?' She was referring to Gabriel.

'If you say not. Though I'd want to show them to everyone if I were you. And I'm sure Barbara would like that sketch. After she's championed you.'

'Championed me?'

'Yes — that time you were ill. She understood Gabriel's concern.'

'She was most kind.'

'But she understood particularly how keenly Gabriel feels about you.' Emma noted Lizzy's lack of reaction. 'Has he not told you her story?'

'No.'

'Well, it's supposed to be a secret. But I got my husband to tell me after I'd overhead them talking about it. I'll tell you if you promise not to let on.'

Lizzy nodded and waited, while Catherine tightly grasped her finger.

Emma did not look at Lizzy as she spoke, and kept her voice low. 'Well, you see her parents were not married.'

This item of information seemed to hang in the air, and both girls were silent for a moment. Emma enjoyed talking about people's lives — such discussions were the life-blood of the small village she came from — but she was not a malicious gossip, and she wondered now if she should be repeating this particular story after all. Lizzy meanwhile waited with some trepidation to discover how such a curious fact could link to herself.

'Are you sure?' she asked.

'Yes. You see, it came out of William Allingham being the first

144

person to find you.'

'Mr Allingham?' She remembered the courteous Irishman whom Ellen had loved, and whose poetry Gabriel sometimes read aloud.

'Yes — he's a particular friend of Barbara's, and he told her how he had seen you in the shop, and then brought Walter Deverell who had wanted you to pose straight away. And then Gabriel told Barbara the effect on him of first seeing you. And so when you were in trouble . . . ill . . .' Emma looked flustered. 'Oh dear, I'm missing the point of the story.'

Lizzy waited.

'You see her mother, Barbara's, had worked in a milliner's shop too. Her father saw her one day in the street when she was seventeen. He was about forty — a bachelor. And he thought she was so beautiful he just followed her and talked to her. And they were like man and wife. They had five children, but she died of consumption when Barbara was still very young.'

Lizzy did not much care for this story. 'Why did he not marry her?'

'I don't know.'

'Because she was just a shop girl, I suppose.'

'His family might have objected.'

'You said he was forty years old. Old enough surely to make up his own mind.'

'You know how snobbish people are. Certainly I have plenty of experience of it. No one in Bruno's family wanted him to marry me.'

'But he did. He has good principles.'

'Yes — he has. He's done his best to educate me too.' She suddenly laughed. 'I hear that Holman Hunt is following Bruno's example.'

'In what way?'

'Trying to educate the girl he may one day wish to marry, but she won't go to her lessons.'

'Do you mean Annie Miller?'

'Yes. Have you met her? I've never seen her.'

Lizzy pursed her lips. 'Yes.'

'I understand she's rather a hoyden.'

'I prefer not to speak of her.'

'Oh dear. Is she vulgar?' But Lizzy was not to be drawn out on the subject. 'Well, anyway,' Emma went on, 'You understand now why Barbara took such an interest in you.'

Lizzy was not at all sure that she did understand, or — if she did — that she liked what she saw.

'Do you know what Gabriel plans to do?' Emma asked.

'In what way?'

'Well . . . for the future. I mean — he so admires you, doesn't he?'

Lizzy did not know what to say.

'Perhaps you'd rather not talk about it. He's got some way to go yet with his painting, Bruno says. He seems to find it so difficult to settle down to compositions. And I know William is anxious that he gets more secure financially. Well . . . I suppose that is understandable. William has to do such a lot for the family. Though he *is* rather pompous about it. Do you know, he hinted to Bruno that he wasn't sure whether a party like Mr Westbury Jones's was quite suitable for launching me, and that he couldn't understand why Mrs Deverell had decided to sponsor you.'

Lizzy flushed a deep scarlet, and the moment Emma had finished her disclosure she realised how indiscreet she had been.

'Oh . . . I am sorry, I didn't mean to be hurtful. It's just William . . .'

'He thought . . . he thought Mrs Deverell's reputation had suffered because of me?'

'No, I'm sure . . .'

Quietly, with the baby asleep now in her arms, Lizzy said, 'I won't have *anyone* thinking I would presume upon the Deverells. Mrs Deverell has . . . has shown me all kindness.'

'And Walter? Walter Deverell?'

But Lizzy could not bring herself to answer.

Emma watched her. 'Oh,' she said, unable to ignore her intuitive discovery, 'I do believe you love Walter Deverell. Not Gabriel.'

'Please . . .'

Emma waited for her to continue, but Lizzy just sat mutely looking down at the baby. 'I'm sorry . . . we'll say no more. And I won't breathe a word about anything. I'll just tell Bruno I dropped in to pay my respects and to show off little Catherine.'

She stood up, thinking it best to go, and waited for Lizzy to hand over the baby. But Lizzy took no notice; she had begun to murmur to the child, and was stroking its fine dark hair with her finger. 'Catherine,' she whispered, 'Catherine.'

146

Emma waited a little longer, then rather awkwardly she said, 'We've got a silly baby-name for her — Kitten. When we're alone, we call her that.'

'Kitten,' said Lizzy. 'Kitten.' Then she stood up, and handed Emma her daughter.

When she was alone again, she continued tidying the studio in a state of excitement. Hearing her love for Walter named by somebody else made it so much more palpable. If Emma could discern her feelings that easily, then they must have real strength and perhaps something would come of them after all. As for what had been said about Gabriel's feelings for her, she was convinced that Emma had misunderstood. She knew she was important to his art — he had told her that often enough himself — but definitely not to his affections.

He came to the studio that afternoon. 'What has been happening?' he asked. 'You look so lively, Lizzy.'

'Emma Brown called to see me. She brought the child. It's such a lovely little baby.'

'All babies are little. It's certainly got a good pair of lungs.'

'It didn't cry at all. Just gurgled. It was sweet. It went "gug, gug, gug," ' she started to laugh.

Gabriel laughed as well. 'Gug, gug, gug,' he mimicked. 'You're nothing but a baby yourself. A little gugguming baby.'

'Emma says they call it Kitten. Isn't that nice?'

'No, it isn't. For I prefer real kittens.'

'Oh, Gabriel! How *could* you?'

'Quite easily. I look at a baby and I look at a kitten, and I feel much more tender towards the kitten. Particularly if it's got long hair. But I like grown-up babies. Gugguming babies. Like you. I shall call you Guggums. What do you say to that?'

'Gug, gug, gug . . .,' she giggled, still light-headed from the morning.

He seized her hands and whirled her round, like children playing ring-a-roses.

Anna was the first to tell Lizzy that Millais's *Ophelia* had been hung 'on the line' at the Royal Academy exhibition.

'What does that mean exactly?' she asked.

'That it's hung at eye level. They so overcrowd the pictures that some are right up by the ceiling and others down by the floor. They put the ones they consider best in the centre. Everyone's been talking about it. Mama and I plan to go to the exhibition later this week, and we would love it if you will come with us. Or will Gabriel be taking you?'

'I don't think so.' Gabriel did not, apart from occasionally inviting her for a walk on the Heath, take her anywhere.

'Then you must come with us. We'll feel ever so proud standing by the painting with you.'

Lizzy longed to go, but she was cautious. She suspected Gabriel would be put out if the painting received too much praise, and she did not wish to add to his displeasure.

'I would like to, Anna. But . . . I think I might feel strange, seeing the picture after all this time.'

'Of course. How stupid of me. We don't want to remind you of your illness.'

Gabriel did not appear for several days and at first made no mention of the Royal Academy. But then, after he had been drawing Lizzy for more than an hour, he said casually, 'My sister Christina doesn't believe you can be as beautiful as Ophelia. So I've promised to take her a lock of your hair, to show how bright it is. Will you allow me to have one?'

She did not break her pose, but remained looking away from him, her chin tilted slightly upwards. 'I thought your family looked down on people like myself. Surely a lock of hair could not alter my position.'

Gabriel threw his pencil to the floor. 'Oh dammit, Lizzy! Don't make it worse. I want so much for her to like you. But she gets strange ideas. She leads such a secluded life much of the time, and leans so heavily on spiritual thought. But she loves all beautiful things. And she was very moved by Johnny's painting.'

Since he had stopped drawing, Lizzy got up and went to the table where there was a pair of scissors. Carefully she pulled forward a thick strand of hair and cut off four inches which she wrapped in a piece of paper and gave to Gabriel.

'Her life cannot be so secluded when compared to mine,' she said. 'She has at least visited the exhibition.'

'Yes, I persuaded her.'

She looked into his eyes, and he knew she was reproaching him for not inviting her.

His gaze shifted. 'One day, Lizzy. One day.'

No mention was made of the lock of hair when he next visited, for

148

the only subject on his mind was Thomas Woolner's imminent departure to Australia. He was going in the company of two friends to dig for gold, and hoped to come back with the fortune he was failing to earn from his sculpture.

'Mad and I and William have been helping him pack. So many corduroys and jerseys and fire-arms. And belts with little bags for the gold nuggets. I'm going with Bruno to see him off on the ship. What an adventure it will be for him.' He looked rather wistful.

'Would you like to seek gold?'

'No, Lizzy. Not in the wilds of Australia. I feel comfortable only in London. I'd like to *have* gold . . . but not to dig for it.'

'Mr Woolner has the constitution,' she remarked tartly.

'Yes, he's strong. But it's the end of our dream. He was one of the original PRBs, you know. We were going to succeed through our art, not have to grub in the mud of the antipodes for raw gold.'

'Will he be in the same place as Mr Howitt?'

'He hopes to see him. But Mr Howitt is thinking of returning, I believe.'

'Oh?' She had not heard of this.

'Mrs Howitt mentioned it.'

'So this studio will no longer be free?'

'Early days yet, Lizzy. Nothing is fixed. But I'm making plans.'

Lizzy did not ask what the plans were, but after that day she began to feel anxious about her life.

She suffered from headaches and lost her enthusiasm for reading. Once again, she could see no path into the future.

Gabriel arrived one afternoon in an angry mood. He was growing a beard, while the hair on his head was beginning to recede leaving a wide widow's peak. When his eyes were clouded and sombre, Lizzy thought he seemed almost diabolic. He was twenty-four now, and looked more of an untidy young professor, less of a perpetual student.

'Lizzy, do you not trust me at all?' he asked.

'Why do you ask?'

'*Answer* me! Do you trust me?'

'Yes . . .'

'Say it!'

'I trust you.' She did not sound confident.

'Then why do you show your drawings to Emma Brown of all people? Why to her? Why not to me? You must know I'd want to see anything you did. Any artistic endeavour.'

She did not know anything of the sort. 'I did not think ... they're not good. I just practised a little with Anna.'

'Emma was full of praises — not that she would know — but she said you could catch a likeness. Lizzy — you must know I want you to prosper in our ways, my ways. Show me your drawings. You must show me your drawings.'

Thoroughly confused and nervous, she went upstairs and fetched her sketchbook.

As Gabriel looked through its pages, the anger went from his face and he became almost spell-bound.

'Oh Lizzy!' he said, 'Wonderful Lizzy. Gorgeous Guggums. You can do it! You can draw. You draw much better than Christina and she's been trying for years.'

Lizzy was about to enquire a little tartly as to the effect of her lock of hair on Christina, when something ominous occurred to her. If Emma had broken her word about keeping her sketches secret, what if she also spoke of Walter Deverell? For if Gabriel thought she was emotionally bound to Walter, might he not lose all interest in her? And with Mr Howitt returning from his prospecting, where would she go?

After he had closed the sketchbook, he made her promise to continue with her drawing and show him everything that she did.

'I will coach you, Lizzy, and then we'll show everyone how clever you are. I'll find somewhere soon, somewhere permanent, where we can both work.'

She tried to absorb this idea. 'You mean when I can't stay here any longer?'

'Somewhere central — near the river. This is so far out. And you'll sign all your drawings Siddal, with one 'l'.'

'Just Siddal?'

'Well, E. Siddal perhaps. Yes — you must never use those two "l"s again. You must keep up your old family name. Now — will you give me one of your sketches? Tear it out carefully, then sign it.'

'Which one?'

'Whichever you choose.'

She chose a drawing of part of the studio, showing his easel in the background and a jug of jasmine on the table in the foreground.

'Now sign it,' he commanded.

Carefully, she wrote 'E. Siddal' very small in the bottom right-

150

hand corner. As she did so, complying with his instruction about the spelling, she had the feeling that she was signing something away, something intangible which she knew she could not afford to keep.

Chapter Ten

Lizzy knew, without anything specific being said, that Mrs Howitt was anxious she should be out of the studio well before Mr Howitt returned from Australia. She guessed that people had begun to question her continued presence, and had sought clarification of Gabriel's role in the matter. What had been a simple act of charity, heightened by the romance of art, had become a somewhat clouded issue. This became particularly apparent when Gabriel showed Lizzy's sketches to Mrs Howitt, praising them extravagantly. Lizzy could tell at once that Mrs Howitt thought he had very much exaggerated her talent, and that she was sceptical of Gabriel's stated intention of finding a studio where Lizzy might work as his pupil. Gabriel had completed no major painting with her as model, just the Dante and Beatrice watercolours, and literally scores of sketches. So Mrs Howitt's kindness had not led to the creation of a notable work of art, and Gabriel's insistence that Lizzy was a 'real artist' did not seem to impress her.

Lizzy was relieved, therefore, when Gabriel came to see her early in November and announced dramatically that he had everything fixed. For himself he had found a suite of rooms overlooking the river by Blackfriars Bridge, and he had persuaded William to sign the lease as co-tenant so there would be no problems over rent. William would, of course, be entitled to share the rooms whenever he wished, but Gabriel did not suppose that he would use them very often. As for Lizzy, he had arranged for her to have a nice little room in a surgeon's house in Weymouth Street, Marylebone, and she was to come most days to Blackfriars to sit for him and continue with her drawing. The surgeon had connections with Barbara Leigh Smith, whose cousin Florence Nightingale managed a sanatorium nearby, and he was pleased for the room to be made available rent-free.

'How does that all sound?' Gabriel lolled back triumphantly.

'What is the surgeon's name?'

'Mr Foxall.'

'And that will be permanent? He won't change his mind?'

'No, Lizzy. I explained — he is indebted in some way to Barbara's family.'

'Marylebone is a long way from Blackfriars.'

'Lizzy! You used to walk from Star Place to Covent Garden and back every day, which must be twice as far.'

'I hadn't been ill then.'

'Well . . . We'll be able to afford the bus. My work will go really well. They're lovely rooms — the studio has two little balconies overlooking the river which are just big enough to sit out on. I thought you'd be thoroughly pleased, Guggums. What's the matter with you?'

'Nothing is the matter.' She could not formulate details of a plan she would have preferred, but she did not immediately feel very enthusiastic about this one. Too much about it was problematical.

The day she moved to Weymouth Street, the eighteenth of November, was the Duke of Wellington's funeral. Festoons of black and white calico hung from buildings, and many of the people in the streets were dressed in black as she and Gabriel drove into central London in a cab. Lizzy had to admit to herself that the houses in Weymouth Street were very elegant, and she felt a twinge of pride when their hansom stopped outside an imposing door whose brasswork gleamed in the grey afternoon. The surgeon's housekeeper, Mrs Burton, showed them up to a room on the third floor, and remained with them until Gabriel left. She was a tall, definite woman, who gave exact information about coal, water and linen in a down-to-earth way that appealed to Lizzy. It was explained that Mr Foxall would meet her later, and that she was to feel free to enquire for anything she needed.

It was a pleasant room, well furnished, with a window which overlooked the street. Once she was alone, Lizzy unpacked her things and discovered that the drawers of the mahogany chest were sprinkled inside with dried lavender and rose petals. Then she set a chair by the window and looked at the copy of *The Times* Gabriel had handed to her with the words, 'You'll want to read the great man's dirge.' He was refering to Tennyson's ode to the departed Duke, which was published that day. Lizzy grappled for a while with its somewhat irregular metre and trenchant sentiments, but then fell into a kind of daydream. Her return to central London had

153

aroused unexpected feelings of excitement and hope; in a little while she would go out and walk around, take soundings of her new neighbourhood. To have a room at such a respectable address was perhaps going to please her after all.

The next day Gabriel took her to see his new rooms in Chatham Place. They were on the second floor of a modern red-brick block, immediately by Blackfriars Bridge. Most of the streets around had old, ramshackle little houses, and the wharves along the river competed to taint the air with their peculiar smells — coal, copper, lime, iron and the pungent Gas Light Company. On their way into the building, Gabriel introduced Lizzy to the caretaker, Mrs Wirrell, as 'My pupil and fellow artist', and Mrs Wirrell gave her a direct look and said she would be pleased to bring up a tray of tea for sixpence should they ever require it.

The rooms were still rather bare, and Gabriel allowed Lizzy only a cursory look at the living room and small bedroom before taking her across the connecting corridor to the studio.

'There!' he exclaimed. 'Isn't that magnificent? It makes me feel established at last.'

It was a large, well-proportioned room, with superb views from the tall balcony windows. Eastwards the river stretched away beyond St. Paul's, its grey surface busy with craft of all sizes, and its banks lined with tall black cranes, while westwards the gardens of the Temple ran to the water's edge before the river curved in front of the handsome buildings of the Adelphi. Immediately below, the water slopped and sucked against the stairs and piers of Blackfriars Bridge, and Lizzy remembered crossing it on windy, wet nights, and the occasion she had walked down those steps to eat six peaches in privacy. She looked across the water and found she could pick out in the distance the region which had once been her home. It was a year since she had been spirited away from Star Place and although she had several times thought of writing to her family, she had never done so.

'We'll take up Mrs Wirrell's offer.' Gabriel's voice startled her. 'We'll have tea.'

She turned quickly from the window and caught the look of delight on his face. He was like a child with a new toy, testing the capabilities of his new home.

She returned to Chatham Place the next day to pose for him shortly after some more furniture had been delivered. Mrs Rossetti had turned out various pieces from the family home, and Gabriel had bought some old but exotic draperies to hang at the windows. He also now had his books, which he placed in piles to be used as tables and vase stands. Amid the general disarray was a large blue urn containing peacock feathers and dried sunflowers.

'Sit by that, Guggums . . . Yes . . . Yes!'

He told her that two of his Dante and Beatrice watercolours were to be hung at an exhibition in Pall Mall, and that the annunciation painting she had seen in the Free Exhibition two years ago had probably at last found a buyer.

'I shall have to work up the angel a bit. I used William for the head, so he'll have to come and sit. Then when that's finished and I've got some tin, we must get down in earnest to your lessons.'

'Am I to come here every day?'

'Of course. Is there anything else you have to do?'

'Nothing.'

'Well then . . .'

It had been stupid of him to ask, she thought. What else could there be for her to do? He arranged her life. 'What time shall I come tomorrow?'

'Ah — tomorrow. I won't be able to work tomorrow. I'm entertaining in the evening. So I shall have to prepare.'

'So you won't need me tomorrow?'

'No, Guggums. You'll be all right at Weymouth Street, won't you?'

'Who are you entertaining?'

'Why — the old crowd of course. Show them my new rooms. Brown, Hunt, Millais, Stephens — and poor old Deverell. He's going to try to come.'

She did not speak for twenty minutes, keeping her pose. Then suddenly stood up, stamped her foot, and with her teeth clenched said venomously, 'No!'

'Keep still!' cried Gabriel, lost in yet another Beatrice interpretation. Then he realised she was bitterly angry. 'Guggums — what is it? Whatever's the matter?'

She walked stiffly to the window, standing with her back to him.

'Lizzy . . .' He came and stood just behind her.

'It didn't used to be like this. At Red Lion Square. You used to let me come any time. I was there when your friends came. Walter never said. . . don't come.' Saying Walter's name, and thinking

155

about those evenings in the past, she began to cry.

'Lizzy, I'm not banishing you. It was just planned as a gathering for the men. None of them will bring ladies.'

'If I'm supposed to be an artist, I don't see why I can't be there.'

He sighed. 'You can, Lizzy. If you really want to. Come along for an hour or two if it would please you.'

She wiped her eyes. 'No. I don't want to.' It was like stepping deliberately in front of a carriage, throwing away this chance to see Walter. But the phantom carriage passed on its way, and she remained.

'But what's all the fuss about then?'

She said nothing.

'Lizzy, I see you more than anyone else. We're going to have our world here. Painting and drawing. And I've been writing again — I've even outdone Tennyson in a poem about the Duke. I thought I'd read it tonight.' He touched her on the shoulder. 'Is that it? You feel left out if I read just to the men? I'll read it to you now, if you like.'

She turned her head, staring at him with pale, proud eyes. 'I have no interest in the Duke.'

Gabriel's expression of concern evaporated and he burst out laughing. 'Oh Lizzy — that's wonderful!' He mimicked: 'I have no interest in the Duke.'

'Don't laugh at me. Don't you dare laugh at me.'

This time he went closer to her, holding her shoulders from behind. 'I'm not laughing at you. I'm delighting in what you said. And how right you are. What's the Duke to us? Nothing. And I've written a most uninspired poem which proves it.'

She stood mutely, feeling the pressure of his hands, and gazing out of the window to the smoke-smudged horizon.

Then in an expressionless voice he said, 'It's Walter, isn't it?' and involuntarily her body went rigid. He took his hands away, but she knew he must have felt her stiffen. 'You want to see Walter, don't you?'

Tears began to fall down her cheeks again.

'Does this mean nothing to you, Lizzy? Our work — this place?'

She faced him, her hair aureoled by the winter light behind, her dignity fragmented by unhappiness and anger. Her skin was damp and mottled, the rims of her eyes red. She seized on the first weapon she could think of that would take his attention away from Walter.

156

'Mrs Howitt knows I'm not a real artist. She could tell that I won't become anything.'

'Oh, damn what Mrs Howitt thinks! I know you will. I know what you're capable of, how extraordinary you are.'

'Will I be somebody?'

'Yes, Lizzy. *Yes*.'

She stared at him, willing him to say more.

'I promise you will be remembered. As Beatrice is. And Guinivere. And Saint Cecilia. As threads of gold in the history of poetry, painting and music.'

His words encircled her mind like a spell.

'What do you want of Walter?' he asked. 'He is striving to take his father's place.' He paused. 'And he is ill himself too, I believe.'

She wanted Walter as he had once been — carefree, kind and beautiful. But she would have adapted to the new circumstances, had she been asked. If there were a way for it to be allowed, she could have helped the Deverells. Sewing, cleaning, cooking — she could have done all those, as well as sitting for Walter. And, after all, Mrs Deverell had once accepted her. But Walter had given no sign of wanting her help.

'Do you still not trust me at all, Lizzy?'

Gabriel was looking at her with that intense stare which made her feel uncomfortable — as though he could see right inside her, and knew things of which she was unaware. She was not sure exactly what it meant to trust someone.

'I trust you,' she said.

The solitary hours she spent at Weymouth Street were not unhappy; she could watch the street below, and the servants accepted her presence in the house without question. Mr Foxall had said she might take meals either in the kitchen or her room whenever she liked provided she gave notice, and once Cook had discovered how small her appetite was she said notice was quite unnecessary: 'It's like putting crumbs out for the sparrows.' Lizzy gathered they thought she was a kind of apprentice to Mr Rossetti, and she never talked about her earlier background, though she would sometimes sit and listen to Cook's reminiscences while helping to clean the silver or darn some linen. Mr Foxall was a bachelor and the running of the house was left entirely to Mrs Burton, who appreciated Lizzy's occasional domestic helpfulness. She was accustomed to her employer's generosity to the temporarily homeless, and Lizzy was far less trouble than some of the strays they had housed.

Sometimes she sat for long spells at her window, letting vague thoughts drift through her mind. Once it had been impossible not to include Walter in any daydreams that developed, but after her talk with Gabriel she tended to avoid thinking of him. Occasionally she looked through her poems, and they reminded her of the nebulous, exalted moods she had experienced when first with the Howitts.

> Love floated on the mists of morn
> And rested on the sunset's rays;
> He calmed the thunder of the storm
> And lighted all my ways.

But now she seldom felt those warm, energizing spurts of joy, and drifted from one day to the next, obeying Gabriel's erratic timetable, and taking a certain interest in the progression of her drawing. He was proving to be a good teacher, and he promised that one day she would be able to sell her drawings — a prospect that pleased her, though she was sceptical of it actually happening.

Once she was at Chatham Place when William — to her the most uncelestial of men — came to pose for the angel in the anunciation painting. He was civil to her, but when she made a sharp little joke at Gabriel's expense he looked displeased, and shortly afterwards Gabriel told him to stop posing since his expression was far too malevolent. Lizzy felt he regarded Gabriel as a kind of wayward prince, whom no one might criticise because of his royal blood, while at the same time being infuriated more than most by his unreliable habits. The brothers then talked at some length about the man who was going to buy the painting, and she realized that William was even more anxious than Gabriel that the sale be completed quickly. The would-be purchaser was a Belfast shipowner called MacCracken, and Gabriel heaped abuse upon the man because he had sought John Ruskin's advice as to the soundness of buying a Rossetti. When William heard that Ruskin — who had recently seen the exhibited Dante and Beatrice watercolours — had told MacCracken that Rossetti's colouring was superior to anything else in modern art he became very excited.

'But that's wonderful praise! If Ruskin backs you, you will be made. Now that Turner is dead he has no giant to promote.'

Gabriel shrugged. 'He's running around after Johnny like an excited sheepdog. But it was a ridiculous letter he wrote MacCracken. I suppose the only thing that's even more ridiculous is that MacCracken should think I would be pleased to know its contents.'

'What else did Ruskin say?'

Gabriel looked wearily around the assorted piles of books, each topped with a scattering of papers and letters. 'Who cares?'

Lizzy could tell that William cared very much indeed, and that Gabriel was pretending very hard not to.

'I believe,' said William, 'that Ruskin's influence is beneficial. He loves art. He isn't just seeking power and influence.'

'Hmm.' Gabriel looked across at Lizzy. 'Guggums — do you think Mrs Wirrell would do one of her Blackfriars teas? As it's for three, I suppose it will be ninepence. But you must sample her seedcake, William. It's positively epicurean . . . And I expect you have the ninepence.'

After William had left, Gabriel said slyly, 'William's in love.'

'How do you know?'

'Christina hinted at it the last time I was home. And he's very touchy.'

Lizzy found it difficult to imagine William as a romantic figure. 'Do you know the girl?'

'Henrietta Rintoul. Daughter of the editor of *The Spectator* — you know, he writes reviews for them. Keeps him occupied after his days at the tax office.'

'You are unkind. He works much harder than you do.'

'Hush, Lizzy. My family remind me of that all the time. You mustn't start too.'

'Have you met Miss Rintoul?'

'Yes. She is intelligent, retiring, not very young, and a born spinster.'

They both began to laugh.

'Family life is so predictable,' said Gabriel. 'Christina daren't marry, William would only do so if it were utterly safe, and no one will ask Maria — which is a shame. It's much nicer here, away from plots and ploys.'

Nevertheless, over the New Year, when families gathered for dinners and parties and exchanges of news, Gabriel was often absent from Chatham Place on visits to his home. So Lizzy, more

159

out of pique than sentiment, said she would visit Star Place. She had the feeling he preferred her not to move outside the restricted routine he had created for her, but he made no attempt to interfere. Privately she decided that if the atmosphere was not too unbearable, she would stay with her family for a few days. She had been saving from the limited money Gabriel gave her, and she would give these savings to her mother.

It snowed on the morning she chose for her visit. The horses that pulled the omnibus slipped uncomfortably on the cobbles, and the flakes almost blinded the driver. After a draughty journey she was put down a quarter of a mile from Star Place, and as she battled against the white wetness hurled by the wind, she wondered what had spurred her to leave the calm and warmth of Weymouth Street.

She went to the back of the house, giving a little tap on the kitchen door before lifting the latch. Tump, now much taller and thinner, was standing at the table peeling potatoes, while Harry sat by the fire whittling a piece of wood. As soon as he saw Lizzy he said, 'You're a wicked girl, you never came. You're a wicked girl.'

The tone of his voice, as well as his words shocked her.

'Don't let the cold in, Lizzy,' said Tump. 'Shut the door. He's only imitating what mother said. What's happened — lost your carriage?'

'I came to visit you. Why did Harry say that? What do you mean, he's imitating mother?'

'Father died. In November. She felt you should have been here.'

'Father died?'

'He had a chill. It went on his chest, and he got pneumonia.'

'Mother . . .?'

'She's away. Staying with Cousin Lily. She almost collapsed after nursing father. The doctor said she needed a rest.'

Lizzy sat down at the table. 'I can't believe it.'

'Well, it's all true.' The flounciness of Tump's youth had changed into a brisk indifference.

'How are you managing?'

'Lyddy's still at the shop. And I'm going to join Annie in Sheffield once mother's back. I was planning to go there anyway when I was sixteen — and I almost am. Father's shop's closed. James is working at the butcher by the tannery. He doesn't like it — he misses the shop.' She went to the back door and threw away the dirty vegetable water. 'And Harry's whittling as usual as you can

160

see. There is one more piece of news, but I'll leave Lyddy to tell you that.'

'How about the house?'

'Mother plans to try to stay. Lyddy will explain.'

'I'm sorry, Tump. That I wasn't here.'

'I don't blame you. I'd go with anyone who sent a carriage like that for me. Oh — by the way, they call me Clara now.'

Lizzy smiled briefly. 'I can see why. You've grown up so much.'

'Yes — mother's anxious to see me settled away from home. She's terrified of us girls bringing her trouble once we're grown up, isn't she? Lyddy's the only one she didn't mind. But then she's the least pretty.'

Lizzy was taken aback by this forthright honesty. In a few words Clara had summed up their mother's attitude to her daughters' womanhood, and metaphorically snapper her fingers at it.

'Are you rich yet, Lizzy? Or has it all come to an end as father predicted?'

'Did he?'

'Oh yes. He boasted about you for a few weeks, until the effect of the carriage had worn off. And then when we didn't hear from you he decided you'd lost all your fine friends and were too proud to come home.'

'No. I was in Hampstead for a year. It took me some time to get better. And it was a long way from here. But now I have a room in Marylebone, in the house of a friend of Miss Leigh Smith.'

'And do you still pose?'

'Yes.'

'For Mr Rossetti?'

'Yes.'

Clara nodded sagely. 'I thought he was very handsome. Even though his hips are rather broad.'

'Tump!'

'It's true — they are. You know, I've thought about getting a protector. But I like to be independent. Annie says she can get me a good post in Sheffield.'

Lizzy did not know what to say. The word 'protector' sounded very ambiguous on Clara's lips. She looked towards Harry, uncomfortable at feeling a stranger in her own home, and when he stared at her blankly for a few seconds and then suddenly smiled with all his old warmth, as though remembering who she really

161

was, she found herself crying.

'I suppose it's the shock of hearing about father,' said Clara matter-of-factly.

When Lyddy came home, she was accompanied by a young man. At first she seemed flustered to see Lizzy, as though suspecting she was the harbinger of more bad news. Only when she had gathered it was just a visit did she smile and touch her shoulder. But Lizzy could tell the old affection, admiration, had diminished.

'I should have written, Lyddy. Sent you my address.'

'We did wonder. Has Clara told you about mother?'

'Yes.'

The young man stood just inside the door. He wore a shabby but well-tended suit, and had carefully knocked the snow off his boots before coming in. His pale, anxious face was remarkable only for its deep brown eyes fringed with thick, curling lashes. He was looking at Lizzy with curiosity tempered by shyness.

'I don't suppose you remember Bill Sawthorne, Lizzy. But he remembers meeting you once, years ago.'

Lizzy looked straight into his eyes, and their expression of slight melancholy took her back to the Sunday afternoon she had striven to find something to say as she and Violet walked towards Clapham Common with a strange boy. 'William?' she said.

'Yes.' He came and shook her hand. 'They all seem to call me Bill now. But you remember that walk?'

'Oh yes.' All those princes in all those dreams who had been invested with William's eyes.

'Has Clara told you?' said Lyddy. 'Bill and I are engaged to be married.'

For some reason Lizzy found herself blushing. So this was it — the children, Lyddy and Clara, had grown up. Clara was travelling north, and Lyddy was to marry the boy who had been the first to stir her own imagination. And her father was dead. The family centre had split apart, and she had no centre of her own that she could tell them about in exchange.

'What lovely news,' she said. 'I'm very pleased.' And she was. Pleased for Lyddy, and glad that Bill Sawthorne seemed a gentle and responsible young man who would look after her well. He had a job as a junior clerk, and they were planning to stay at Star Place after their marriage so that Mrs Siddall could remain secure in her own home.

162

'You see,' said Lyddy, 'there's Harry to think of. And James is not yet fifteen.'

Lizzy was shocked by the appearance of James when he arrived home. He was small for his age, and his face was lined and careworn. She realised that their father's death had taken away his whole future, and it was as though at fifteen he had surrendered to the treadmill of work just in order to keep his head above water until death. There was something fatalistic about James, he had none of Clara's verve and attack.

Trying to reintegrate herself into the household, Lizzy started to lay the table as soon as she saw that Clara had almost finished preparing the food. Automatically she picked out the knife and fork which her father had always preferred to use, and then hesitated before putting them on the table. To whom should she give them?

Had it not been for the snow she might not have stayed the night, and she was relieved to set off for Chatham Place in the morning. She felt displaced and undermined by events, even though she had been living for quite a long time now outside the influence of her family. She turned and looked back down Star Place to where the shadow of the children's asylum fell across the end of the street, darkening the already stained and scumbled snow.

Gabriel was sitting by a balcony window when she reached Blackfriars, finishing off a long letter to Woolner in Australia. An unexpected gladness came over her, as though she were back from a much longer visit.

'Oh, Lizzy. I was waiting here for you.'

She knew that was not strictly true, but she did not mind.

'How are the Siddals of Sheffield?'

'My father has died.'

Gabriel put down his writing things and looked at her gravely. 'How do you feel?'

'I'm not sure. It happened in November.'

'Come and sit by me.'

She drew up a stool by his feet, and he put an arm around her shoulders and slowly stroked her hair. She felt secure and warm, and after a while would have liked to turn her head and kiss the hand that lay on her upper arm.

After a long silence he asked her the cause of her father's death and the present circumstances of her mother. He listened to what she had to say, and then murmured to himself, 'Death, death

163

already. When we had barely started life here.' Then he asked if she would make a drawing, 'To establish that art must go on, Lizzy.' His voice was compelling.

She did not remotely understand his urgency, and would have much preferred to stay resting by his knee. But she did as he requested, laboriously sketching the peacock feathers and sunflowers. Dead feathers and dead flowers, she thought.

It had become their custom to eat an early supper in a nearby chop-house before he put her on the omnibus for Oxford Street. On their way they always passed a bigger, gayer restaurant which Lizzy occasionally glanced into, attracted by the lights and the bustle, and that evening they almost collided with a girl who came quickly out of its side entrance.

Apologies were being made, when the girl gave a little shriek, and cried: 'Why! It's Mr Rizzetty. So sorry, duck, didn't recognize you.'

Gabriel bowed, tightened his grip on Lizzy's arm, and hurried on. She meanwhile was absorbing the image of the girl she had so fleetingly seen: full-lipped, fair-haired, vibrant and vulgar.

'Who was that?'

'I don't know her name . . . Phoebe . . . Phyllis . . . something. She works in that restaurant.'

'How does she know you?'

'Oh . . . I've eaten there once or twice . . . with Mad and Bruno.'

'Why don't we ever go in there?'

'It's a noisy place.'

Something in Gabriel's demeanour when confronted with the girl, and the look of the girl herself, reminded Lizzy of the way he had behaved in the company of Annie Miller.

'Do you go there with other girls?'

'No, Lizzy, of course I —'

'I don't mean you. I mean, do the others have girls with them?'

'They may do. Occasionally.'

'Why do you never take me out in company?'

'Because I like to have you all to myself, Lizzy. Because I don't like to see you in a rowdy place.'

Quite without premeditation she said sarcastically, 'Has Miss Miller learned to read yet?'

Her voice was quiet and sibilant. A carriage clattered by and Gabriel seemed not to hear.

She said very little throughout their meal. She was thinking of all

164

the hours she was not with Gabriel, and how she really knew nothing about how he spent them. Work was the only activity he ever emphasized to her, yet where was his *Ophelia,* his *Twelfth Night?*

In the early spring, the reason for Gabriel's current distraction and absences was explained to her: his family was moving down to Somerset. Their day school had proved a failure, and Mrs Rossetti's well-placed sister — who regularly saved Gabriel from Queer Street — had found an opening for them in Frome. Maria and William were to remain in London, but Christina and Mrs Rossetti would teach the children of nearby farmers, and it was hoped that Mr Rossetti, now elderly and ailing, would benefit from country air. A farewell dinner was arranged at Mornington Crescent, to which Lizzy discovered that the Browns and Holman Hunt were invited.

'But of course I may not come!' she sneered.

'It isn't my choice, Lizzy.'

'You get your choice in most things. You won't ever try for me.'

She deliberately refused to come to Chatham Place for a few days, saying she was bored with drawing and posing. Since her father's death she had taken to visiting Star Place every two or three weeks, and she spent a night there helping Lyddy cut out her wedding dress. Clara had gone to Sheffield, and Mrs Siddall seemed stoically resigned to widowhood. Only James appeared irredeemably displaced in a regime without his father. Bill Sawthorne was going to make a steady husband for Lyddy, but Lizzy could see that he would not be able to provide opportunities for James, nor solve the problem of Harry.

'And how about you, miss?' her mother asked when they were alone. 'I don't suppose anyone is going to marry you. Will you be able to help support Harry and myself? It can't all be down to Lyddy and James, you know. Annie's doing her bit by taking care of Clara.'

The tone of the statement angered Lizzy, but she could see the sense of it. 'I'll try, mother. I'll think about what I can do.'

'The number of times I've told you that thinking never did any good.'

When Lizzy next went to Chatham Place she had every intention of telling Gabriel she must work for some of the other painters in order to earn money to help her family. This was so uppermost in her mind that she had put aside the fact he might be annoyed by her recent absence. And in fact he greeted her warmly, with no trace of resentment — rather he seemed most anxious to please her. Since the snow had cleared, would she like to go to the Photographic Exbition with him, once he had finished writing a letter? Or would she prefer to work alongside him for a while in the studio?

Her eyes strayed to his writing-table: a sheet covered with a round, feminine hand lay by his own half-written page.

'Who are you writing to?'

'Emma Brown. She sent an invitation. She included us both, of course.'

'When is it for?'

'Tuesday. I'm afraid I shall have to tell her we cannot go.'

'Why is that?'

'A long-standing arrangement. Several of Woolner's friends are to meet to sketch mutual portraits to send out to him. I promised him in my last letter the ceremony would take place at noon on April 12th.'

'For what time is Emma's invitation?'

'Six o'clock.'

'Then why may we not accept? It can scarcely take several hours to sketch pictures for Mr Woolner.'

'Ah! We have arranged to make a day of it. Meet at Johnny's for breakfast and then go out into the country.'

'And apparently make an evening of it as well.'

'Lizzy . . .'

'Bruno is not going, presumably?'

'No. He hates doing things in a crowd.'

'And you love it.'

'Gug, you've just come back. And you're angry already. It's just a sketching party. To meet a promise to old Woolner.'

'And so the first invitation that comes where I may accompany you to a proper supper in somebody's house has to be refused. Just so you can go on an outing . . . like children. To make little pictures for great big Mr Woolner who's gone all the way to Australia!'

Gabriel said no more. He turned from her and went back to the table and completed his letter.

She was left seething with anger, pacing up and down the studio.

Finally she burst out: 'I've got to earn money, Gabriel. Listen to me. I must help with my family. I must pose for other artists. I shall send cards to those I have met. See if they will use me.'

His olive-skinned lids half concealed his eyes as he watched her. Her meek, dove-like side was invisible; she flung her head back, and whirled her soft, hoopless skirts as she turned, like a dancer.

'No, Lizzy. If you need money for your family, I will give it to you.'

'How can you? You even have to ask William for the rent.'

'That is none of your business. My family undertstands my needs and my position.'

'Oh, do they? Then what is their understanding of me? Just your paid model. Your hired, paid girl!'

She burst into violent sobbing, and he ran to her. He held her painfully hard against his chest, and for the first time she felt a man's lips touch every part of her face — her eyes, brow, cheeks, mouth. Her tears were wiped by his beard, her lashes crushed against his cheek.

When she was calmer she felt his heart thudding, saw the un-familiar brilliance of his stone-grey eyes.

As he finally let her go, he said, 'Lizzy. Will you come now to the Photographic Exhibition? Be by my side to reassure me that artists aren't obsolete in this modern world?'

'If you want me to.'

Now he held her very tenderly, kissing her on the lips, and running his hand down her loosened hair.

'Yes, Guggums. I want you to. I want you to.'

Chapter Eleven

Only two segments of the brilliant May sunshine were allowed to pass the dusty purple and gold drapes into the studio. They fell like shafts of light from heaven, creating the effects Gabriel wanted for his medieval settings. While other girls were taken to dance under the budding trees in the gardens of Vauxhall and Cremorne, Lizzy was posing as a friend of Dante — watching sadly as he drew Beatrice from memory a year after her death. She seldom questioned Gabriel's subject matter, and grew accustomed to the blotting out of the light.

During breaks she would go and stand on one of the balconies and watch the barges unloading below. The smell from the wharves grew more redolent in the warm sun, and she would hold a handkerchief in front of her face and take shallow breaths. Gabriel gave her money regularly now for her mother — juggling, she supposed, his earnings from MacCracken and windfalls from his aunt — and he also kissed her closely for a few minutes each time they were about to leave Chatham Place. These kisses made her tense and excited; she half dreaded them, yet would have been crestfallen had they not occurred. She would think about them as she lay in bed at Weymouth Street, remembering her mother's old warnings about girls who 'touched'.

In June the heat was intense, and small outbreaks of cholera were reported in the city. Gabriel became listless and irritable, and a series of boils broke out on his neck and refused to heal. A doctor gave him ointment and pills, but the eruptions remained poisonous and painful. One evening, after Lizzy had accidentally grazed the dressing on his neck with her hand as he kissed her, he broke from her abruptly, breathing heavily.

'I must go away — get some air. Go to the country, or I'll never get well.'

'Will you go to your family?'

For a second he looked at her as though she were half mad, then checked himself. 'No . . . no, I don't think so. Perhaps later. I shall go to Newcastle. There is a painter, William Bell Scott, who will make me welcome, Tynemouth is not far away — I shall bathe, the salt water will do me good.'

'And I . . .?'

'I must get well, Lizzy.' His breathing was still heavy, and he kept looking at her as though about to do something reckless. 'What do you want to do?'

An idea occurred to her — an ambition that flashed bright and brief as a kingfisher. 'I should like to stay here. To do my work. By myself. I shall try to finish a painting.' He had been teaching her to use oils, supplementing his practical lessons with visits to the National Gallery.

His expression was one of pride now. 'Good for you, Lizzy. Good for you.'

He had to borrow his fare to Newcastle, and a carpet bag for his belongings, but in two days he was gone and the rooms at Chatham Place were all hers. He had told her to keep the door locked against stray callers, and at the last moment had hurried from the studio without embracing her. She was left feeling irresolute and empty, yet also pleasantly untramelled.

A clean palette, brushes, colours and mixing materials were set out for her on a table. After wandering around, changing her dress, looking at a journal, and just gazing out of the window, she went up to the table. She looked at the objects on it for a long time, and then touched each one tentatively with the tips of her fingers. Energy seemed to run through her at each brief contact, and she had a gratifying sense of individual, independent power.

There was no question what her first oil painting would be; the only thing she wanted to attempt was a portrait of herself. There were so many images of her by Gabriel that she felt impelled to find out what would happen when she observed her mirrored reflection and tried to reconstruct it in paint.

For many days she did not go out. Mrs Wirrell brought up her meals, and late in the evening when the sun went down she would sit out on the balcony for air. The heat and smells faded then, and sunset brought landscapes of colour and cloud that lifted her imagination into a state of hallucination, where gold and crimson, damson and leaden grey, became the whole universe, staining her emotions with their intensity, floating free of the nagging demands

169

of daily life.

When she turned back into the dark studio, her developing portrait was almost invisible. But when she lit the lamp it stared at her with all the affront of a spirit brought to life and then denied the succour of dreams. Without really meaning to, she had imitated the flat, precise style of Elizabethan portraits with their challenging stares and bleached complexions. It made her look older, but was more truly like her, she felt, than Gabriel's pictures. The pale lashes, slightly pursed or pinched mouth, elongated nose, and heavy lids, all emphasized in their pallor by the dark copper and brown shades of her hair and dress, combined to indicate her exact character seen without the intervening veil of myth. It frightened her sometimes, its exactness. She, the living she in the flesh and nerves behind the skin of her face, was in a way less real than the amalgam of paints on the canvas.

But self-reproduction did nothing to lower the barriers between her isolated present and a more integrated and secure future; in fact is seemed to stress her solitude, pinpoint her precarious position. Yet even though loneliness magnified her fears, it also brought a measure of relief. She realised, not without humour, that to have Gabriel completely absent for a period was in itself a holiday.

One afternoon, when she was sitting half-asleep over a book, Mrs Wirrell came and informed her that there were two people downstairs who said they knew her. 'Mr and Mrs Madox Brown, they call themselves. Will you see them?'

At first she felt panicked and shy, but then became curious and rather pleased. 'Yes. Yes. Do show them up.'

So Madox Brown and Emma came into the studio before she had time to cover the portrait, or make things tidy, and in that atmosphere, aided by one of Mrs Wirrell's teas, and without Gabriel's dominating presence, real friendship grew. The Browns had learned that she was on her own, and they decided that since they were passing through central London they would come and see if she was all right. Bruno quickly spotted the portrait, and when he realised it was her work, he was full of praise. He kept shaking his head and saying, 'Remarkable, remarkable,' and Lizzy felt exhilarated each time he repeated the word.

Emma was the first to comment directly on the peculiar stench from the river — the mud of low tide mingling with the chemical smells. She was concerned that Lizzy seemed resigned to it, and

170

suggested she ought to go back to Hampstead with them, where the air was pure, rather than risk disease.

'Thank you,' said Lizzy, 'But I'm used to it. And by late evening it is much fresher.'

'You shouldn't take chances,' said Emma. 'We've just been to see poor Walter Dev —' she bit back the rest of the sentence, and blushed.

Bruno looked at her in surprise. 'We've been to see Deverell,' he explained. 'He's in a very bad way, poor fellow.'

'I am sorry.' Lizzy spoke with deceptive calm. 'What is the matter with him? It is so long since I last saw him.'

'The doctors don't seem to know. In that respect it's a repetition of what happened to his father, though the symptoms aren't the same.'

Emma, speaking over-brightly, said: 'He has hopes of recovering soon. He thinks he's better than he was last week.'

'Then I'm glad we didn't see him last week,' said Bruno grimly. 'He looked quite bad enough for me.'

Emma quickly tried to change the subject, but he interrupted. 'In fact that first picture you sat for, Lizzy, the *Twelfth Night* one, may be coming to the family's rescue. Evidently Millais told Ruskin of their plight, and he's persuaded MacCracken to buy it.'

Lizzy nodded, she could not speak. She wondered, vaguely, what kind of man it was who, when reassured by Mr Ruskin, could give money to the one-time tenants of Red Lion Square for their pictures, and would have an image of herself in boy's clothes, painted, oh, so long ago, hanging in his home. She remembered the first time she had changed into those clothes, and how Walter had come to reassure her. Her eyes brimmed.

Later, when Bruno stepped out on to the balcony and became absorbed by the view, Emma said quietly, 'I'm sorry — sorry if we've said anything to upset you.'

'No . . . I knew Walter had not been well. Gabriel told me. It was just sad to think how hopeful he had been when he did that painting.'

'Of course,' Emma hesitated awkwardly. 'You must miss Gabriel?'

'I suppose so.' There was no expression in her reply.

'When do you expect him back?'

'I don't know.'

Emma gave a little sigh. 'You are brave. Being here on your own. Having the courage and talent to paint.'

'I don't find it too difficult. I like being in these rooms.'

'I hate it when Bruno goes away.'

'But he's your husband.'

They were both embarrassed.

'Well . . . yes.' Emma's curiosity got the better of her. 'You don't feel . . . well, *feel* for Gabriel?'

'It's not like that.' She remembered his kisses. 'It's not really like that.'

'He ought to let you know how long he intends to stay away.'

'He never knows his plans in advance. Or he certainly never tells them.'

Emma laughed. 'We've noticed that.' Bruno was coming inside, closing the long window. Lowering her voice, she said, 'Lizzy, if ever you need friends, remember we'll always try to help.'

When they had gone, Lizzy knelt in a high-backed chair with her face bowed against the knobbly, carved wood. Instinctively she had assumed the position of prayer. Marriage had to be perfect and was therefore out of her reach. She would never be married with the unquestioning certainty that Emma had. Walter was gravely ill. She had never wanted anyone else. He had excluded her. Gabriel kissed her now. And that made her imperfect for anyone else.

Her tears crept into crevices in the carving and mingled with the dust.

She dreamed of Walter so clearly. He was standing in a wild garden, in dappled sunlight under a hawthorn tree, and the blossom smelled yeasty and sweet. His dark hair was ruffled, and he was singing. The tune was that of an old nursery rhyme, and his voice was baritone and slightly husky. She strained and strained to hear the words but could not. When he had finished he walked towards her and she knew he was going to kiss her. She waited, tranquilly ecstatic. Everything was about to begin.

As he came towards her, so she seemed to diminish, until her dreaming self disappeared and she was most reluctantly awake. The heavy red curtains kept fresh air and dawn light out of the small bedroom, and the prevailing smell was that of Gabriel's old books stacked against the wall. She turned distractedly, burying her face and succumbing to the disappointment that drenched her. Soon she was unconscious again, drawn back into the dream territory of

172

earlier years. A dismal interior, long and wood-panelled, stretched all round her, with no windows or door. The old shape, the old red shape, was where a fireplace might have been. It grew from the size of a compact violin into an ill-shaped tunnel-mouth, capable of receiving a monster locomotive. She threw herself on to the floor, forcing her nails between the boards as though to prise one up and find air. But in that prone position she became less frantic, more passive and she was on the verge of double sleep as the dream vanished.

It was late when she woke. Her abdomen ached in a grinding non-specific way for which she could find no relief. When Mrs Wirrell brought her morning tea she had not washed or dressed and sat on her bed clutching her knees, rocking slowly backwards and forwards. Once it was established that her problem was menstrual and not infectious, Mrs Wirrell became sympathetic. She questioned Lizzy on her past experience, and on hearing that she used to resort to drops, offered to go to the pharmacist and get her some more. Remembering the blessed relief that they brought, Lizzy nodded emphatically.

When the pain had lessened, and the drug was working on her imagination, she began to speculate about Walter. Surely she ought to be able to see him, to talk to him just once about her feelings? It seemed so unfair that other people could visit him, while she was quite cut off. Perhaps she should send him a letter, saying she had been upset by the news from the Browns. Or just send a short greeting to him and his mother. Gabriel had some particularly nice ivory cards; could she compose a message to go on one of them?

She went to look for the cards, shuffling dreamily through the untidy piles on the writing-table, and then looking inside the single brass-handled drawer. She saw the cards immediately, but she also saw the letter pushed underneath them. It was on cheap paper and written in pencil, not at all like the letters he received from Woolner and Allingham and Tupper, and many other of his friends. Curiously, she pulled it out.

Dear Mr Rizzetty,

A pity you did not come. We had a good
time. I wish you had been there. I missed you.

     Your
      Phoebe

Phoebe . . . Phyllis. How dare he say he could not remember her name? That flouting, common girl. 'I don't like to see you in a rowdy place.' How very convenient to have such a feeling. 'Your Phoebe.' Damn Phoebe. Damn, damn Phoebe!

She did not tear the note up. She folded it very carefully and put it in her pocket book. Then she took some more drops and went back to bed.

The pain was not severe the next day. She felt lethargic and heavy, but not uncomfortable. It no longer seemed thinkable to write to Walter. There was no point. The vibrant face of the girl coming out of the restaurant nagged at her mind. She had draped a cloth over her own portrait, over that pale, disapproving, *Governessy* face.

On the following day she went to Star Place, and stayed for two nights. In her subdued mood she got along well enough with her mother, and she spent several hours playing simple games with Harry in the yard. Lyddy and Bill were to be married in July, and most of the family's energy and anticipation were directed towards that event. Even Lyddy did not bother to ask any questions about her life. It was as though they had written off her prospects altogether. She was twenty-one, and it felt old.

Gabriel was back when she returned to Chatham Place. He was standing in front of her portrait, hands in his pockets, the carpet bag thrown carelessly on the floor beside him.

He did not immediately turn to her, but had recognized her step and said in a low voice, 'Lizzy, it's a wonderful painting. A miracle. I'm so proud of you.'

She was confused. Mrs Wirrell had warned her at the foot of the stairs that Gabriel was there, and she had walked up with the intention of being very reserved and distant. At some point she would ask him coolly about Phoebe. And she had temporarily completely forgotten about the portrait.

Now she was abruptly thrown back into the world where paintings took precedence over everything — only this time there was a difference. It was her own painting that was being given consideration, and she did not feel that Gabriel's eulogy was totally misplaced.

He made one or two suggestions, constructive criticisms, but mainly he was full of praise for her precision and subtle observation. She could not make the words he used match the experience

174

she had when working on the picture, but nevertheless the praise was sweetly welcome. As the afternoon wore on, and they settled into old ways, familiar routine — tea by the window, Gabriel reading some verses he had written on the train — it seemed increasingly inopportune to introduce the carefully-folded note in her pocket book into the conversation. But when the time came for her to collect up her things and leave for Weymouth Street, and he came to embrace her, she stiffened and turned her face away.

'Lizzy?'

She said nothing.

'Guggums, what is it?'

Her face was still turned away and he dropped his hands from her shoulders. Then he went briskly to his carpet bag and started to unpack.

'I'll go then,' she said.

'Yes, Lizzy. Goodbye.' He sounded neither angry nor disappointed. But there was an unfamiliar edge to his voice that unnerved her.

She left the studio, and just as she walked round the corner of Chatham Place to go up to Ludgate Hill, she heard voices and footsteps behind her. It sounded as though they went into the building, but she did not turn round to look.

No plans had been made for the following day, and she woke with a feeling of unsureness and disappointment. She was secure enough in her clean Weymouth Street room, and there would be an ample breakfast, should she want it, in the kitchen; but what after that? She had to go to Gabriel if anything were to happen that day at all.

He was very despondent when she arrived.

'It's perhaps as well you went so quickly yesterday, Lizzy. You must have had a premonition. As soon as you'd gone, William Allingham arrived with Walter.'

Those voices she had heard. . .

'Oh Lizzy, he looks so ill.'

She could tell from the way he spoke that he was completely absorbed in his own feelings for Walter, that any previous conjecture he'd had about her emotions was not concerning him. She sat down and waited.

'It's no use. He's been to see a doctor on Bruno's recommendation — Dr Marshall — and he says he won't live more than six months. Perhaps if he's very careful he may last a little longer. I asked him to come and stay here. I could fix up the sitting room. It would have been more cheerful for him perhaps. But he says he must stay at home — and oddly enough he says he's able to work quite hard. He's started up again on that big painting, *The Doctor's Last Visit*.'

Lizzy buried her face in her hands, remembering how he had said, 'It seems almost . . . criminal. Tempting fate,' when he had begun the painting during his father's illness.

'Johnny and Mad have acted well. The last painting he finished was shown at the Liverpool Academy, and they've clubbed together to buy it.'

'What is it?'

'A girl feeding her pet songbird. One of his sisters, I believe.'

She remembered him saying, 'My sisters are no good for posing. They talk all the time. And they're not very pretty.'

'Well, Lizzy. We mustn't despair. He certainly isn't. He was as cheerful as anything . . . Both he and William asked after you, and they were immensely taken by the way you didn't flatter yourself in your portrait. They thought it a very strong painting for a woman.'

'Do they know now what is the matter with him?'

'It's called Dr Bright's disease. Kidneys. He has dreadful trouble with his stomach.'

He used to eat the gingerbread so eagerly, saying he was hungry enough to eat a horse.

Instinctively she went and covered her portrait with a cloth.

'Why did you do that?'

'I don't know.'

'You reminded me of Christina. When our canary used to sing for too long, she would cover its cage. She said she couldn't bear the way it made up songs so effortlessly, when she found it so difficult to write good verses.'

'I don't want to see myself staring out. I don't want to paint any more.'

Much later in the day he said, 'It would be treasonous not to paint, Lizzy. That would be letting the dark side take over; we've got to create light through art. We can't give up.'

She didn't see how an image of her face could affect the forces of good and evil.

The weeks that followed were desultory. Lizzy barely drew at all,

176

and Gabriel produced very little. His boils returned, and it rained a great deal. He had not attempted to kiss her again. They took to wandering around the City, slipping into the Wren churches where each developed their private thoughts, and walking up and down unknown streets of shabby houses. She did not know the reason for these journeys, but she found the action and ensuing fatigue comforting. Sometimes Gabriel would deliver her back to Weymouth Street with wet feet and clothes, and Cook would give her a jug of hot water and a warm towel. Then she would change and spend the rest of the evening reading and drowsing and gazing out at the clouds and the rain. If she became depressed, or developed a headache, she would take a few of her drops. They helped time to pass without effort. During this period Gabriel visited Walter fairly frequently, as did the other PRB's, and each time they saw signs of deterioration though not one of them ever reported finding him in low spirits.

She knew that he was dead from the expression on Gabriel's face when she arrived at the studio one morning. He led her to the writing-table and pointed to the letter he had just finished to Madox Brown.

You will be grieved to hear that poor Deverell died yesterday about 4 o'clock. He retained his senses to the last, and died without pain, I believe. He had been told in the morning that he could not live thro' the day; and appeared to receive the announcement without either emotion or surprise, saying he supposed he was man enough to die. His sister wrote (or rather got a cousin to write) to me this morning telling me of their loss. It seems Millais was in the house at the time of his death, but did not see him. I saw him about a week ago for a few minutes. He appeared to congratulate himself at that time that his present doctor was succeeding in reducing the swelling of his legs and feet: but I believe this was in reality a fatal symptom. He said, 'However, I must not holloa before I am out of the wood.' We shall all sincerely regret his loss; but no one more than — or perhaps so much as — I, for I had known him longest and most intimately.

The letter emphasized her exclusion. There was no one she could write to about Walter, no claims she could make about the importance to her of their friendship.

Her crying was brief and controlled. Death did not make much difference. They had been apart for too long. She had not felt very much when she learned of her father's death, she remembered. It was as though her feelings were benumbed, protected, like wax flowers under a glass dome.

When Gabriel said he would go and tell Hunt what had happened, she elected to stay in the studio. She had an urge to read something very simple, such as might absorb a child. She remembered Wordsworth's ballads, with their country stories and swinging rhymes, and found the volume in the bedroom. After reading two or three, she fastened on *We Are Seven,* which told of a little girl who could not feel that relationships were destroyed by death or absence. Even though two of her brothers and sisters were dead and the other four gone away, she would always reply to the narrator's question, How many are there in the family? 'O Master! we are seven.' Lizzy repeated that phrase over and over, 'O Master! we are seven.' People weren't taken away like counters in a game. Everything they had ever done, ever been, stayed in the world's memory.

For the first time for weeks she found her sketchbook and started to illustrate the poem. She did not just draw the little girl with her 'rustic, woodland air', but she also included in the picture the two brothers who had gone to sea, the sisters who had moved away, and John and Jane who 'in the churchyard lie, Beneath the churchyard tree.'

When she had finished, she tried to draw her father from memory. By barely looking at the paper, but reaching far into her memory, she produced a fair likeness. She looked at it for a long time, wondering what she had felt about him. He had always frightened her a little. And without warning, she remembered Mr Greenacre. She slammed the sketchbook shut. Mr Greenacre's image frightened her more than any she had ever seen. It was almost as though he was begging to be drawn: to be remembered, to be immortalised.

She could not stop thinking about the old newspaper cutting, tucked into the back of the family scrapbook. She had read it only once, and had never tried to analyse the information it contained. But now the facts martialled themselves with pressing clarity: Mr

178

Greenacre had killed a forty-year-old woman on the day before their wedding, in the house of a younger woman with a baby.

It was possible for a man to murder to avoid marriage.

When Gabriel returned, he found her huddled in a chair, shivering. He held her, and warmed her, brought her brandy and water.

'We're all upset, Lizzy. We were all so fond of him.'

'It . . . it's not just that. It's the whole world. Dark and cold.'

He knelt by her chair, drawing her to him, stroking her hair forward so it encircled his neck.

'We make our own light, Lizzy. Our own fire.' She breathed the warm air between his collar and beard, seeking blind comfort like a fledgling under a wing.

Later on he said she must not try to get back to Weymouth Street. 'I shall doss down on the chaise. Mrs Wirrell will not mind. She knows we have lost a friend.' He straightened the bedroom and took in an extra rug they kept in the studio. It was unusual for him to do household tasks, and his homely actions smoothed away her doubts. She was so relieved to lie back in the bed, warm and semi-conscious, knowing that he was next door; and when he tapped on the door and came in and lay beside her on the coverlet, she did not mind. He stayed until long after she was asleep, as still as a knight on vigil. She slept deeply right through the night, but before she opened her eyes in the morning recalled enough of the evening before to touch the space beside her to make quite sure it was empty.

Chapter Twelve

Throughout the rest of the winter Gabriel referred to Lizzy as being 'ill'. She had little appetite and was losing weight, and all her quiet yet steely impulses seemed to have been attenuated. She did not complain, but just allowed the days to pass, posing on request, and sleeping a great deal. He once asked her if the drops she took were doing her any good, but she assured him she had used them before and found them satisfactory.

More and more frequently she stayed at Chatham Place overnight, finding the journey back to Weymouth Street too much of an effort. Mrs Burton had asked her searchingly on two occasions if she were all right, while Mrs Wirrell accepted the situation with a broadminded shrug. Lizzy and Gabriel were no bother, and she found them more interesting than the other tenants.

The only thing that gave a stimulus and regularity to Lizzy's days was the grey linnet Gabriel had carried back after attending Walter's funeral. The bird was the one featured in the painting that Millais and Hunt had bought, and the Deverell family were upset they would not be able to keep it when they moved in with relations. Knowing Gabriel liked pets, they had asked if he would look after it. From the start, Lizzy had taken over its care; talking to it, giving it food far more often than she herself would eat, and cleaning its ornate wire cage every morning. She called it Lancelot, and when it sang tirelessly and sweetly, lines would repeat inside her head with the insistency of a waltz tune:

> In the desert a fountain is springing,
> In the wide waste there still is a tree,
> And a bird in the solitude singing,
> Which speaks to my spirit of *thee.*

Gabriel watched her tend the bird, and drew the caring attitudes of her thin body. Sometimes when he left Chatham Place on his

180

own he seemed to throw off an invisible pall, becoming immediately more brisk and forthright as he stepped into the street.

In the early spring he told Lizzy that his family had decided to return to London. None of them had benefited from the country, and a recent rise in William's salary plus a small family inheritance made it possible for them all to be reunited in a house in Albany Street by Regent's Park. All, that is, except for Gabriel himself.

'I shall remain independent.'

'I won't stay if you continue to refuse to introduce me to your family.' Her statement, instinctive and bitter, hung in the air.

Finally he said, 'No, Lizzy. I understand.'

Three weeks after the move had taken place, he came in and told her that Christina would be coming to tea the following day.

'My father's health has deteriorated so much since the move, it isn't possible for mother to have visitors at the moment.'

Early that evening Lizzy said she would spend the night at Weymouth Street. She knew that Gabriel would publicly describe her as being present only during the day at Chatham Place and Christina's impending visit made her touchily observe this convention. Neither she nor Gabriel ever mentioned their false position to one another.

One and a half walls of the studio were already covered in the sketches and paintings he had made of his 'dear Guggums', and before Christina came he arranged Lizzy's own drawings and self-portrait on another wall. As she sat in a severe dark-blue dress, waiting for the hands of the clock to reach three-thirty, she sensed that he was more nervous than she. It would have been simple to start a neutral conversation, but she chose to remain silent and to observe his discomfort. Her expectations of Christina were confused. On the one hand there was the pinch-faced, anxious girl in the annunciation painting, and on the other she envisaged an intellectual genteel woman of authority.

What she was not prepared for was the small, pretty, pale young woman whom Mrs Wirrell escorted to their door. Lizzy was two years younger than Christina, but there was something untested, veiled in the latter's expression that made Lizzy feel much older. In conversation, however, although she spoke little, Christina was disconcertingly definite and caustic. She addressed virtually all her remarks to her brother, directing only the absolutely essential social niceties to Lizzy. Gabriel did his best to weave the fabric of

181

their nervy posturing into a resemblance of compatibility, but the history of his four-year relationship with Lizzy gaped between the two women.

Throughout tea Christina cast covert glances at his drawings, which were on the wall facing her, and after questioning admitted she had brought some poems for him to read.

'But perhaps I will not leave them with you.'

Lizzy knew that this was said because Christina did not want her to see them.

'We have always shared our things, Christina,' said Gabriel. 'Come, I'll show you what Lizzy and I have been up to.'

He took her first to his own work, which Christina looked at slowly and carefully, mentioning only colour effects and the particular passages from Dante that he had illustrated. Then he led her to Lizzy's wall. 'My discovery,' he said. 'You'll find no better natural talent.'

Lizzy's fingers and toes were clenched tightly as Christina stood in front of each of her drawings in silence. Finally she came to the self-portrait. 'You have an inscrutable method, Miss Siddall.'

Gabriel sighed. 'We're all very impressed. Bruno, Mad, William Allingham, Frederic . . . and, of course, poor Walter was too. When he made his last visit.'

'Yes,' said Christina.

At that moment, Lancelot suddenly hopped on to his perch and erupted into loud song. Lizzy, who had been fuming, released her resentment in hard laughter. 'He won't let his master's name go unnoticed.'

Christina looked baffled.

'He was Walter's song-bird,' explained Gabriel.

'Now,' said Lizzy, 'He is ours.'

'Ours', the abrupt pronouncement of joint possession and all that it implied, with Lizzy's sibilant 's' slightly prolonging the word, was, they all knew, a deliberate challenge. But it was a challenge that could be ignored — as a lady's dropped silk glove, hidden in the grass, may be passed over, whereas a man's steel and leather gauntlet, thudding to the ground, must be avenged.

It had been previously arranged that Gabriel should see his sister home, and Lizzy made quite a play of finding coats and saying that she herself would have left for Weymouth Street by the time he returned. And indeed she did intend to leave, but after she had

182

helped Mrs Wirrell tidy away the tea things she picked up the manuscript poems which Christina had, after all, left behind. And although she started to read them in a critical mood of jealousy, she became completely mesmerized by the longest of the three, and just sat reading it over and over. It was a poem which, if she had had the power, she would have written herself.

Sleep, let me sleep, for I am sick of care;
Sleep, let me sleep, for my pain wearies me.
Shut out the light, thicken the heavy air
With drowsy incense; let a distant stream
Of music lull me, languid as a dream,
Soft as the whisper of a summer sea.

Pluck me no rose that groweth on a thorn,
Nor myrtle white and cold as snow in June,
Fit for a virgin on her marriage morn:
But bring me poppies brimmed with sleepy death,
And ivy choking what it garlandeth,
And primroses that open to the moon.

Listen, the music swells into a song,
A simple song I loved in days of yore;
The echoes take it up and up along
The hills, and the wind blows it back again. —
Peace, peace, there is a memory in that strain
Of happy days that shall return no more.

O peace! your music wakeneth old thought,
But not old hope that made my life so sweet,
Only the longing that must end in nought.
Have patience with me, friends, a little while:
For soon, where you shall dance and sing and smile,
My quickened dust may blossom at your feet.

Sweet thought that I may yet live and grow green,
That leaves may yet spring from the withered root,
And buds and flowers and berries half unseen.
Then, if you haply muse upon the past,
Say this: Poor child, she has her wish at last;
Barren through life, but in death bearing fruit.

She was re-reading it for the dozenth time when Gabriel returned.

At first he was glad to find her still there, and relieved that she was so taken with Christina's work.

'Wouldn't it be a good idea if you were to illustrate some of her poems? I hope one day she will publish a volume, and it would be so nice if you provided the illustrations. Nothing would please me more.'

'It wouldn't please her.'

'Oh, Guggums . . .' He reached out for the manuscript in her hand. When he had finished reading it, he let out a deep sigh. 'It's no use . . . no use, all this anguish.'

'You don't think it a fine poem?'

'Yes, Lizzy. It's a fine poem. But Christina's a young woman. She can't drown in self-suffering for ever.'

'That poem,' said Lizzy, her chin held up and her eyes reflecting the pale flame of the lamp, 'expresses exactly what I feel.'

She always used the servants' entrance to Mr Foxall's house, and she was going down the steps to the basement area a few days after meeting Christina, when she heard a hearty shout from above.

'Hulloo . . . Miss Siddall . . . Lizzy!'

It was Barbara Leigh Smith. Lizzy climbed back up the stairs to the pavement.

'Lizzy! What good luck. I've just been talking to Mr Foxall. And I wanted to see you.'

'Please . . . come in. I was just . . .' Lizzy stopped, confused, realising she could not invite Barbara in through the back door.

'May I? If I could just come and talk to you for a few minutes. In your room.' Barbara solved the matter by leading the way down the steps.

Mrs Burton did not seem surprised to see the visitor she had just shown out of the front door returning through the kitchen, but merely said, 'Will you require anything, Miss?'

'No thank you, Mrs Burton. Not after your splendid tea. But Lizzy . . .?'

'It's a feast day if Lizzy eats a scone.'

'I've got something she'll take,' said Cook. 'Some freshly squeezed oranges.'

Lizzy smiled. 'Thank you — ever so much.' She accepted the white china jug half-filled with juice.

'Cook's so kind to me,' she said, once she and Barbara were in her room. 'I have a suspicion she makes fruit drinks especially

184

for me.'

'You are happy here then?'

'Oh yes. I couldn't be in a nicer place. Everyone is good to me.'
She set the bedside chair next to the one already in the window.

'I'm glad. You see, we're rather worried about you.'

'Why . . .?'

'Worried about your health. Gabriel mentioned it when I saw
him at a party a few days ago. And I received a note from Mr Foxall
this morning saying that Mrs Burton was worried about you too.
You've got much thinner. Lizzy. And I gather you have very little
energy.'

Lizzy bowed her head. It was true. But difficult to bring into the
open and discuss.

'I wonder if perhaps you should see a doctor? Whether you have
any actual symptoms that worry you?'

'No . . . no, I can't think of any.'

'Then if it's just weakness, I think a change of air might do you
good. Particularly as I'm told the atmosphere at Blackfriars is
frequently positively murky.' She gave a good-humoured chortle.
'Now, I've talked to Mr Foxall, and he agrees with me that a spell by
the sea never does any harm. Would you like to go to the seaside?'

Lizzy smiled faintly. 'I don't know. I've never seen the sea.'

A fleeting look of pity passed across Barbara's face. 'Then I think
that settles it, my dear. It's high time you did see the sea.' She
paused, waiting for Lizzy to say something; but she just sat quietly,
looking at her hands. Barbara cleared her throat. 'Well, then. You
leave everything to me. I shall talk to Gabriel. Get him to see sense.
And we'll decide what would be best.'

Lizzy looked up. 'Thank you. You know . . . I shan't ever be able
to thank you for everything you've done for me.' She spoke in a
rush.

'Get well. That's all the thanks I need.' She reached across and
held Lizzy's hand for a few seconds.

Barbara came back to see Lizzy the next morning. She had
discussed her case with a friend, Dr Wilkinson, a believer in all sorts
of modern theories, and he would very much like to see Lizzy, if she
would consent to a consultation. His rooms were in a street nearby,
and he was particularly sympathetic with women — unlike so
many of his profession. It seemed strange to Lizzy to go to a doctor
when you had nothing absolutely disabling the matter with you,

but she was anxious to please Barbara, so she agreed.

Dr Wilkinson was tall and pale and bearded, with a dreamy expression in his eyes. His voice was gentle and melodious, and he asked her innumerable questions about her background and previous illnesses. Barbara sat in the corner of the consulting room, and Lizzy found her commanding presence rather more inhibiting than Dr Wilkinson's shadowy one. It was easier to say 'yes' or 'no' to his questions than to elaborate, even if such monosyllables tended to be half-lies. At one stage he gently felt the bones in her arms and back, and looked inside her mouth, and at the end of the consultation pronounced there was nothing wrong with her other than slight curvature of the spine induced by long hours at the sewing-table, and that this could be cured by fresh air and exercise.

Barbara's indignation about the fact that in order to earn a meagre living people must work until their bodies were deformed, knew no bounds. Lizzy privately thought that her back was perfectly straight when she chose to sit up, it was just that she preferred to curl round in a chair. However she entered willingly enough into plans to send her away. They drove over to Chatham Place, and Barbara explained that her father had a country house called Bredelands near Hastings, and that she would be able to arrange for Lizzy to stay in the home of his groom's sister, who kept lodgings right by the sea. This plan was put to Gabriel, who expressed enthusiastic relief.

'Then you really will get better, Lizzy. I get so worried when you just lie on the chaise all day.'

Lizzy had noticed before how his tone of voice seemed to become pompous and buoyant when rich or influential people smoothed away difficulties in his life. 'What shall I do all day?' she asked.

She watched Gabriel catch Barbara's eye.

'You'll take exercise,' said Barbara, 'and eat good meals. And there'll be ample opportunity for you to draw.'

'Lancelot must go to Mrs Wirrell,' said Lizzy, 'Because you will forget to feed him, Gabriel.'

When Barbara had left, she asked him if he would take her down to Hastings himself rather than arrange a chaperone as had been discussed.

'Can't you do without me, Lizzy?'

She blushed. 'I've never travelled right out of London before.'

Two days later the train rattled between fields and orchards whose winter bleakness had only recently been softened by new spring growth. Perspectives of misty greens and greys were broken by snowy daubs of blossom, and sometimes the banks by the rails were smothered in primroses. Lizzy discovered that the very act of travelling made her feel hopeful. The plumes of smoke from the engine streamed against the pale sky, and when it whistled loudly at each new station the noise made her nerves tingle. She looked at Gabriel, who was reading, and seeing him in these strange surroundings made her realise how he had become more familiar to her than anyone she had ever known — including even her own mother and sisters.

A cab took them from the station to a weather-boarded house in the High Street, and when the driver suddenly turned into a road with a view of the sea, Lizzy gasped. The pearly-grey stretch before her was so bright — so wide and flat and dazzling.

Gabriel looked at it rather morosely. 'Funny old Turner,' he said, 'Spending a lifetime chasing that light.' He was travelling straight back to London that evening because Ruskin had written to ask if he might call at Chatham Place the following day. It would be their first meeting.

'You're worrying about Mr Ruskin?'

'No. Of course I'm not. My only worry is your health.'

His tone did not convince her.

They were made very welcome by a Mrs Marriot, a garrulous lady who seemed to believe that everyone liked to know as much as possible about the minutiae of her life. Gabriel stayed to see Lizzy settled in a pretty low-ceilinged room, and then fled back to the station, interrupting a convoluted saga about spring cabbage and mackerel. He had arranged to take one of Mrs Marriot's other rooms at the weekend, and there was a message waiting for Lizzy to say that Bessie Parkes, a close friend of Barbara, would call to see her in the morning.

She felt apprehensive about seeing Bessie alone. They had met before at the Howitts, and she had been in awe of the handsome young woman who seemed to know everything about politics and literature, and had even published a book of poems. However Bessie made her feel at ease immediately — bringing bottled greengages, for she had been told by Barbara that Lizzy liked fruit, and joking about Mrs Marriot's stories which were locally renowned for their length and triviality. After a while she suggested taking

187

Lizzy down to the promenade for her first proper look at the sea.

'If you feel strong enough, that is.'

'Yes. I feel quite . . . '

'Quite . . . ?'

'Well — *new!*'

Bessie laughed. 'That's excellent. That's what the sea air is for.'

Lizzy was fascinated by the waves. They were very small — wavelets, Bessie called them — hurrying conscientiously towards the shingle and then curving over like grey brandy snaps and slapping on to the pebbles, making a creamy rim of froth. 'I keep waiting for them to stop.' she said.

'It's *lovely* showing someone something for the first time. Something really big, like the sea.'

Bessie was staying at Bredelands, which was several miles inland. Lizzy and Gabriel were invited over for Sunday and the carriage would be sent for them. 'Barbara will be down, and there'll be just the four of us so you won't get too tired. It's a most beautiful place. You will love it.'

'Mr Leigh Smith must be very rich.'

'Well, fairly. And *very* kind. He lets his children lead proper independent lives. As does my father. But most don't.'

'She has no mother?' Lizzy wanted to test Emma's story.

'No. She died when Barbara was small.' Bessie looked at Lizzy speculatively. 'Have you heard about her at all?'

'I . . . think so.'

'What did you hear?'

'That she was once a millinery girl . . . like me.'

Bessie nodded. 'Anything else?'

Lizzy gave a barely perceptible nod.

'I think those people who follow the dictates of their hearts are wonderful,' pronounced Bessie. 'People like yourself, who devote themselves to people dedicated to art. And it is so thrilling that your own talent has flowered as a result. Women really begin to discover themselves when they are not totally hampered by the chains of domesticity or menial work. We all think it's marvellous the way you and Gabriel draw and paint together.'

Lizzy was amazed by the vibrant, almost reverent, tone in her voice as she delivered this speech.

After Bessie had left, she felt physically exhausted yet mentally agitated. She picked at the supper Mrs Marriot prepared for her, and was treated to a long tale about a second cousin with a missing finger whose dresses hung from her like farmers' smocks because she would not eat her food. Lizzy's head by then was throbbing, and when she went to bed she poured herself a generous dose of drops so that she might sleep very deeply.

She was almost light-headed in the morning, answering Mrs Marriot's solicitous enquiries in a vague, disconnected manner.

'I'd better fetch the doctor, miss.'

'No . . . I'll be stronger soon.'

'Well, if you're not, the doctor's coming. It'll be more than my life's worth if I allow you to become more poorly.'

'By midday. I'll be down.'

Lizzy knew from experience that by then the layers of her mind would have merged together, and that she would be able to get up without too much dizziness.

The day before Gabriel was due to arrive, she realised that her drops were almost finished. She had noticed a pharmacist in the High Street, and told Mrs Marriot that she was going to do a little shopping and then take a look at the sea.

'That's right, my dear. The air will do you good. And you seem to have taken a turn for the better.'

The pharmacist was an elderly man with a kindly but firm manner. He took the bottle that Lizzy showed him, took out the stopper and sniffed.

'Hmm. How long have you been taking this, young lady?'

'About four years.'

'You have taken it regularly all that time?'

'No. Not regularly. I first had it four years ago.'

'And why did you first take it?'

Lizzy was embarrassed. She very much resented all these questions. In London, the pharmacist just filled up her bottle and that was that.

'I presume it was prescribed for ladies' complaints?'

She nodded.

'And do you just take them on the bad day once a month, or do you use them for headaches and other minor matters?'

'Yes . . . headaches.'

'Hmm.' He looked at her very hard. 'I would estimate you are . . . twenty-two years old?'

She found his accuracy uncanny. 'Yes.'

'Well, I'm afraid I am going to say to you what I have said to other young ladies before you. And young gentlemen too. That unless the dosage of this drug is *strictly* regulated to absolute need, it is a pernicious destroyer of health. No one needs laudanum for the occasional headache. And anyone who has become accustomed to using it in that way is in danger. So, I am very sorry young lady, but I'm afraid I'm not going to give you any more of this medicine. My recommendation for monthly upsets is warmth, rest, and hot sweet tea.'

Lizzy was too mortified and angry to reply. She was about to hurry from the shop, but remembered he still held the bottle. She reached out her hand.

Very reluctantly he placed the bottle in her palm. 'I had hoped you might leave this with me. But if you think you need it that badly. . .'

He watched her leave, saying, 'Please remember, my dear. I have given you good advice.'

Lizzy walked quickly and agitatedly towards another street which had shops in it. She found a second pharmacist, and this time an unctuous young man gave her a new bottle of medicine complete with a fancy label. 'The sea air is so beneficial to young ladies,' he said ingratiatingly.

She looked forward to Gabriel's return, and when the time came walked up to the station to meet his train. As the slamming of the carriage doors ceased, the smoke dispersed, and the porters hurried towards the line of cabs with passengers' bags, she was disturbed to see him trailing slowly behind everyone else, his normally warm olive complexion drained to a sickly yellow.

He brightened when he saw her, exclaiming how well she looked, and fussing about the distance she had walked. She noticed that his breath smelled sour and that there were dark circles under his eyes.

'What is the matter with you, Gabriel? You look so ill.'

'No, Guggums. I'm fine. Tired, that's all. And the movement of the train made me a little queasy.'

'It didn't affect you the other day.'

'No. It's just on top of being tired.'

'What have you been doing then?'

He took her arm and they started to walk away from the station. 'Celebrating. Ruskin has been most encouraging. It seems he really wants to take me up. So I invited a few of the old crowd over to

190

Chelsea to tell them all about it and to celebrate.'

Sharp as a whip she asked, 'Why Chelsea?'

'Well, whyever not?'

'Holman Hunt's still away. Who else lives there?'

'My dear Lizzy. Just because Mad chooses to go and paint in Palestine doesn't mean we must all forsake Chelsea as a meeting place. It has some of the jolliest inns in London. And I'm afraid I've got a head that proves it.'

'Did you see Annie Miller?'

'Whyever do you ask that?'

'She lives in Chelsea.'

'So, Miss Sid, do hundreds of other people. That is a perfectly ridiculous reason for the question. Now . . . will you tell me how you have been getting on? You look so much better.'

She would not reply.

'Oh Lizzy! For goodness sake don't sulk. We're supposed to be on holiday. Aren't you even going to ask me what Ruskin said?'

Woodenly she enquired about Mr Ruskin. But it was uppermost in her mind for the rest of the day that he had not answered her question about Annie Miller. Even if it were an unreasonable question, surely he could answer it when he saw how much it meant to her?

In the morning she had a headache and took a few drops. They made her feel detached and inconsequential, and she elected to stay in the house while Gabriel went walking on the cliffs. Mrs Marriot was out during the afternoon, and he persuaded Lizzy to sit next to him on the couch in the little chintzy sitting-room. He read some ballads by William Allingham to her, and she listened drowsily to their evocations of Celtic myths and magic.

'He's asked me to do some illustrations, Guggums. For a special edition. Would you like to help me? You could choose the ones you liked best to illustrate.'

A spark stirred in her mind. 'They would be printed? My designs?'

'Yes. Will you do them?'

'If you like.'

He moved nearer and took her in his arms. 'Oh Lizzy. Silly Lizzy. You make such fusses sometimes. You know there's only you. Only you who matters.' He started to kiss her brow and temples very gently. His breath was sweet again, and his hair smelled of the sea.

The kissing moved her: she felt a soft, slow surge of joy swell up through her body. She put her arms round him, and her mouth became pliant against his. She allowed him to kiss her for a long time. The feeling of joy and desire rippled again and again, like the little waves she had first seen on the beach.

· Early in the evening she pleaded tiredness, and went to bed and slept like a child.

Barbara's carriage was to collect them at ten the next day, and when Lizzy woke her euphoria had ebbed and she was apprehensive about visiting Bredelands. Anticipating that it might be an intimidating experience and bring on a headache, she took a few of her drops.

The carriage took them along small country roads, between hedges whose severe winter trim had burst into shoots of bright leaves. The last mile of their journey was uphill through a greenwood of beech and larch, and then suddenly the trees ended and there, on a wide slope, was the house, surrounded by lawns and wild gardens, and seeming to reach out to welcome visitors with its long low lines of warm brick, and sparkling diamond-paned windows.

Bessie and Barbara came running out to meet them, both dressed very informally and followed by no less than six dogs. Gabriel embraced the dogs first and then the girls, while Lizzy was greeted with kisses and pronounced to be looking 'Perfectly beautiful.'

Everything was so different from London. Barbara seemed much less commanding, and while it was the biggest house Lizzy had ever been in, she had never before felt so relaxed and comfortable. There were log fires in every room, and the most wonderful views looking down over the tops of the trees to the valley. After a meal consisting mainly of produce from the home farm, they walked round the garden, admiring the flowers, and Bessie picked a sheaf of blue irises. Then they sat on the verandah and she wove them into a crown which she asked Lizzy, who was sitting in the full sunlight, to wear. 'Only first, you must let down your hair.' Obediently, Lizzy pulled out her ribbon and shook her hair so that it fanned out in a springy mass over her shoulders. Bessie exclaimed with delight, and placed the iris-crown gently on her head.

'Now,' she said to Barbara and Gabriel, 'You must both draw

her.'

Lizzy could not remember a happier pose. She knew they all found her beautiful, and she had never been in a lovelier setting.

When it was time to return to Hastings, Barbara took her aside. 'Tell me honestly, Lizzy. Have you enjoyed it here?'

'Oh . . . You can't need to ask?'

'No. No, I can see you've been happy. And I'm so glad. The place always seems to work its magic. But I know I mustn't expect everyone to love it as much as I do.'

'How could anyone not love it? It's . . . it's like coming to paradise.'

'Oh, my dear — what a lovely thing to say. And you've told me what I need to know. You see I want to invite you and Gabriel back. To stay for a night or two, as soon as he's got the time. But I didn't want to inflict an invitation on you that would be unwelcome.'

'I would love to stay here.'

'Then it's settled.'

A thought occurred to Lizzy. 'But . . .'

'Yes?'

'Well — I expect often you have many visitors . . .'

'I quite understand. I don't like large parties either. Just the four of us again. Oh — perhaps with Anna, Anna Howitt?'

'Yes. I would like that.'

During the next fortnight, letters and messages passed between Hastings and London and Bredelands. Bessie came over to visit Lizzy on three occasions, and she also arranged for two of her acquaintances in Hastings to call. Lizzy found herself enjoying these attentions, though on the third occasion Bessie came, she was in bed, having had very bad stomach pains which she alleviated with doses of her medicine. Her condition caused Bessie to write to Gabriel, but he was unable to come to Hastings immediately. As he explained in quick notes both to her and to Lizzy, he had been dining formally with the Ruskins in Denmark Hill, when a messenger had come from Albany Street to summon him to his father's bedside. Four hours later, old Mr Rossetti had died, and he would have to remain in London until the day after the funeral.

However, in the event, he arrived at Mrs Marriot's late in the evening of the day the funeral had taken place. 'I couldn't wait any longer, Lizzy. I had to be with you.'

She hugged him, incredulous that he had hurried to her so

quickly at such a time.

'I think death brings out the best in families,' he said later, 'for the space of about six hours. And then for six days the funeral plans bring out the worst.'

'Do they know you've come here?'

'Yes, they do. In fact one of my aunts gave me a warm shawl for you — only I forgot to bring it.'

'Didn't they object to your coming?'

'No, Lizzy. They are beginning to understand me better. And Christina has spoken up a lot for you. Mother wants to meet you as soon as we all can manage it.'

Had she not read Christina's poem she would not have believed what he said; but it had made her realise that Christina's manner concealed rather than revealed her feelings.

'Oh,' he sighed, 'So much has happened. Are you tired, Lizzy? Shall I tell you now, or leave it until morning?'

'Tell me now.'

Mrs Marriot, who was pleased to see Lizzy looking so animated, produced a cold supper for Gabriel, and left them in the sitting room. It was two o'clock when they finally finished talking, and Gabriel made a move to go to bed. He kissed Lizzy on the brow, and said, 'Good night, my dearest, closest friend.'

She smiled and yawned. Then she kissed him of her own accord. 'I'm so glad you came tonight.'

Before she went to sleep, she thought over some of the things he had told her. How his old father, after a lifetime of radical political beliefs and disregard for religion, had suddenly cried out to God just before he died. Gabriel had sat quietly for a few seconds, and then asked her, 'You believe in God, don't you Lizzy?' She had pictured how the waves on the beach kept on coming, kept on breaking, kept on receding, for ever and ever, for ever and ever without end, and had replied, 'Yes.' And then there was Ruskin . . . Gabriel did not seem to know quite what to make of the favours Ruskin was showering upon him. 'It's an odd business, Lizzy. He's given me copies of all his books — fine, expensive editions — and a large piece of opal from his gem collection. And he's commissioned a watercolour, and has the apparent intention of commissioning many more. He showed me endless Turner drawings that he owns, and I get the feeling he wants me to occupy a similar place in his collection. But he says such strange things. He's all deference one minute, and behaving like a schoolmaster the next. And to cap it all, London's seething with rumours about him.'

'What kind of rumours?'

'Best not say. But he's going abroad in a few days.'

'He won't be much use to you there.'

'He'll come back, silly Lizzy. When it's all blown over.'

'What's he done to make him leave the country?'

Gabriel had given a rather quizzical smile. 'It's more a case of what he hasn't done.'

Lizzy's mind flickered sleepily back to an afternoon earlier in the year when William Rossetti had called unexpectedly at Chatham Place. Millais's name was mentioned, and William had lowered his voice and pronounced in a dramatic whisper — which she could hear perfectly clearly — 'Johnny's making a fool of himself with Mrs Ruskin. She's in his studio daily.' To which Gabriel replied, 'Johnny'd never do anything to mess up his professional reputation.'

She wondered if the rumours Gabriel had referred to were connected at all with that earlier conversation, finding the notion that the ambitious Johnny Millais might be involved in a scandal rather intriguing. The final wandering thought that drifted into her head before she slept was that she and Gabriel had now both lost their fathers, and that on the last occasion she had seen hers, he had had Millais's cheque for the doctor tucked into his top pocket.

Chapter Thirteen

Lizzy was lying on the bed in one of the guest rooms at Bredelands. It was afternoon, and she had been encouraged to take a rest. Gabriel, Barbara, Bessie and Anna were downstairs reading poetry, and outside a light rain was falling.

If she swung her bare feet to the ground, they would touch the silky pile of a Chinese carpet, and the linen sheet under her hand was bordered with fine hand-made lace. Next door was a bathroom — the first she had ever used — where she had bathed that morning in a porcelain tub patterned with roses. Everything was done for her comfort, and everywhere she looked her eye found something beautiful. She wriggled her spine against the soft bed and breathed in the scent of lilac. Sprays of the white and mauve blossom stood in a pitcher by the Dutch-tile fireplace, and a small coal fire warmed the air.

There was a knock at the door. It was Bessie.

'You're sure I'm not disturbing you?'

'No. I'm just lying here smelling the lilac and thinking how nice it is to be warm and dry when it's raining outside.'

'*Isn't it?* I like the feeling too.' She drew a chair up to the bed. 'They've started gossiping downstairs, and I got bored.'

'What are they gossiping about?'

'Oh, the Ruskins. No one ever seems to talk of anything else.'

'Gabriel won't let me know what it's all about.'

Bessie laughed heartily. 'What a selectively chivalrous knight he is! He makes us talk about it, but protects you.'

'Will you tell me?'

'If you wish. It's quite startling.' She paused. 'Effie Ruskin has petitioned for her marriage to be annulled. She says that Mr Ruskin is impotent. And he is not contesting the case.'

Lizzy looked at her uncomprehendingly.

Bessie's forthrightness wavered. 'Oh dear — you don't understand. Perhaps I shouldn't . . .'

196

'Please explain.'

'I hope Gabriel will not think it wrong if I do. Though I always believe one needs to know about the meanings of things before one can understand about life and act freely. Barbara thinks so too.'

Lizzy waited.

'Well, it means she is claiming that Mr Ruskin cannot give her any children. That they don't lead a full married life.'

'Oh.' Lizzy looked past Bessie at the rain on the window. It was not a subject to be talked about. One of those hidden themes that should not find expression in words.

'Half London thinks she's wicked to have brought the case, and accuse her of running after Johnny Millais. And the other half thinks Mr Ruskin is wicked, and that he has treated her cruelly and more-or-less thrown her into Johnny's arms to get rid of her.'

There was a silence.

'Are she and Mr Millais in love?' Lizzy asked.

'Oh surely, they must be. He has done so many lovely drawings of her.'

Lizzy blushed, and Bessie realised the embarrassing implication of her remark. She quickly changed the subject.

By early evening the weather had completely changed. Sun rays slanted across the woods, turning the treetops into a prospect of pale gold. Lizzy gazed out of the sitting-room window, while behind her Anna quietly played the piano, and Barbara and Bessie discussed plans for the next day in order to instruct the servants.

Gabriel came and stood beside her. 'It's quite hard work being rich,' he murmured.

She turned and smiled. 'I'd like to go outside.'

'Would you like me to accompany you?'

'Yes.'

They took a wide path into the woods, which smelled peaty and fresh after the rain. The sun shafted through the trees, and the young, translucent beech leaves flickered in the wind like green and gold coins. Birds were singing loudly, and Lizzy felt it was as though the whole wood were poised on the edge of a celebration.

Gabriel had his arm around her waist, and when they turned a bend in the path they both looked down the slope that fell away to their left. Simultaneously they gave a gasp.

'It's like . . .' she began.

'A lake,' he completed. 'A secret lake under the trees. Oh Lizzy,

197

I've never seen so many bluebells!'

They stood for a long time above the unexpected vista of blue. 'Will you plunge in with me, Lizzy?'

His face was only inches away, his eyes searching hers as though desperate to find a response more complete than any she knew how to give.

She looked past him, upwards through the trees to the heavens, and then down to the flowers that were like a tangible heaven laid out at their feet. Then tugging violently at his arm she cried, 'Come on! Come on!'

They ran headlong down the slope, their boots sinking into the soft leaf mould, until they reached the bluebells, where they both flung themselves to the ground and buried their faces in the sweet flowers.

Their kisses followed soon, and as every touch and gesture Gabriel made seemed to her unwontedly more exquisite than the one before, she did not prevent him undoing her bodice and placing his hand on her breast. Her breathing came fast and unevenly, and she did not properly realize and experience everything that was happening to her. All the time she was dimly aware that Gabriel's body, which lay half over hers pressing her back into the white, juicy stems of the bluebells, was undergoing dominant yet inexpressible sensations.

When they returned to the path, they were mute and shy. Gabriel had stepped aside to straighten his clothes, and now he attentively smoothed her hair and brushed the back of her dress with his hand. The wet ground had left damp marks on the material and mud and leaf mould clung around the hem. She began to shiver.

'Darling Lizzy. Are you cold?'

'No . . . I'm all right.'

'But you're shaking.'

'It . . . it isn't cold.' She laughed a little hysterically. 'I'm quite warm.'

'I haven't frightened you?' He put his arms around her, warming and soothing her. She nestled against him, and the shivering ceased. 'You aren't afraid?'

'N. . .no.'

'You don't sound very sure.'

'Not if . . .'

'If . . .?'

'If you love me.'

'I love you, Lizzy.'

Her mind pictured all the drawings he had ever made of her being sucked up and swirled round and round by a whirlwind.

'I give you my pledge,' he said.

They walked back to the edge of the wood. Looking towards the house they could see the girls on the verandah. A labrador started to bark and ran towards them wagging its tail.

'And are you pledged to me now?' he asked. 'Are you freed from the past?'

She looked him straight in the eyes. 'Yes,' she said. There was no other answer to give.

He kissed her on the lips, and then he ran to meet the dog, his arms outstretched.

She stayed on the fringe of the wood for a few moments. Bessie and Anna were leaning on the balustrade of the verandah, looking towards them and waving. Bessie was shouting something she could not hear. Barbara was standing back, but also looking in their direction.

An involuntary surge of power went through her. She had Gabriel's pledge. The three on the balcony had education and means; but none of them had a lover.

Gabriel returned to London two weeks before Lizzy. She stayed in Hastings, preparing two illustrations for William Allingham's book and wandering by the sea in a hazy early heatwave. Her face became lightly freckled, and the salt in the air made her hair stand out more thickly than ever.

'When you came in just now,' said Mrs Marriot one afternoon, 'I could tell myself truthfully you looked a real picture of health.'

But then suddenly for two days she was crippled with excruciating stomach pains. They were not menstrual, and she had no sickness or diarrhoea. She had to stay in bed, but refused to let Mrs Marriot call a doctor, submitting instead to doses of Epsom salts. Relief came, however, only from her own drops, so she sipped these in water and took a little meat broth. Then on the third morning the worst pain had gone, and she was able to walk unsupported to the privy in the back yard. The days without food left her feeling very weak, and for the last part of her stay she went out little, taking some drops each afternoon to revive her spirits. There was no one staying at Bredelands, and her only visitor was an elderly acquaintance of Bessie's who kept advising her to take up sewing to pass the time. Lizzy wondered how she would react if she told her that every stitch in every dress she owned was done by herself.

She travelled back to London alone, and was met by Gabriel at the station. He kissed her anxiously, knowing she had been ill again and searching her face for signs of strain. Then he took her back to Chatham Place where Mrs Wirrell came out to greet her.

'You're looking so much better dear, and Lancelot's waiting for you upstairs. I took him there just an hour ago and he sang away the minute I put him down. Not that he's been unhappy — he hasn't pined at all. But he was pleased to be back in his old home.'

Lizzy flushed. She hadn't thought of Lancelot for a long time. Guiltily she ran up to the studio and looked in the cage. The linnet stared at her with his beady yellow eyes. He was looking very sleek. She poked a finger through the bars and scratched his head. When she stopped, he started to sing. *In the desert a fountain is springing* . . . She had forgotten.

Gabriel watched her closely. He started to say something, but she was absorbed by the singing bird. It was some time before he had her attention and could begin to explain his immediate plans.

He was going to embark on a really large, intricate, theme-painting — it was the only way to success. It would mean he would be away a good deal since he must paint meticulously from nature, just like Millais and Hunt. The subject he had chosen would necessitate, among other things, painting a calf and a farmer's cart. He was sure he would be able to find both of these at a farm in Hampstead, and while he worked on them he could stay with the Browns. He also needed a long brick wall, and was still looking for a suitable one. Then when the painting was finished, Ruskin would be able to find a buyer, and the price would be enough to keep them for a year.

'What is the subject?' asked Lizzy.

'It will be called *Found.* I'm tired of long titles. I got the idea from a poem William Bell Scott wrote.'

'But what is the idea?'

'Oh — a young farmer comes into town to sell a calf, and finds his childhood sweetheart has fallen on bad times in the city.'

Lizzy pursed her lips. 'Taken to the streets, you mean.'

'Why do you say that?'

'Because you're all fascinated with street women.'

'Lizzy!'

'You are. There's that woman in Holman Hunt's painting — *The Awakened Conscience*. And that poem you've been working on for years and won't let me read — *Jenny*.'

'How do you know what that's about?'

'Because I looked at your manuscript when you left the room once.' Trying to imitate his poetry-speaking manner, she intoned:

Lazy laughing languid Jenny,
Fond of a kiss and fond of a guinea . . .

'Lizzy, I wish you'd leave my papers alone. And not talk about things you don't understand.'

'Don't understand? Don't *understand!* I understand perfectly well.'

'You've only just come back, and already you're abusing me. Why?'

'Because you aren't going to be here. You're going off painting some street woman. I'll be here on my own for days on end. And the smells from the river are worse than ever.'

'You can stay at Weymouth Street.'

'And what am I supposed to do there?'

'Lizzy, please be patient. Ruskin will be back in England soon. I know he'll buy another watercolour. And he might give me an advance on the big painting. Then we can make plans for the autumn.'

'What kind of plans?'

'Well . . . plans.'

She waited for him to say more, but obstinately he turned away and busied himself at his desk. Then he noticed an envelope which he picked up and handed to her.

'This came for you this morning.'

She saw that it was from Lyddy and had a feeling of apprehension. But it was to tell her that Lyddy was expecting a baby and would very much like to see her. Tears filled Lizzy's eyes.

'Bad news?'

She shook her head. 'No. Lyddy is going to have a child.'

He looked uncomfortable. 'Why does that upset you?'

'It doesn't upset me. I am very glad for her. Only . . . '

'What?'

'Everything is so settled for her.'

'And not for you, you mean?'

'I suppose so.'

'Lizzy. The most influential critic in London has taken me up. In six months time the whole world will be available to us. Your work develops all the time. We make our own magic. We're different from everybody else. Unique. Do you really want to be tied to cooking and washing and babies? I can't believe it. I won't believe it.'

'Don't you like babies?'

Gabriel looked baffled. 'Well . . . one can't say one *doesn't* like babies. But they're not exactly intoxicating.'

Despite herself, Lizzy laughed, and he looked singularly relieved.

'I shall go and visit Lyddy. She would like to see me.'

'Of course. You must visit her whenever you please.'

Although the matter rested apparently amicably there, she felt curiously disturbed. The event which she should have anticipated, but in fact had never thought about, of her younger sister having a baby seemed to upturn all the history of their relationship. Little Lyddy a mother. And she . . .? She had never considered motherhood for herself. But now the idea loomed as a dark yet tantalizing possibility.

She stayed at Chatham Place that night and went to Star Place in the morning. The summer air was stale and tepid compared to the sea air of Hastings, yet there was something comforting in its familiar dusty smell. And there was something comforting too about the atmosphere at Star Place. Since their marriage, Bill and Lyddy had made small improvements to the house, and it seemed much more welcoming. Lyddy was half way through her pregnancy, and in excellent health. Mrs Siddall grudgingly admitted that she quite looked forward to having a grandchild in the home; and Harry spent hours whittling pieces of wood into 'toys for the October baby'. He was fourteen now, lanky and withdrawn, spending long hours with his own thoughts that no one attempted to penetrate. James had recently moved away from home to a living-in job with a butcher in Wapping, and returned each Sunday with a contribution from his wage.

Lizzy apologized for not having sent any money herself for some time. 'I have been ill. Miss Leigh Smith arranged for me to stay in

Hastings. For the sea air.'

'Did you see a doctor?' asked Lyddy.

'Yes. He advised the rest.'

'You need a strong iron tonic,' said Mrs Siddall. 'Something to strengthen your blood.'

'I have my drops.'

Mrs Siddall laughed. 'What? Do you take that stuff? It's worse than spirits my girl. It'll addle your brain. No wonder you've got tired blood.'

Later when they were alone, Lyddy said to her, 'Lizzy, I've known one or two instances of people who could not stop taking drops. You will be careful?'

'Of course. But I'm sure they do no harm.' Lizzy remembered the elderly pharmacist in Hastings who would not serve her, and waited rather anxiously for her sister's reply.

'I'm not so sure. Bill's very set against them. He thinks they make people act rather peculiarly sometimes . . . when they take them too often, that is.'

They were sitting in the little front parlour — a more cheerful room now, with new yellow curtains, a velvet-covered sofa, and a table of burgeoning ferns.

'Not,' said Lyddy awkwardly, 'that I mean to imply that you act . . . out of the way.'

Lizzy was silent for a while. Then she said, 'It's so nice here now. You and Bill seem to have made it . . . a happy place.'

'I wish you'd come and see us more often. Now that James is away, it would be easy for you to stay the night.'

Involuntarily, Lizzy replied, 'I would like that.' She realised she did not want to return to her room in Weymouth Street. Despite its cleanliness and comfort, its good address, it was a lonely place. A place to go when Gabriel did not want her, or she was out of temper. It would be much nicer, or so it seemed on the spur of the moment, to come home.

'Then please do it, Lizzy. Mother never speculates out loud about you now. But I know she worries. It would be a comfort to her to see you regularly.'

'Oh, she needn't worry.' Lizzy spoke in a funny, high little voice. 'Gabriel has given me his pledge.' She paused. 'But it is a secret. No one must know. You're not to say anthing, Lyddy.' She was beginning to sound a little hysterical.

'Of course not. Of course I won't say anything. And I'm very glad for you Lizzy.'

'Yes,' said Lizzy without expression.

That evening she told Gabriel she was going to give up her room at Weymouth Street and visit Star Place more often. She delivered the information flatly, standing by the window, while he lolled on the chaise with a book.

'Whatever for, Lizzy? The room doesn't cost anything. And you always say how kind they are.'

'I'm not going back. I want you to tell Barbara. I will go and see Mrs Burton.'

'Do think it over.'

'Don't you want me to go on staying here — like I did in the winter?'

'If you wish, Lizzy.'

Later on he drew her down on to the chaise beside him and held her in his arms. 'Now, Guggums. Are you going to be kind to me? No crossness and tantrums, while I embark on my big painting?' He kissed her gently on the eyes and cheeks, and then fully on the mouth. 'Be nice to me. Close. Like we were in the bluebells.'

But she no longer felt as she had felt in the bluebell wood. No headlong current of excitement flowed between them. She rested in his arms passively and apprehensively.

Rather roughly he pushed her to one side. 'I'm going out for a while. I might call in on Stephens.'

She was quite glad to see him go, to be on her own. Yet she lay awake in the bedroom listening out for his return, noting the hour from the strike of a distant clock. It was two in the morning when the front door opened, and it was not so much the lateness of the hour she resented, as the fact that he had the choice of a wide circle of friends to visit at all hours of the day and night. Why should she be close to him, as he asked, when for so much of the time he was out and about, quite separate from her?

She knew when she left Weymouth Street, having lied to Mrs Burton that her sister needed her, that she was making difficulties for herself. She also knew that Mrs Burton did not believe her story, but assumed she was living clandestinely with Gabriel. Her attempt to convey a message of thanks to Mr Foxall was virtually brushed aside, and only Cook's impulsive, affectionate kiss gave any cordiality to her manner of leaving. Yet she did not regret what was

204

happening. She had a strong need for things to change. The experience of Hastings, of Bredelands, of travel, had made her more impatient.

During the following weeks she spent quite a lot of time at Star Place, and she developed the habit of comparing Lyddy's situation with her own. At first the small domestic improvements to the home, together with Bill's regular habits and gentle temper, made everything seem rather idyllic, in a limited, safe kind of way. But then Harry's sudden bursts of boy's anger, or her mother's critical assessment of mankind, or Lyddy's mild acceptance of confining circumstance, would make her suddenly impatient; make her long for Gabriel, or Bruno, or Barbara; for extravagent words and improbable scenes. She could never, for example, have told her mother of the impromptu moment she was crowned with irises and sketched in the sunlight, though she did try to tell her about Bredelands and, with pride, the fact that she had been Barbara's invited guest there.

But while she had a sense of enclosure and restriction at Star Place, she experienced uncertainty and growing anger with Gabriel. He did not seem to show any concern for her when he left the flat for days on end to stay in Hampstead to paint, and apparently came back only to see if a letter from Ruskin had arrived. It was true he caressed her, and wanted to be near her while he was present; but she felt that should she suddenly cease to exist altogether, his life would not really change very much.

Then one day she came back from Star Place and heard Mrs Wirrell talking to a woman on the stairs. Something about the husky, coarse timbre of the stranger's voice alerted her, and as she rounded the corner it came as a shock yet no real surprise to see a coil of thick orange hair and Annie Miller's vibrant profile.

'Why,' exclaimed Annie, after staring at her a few seconds. 'It's Lizzy. I only just recognised you dear. You're so thin . . . But it suits you. Ethereal like.'

'I have explained to Miss Miller that there is no one at home in the studio,' said Mrs Wirrell, looking rather anxiously at Lizzy.

'I wanted to see Mr Rossetti,' said Annie. 'But it's nice to meet you again. Will he be back soon?'

'No. He is away painting.' Lizzy hesitated, and then pushed past Annie and went upstairs. As she slowly closed the door of the flat she heard Annie say, 'Well, I don't know. I thought at least she'd ask me to sit down for a bit. It's a fair walk from Chelsea. I only wanted to find out if he still wanted me to model for a painting he told me he had in mind.'

Lizzy stood in the middle of the hallway, trembling. Shortly there was a tap at the door, and she could hear Mrs Wirrell saying nervously, 'Miss Siddall? Miss Siddall?'

She made an effort and called out, 'Come in.'

'Miss Siddall, are you all right? You went so pale, and rushed by so quickly. I wondered . . .'

'Has she been here before?'

'I . . .'

'You are to tell me the truth.'

'I believe so.'

'How many times?'

'You know I do not see all visitors.' ·

'More than once?'

'Perhaps.'

'Up here?'

'Just . . . to call.'

'While I was away — ill. Or recently?'

'Not recently.'

'I see. Thank you.'

Lizzy gave a vague smile and went towards the studio door. Mrs Wirrell sighed, and watched her until she had disappeared inside.

Late that night, Gabriel returned. He was feeling quite pleased with himself since he had at last made a start at painting the cart from the Hampstead farm, though the calf was a damn nuisance — struggling and wriggling and lowing in its net and not keeping still for one second. There were no lamps lit in the studio. When he stepped inside there was a movement at the far end, and in a high-pitched shriek that made the back of his neck tingle, Lizzy screamed: 'How dare you! How dare you bring her here! How dare you let her pose for you!'

As he stuttered, tried to speak, the words went on pouring out of her, until they tumbled into a torrent of sobbing.

He went to one of the windows and pulled back the draperies so that the light from the street lamp below shone into the room. Then he stood over Lizzy, staring in amazement at the choking, gasping figure huddled face down on the chaise.

'Whatever . . . Lizzy, whatever has happened?'

206

She lifted her face, disfigured by hours of weeping, and hissed, 'That woman! Annie Miller. She came here.'

He raised his eyebrows, and flicked his fingers rhythmically against his thigh. 'Did she do something dreadful to you?'

'She wanted to pose for you. She knew about your painting.' She started to cry again. 'She was here when I was away ill. You told her you wanted her for the painting.'

'I did not, I said I'd consider her. But she's not the right type. I was going to let her know, but it slipped my mind.'

'How *could* you consider her?'

'Lizzy, for goodness sake! I wish you could hear yourself. Annie is a good model. And Hunt did not want her to be posing for every Tom, Dick and Harry while he was abroad. He asked me to keep an eye on her. Said he didn't mind if I employed her sometimes. And she could do with the work. That's why I said I'd consider her. It's the least Mad would expect me to do.'

She did not reply, but lay with tears still running through her fingers into a cushion. He sat down on the arm of the chaise and put his hand on her shoulder. 'Now, Lizzy. What is this all about?'

'You'd go to her, I know you would. If it wasn't for Hunt. She's a flirt. She doesn't get ill all the time.'

'Of course I wouldn't go to her. She's Mad's girl. But we all know her. Like to work with her. I often wish you'd tried to make friends with her that first time.'

'Make friends!'

'All right, I know she appears a bit . . . loud. But she's a good-hearted person. And there is absolutely nothing that justifies your getting in a state like this. I can't understand you, Lizzy. You're such a quiet soul most of the time.'

He slid down beside her, and pulled her gently so that she lay with her head on his lap. Sobbing had left her purged of all feeling for the moment, and she allowed his hand to stroke her hair and neck and the upper part of her breast rather as though it were happening to somebody else. After a while he said, 'Do you want to try to explain to me, Lizzy?' And in a distant little voice she said, 'I can't.' Which was true, for it was as though her violent grief had made a barrier between her and the rest of the world, leaving her alone and unable to communicate.

He picked her up in his arms and carried her through to the bedroom, where he took off her dress and then helped her to get

207

into bed, still wearing her underclothes. She collapsed on to the pillows, like a bird finding sanctuary after a buffeting storm. He lay beside her, on the coverlet, his arm around her.

'Please, Lizzy. Let this be the end to jealousy.'

She felt his arm tighten, and his breathing quicken. She turned her head, knowing he would kiss her. The caressing went on for a long time.

But she knew she was right to be jealous of the image of Annie Miller. She knew that type of woman would have given him much more. Would both have apeased and further excited the emotions he wanted to demonstrate. Emotions which on the few occasions they were matched by her own seemed heady and sweet; but more frequently clashed with her mood, seeming dark, and awkward and wrong.

She woke in the morning while he still slept beside her, and looked for a long time at his head on the pillow. The dark hair was thinning slightly at the forehead, the beard was badly in need of a trim, and the skin below his eyes looked like twin bruises. Yet she could imagine no other man's face beside her, actually in the flesh. The rage caused by Annie acknowledged that. If he should be taken, she would have nothing left.

The early post brought a letter from Ruskin, announcing among other things his imminent return from Switzerland. It was a long letter, and Gabriel sighed once or twice while reading it. Then he gave a triumphant shout.

'Listen to this, Lizzy! We're going to be all right. He says, "I am not going to make you any offer till you tell me, if you are willing to do so, what your wishes and circumstances really are. What I meant was to ask if an agreement to paint for me regularly, up to a certain value, would put you more at your ease; but I will not enter into more particulars at present . . ." And listen to this bit! "I forgot to say that I really do *covet* your drawings as much as I covet Turner's." Well, if he buys half as many as he bought from Turner, we're made for life.'

Slyly, she said, 'You don't paint half as many as Turner did.'

Gabriel roared with laughter. 'You're right. But from today I'll reform. I won't go back to that confounded calf today. I'll get a nice little watercolour in the bag ready. And another tomorrow.' He looked up at her. 'And you're to get to work as well. No more Sarah

208

Siddons stuff. You're a painter. And Ruskin's going to like your work too. He's going to like it very much.'

Chapter Fourteen

It was several months before Lizzy met John Ruskin. Lyddy had her October baby — a son called George — and throughout the winter Gabriel went on playing long visits to the Browns in order to work on his big painting. They finally had to ask him to leave because of the imminent arrival of their second child, and Lizzy learned later from Emma that Gabriel had eaten them out of house and home and had frequently kept Bruno up until the early hours talking about suicide and death. There were times when they thought he seemed on the verge of madness with his stream of unstoppable, morbid talk. Towards Lizzy he behaved more restrainedly, but he sometimes made sarcastic references to her outburst over Annie Miller, and she did not dare question him about his doings away from her. As it was, vague anxieties and suspicions eddied in her thoughts when she spent long, cold evenings on her own, and recourse to her drops tended to transform her waking fears into terrifying dreams. If Gabriel came home when she was in one of these drugged, nervous states, he would become extremely agitated, asking her questions she could not answer, and pacing up and down. When she was well he would watch her like a hawk, and while embracing her he often clutched her in a motionless grip of iron. Once he said, 'You've got to find out about your real feelings for me, Lizzy,' and she replied coldly, 'We were pledged at Bredelands, in May.' Adding, after a pause, 'It is December now.'

Ruskin had been twice to Chatham Place to buy drawings, and both times it had been carefully arranged that Lizzy was absent. Gabriel was quite open about the fact that he did not want Ruskin to know she stayed there. 'I have been telling him about your work, and when the right time comes I shall ask him to take a look at it. But I should not like his view to be influenced by too much concern over our relationship.'

'You mean he would think I was improper?'

'He would see that you are not. But I believe that close relationships between people confuse him.'

Lizzy smiled rather tartly. 'Did his wife confuse him?'

'I think she must have done.'

'Bessie told me about that. Since you wouldn't.'

'It was a strange business.'

'Is she going to marry Johnny Millais?'

'I suppose so.' He spoke off-handedly and quickly changed the subject.

On the morning it was arranged for Gabriel to show Ruskin her drawings, Lizzy decided she would go shopping for material and trimmings for a new spring dress. As usual, she knew exactly what she wanted and it took her some time to find it. Her search led her past Mrs Tozer's, and she felt an odd mixture of dread and nostalgia as she glanced at the displayed bonnets. She hesitated ever so slightly by the doorway of the shop opposite; it was six years since Walter had stood there wearing a floppy silk cravat that matched his eyes. And now he had been dead for over a year. She hurried from the street towards Leicester Square.

When she returned, Gabriel seized her in his arms and waltzed her into the studio. 'Ruskin's bought all your sketches. He says they're every bit as good as mine. And we're invited to dine next Wednesday.'

'At his home?'

'His parents' home, where he lives now. In Denmark Hill.'

'Bought all of them?'

'Yes. He's taken them off to be properly mounted. And there's a cheque on the mantlepiece. He begged to see your portrait, but I told him you didn't want it shown.'

'I can't take it all in.'

'He says we must be the most talented couple in London.'

Before she had time to extract a longer description of the encounter, to assimilate properly what had happened, he was getting ready to go out, giving as his pretext that he must go and tell his brother the good news. At her look of disappointment, he said, 'Rest on your laurels this evening, Lizzy. Relax with some poetry. Then tomorrow you can start making your new dress. We must see that you look sublime on Wednesday.'

But she could not do as he wished, could not fill her time alone contentedly — neither on that occasion nor on countless others.

211

Restlesness marred her concentration, and anything she attempted was done so half-heartedly that it was bound not to absorb her. He had claimed the need to see his brother, but William still lived with his mother and sisters so presumably he would see them too. Christina had not made a second visit to Chatham Place, and no invitation had been issued for her to meet Mrs Rossetti.

She tried to think what it meant — that Ruskin had praised and bought her drawings. In a way she supposed it put her above caring what Gabriel's family thought of her. She went into the corridor and fetched the self-portrait which she kept hidden behind a chest. She no longer liked it at all, nor could she remember how she had set about doing it. Those days of solitary excitement during the creation of the picture seemed to belong to another world.

She put the painting away, and went to feed Lancelot. As she watched him dart his beak eagerly into the little bowl of seed, she thought, Walter must have watched him do this, just fourteen or fifteen months ago . . .

Suddenly Gabriel's good news seemed meaningless. She remembered how hard Walter had struggled with his paintings; the evenings at Red Lion Square. Slowly, she went and poured a few of her drops into a glass of water. Then she fetched her private writing book. After a while, the lines flowed easily.

> Oh, never weep for love that's dead,
> Since love is seldom true,
> But changes his fashion from blue to red,
> From brightest red to blue,
> And love was born to an early death
> And is so seldom true.

The closing of the front door woke her from a trance-like sleep. The coldness of the room, and the grey light seeping round the edges of the curtain told her it was already early morning. As Gabriel came into the room she grabbed her open writing book from the floor and thrust it behind a cushion guiltily.

'Guggums, what are you doing?'

'I must have fallen asleep. I just put my feet up for a minute — I was tired after shopping.'

'Silly girl. You'll be all cold and stiff.' He lit one of the lamps and came and looked at her. 'You're sure you haven't been taking too many of those drops?'

'Of course not. It must have been all the walking I did.'

She did not remember exactly what words she had written in her book, but she knew they were connected with Walter and that pulsing shapes of red and blue had pounded behind her eyes before she slept. While she was writing, Walter had seemed immanent in everything, and now she had difficulty in suppressing her awareness of him and readjusting herself to reality, to Gabriel.

'I had to go and see Woolner,' he said. 'Tell him the good news. And we stayed up jawing.' She could smell the wine on his breath. Then she remembered what the 'good news' was. A little quiver in her stomach indicated that she felt some pleasure, or at least interest, at being taken up by Ruskin.

'And William was *most* impressed. Though why he couldn't have used the evidence of his own eyes months ago . . . Anyway, that's all over. Mother wants us both to go to tea on Thursday, so we can tell her all about our day at Denmark Hill. And Maria is madly jealous because John Ruskin is her hero. And Christina says she's written a poem about you, but won't show it to me.'

'Why not?'

'Well . . . she said she would only show it to me when you became her sister.'

She looked into his eyes, confused by the shifting state of everything. And he bent over and gazed solemnly back. 'Oh, Lizzy. It's weeks now since you looked at me like that. As though you trusted me enough to drown in my eyes.'

There is only him, she thought, only him.

'Lizzy — reach for me.'

Her hands came tentatively towards his shoulders, and he waited as they clasped behind his neck and drew him down into a kiss. He refrained from quickening their contact, but remained peaceful while she stroked and kissed him, and finally hugged him tightly.

'Will you do that?' she asked.

'What?'

'Make me Christina's sister.'

'It's inevitable, isn't it?'

'How soon?'

'May is our month. The bluebell month.'

Then he was no longer passive, but kissing her deeply.

Silently he stood up, pulled her to her feet, and led her to the bedroom. Still without words he undressed her and then said, 'My

213

Beatrice. My bride. My Lizzy. My life.' She stared and stared at him, shivering, and he tore off his jacket and shirt and shoes and carried her to the bed. Once under the covers, he removed the rest of his clothes.

'Don't be frightened,' he said.

She liked only the closeness afterwards, when he held her gently against his chest. It felt as though they were cut off completely from the rest of the world. Rather like the sole survivors of a storm.

They did not get up until the afternoon, and for the rest of the day Gabriel was unusually quiet. He spent most of the time writing, and Lizzy felt a separation form between them that seemed to deepen and widen by the hour. He was so absorbed in his work, and her heart cried out for him to speak. She wanted to hear him talk enthusiastically about love, about her, about their future. Just as so often in the past he had eulogized her looks, their life in art, now she wanted his words to praise their future together so that she could sever the past for ever.

Late in the evening he handed her a poem. It did not give her the concrete reassurances that she needed. It showed that he, too, had experienced feelings akin to being a survivor from a storm.

> Sometimes she is a child within mine arms,
> Cowering beneath dark wings that love must chase,
> With still tears showering and averted face,
> Inexplicably filled with faint alarms:
> And oft from mine own spirit's hurtling harms
> I crave the refuge of her deep embrace, —
> Against all ills the fortified strong place
> And sweet reserve of sovereign counter-charms.
>
> And Love, our light at night and shade at noon,
> Lulls us to rest with songs, and turns away
> All shafts of shelterless tumultuous day.
> Like the moon's growth, his face gleams through his tune;
> And as soft waters warble to the moon,
> Our answering spirits chime one roundelay.

She read it slowly, and then gave it back to him.

'Have you nothing to say, Lizzy?'

She could not think of anything. No part of her felt willing to respond to the words, to praise their beauty or affirm their truth. She wanted Gabriel to speak directly to her — about their love and

214

its manifestation in terms of plans and permanence.

'Talk to me,' she said.

'I am talking to you. I'm talking to you in that poem with my innermost soul.' He took her in his arms and kissed her. 'Are you very happy, Lizzy? It's been such an important day.'

She sighed. 'Yes.' But her thoughts were anxious and capricious.

She devoted the next four days to making her new dress and shopping for accessories. She sat hour after hour at her sewing table, diligent and concentrating, until she was satisfied with every detail. On the day of their visit to Denmark Hill she got up early and spent almost two hours getting ready. When she finally came into the studio she was quietly confident.

It was some time since she had taken so much care over her appearance, and Gabriel was patently pleased. 'I always said you were a stunner, Lizzy. And what beautiful colours.' Her dress was a shade of soft brown that resembled moths' wings, and she had used the same brown together with shades of old rose to complete the outfit. Her hair was fastened at her neck with tortoise-shell combs, and it curved out in wings on either side of her face.

When she had questioned Gabriel about the Ruskins' home he had been rather vague. As their cab turned into the gateway she was unprepared for the wide, curving drive, the immense cedar of Lebanon on the spacious lawn, and the footman at the door. She became very tense, fearful that she would not know what to say or how to behave.

John Ruskin met them in the hallway, taking her hand tightly in his thin fingers and bending over to greet her rather like a heron peering down into a pool. His words of welcome were effusive, and he was cut short by his bushy-eyebrowed father whose jovial manner put Lizzy more at her ease. They were taken immediately to a long drawing room lined with pictures where Mrs Ruskin greeted them in a manner that was both grand and astringent, announcing that she herself would escort Lizzy upstairs to remove her bonnet.

'Mother, are you sure — ' John began, hovering and anxious.

'I am perfectly capable of making an extra journey upstairs.' Mrs Ruskin glared at her son, smiled graciously at Lizzy, and led the way slowly from the room. Lizzy was taken aback to see that London's greatest authority on art was apparently terrified of his seventy-five-year-old mother.

215

Mrs Ruskin had been told of Lizzy's poor health, and seemed keen to diagnose the cause for herself. After questioning her about her diet, she asked, 'Do you sleep well?'

'Yes, thank you.'

'Not too well, I hope? Lethargy is as bad as wakefulness. Come here, near the window.' Lizzy obliged. 'Hmm. You have a natural colour. Clearly there is no danger of your being in a decline.' The old lady spoke with unassailable authority. 'But you suffer from weakness. I shall arrange for a packet of Ivory Bone Dust to be sent to you. It is difficult to obtain, and a most powerful restorative.'

Lizzy was relieved when they returned to the drawing room, where she soon realised that Gabriel did not entirely enjoy being with the Ruskins. This was not because of any lack of hospitality or kindness, but because of the super abundance of pictures. In their places on the walls they could be viewed without too much effort, but John and his father were forever hurrying away to lift a picture from the wall in order to give it to Gabriel so that he could see it in the best light. Gabriel, Lizzy knew, had a very limited interest in Turner, so she was not surprised to see a glazed expression come into his eyes as yet another watercolour by the great man was lovingly deposited on to his lap.

At last the conversation turned to the illustration of poems, and for the first time John referred directly to her own drawings. She found she was able to talk quite easily of her pleasure at interpreting poetry, most particularly Tennyson's. Staring at her fixedly with his mild blue eyes, he said rapidly, 'His poem *The Princess* might almost be about someone like yourself. Princess Ida, so bravely claiming the right to study and develop her talents. Perhaps I might be permitted to say that Ida would be a very suitable by-name for you, Miss Siddall.'

'John, stop talking nonsense that will embarrass our guest.'

'Yes, mother. Forgive me.'

'His flights of fancy unfortunately know no bounds,' said Mrs Ruskin disapprovingly.

Lizzy tried to assume an expression that would displease neither the dictatorial old lady nor her son. She did not dare glance at Gabriel. *The Princess* was a poem they had once laughed over, agreeing that Ida's defence of women's rights and the founding of a female university were not subjects that settled easily into penta-meters. 'Rather as if Barbara had decided to become a ballerina,'

216

Gabriel had said at the time.

Old Mr Ruskin restored the situation by moving nearer to Lizzy and saying to her quietly, 'I went through all your sketches with John. They show a remarkable touch. I hope very much you will be able to continue. Especially your illustrations to poems. It is so satisfying when words and pictures chime together. Mr Rossetti must be a good teacher and you must be an excellent pupil.'

She smiled at the kindly old man. He made everything sound so safe. So safe and simple. 'I am very glad *you* like them,' she said.

He patted her hand. 'Now listen. I think John is talking to Mr Rossetti about a project dear to his heart. It is to do with teaching art to working men in the evenings. He wants very much for artists of talent to aid and abet him. And you have given ample proof of Mr Rossetti's teaching powers.'

They turned to catch the tail end of some remarks by John, followed by Gabriel's reply:

'I would very much like to try it out. But you know I've never done any formal teaching. And I was not at all an exemplary class pupil.'

John clapped his hands together with enthusiasm. 'That is exactly why I want you to share a class with me to start with. We will explore teaching in a completely new way. We will enable good folk to record the colours and forms and objects of their everyday life.'

'No plastercasts?'

'Definitely no plastercasts.'

'Then I'll gladly help if you think I can be of use.'

'John is always so anxious to help people,' said his father. 'I'm sure he will be able to enlighten many working men and enable them to see the beauties that surround them.'

An image of her brother James on the first occasion she saw him after her father's death flashed into Lizzy's mind. She remembered his careworn boy-man's face, the blood from the butcher's bespattering his clothes and boots, and above all his look of resignation.

'I hope they will appreciate what is to be done for them,' said Mrs Ruskin. 'And be of clean appearance.'

When it was time for Lizzy and Gabriel to leave, old Mr Ruskin insisted that his carriage should take them home. Gabriel said that they would need to go first to Weymouth Street and then to Chatham Place. Once inside the carriage, after very warm farewells

217

from their hosts but before they had even turned out of the drive, Lizzy whispered, 'I can't go to Weymouth Street. I won't go.'

'Sshh,' he whispered back. 'We will change our mind in due course.' And when they had passed Elephant and Castle, and were approaching the river along Blackfriars Road, he leaned up to the coachman and said, 'We have changed our plans and will now both be going to Chatham Place.' The coachman touched his hat with his whip, 'Yes, sir.' Lizzy did not like the knowing look on his face.

Once in the privacy of the studio she said, 'I suppose you will lie to your family too. Tell them I still live at Weymouth Street.'

'I don't mind. We can say you stop with your family. That's nearer the truth since you go there sometimes. And William might hear something about Weymouth Street from Barbara.'

'You don't mind lying, do you?'

'Not about things that don't matter.'

'If it doesn't matter, why don't you tell the truth?'

'You know why.'

'Because then they'd never accept me.'

'Do you tell your family the truth?'

'They don't ask questions now.'

'We aren't sinners, Lizzy.'

'When we go to your family tomorrow, will you tell them we will marry in May?'

'Not tomorrow.'

'But it's only a few weeks away.'

'We don't need to give long notice. We'll make it a surprise.'

'You're not completely sure, are you?'

'Are *you*?' His voice had an edge of accusation in it; as though he had some evidence of uncertainty.

'How can you say that?' She felt the old anger and desperation begin to well up. 'After what has happened between us.'

He made no reply.

She started to weep, and then he spoke. 'No, Lizzy, no. Stop. Take control of yourself. We are in a position to choose now. Ruskin hinted to me privately this afternoon that he wants to make a practical proposal to you. That means money. He's eating out of my hand and will buy pretty well anything I do. We can decide what we really want. And there's one thing I particularly want for you.'

'What?'

'Health. I want you to get really well. Ruskin knows that.'

'You don't love me.'

'It was the proudest moment of my life this afternoon, seeing how the Ruskins, the pernickety rich Ruskins, all admired the woman I love.'

'Do you think they really liked me?'

'Lizzy, even *Mrs* Ruskin liked you, you behaved so beautifully and looked so stunning. And I can't see her taking to many people.'

She suddenly laughed. 'It was funny — about Princess Ida.'

'That's better.'

She looked up quickly. 'We won't do that again. In bed. Until we're married.' She could not read the expression on his face, and when he did not speak she began to sense a deep anger from him that frightened her. 'You see,' she said, speaking very quietly, 'There could be a child.'

His mood seemed to soften. 'There are things to talk about, Lizzy, ways to manage.'

She looked uncomprehending, then she shook her head.

'Well,' he said coldly. 'You will have to change something. We cannot both live here together as brother and sister. I will not endure it.'

She just wanted to cry out, 'Then why don't we marry?' but did not dare. Nor did she dare submit to a night of tears. An element in her knew she must stay composed, be at her best when she met Gabriel's family the next day. As impassively as she could she said, 'I will try to think what to do.'

She was still in the bedroom the next morning when she heard knocking at the front door. It went on for some time and Mrs Wirrell called out, 'Mr Rossetti. Mr Rossetti. Someone to see you.' At last the studio door opened, and Gabriel went down the corridor. She could not hear what he said, but knew he would not be pleased at being roused. Ten o'clock was not to him a civilised hour for calls.

Then another voice joined in. It was slightly familiar to her, but she could not identify it. She opened her door a crack and was just in time to glimpse Ruskin following Gabriel into the studio. She sat for what seemed like hours, waiting for Ruskin to leave. Hiding away like this was humiliating. If only Gabriel could be straightforward.

At last she heard the voices again, and after the front door had slammed he came straight to her door. 'Lizzy? Lizzy?'

'Yes. Come in.'

He was wearing his old flannel dressing-gown and seemed very elated. 'You'll never guess who that was!'

'Yes I will. It was Mr Ruskin. I heard his voice.'

'He wants to settle a hundred and fifty pounds a year on you!'

'Whatever do you mean?'

'He will give you that sum and take any work you do up to that value.'

'I can't take money like that from him. I don't want to.'

'Oh Lizzy, don't be so —' He broke off, checked himself. 'Please think about it. Please consider it. He values you so highly. He kept saying how much his parents had taken to you. How sensitive you were. And he wants an answer. Please let me send him a note saying you are thinking about it. I'll express your reluctance. Which is in any case perfectly proper. I'll say that to him — shall I?'

'If you want.' She had not the will to argue about it just then.

Almost the whole of her visit to the Rossettis seemed to revolve around the subject of Ruskin's appreciation of her. Gabriel had promised not to mention the proposed settlement, but she thought he would never stop quoting Ruskin's opinion of her drawings. Mrs Rossetti, who looked like an older, more ordinary version of Christina, was wary throughout all the rhetoric. Lizzy could see she was long accustomed to Gabriel's 'going on'. She could also see that, like her own mother, she expected people to be hard-working, god-fearing, and uncomplicated. Gabriel, and to a lesser extent Christina, were an enigma to her. Maria, whose practical kindness Lizzy warmed to, fell beneath her mother's ideal too because she was plain and over-compassionate. William was clearly her favourite, moving in established artistic circles, but behaving circumspectly and slightly pompously, as a man should.

From the start Lizzy realised Mrs Rossetti had chosen to pretend that she and Gabriel had not known one another for very long, and she refused to collude in the pretence. She did not contradict or make controversial remarks, but she quietly made it clear that if anyone had been close to Gabriel over the last few years it was she. The conversation eddied and flurried without actual conflict, but it was not a comfortable occasion. Christina's clear hazel eyes seemed almost to devour her, as though seeking for clues and answers, and Lizzy thought uneasily of the poem Gabriel said she had written about her. She felt no warmth from Christina, no hint that she wanted her to become her sister-in-law; just that disconcerting, almost pitying, scrutinization. If she was 'on trial' with this family as a suitable bride for Gabriel, she wanted no part of it. Compared to the Ruskin household theirs seemed very ordinary, and she thought the way they went on about her success at Denmark Hill was in very bad taste. Why should she not be a success with gentlefolk?

As soon as the visit was over, and they were standing outside the house in Albany Street, Gabriel gave an enormous yawn. His face seemed almost to split apart, and he could not control the spasm that affected the whole of the upper part of his body.

'I'm sorry. Very rude of me. But it exhausts me. Absolutely exhausts me, being with all the family.'

Suddenly she found herself yawning too, and they both began to laugh.

'Let's stay out in the air a while,' he said. 'Clear our heads. I know — would you like to go to the Zoo? It's just over there.'

'I'm not sure.'

'Have you ever been?'

'My father took us once, when I was small. A woman stood in front of me by the elephant's cage, she was wearing a blue velvet cloak. A lovely blue. And I remembered the colour and used it years later to trim the first dress I ever made.'

'And how about the elephant?'

'I thought he looked sad. I thought most of the animals looked sad.'

'Yes, Christina always said that. Perhaps we'd better not go. In case they're still looking sad.'

'Did you go often when you were children?'

'Quite often. And we used to play in the park, and collect frogs from the pond. I found a dormouse and a hedgehog there too. I took them home and kept them as pets.'

'Didn't your mother object?'

'Yes. Especially when I gave the hedgehog some of father's beer and it got tipsy!'

They wandered through sidestreets to Tottenham Court Road where he asked, 'Would you like a cab?'

'No. Let's walk. Tell me more about when you were children.'

'Christina and I used to make up poems. And I used to draw pictures for them. I remember I used to envy her because her

221

dreams were better than mine. She once had a lovely one about Regent's Park. She dreamt she was walking there at dawn, and what looked like a band of yellow light in the sky surged towards her and became a huge flock of canaries. All the canaries in London used to meet in the park every morning at daybreak before going back to their cages.'

He told her more stories, and finally she said, 'This is the first time you've really talked to me about your family.'

'Well — now you've met them. . .' He paused, and his tone of voice became more sombre. 'Was it all right, Lizzy? Not too much of an ordeal?'

She shrugged. 'It doesn't matter. They just don't care for me.'

'Lizzy —'

'I don't want to talk about it any more. I think tomorrow I will go and visit my family for a few days. I would like to see the baby again — he grows so fast.'

'You can't go for long. Ruskin will be wanting an answer. And we must both get on and do lots of work for him. I want to do some fresh drawings of you.'

'How about your big painting? Have you abandoned it?'

'Of course not.' He spoke impatiently. 'But it will take so long to finish. And I have some ideas for watercolours which Ruskin will love.'

'I will go just for a day or two.'

'Yes, all right.' He kicked a loose stone along the pavement. 'I'll never understand you, Lizzy. A chance in a lifetime, and you choose to disappear to your family.'

'I never asked to be taken up by Mr Ruskin.'

'Aren't you interested in being an artist, after all?'

'Not all by myself.'

'You aren't all by yourself.'

'I often feel as if I am.'

She could tell that neither her mother nor Lyddy was particularly pleased to see her. George occupied the centre of their attention now. Lizzy watched them sharing the household duties without any hint of friction, and realised that life had become more pleasant for them both. There was enough regular money coming in to guarantee the family's basic needs, and the presence of the baby, in his helpless, engaging early months, gave a zest to the simplest of routines. She sat while Lyddy washed napkins and her mother sewed baby clothes, and could not begin to try to explain to them John Ruskin's proposal. Half-heartedly she told them she had sold a few drawings, and had recently spent a pleasant afternoon with Gabriel's family, but otherwise she just tried to enter their concerns. She sensed that until she came home with a wedding-ring on her finger, her mother was not going to mention Rossetti.

Harry had a job now, working in the boiler-room of the asylum at the end of the road. Lizzy's heart sank, for he had always been so frightened of the deaf and dumb children who huddled weirdly behind the railings, but clearly her mother was very relieved he had been able to take up employment, and she remained silent. When Harry came home, however, she found it hard not to protest.

Bill was already back, sitting contentedly at the kitchen table and being tended by Lyddy, when Harry opened the door. He was covered in grime and ash, and when he had washed his face Lizzy felt sure he must be ill. But the others seemed to take no notice of his subdued, exhausted state. She did have a brief opportunity to ask Bill quietly if he thought Harry was strong enough for his job, and he replied. 'Oh yes. When the head's a bit weak the body's usually resilient, and he doesn't complain.' By that time Harry had already gone to bed, having barely acknowledged Lizzy's presence.

During the night, which she spent on the chaise in the parlour, she woke with the same excruciating stomach pains she had experienced in Hastings. It was all she could do not to cry out loud, and at dawn she went to the privy to see if she could get some relief. She was bent over, groaning into her knees, when her mother appeared in the doorway.

'What's the matter with you, Lizzy?'

She tried to look up, gasping. 'I don't know. It...hurts so much.'

Her mother half lifted her, and having ascertained that it would do little good to remain at the bucket, took her indoors. She supported her back on to the chaise, and fetched a hot stone bottle.

'Now my girl, we must find out what the matter is with you.'

She asked a few questions, and soon decided that constipation was the cause. Lizzy was vague about the extent and frequency of the complaint since she usually acted on the principle that the fewer journeys she had to make to the uncomfortable privy at Chatham Place the better. Her mother reprimanded her for laziness and irregular eating habits. Then, when another spasm of pain made her draw up her knees and bite her hand to stop her cries, Mrs Siddall suddenly became even more severe. She waited for the spasm to pass, then said, 'Do you still take those drops?'

'Yes,' Lizzy replied weakly. 'Perhaps I should have some now.'

'You mean you carry them around with you?'

'Sometimes.'

'And you take them *often*?'

'No,' she lied.

'If you find it necessary to keep them by you, you're bound to take them too frequently. I warned you about them, Lizzy.'

'They don't give me pain. I took none yesterday.'

'But they cause bad constipation. There have been cases of death — people who just seize up. Now, you're to tell me the truth. When did you last relieve yourself properly? How many days ago.'

'I'm not sure.'

'More than a week?'

'I don't think so,' she lied again.

'Don't be sly with me. It's longer, isn't it? Dangerously long?'

Lizzy shook her head and began to cry. 'No. Not dangerously.' Then another spasm overcame her completely.

The rest of the morning was a nightmare. Two neighbouring women were brought in to look at her, and finally one of them fetched a most unpleasant-looking apparatus and gave her an enema.

During this procedure, Lizzy felt she was going to expire in a miasma of humiliation and pain. But at last the bustle and the voices, the smell and the discomfort, subsided, and she was left alone to sleep.

When she woke she felt weak but better, and resolved that she must get back to Chatham Place at once.

'Stay one more night,' urged Lyddy. 'You look as though you might easily faint.'

'You needn't think you're slinking away to swallow drops,' said Mrs Siddall. 'I've thrown away the bottle that was with your things.'

Lizzy felt an unconscionable anger. She tried not to let it show, though the power of the emotion was overwhelming. The intensity of the rage frightened her, but it also gave her strength to act. Mechanically, she began to make preparations to leave.

When she was ready, she went to take a last look at George

224

sleeping peacefully in his crib, and her anger ebbed. For a few seconds she tried to fathom what it was that was driving her out of the house, unsure whether she had even enough strength to walk to the bus route. But then Lyddy came in from the garden with some washing, her mother started to heat the flat irons, and she felt excluded. In this setting she was useless, a liability.

As she walked falteringly along Star Place towards the main road, she had it fixed at the back of her mind that she must call in at the pharmacist near Blackfriars Bridge before she got back to Chatham Place.

Chapter Fifteen

When Lizzy staggered wanly into the studio she was greeted by four strong male arms — Gabriel's and Bruno's. Both men exclaimed at her appearance as they helped her to a chair, and begged to know if she was really ill. She tried to pass the matter off as a stomach upset, but Bruno said in a concerned, gruff way, 'It looks worse than that, my dear. Isn't it time you saw a doctor again?'

'I'll be all right.' She glanced around the room and saw evidence of company — glasses, pipe ash, empty bottles — among the usual clutter of books and painting materials.

'I meant to ask Mrs Wirrell to clear up,' said Gabriel. 'We had a good session last night with Allingham and Woolner. I read all my new stuff to them.'

'And I stopped over,' added Bruno. 'It was too late to walk back to Hampstead. And now I've lost a day's painting because Gabriel's been talking to me ever since I woke up.'

She sighed. It seemed that Gabriel could enjoy himself better when she was away. He did not notice the sigh, having gone to the mantelshelf to fetch an envelope, but Bruno did and looked at her as though he wished to comfort her but did not know how.

Gabriel placed the envelope ceremoniously on Lizzy's lap. 'Do open it, Lizzy. It's from Ruskin. And we're dying to know what he's got to say to you.'

She saw the letter was addressed to her, but made no attempt to undo it.

'I think,' said Bruno quickly, 'that I shall in fact survive very well without further words of Ruskin's. I'm glad he wants to help Lizzy, but I can't abide his writings. And I must get back to Hampstead.'

Gabriel, seeing that Lizzy had now put the letter to one side, looked disappointed but did not protest. 'As you like, old chap,'

While Bruno was preparing to leave, she went hesitantly up to him and said quietly, 'Please greet Emma for me. And the baby and Kitten. Do you have a nickname for the baby?'

226

'Oh yes, he's called Nolly — because Kitten can't say Oliver. When you're properly well you must come and see him. Emma would love to show him off to you.'

'I would like that.'

While the two men went to the door, she picked up the envelope again. Cautiously she opened it and drew out two sheets of thick writing paper closely covered with a fine script. Ruskin was quite adamant that she should accept his offer. He did not want her to think he was helping her just for Rossetti's sake, but for 'the plain *hard fact* that I think you have genius and I don't think there is much genius in the world'. She read on, and just as Gabriel came back into the room, started to shake with laughter.

'What does he say? Why are you laughing?'

'He seems to think I'm like a crumbling cathedral!'

'What *do* you mean?'

'He says he wants to preserve my genius, just like . . . wait a moment, I'll read it out . . . just "as I should try to save a beautiful tree from being cut down, or a bit of Gothic catheral whose strength was failing".'

They were both laughing. 'Only a *bit* of a cathedral, Lizzy, not a whole one.' He took the letter and read it through. 'You'll accept, won't you? The comical old thing means well.'

'I must still think it over. I'm not sure how much painting I shall be able to do.'

'Were you very ill at home?'

'It was like the bad time I had in Hastings.'

'You looked frightful when you came in. Bruno's right — it's time you saw another doctor.'

She did not want to pursue that suggestion. 'It's all over now. But I am tired. I'd like to go to bed. Do you think Mrs Wirrell would bring me some tea?'

He sat on the end of the bed while she drank the tea, passing on stories that Allingham had told him about Tennyson, and explaining his ideas for two watercolours for Ruskin. 'I know he'll like them. And you *will* let him help you, won't you Lizzy?'

'I'm going to think about it.'

After he'd gone, she tried to think about it. She knew that if she accepted the offer, it would make Gabriel's life easier. She would not need money from him, and if she complained that he left her alone too much he would be able to say it was an opportunity for

227

her to get on with her work for Ruskin. But why should she provide him with these advantages? Though it would be lovely to have some money of her own, and it *was* exciting to be taken seriously by Ruskin. Yet the idea of having to draw regularly to please him was very daunting. Sometimes, when she wasn't well, it was difficult to concentrate on anything, and it was a particular torment then to try to co-ordinate hand and eye and make pictures.

Then she remembered how Ruskin had gone on at length about his ideas for teaching working men. Was he only interested in her because she came from a poor background? What would he have felt about her drawings if they were the work of Barbara or Bessie? After all, Bessie did draw very well and had also met Ruskin, but she had not been labelled 'genius'. She pressed the back of her hand against her throbbing forehead and looked across the room to her purse, which revealed the solid comforting shape of the pharmacist's bottle. But her mother's words and the agony of the constipation were still too close for her to ignore. She turned on to her side and after what seemed like a long time went into a deep sleep.

She woke late the next morning to see Gabriel standing in the doorway staring down at her.

'At last, Lizzy. I was beginning to fear you had gone to sleep for ever.'

Her mind felt very clear and sharp. 'Which would suit you quite well, I suppose. I wouldn't be a nuisance to you all then.'

He came and sat on the bed, taking her hand and stroking her hair. 'Don't say things like that.'

She could tell he was about to embrace her, and pushed herself up to sit against the pillows. 'I must get up, Gabriel.'

'Won't you kiss me first?'

'Just once.' She pecked him quickly on the cheek and then drew away.

'That's a travesty of a kiss.'

But he got up and left the room.

When she joined him, he behaved in the distant manner that frightened her. She didn't mind when he hectored, but when he was cool or sarcastic she became desperately anxious to please in order to dispel his disapproval.

'Ruskin called earlier, Lizzy. We had a long talk, and he is very concerned about your health.'

228

'Did you say anything about his letter?'

'I explained that you were too tired yesterday to reply to it.'

'I feel much better today.'

'So what will your answer be?'

She hesitated, and then said very quickly, 'I'd better say yes, hadn't I?'

'There's a sensible girl.'

She expected him to become friendly again then, but there was more to come.

'As I said, Ruskin's very anxious you should get completely well. And he'd like you to go to a Dr Acland in Oxford. You'd be able to stay in his house until he knew exactly what was the matter with you, and how you should be treated.'

She was even more frightened now. 'But —' she began.

'Now Lizzy, listen. Dr Acland's an old friend of Ruskin's, and he's one of the most respected men at the University. He is especially interested in young people, and Ruskin says he's the kindest man in the world. He understands about art, and he'll take care of you as though you were his own daughter. It won't be for very long. And Ruskin will see to the train fares and everything like that.'

'I won't travel alone.' She realised as she said it that she had committed herself.

'No, Lizzy, of course not. Someone can chaperone you on the journey. The important thing is that you get to Oxford.'

'I won't travel with anyone but you.' She was quite lost now, not knowing what she had got herself into.

Gabriel at last looked cheerful. 'I should think Ruskin'll stretch to two railway tickets. And it'll be jolly to pay a flying visit to Oxford. It's a grand place, you're bound to like it.' He paused, and then laughed. 'You'll feel quite at home. Every other building in Oxford resembles a crumbling cathedral!'

Oxford — apart from its old stone buildings — took her completely by surprise. She had expected to feel intimidated and lonely, whereas in fact she was flattered and sought after. The doctrines of the pre-Raphaelites were all the rage, and the presence of one of their favourite models caused great excitement.

Dr Acland himself was a courteous, imaginative man and Lizzy liked him very much. He was apparently one of the most popular people in the University, and introduced her to many of the

229

undergraduates and professors who dropped by for a chat or advice. One beady-eyed professor of botany peered at her closely and said, 'Wonderful! Wonderful! To the life!' Adding by way of explanation, 'I took my students to see *Ophelia* because the river-bank flowers are painted so accurately. And so, my dear, are you. Millais's a marvel!'

Lizzy did not care so much for Mrs Acland, finding her brisk manner and continual concern for religion and moral welfare rather daunting. However Dr Acland's very sympathy, and way of making her feel he understood her, meant the prospect of a medical examination gradually became increasingly alarming. For it would not be easy, as it had been with Barbara's doctor, to avoid telling the complete truth, and above everything else she was terrified he would discern she was a girl 'who touched' and might diagnose this as being the main cause of her ill-health.

When, after a few days, he finally invited her into his surgery for 'a little talk' she made a pretext to go briefly to her room and took a few drops to calm her nerves. It was the first dose she had taken since her mother's condemnation.

Dr Acland centred his gentle questioning around the fact that he thought she was far too thin. Gradually he discovered the few foods that she did enjoy, and managed to glean that she had experienced sickness and stomach cramps. He also found out that she was capable of sleeping a great deal. Then he talked about her drawing, about Mr Ruskin's enthusiasm, and about Mr Rossetti's tutelage.

'Do you feel that your health is holding you back from the future you hope for yourself?'

'I don't know. I can't always draw. I don't know whether Mr Ruskin realises.'

'Yes he does, he has written at length to me about how he never wants you to overtax yourself making drawings for his sake. But he does want us to try to get you really well — so that you will enjoy your work, and we will all enjoy the results.' He paused and looked at her. 'Miss Siddall, you do enjoy your art, don't you?'

'Yes, Dr Acland.'

'I just wondered whether these clever men were pushing you too much. Whether because they thought so highly of you they were preventing you from leading a different sort of life. You mentioned your sister and young nephew, living with your mother, the other afternoon. I wondered if sometimes you would prefer to live like

230

them?'

'Oh no, Dr Acland.'

'I see.' He smiled encouragingly. 'But one day Mr Rossetti's attachment to you may lead to a family life?'

She blushed. _

'You would care for that?'

She nodded.

'But various things stand in the way at the moment?'

Lizzy suddenly found that she was crying.

Dr Acland took the interview no further. He rang the bell for the maid and ordered tea, soothed Lizzy and apologized for upsetting her, and then spent half an hour telling her inconsequential anecdotes until she appeared to be quite restored.

He wanted her to stay on in Oxford for a prolonged rest, but two days later she insisted on going back to London. She suddenly could not face any more encounters with polite society, and had a longing to be back with Gabriel in the familiar surroundings of the studio. He took her into his surgery for a last brief talk.

'I shall have to write to Mr Ruskin and give him my opinion of your health, as promised. And I'm going to emphasize my belief that you should rest completely for a while — away from your present life, and in a place where you can eat good, fresh food.' He spread out his fingers on his desk, and looked down at them for a few seconds. 'There is just one thing. Do you ever take laudanum drops for headaches and pains?'

'No, Dr Acland.'

'Good girl. They do not, in my opinion, serve much purpose, and I have observed that they cause some sensitive people to become overtaxed.'

Lizzy noted that he did not suggest the drops had any more precise medical effects, and therefore privately dismissed her mother's claim that they were the cause of her recent attack. It must be just another old wives' tale.

Gabriel was at Paddington station to meet her train. When she saw him walking towards her she was apprehensive, afraid he might be angry with her for not remaining in Oxford. But he was in the highest of spirits.

'You've come back just at the right time! Bruno was with me when your note came and he's gone to collect Emma. I thought we could all spend a couple of days together at the studio and

231

celebrate. There's plenty of room.'

She was somewhat taken aback at the suggestion, but not displeased.

'And what's Dr Acland's verdict?' he asked.

'Well — nothing very much. He's writing to Mr Ruskin. He wants me to go away somewhere. For a rest.'

'I expect Ruskin'll see to that,' said Gabriel airily. 'Come on, let's get home.'

Bruno and Emma were already at Chatham Place when they arrived, with Nolly asleep in a big rush basket. Lizzy felt a surge of pleasure at seeing them. 'It's so nice to be back — with friends.' She knelt by the basket and looked at Nolly. 'He's even more beautiful than Catherine was.'

'Surely we seem dull fry after Oxford life?' said Bruno, smiling.

'Why, you're famous in Oxford. The young men want to know all about the PRB's.'

'Millais and Hunt perhaps. But not me.' His gruff voice was rueful.

Emma went and stood on tiptoe and kissed him. 'No regrets today,' she said.

Lizzy watched her gesture. It was so unaffected and loving. Things were never quite like that between her and Gabriel.

'Why don't we have a picnic here?' Emma suggested. 'Lizzy's probably tired, and it's past dinner time.'

It was agreed that she and the two men should go and shop, and Lizzy would stay with the baby.

After a while he started to whimper, and she lifted him on to her lap, sitting in a low chair by the window. 'See,' she murmured, 'Look at the steamboat, and the frothy wake it leaves along the river. And the way the water sparkles as it flies off the paddles.' The sound of her voice took his attention and he gazed up at her face as she enjoyed the familiar view.

They were still sitting there when Bruno came back, preceding the others with his energetic stride up the stairs. She turned, looking as though she were about to rise.

'Stay there, Lizzy. Stay there. Don't move.'

Obediently she leant back into the chair, while he dumped the parcels he was carrying untidily onto the table and grabbed one of Gabriel's pencils and sketchpads. By the time the others came in, he was engrossed in a drawing.

232

They both laughed when they saw what was happening, and Gabriel insisted on finding another sketchpad and making a drawing too. As Lizzy remained motionless in her chair, the baby fitting snugly against her and the familiar scratching of pencils just audible over the sounds Emma made as she laid out the meal, she felt as though she really had come home.

By the time they had finished the last of the wine it was late, and Gabriel — a little tipsy — cried, 'Pig! Pig!' as Bruno swept the remains of the meat and pickle onto his plate. Nolly had been put in the bedroom, and when Emma and Lizzy joined him, taking off their dresses and clambering into the soft feather bed, Lizzy had a sense of companionship that was usually lacking in her life.

They talked for a while about the baby, and Emma suddenly said, 'Wouldn't you like to have children, Lizzy?'

They both blushed in the brief silence that followed, and then Lizzy replied, 'Yes. One day.'

'Only,' Emma fumbled for words, 'Bruno seems sure that it's just the matter of your health that keeps you and Gabriel from marrying.'

Emboldened by a few glasses of wine, Lizzy replied, 'I would prefer it if Gabriel would agree to marriage now. After all, if I'm not entirely well every day, that's no more than usual for a great many people. And I certainly haven't got consumption or any kind of wasting disease.'

'There!' exclaimed Emma triumphantly. 'I had a suspicion it was just Gabriel being stubborn.'

'How do you mean?'

'I mean that any man who wanders in and out of people's houses at all hours, calls friends out to taverns when they haven't any money, and wastes days either sleeping or talking, must realise he would have to mend his ways once he was married. And Gabriel just seems to want to go on being a student for ever.'

Lizzy had never looked at it quite like that. She was glad to have Emma make things so clear. And thinking about Gabriel's behaviour aroused her old nagging jealousy.

'Do you think he takes an interest in other girls?' she asked.

Emma was not to be drawn on this one, but her reply was so carefully circumspect that Lizzy came to her own conclusion. She did not try to pursue the subject any further, but just as they were at last settling down to sleep asked rather shyly, 'What do you think I

233

should say to Gabriel?'

There was a silence. Finally Emma replied, 'If he was different I might have a suggestion. But Bruno always claims it's *impossible* to know what to say to Gabriel to get him to behave reasonably . . . But he always adds he'd rather have him as he is than not at all — that life wouldn't be the same without him.' She paused. 'That's all right in a friend. It's not so endurable in a . . . well . . .'

'Husband?' completed Lizzy.

'Yes. I don't think I could manage Gabriel. I mean . . . Bruno's so thoughtful.'

'He's the kindest of men.' And yet, she thought as she went to sleep, she could not imagine marrying him. Gabriel, despite everything, was so much more . . . more *magnetic*.

In the middle of the next morning, when Emma was still barefoot and with untidy hair, and Gabriel and Bruno were in their shirtsleeves discussing Keats, and Nolly was crying because he had wind, John Ruskin arrived.

Lizzy could see at once that he was quite appalled by such hotchpotch domesticity, and as Emma whisked the baby off to the bedroom she hastened to follow. But Gabriel touched her arm and indicated she had better stay.

Ruskin had gone straight to the easel, as though to a harbour of refuge, and was looking at Gabriel's latest watercolour. Bruno joined him and made a few bluff remarks, and Ruskin's reply, clearly influenced by his unease at the whole situation, sounded rather contemptuous. Bruno did not attempt to answer back, but huffily left the room and went after Emma.

'I am afraid I never manage to please Brown,' Ruskin said plaintively.

'He hasn't got over the fact you don't like his paintings,' replied Gabriel.

'It's the subjects I don't like. He paints well enough, but the subjects are ugly.'

'He paints real life,' said Lizzy quietly.

Both men looked at her. 'Yes,' said Ruskin, 'I suppose that is my trouble. I find real life ugly.' He glanced around the studio where the evidence of the picnic, and Lizzy's opened but unpacked bags, were all too untidily apparent. However he made no comment, and suggested they drew up chairs by the window so they could discuss her immediate future. He had that morning received a letter from

234

Dr Acland and understood that she needed complete rest, preferably somewhere bracing. All he wanted to ask her now was whether she would, if proper arrangements could be made, be willing to take a trip to Europe at his expense?

'Well, Lizzy?' prompted Gabriel.

'I . . . I don't know.'

'Perhaps in the mountains?' said Ruskin gently.

Lizzy looked up wide-eyed: the idea of mountains, rugged and glacial, terrified her.

Ruskin misinterpreted her expression as one of excitement. 'I always find a spell in Switzerland gives me the greatest benefit in the world. The pure air, the rushing streams, the dramatic precipices . . .'

Lizzy turned to Gabriel, hoping he would rescue her.

'Perhaps,' he said, recognizing her panic, 'John and I should talk it over. See if we can come up with a plan that will please you.'

She nodded.

'But Lizzy,' he went on, 'is there any place that particularly appeals to you? Just so we have some notion.'

She remembered the illustrated magazines they used to scour for fashion ideas at Mrs Tozer's, and how she used to love some of the picturesque engravings. It was not just the fineness of the clothes, but also something fairy-tale about the settings that made her reply, 'I should like to see Paris.'

It was a reply that, she realised, gave pleasure to Gabriel and annoyance to Ruskin.

Three weeks elapsed between the half hour Lizzy spent huddled in the bedroom with the Browns discussing whether she should or should not allow herself to be sent away by Ruskin, and her arrival at the Hôtel de Fabrice in Paris. She was accompanied there by a chaperone, Mrs Kincaid — a distant cousin of Gabriel's — and according to Ruskin was supposed to stay for a few days to see the sights, and then travel on to Nice, probably for the duration of the winter. Lizzy, however, had made other plans. She had only agreed to go abroad at all if Gabriel joined her — a fact which had been kept from Ruskin — and privately she did not intend to go to Nice. Encouraged by Emma, and with the extra confidence that her stay in Oxford had given her, she had decided to use Paris as a testing ground.

From secretly reading Ruskin's letters to Gabriel, she gathered that Gabriel had inferred her history of illness was more serious than it actually was. Ruskin had assumed this was the only obstacle to their marriage, and earnestly wished to help her recover so that both his protégés could be happy. However Dr Acland's diagnosis, while relieving anxiety, had not made it easy to know the best way to help. 'Mental power long pent up and lately overtaxed' was how he described the cause of her condition, and he made no specific recommendation as to the best place for her to recuperate. Nice had finally been chosen because it was a favourite resort of the English, and Gabriel had persuaded Ruskin that a few days in Paris first would do Lizzy no harm. Privately he promised to join her there, but Ruskin was not yet to be informed of this since he was adamant Gabriel should use his solitude to work. He fully expected that freeing his prodigy from financial worry and the continual spectacle of Lizzy's ill-health would enable him to produce the flood of work he so yearned to see.

The practical proprieties raised by the trip were much on Ruskin's mind. He wanted Lizzy to have a chaperone who would be thoroughly reliable and sympathetic, and he insisted that Gabriel should call on Mrs Siddall to explain that Lizzy was going abroad and under what circumstances. Gabriel undertook this obligation most unwillingly, but when he and Lizzy arrived at Star Place one afternoon only Lyddy was in and explanations were comparatively easy. Indeed afterwards Gabriel claimed he had enjoyed the visit, and that Lyddy was very jolly and the house much more cosy than he remembered. The chaperone problem was solved by William, who reminded Gabriel that their cousin Evelyn Kincaid had been in straitened circumstances since the death of her husband, spoke French, and was both reliable and unflamboyant — or, as Gabriel put it, positively mousy.

In England Lizzy had not objected to the mousiness, finding Mrs Kincaid's retiring character quite appealing, but once they were in Paris it became something of a drawback. They arrived there, complete with Lancelot in his cage, a month after Queen Victoria had made a highly successful state visit, and the Parisians were in an unusually anglophilic mood. The great triumphal arches, painted in imitation of white marble and decorated with banners and flowers, were being dismantled, but many of the smaller displays of fairy lamps and plaster statues were still in place, and often when people overheard them speaking English they would touch either

236

Lizzy or Mrs Kincaid on the arm and point to the decorations and exclaim, 'Ces ornements sont pour votre Reine!', to which one man added, 'Et maintenant, pour *vous*!' Lizzy found these approaches charming, but her companion always bustled her away and refused to allow her to speak to strangers other than in the hotel.

They made two visits to the great international exhibition in the Champs Elysées, and Mrs Kincaid was quite overcome by the horticultural section with its fountains and ornamental gardens and silken tents containing monumental displays of wax fruit and flowers. But it was the shops and the outdoor cafés that particularly appealed to Lizzy. She spent hours just gazing at the elegant clothes and fancy goods, and loved to sit out on the wide pavements at little green tables eating ices flavoured with raspberry, pineapple, strawberry or lemon.

She had liked Paris from the moment they drove away from the Gare de Strasbourg and she discovered that the warm air smelled completely and delightfully different from that of London — much more zesty and sweet. And she liked the comfort of the hotel, which although quite modest, was prettily furnished and provided meals better than any she had ever eaten before. A dish such as roast lamb and vegetables, which she never enjoyed at home, became a subtle and mouthwatering affair at the Fabrice. She realised after a few days that there was only one thing which made her feel uncomfortable — her clothes. In England her simple dresses looked good, but in Paris they were positively dowdy and by the end of the week she had consulted with the manageress of the hotel and had made an arrangement to see a dressmaker. When Mrs Kincaid meekly protested that it would eat into the allowance Ruskin had stipulated for them, Lizzy just looked obstinate.

It wasn't only that she did not like walking along a smart shopping thoroughfare in her slightly medieval dresses. She also wished to present her very best possible appearance to Gabriel when he arrived, for this was all part of her plan. With Mrs Kincaid present, and the formalities of hotel life, Gabriel would not be able to claim any physical intimacies, and freed from that complication she intended that he should see her as a desirable but respectable lady whom he wished to escort straight back to England and marry. She was still his Lizzy, his Guggums, but some of the things Emma had said made her realise she must be something else as well. And Paris had turned out to be the perfect setting.

The dressmaker worked wonders, but when the bills came in Lizzy was appalled. It was the way all the extras had mounted up, for the dressmaker had also advised on the purchase of gloves and shoes and stockings and scarves, and these turned out to be far more expensive than she had expected. If she paid everything immediately they would have no money left for the rest of the month.

As she sat in her room, with its blue and white furnishings, the little brocade settee piled high with dress-boxes, and the hoarse voices of boys drifting up from below as they narrowly avoided colliding their clanking handcarts of vegetables and wine, she looked at the additions she had done on the back of one of the bills and tried to feel remorseful. But she just found herself giggling. There was something about the Parisian atmosphere that made regret impossible.

There was only one thing to do: she would have to write to Gabriel and ask him to come at once and bring some money.

While she waited for a response to her letter, she set aside time each day for sketching so that when she returned to England earlier than Ruskin expected she would at least have some drawings for him. She also allowed Mrs Kincaid to give her French lessons, and rather enjoyed trying to get her tongue round the elusive French 'r'. A week went by with no word from England, and Mrs Kincaid started to make remarks like, 'Letters can so easily go astray, it might be wise to write again,' which irritated Lizzy, for secretly she was beginning to get worried too. But she knew Gabriel did not like to be badgered and was reluctant to write a second time. However it became increasingly frustrating to be dressed more elegantly than she had ever been before while at the same time not having enough money to buy ice creams or lemonade at the boulevard cafés, and in order that these worries should not press on her too heavily at night, she started to take a few drops — something she had not done since being in Paris.

She was in her room one afternoon supposedly sketching, though in fact just playing lackadaisically with Lancelot, when there was a knock on her door and a maid announced that there was a Monsieur Rossette downstairs to see her. Lizzy temporarily forgot all about her plan to be dignified, and went rushing out into the corridor and down the stairs to where Gabriel was standing in the hall. When he saw her new clothes and coiffured hair he exclaimed 'By Jove!' and gave a mock bow, then embraced her murmuring, 'Oh Guggums, it is so lovely to be with you.'

Within an hour they were sitting outside Lizzy's favourite café, hands touching across the table, and a celebratory bottle of wine open in front of them. Most of the passers-by gave her a long, appraising stare, and Gabriel said that her cream silk dress with its fashionable wide frilled skirt made her look like a French countess.

'I want to feast my eyes on you. I've been painting you from memory all week and I want to replenish my store.'

'What were you painting?'

'Paolo and Francesca. As soon as I got your letter I set to work. I knew it was a subject that would not please Ruskin. And he gave me thirty-five guineas for it, so here I am. Just think, only the day before yesterday I was painting you floating through hell with Paolo.'

'Why did they go to hell?'

'Because they were illicit lovers.'

Lizzy blushed and looked away.

'Now,' Gabriel went on, 'I suppose I've got to pay my respects to the International Exhibition. But mainly I want to go to the Louvre with you. And last week I met Robert Browning — he's such a splendid man — and he's staying in Paris now. So we could call on him and his wife. And Frederic Stephens is over here. I must look him up. And then we'll get all your affairs settled up tomorrow. By the way I told Ruskin that any lady worth her salt runs up dress bills in Paris. But we won't talk about that now. We'll enjoy ourselves.'

For two days they did exactly that, and to Lizzy it seemed that her plan must be succeeding. When they accidentally bumped into Stephens in the Louvre, Gabriel seemed so proud to show her off, and in front of Mrs Kincaid he showed her the utmost courtesy. But then the bubble, the bright Parisian bubble of *Joie de Vivre*, burst.

She and Gabriel were walking in the Bois de Boulogne by a lake whose surface was scattered with the first yellow leaves of autumn.

'They remind me of London,' she remarked, 'when the plane leaves are flattened on the pavement after rain.'

'At least you'll avoid that this year. All those London rains and fogs and mists and snows.'

'I suppose so.' She sounded dubious.

'Well, you don't get English winters in Nice.'

'Gabriel . . .'

'What's the matter?'

'Please listen carefully. You see — I don't want to go to Nice.'

'Lizzy — whyever not?'

'I don't want to be away on my own.'

'You've got old Mousy.'

'You know that's no real company.'

'But you've got to spend the winter away. Dr Acland said so.'

'Gabriel, I'm not seriously ill. I've been very well all the time I've been here. I've enjoyed coming away — it's been lovely. But now I'd just like to come back with you.'

'But Ruskin wouldn't hear of it.'

'What difference does it make to him where I am? If I'm not ill, and I'm working, it can't possibly matter.'

'Lizzy it matters a great deal. Look,' he searched his pockets and brought out a letter, 'He didn't even want me to come to Paris for a few days. He wrote, "I am ill-tempered today — you are such absurd creatures both of you. I don't say you do wrong, because you don't seem to know what *is* wrong, but just to do whatever you like as far as possible — as puppies and tomtits do…" Damn cheek, though I must say I'd rather be a puppy than a crumbling cathedral. Anyway, he goes on a long time in that vein. Then near the end he says, "Tell Ida she must go south directly. Paris will kill her, or ruin her." You certainly don't look dead or ruined to me, but it's no good trying to go against him. He wants me safely churning out masterpieces in London, and you improving your constitution and churning out masterpieces in Nice. If we go against him he'll get obstinate.'

'You mean he'll stop giving us money.'

'Exactly.'

They walked on in silence for a while, and then she said quietly, 'Gabriel, if I beg you, will you take me home? Please?'

'We can't afford it Lizzy, you know we can't.'

Already it seemed as though he was slipping away from her, deserting her, and a lump of misery hurt her throat so much that she could not speak.

She was too unhappy to accompany him later when he went to call on the Brownings, shutting herself in her room and swallowing a large dose of laudanum.

The next morning she had to be woken by Mrs Kincaid from an almost comatose sleep, and as they sat downstairs with Gabriel over coffee and rolls she felt as though she might faint. The room seemed to be slowly rotating, while the sounds of clinking china and people's voices merged into an incoherent roar inside her head. Gabriel was in full spate, reporting on his visit the night before — telling how Robert knew more about Italian painting than anyone he'd ever met including Ruskin, and how kind and gracious Elizabeth was despite being so poorly.

'She's a proper invalid, I'm afraid. They'd planned to go south to Florence for the winter, but they've got cholera down there. So Nice is a good choice for you Lizzy — it'll be warm, but healthy too. And you know, my dear, you don't look at all well today. Whatever you claim, Paris hasn't been able to cure you.'

Early the following morning, the Nice train steamed slowly out of Paris with Lizzy and Mrs Kincaid aboard. Gabriel had insisted that Frederic Stephens come to the station with him to see them off, and when the train moved away Lizzy saw the two friends hurry down the platform like boys released from school.

Chapter Sixteen

The dry wind roared along the empty sand, picking up flurries of grit and whipping the grey surface of the sea. It had been roaring like this for over two weeks, relentless and merciless, keeping tetchy-tempered visitors indoors and spoiling all the efforts of the hoteliers of Nice to gratify their leisured clients.

Lizzy left the side door of the little Hôtel Martigues, struggled down the narrow street that led to the promenade, and then had difficulty in standing up against the full strength of the head-on wind. Her predicament was worsened by the fact that she held cupped in her hands a small object wrapped in white linen and so could not stretch out her arms to keep her balance. Slowly, step by step, she made her way down on to the beach.

She looked among the detritus on the water-line, and when she saw a stout piece of wood she took it and proceeded to dig a hole in the sand. When the hole was deep enough she lowered the white-wrapped object into it and covered it over. Then she knelt, her dark cloak flattened against her by the wind, her head bowed, while the roar of the elements failed to obliterate the sadness of her thoughts. Before she finally got up she turned and gazed at the sea, and then stood and allowed the wind to speed her steps back to the hotel.

In the little attic room, she took out her writing-box and started a letter:

> Dear Gabriel,
> Lancelot died this morning

But as soon as she had written those words her eyes filled with tears and she started to sob. She began the letter afresh later, and this time did not attempt to mention the illness and demise of the linnet. Less and less did there seem any point in writing down her real feelings in her letters, and the death of Lancelot was, she decided, just the last of the private losses she had suffered through loving Walter Deverell. But it was so lonely in the room without the little bird.

Mrs Kincaid had left Nice three months before. They had stayed at a large, stuffy hotel that catered for pernickety English people, and 'old Mousy' had blossomed into a simpering widow keen to attract the attention of any eligible widower. Lizzy had grown thoroughly impatient, and one day when her companion asked for money for a new pair of gloves she replied, 'There is no money. Only enough to keep me here by myself. You will have to go back to England.' It wasn't true, but she did not see why she should have to endure the spectacle of Mrs Kincaid's husband-hunting any longer.

On the day of her departure, Lizzy moved to the Hôtel Martigues which had no English guests and a sympathetic proprietor, Madame Colin. Ruskin wrote begging her to proceed to Switzerland or Italy where acquaintances of his would look after her and she would have the benefit of real scenery for her work, but she ignored his pleas. It was not that she particularly liked Nice, but Madame Colin had introduced her to a cooperative doctor who was happy to indulge her needs, and there seemed no point in moving until Gabriel summoned her home. Sometimes she doubted whether that would ever happen and then she took a larger dose than usual of her medicine, but at other times his letters hinted at marriage and mentioned a spring home-coming.

Some days she used her time quite well. She wrote to Gabriel, giving amusing descriptions of the people she met at the hotel or in the shops; she enjoyed the meals which she usually had sent up to her room; and occasionally she dutifully did some drawings for Ruskin. But if anything upset her, or if she felt a mood of grey depression crushing her when she woke, then the day would pass in a drugged haze with no one to disturb or reprimand her.

During the night that followed her solemn journey to the beach, the wind suddenly ceased. The absence of the roar, of the slap-slap of palm fronds, of the banging of a loose board next door, woke her up. She lay in the dark, surrounded by silence, and for a few seconds forgot that Lancelot's cage was empty. Then, when she realised she was completely alone, she became afraid.

The doctor had taught her not to use her medicine out of panic, but to try to relax her mind first. The bottle, glass, and flask of water, were already by her bed, and she could see just well enough to pour a strong dose. Then she lay back on the pillows and tried to

243

conjure up happy pictures.

She was in the studio at Red Lion Square, sitting by the fire after posing, and waiting for a moment when Walter would kiss her. She always imagined the same kiss — the only kiss. 'Lizzy, we don't deserve you. You're like a lovely flower. All smooth and fragrant.' Or she was standing on the piece of wild ground near Star Place, surrounded by scented summer flowers, and Harry, his face still untroubled, was lying on the grass, intoning 'Sky, sky, sky.' She remembered when she did her self-portrait, and could feel the brush between her fingers as she delicately touched the palette with its tip. She tried, too, to remember the bluebell wood, the smell of flowers and leafmould, and how that excitement had been real and how she and Gabriel were surely indivisible now.

But the wrong picture came into her head just as she swallowed the liquid in the glass. She remembered Gabriel coming back from the funeral carrying the birdcage. *In the desert a fountain is springing. . .*

As the doctor had warned, the medicine took her into nightmare and she was hurled through dark and terrifying scenes before her mind finally became too drugged even to dream.

Her first sensation in the morning was of confusion. She could hear voices, and could glimpse the empty bird-cage. The strong light told her it was late. Her mouth tasted rancid, and she ached all over.

Madame Colin was bent over, shaking her shoulder. 'Mademoiselle! Mademoiselle!'

It transpired that the maid had been unable to rouse her and had become afraid. Lizzy struggled to sit up.

Madame Colin looked at her gravely, and told the maid to put the tray with coffee and rolls and a letter from England on the bedside table. Then the two women left the room.

It was five minutes before Lizzy could trust herself to lift the cup, for at first her hands were shaking uncontrollably.

The letter was from Gabriel, and when she finally opened it she discovered it was a Valentine poem, of which she took particular note of the first and last verses:

> Yesterday was St Valentine.
> Thought you at all, dear love divine,
> Upon the beard in sorry trim
> And rueful countenance of him

244

That Orson who's your Valentine?

Come back, dear Liz, and looking wise
In that arm-chair which suits your size,
Through some fresh drawing scrape a hole.
Your Valentine and Orson's soul
Is sad for those two friendly eyes.

Later in the day Madame Colin advised her that she would have
to make plans to return home. She could not take responsibility for
a sick English girl.

Lizzy accepted the decision meekly. It was a relief not to have to
wait any longer. The next morning she went to see the doctor, and
he wrote a letter saying she would obtain no more benefit from a
foreign climate. He also prepared a veritable medicine chest for her
journey and first weeks back at home. She almost wrote to Gabriel
to tell him she was coming, but changed her mind. She would let it
be a surprise.

England was enjoying a few days of premature spring, and when
Lizzy embarked on the train at Dover the air felt like silk after the
rough grip of the gales in Nice. She travelled first-class, for since her
removal to the Martigues she had saved from Ruskin's allowance,
and when her train arrived in London she asked a porter to take her
luggage to the new station hotel. Walking in to the lavishly-
appointed entrance hall she attracted approving stares, and her
request for a room was treated with deference. Besides fashionable
clothes, Lizzy had also returned from France with the confidence
that independence however unsought brings.

When she had rested, she wrote a short note to Gabriel telling
him of her return and asked for it to be delivered by messenger. An
hour later Gabriel arrived at the hotel.

He seemed overjoyed. He was particularly pleased that it was his
valentine that had prompted her return, and delighted at the style
of her arrival. He decided they should dine at the hotel since Lizzy
looked so at home in its grandiose surroundings, and was much
amused when she found the food inferior to that from Madame
Colin's kitchen.

'You see,' he said, 'we were all quite right. The Mediterranean
has done you good. You never used to have an appetite.' He looked
around the huge dining room with its marble pillars and gilt
ornamentation, 'Are you going to stay on here? I don't think I've

ever eaten anywhere quite so vulgar.'

'Only for a night or two. Then . . .' She looked at him squarely and noticed that he shifted his gaze.

'Yes, we must decide what to arrange. I wonder what Ruskin will have to say.'

'I came back to you, Gabriel. Not Ruskin.'

'Oh Guggums, I know. But Ruskin's such a fusspot. We must keep him informed.'

'I have some drawings for him.'

He brightened. 'Oh excellent. I tell you what — why don't you give them to me and I'll take them over to Denmark Hill in the morning?'

'We will go to Denmark Hill together,' she said firmly.

When he came to collect her in the morning, he took one look at her dress and asked if she could change into one of her old ones.

'Why? Are you afraid that Ruskin will be reminded of the money I spent in Paris?'

'Not exactly. But he so loves you in those simple dresses. He's often remarked on it when he's gone through my sketchbooks. I think fripperies remind him of his wife. He likes girls to be unadorned, natural, and young.'

'Well, I'll change my dress if you like. But I can't change my years.'

'You look younger than ever.'

She knew that was not true. Her twenty-fifth birthday had passed while she was in Nice, and her face did not disguise that fact.

Their reception at Denmark Hill was very different from their first visit. Old Mr Ruskin greeted them rather sternly when the footman announced their unexpected arrival, and John was fetched from his study, clearly leaving his work most unwillingly. When he saw Lizzy and Gabriel together, he seemed almost to blanch. However he greeted them with conventional courtesy, and after signalling to his father to leave, asked them what had happened.

Gabriel was about to reply, but Lizzy nervously took the lead. 'The weather in Nice has been very bad,' she began, 'cold, and with a wind that never stops. And the doctor who has been looking after me thought I should come home. I have his letter here.' She produced an envelope and gave it to John, who read its contents slowly.

'Have you seen this, Gabriel?'

'No.'

John handed the letter over to him, and then said to Lizzy, 'Is this doctor one with a reputation among the English colony?'

'Yes,' she lied. 'He is much sought after.'

'Well,' said Gabriel cheerfully, 'He seems to think Lizzy is recovered.'

'But what have you and she planned to do now?'

'I suppose,' said Gabriel slowly, 'she will need a room . . .'

'That hardly seems to constitute the normal family life this doctor appears to think she should lead.'

'The room would only be temporary.'

Lizzy sat quietly staring out of the window while this exchange went on.

'All right then, temporarily I will pay for a suitable room large enough to accommodate her needs. But only while you settle your plans.'

'Lizzy's brought some drawings for you.'

John softened. 'I should like to see those very much indeed.'

Gabriel started to undo the folder.

'I did as you asked,' she said. 'I didn't throw anything away.'

The two men stood side by side as John slowly turned each drawing over. It was not long before Lizzy could tell they were both appalled.

When they had been right through the folder, John seemed too embarrassed to speak, and Gabriel said awkwardly, 'Have you got your more finished drawings somewhere else, Lizzy?'

'No. They are all there.'

'It is just that they are nearly all so . . . slight.'

She shrugged. 'One cannot achieve much in a hotel bedroom.'

'But my dear,' said John, 'why did you not follow my advice and go to Italy or Switzerland? Then you would have had inspiration all around you.'

'I can't go outside to sketch. I find it disagreeable. People come and watch and try to talk to me.'

'But surely your companion . . . whom you so summarily dismissed.'

She was beginning to feel irritated. 'Oh *Mousy* . . . it was even more difficult if she was there. She said such stupid things.'

John sighed. 'But even with interiors and domestic objects. You

247

used to work so hard to get them right. And now you seem content with — to be frank — a lot of lop-sided birdcages.'

'I'm sorry.' She sounded penitent, on the verge of tears. 'I'll take them away.'

'There are just two I should like to keep,' he said. 'The Paris rooftops, and that little study of a bottle, glass and flask. That is carefully done.'

She could tell he thought it a very poor exchange for her six-month trip abroad.

'I'll see she starts working again properly,' said Gabriel. 'It was obviously too soon for my little pupil to fly the nest.'

'Don't neglect your own work. That commission I obtained for you is long overdue.' The tone of the dominie in John's voice hung in the air, deadening any further exchange. Within a few minutes Gabriel and Lizzy were on their way to Chatham Place.

It was smaller than she remembered. The studio no longer seemed to have special areas and corners, but was just a long room filled with clutter. Inevitably some objects had been rearranged and new ones introduced, and this made it feel alien; interesting, but alien. Yet she also felt it was the most important room in her life. Her reality was either here, or else it did not exist at all.

Gabriel was clearing a length of old tapestry away from her favourite high-backed chair which he then placed by the window.

'There,' he said, 'sit down and let me take a long look at you.'

She hesitated, determined not to repeat exactly the pattern of the old days. But to reject her old chair would have seemed merely petty. Cautiously she sat down.

Gabriel was standing by the other window, and they faced one another, their faces harshly lit by the glare glancing off the river. They both gazed into each other's eyes for a long time. Then, with half a smile, he said, 'Please undo your hair, Lizzy.'

She stared at him a little longer before replying, 'No, not yet. We must establish a truth first, Gabriel.'

He clicked his fingernails and looked away.

'What you said at Ruskin's is not true. I did not "fly the nest". I did not want to go to Nice. You know I didn't. You made me go there so Ruskin would go on giving us money. I wanted to come back from Paris with you.' Already she was slightly breathless. It had needed courage to confront him in this way. She bent her head.

'Lizzy.' Sometimes his voice had the impact of notes drawn from

248

a musical instrument; he seemed able to pitch the tone and to pace the syllables with such impelling effect.

'Yes?'

'I understand. Now — please will you undo your hair? Now that you *are* back?'

She lifted her arm and drew out the two constraining tortoise-shell pins.

Gabriel softened the light by partially drawing the curtains, and then sketched her in the high-backed chair.

She did not return to the station hotel that night. After they had been out to dine he begged a favour. 'I want to spend the night by you, Lizzy. Nothing will happen that will lead to harm. I want to have a vigil.' He gripped her arm hard. 'Don't refuse me. It is so important.'

She acquiesced. She did not want to leave him. The prospect of company, of talk after the lonely months, of sharing long hours with Gabriel, was solacing.

He came into the bedroom when she had taken off her dress and stockings and was sitting against the pillows, the sheet drawn up to her armpits. The slightly acrid smell of a newly-lit candle filled the air. He was in his shirtsleeves, and went to the other side of the bed where he lay on the covers propped up on one elbow, separated from her by many inches.

'Do you want to sleep now?' he asked.

'No. I don't feel tired. Tell me news about other people. You've told me about your paintings and translations, and I've told you about those boring people in Nice. But how are Emma and Bruno, and all the others?'

'Dear Bruno. Struggling as ever. He's so *thorough*. D'you know, he's at last finished that painting of Christ and Peter — it's taken him five years.'

'And Emma and the children?'

'Emma's nice as ever. The children nice enough. What *can* one say about children? Though I think Nolly's going to be an exception. He likes me to recite poems to him.'

'You probably mesmerize him. Like a snake-charmer.'

'No, he's going to be a literary child. I leave snake-charming and other exotic practices to Hunt. He's back, you know. Burned and bearded, and with strange, harsh paintings. I'm not sure that the east has done him any good at all. He took some poor goat to the

249

ends of the earth to do a scapegoat painting. And it went and died before he'd finished, so he had to go and find another one. Woolner swears he ate the first goat. But I suppose it's a powerful painting.'

'Lancelot died.'

'Oh, Lizzy . . .'

'Didn't you notice? I hadn't got him?'

'I was so glad to see *you* . . .' He laid his hand on top of hers. 'I really am sorry.'

'I buried him by the sea.'

'Darling Lizzy.' He gave a deep sigh, as though making a supreme effort. 'You must have thought of Walter that day.'

'Yes.'

'We both loved him.'

They remained quiet for what seemed like a long time. Then Gabriel removed his hand and shifted his position.

'Would you like to hear about some new friends? I told you I had been to Oxford. Where, I may say, you've made a great impact. I kept meeting people who were much more interested in the fact that you sat for me than that I made the paintings.'

She turned and smiled. His remark about Walter had seemed like both a restitution and a resolution. 'Tell me about the friends.'

'You will love them. They're dedicated to chivalry and all things medieval, and to look at they're the most extraordinary pair. Ned, that's Edward Jones, is frail and fair, like Keats's knight "alone and palely loitering", and Topsy is like a blacksmith, all fire and force.'

'*Topsy*?'

'William — William Morris. We call him Topsy after that comic character in *Uncle Tom's Cabin*. He's got a huge head of curly hair that I'm sure he never combs out. I've started him writing poetry — he spouts it out like a fountain. And Ned makes the most exquisite designs and paintings.'

Lizzy lay listening while he expounded the charms and exploits of these two young men and then at some point drifted off to sleep. When she woke, Gabriel was sleeping too.

She could only just make out the shape of his head and body, and lay listening to his even breathing which was so slow compared to hers that she wondered he was not gasping for air. She reached across and took his hand, comforted by his presence.

He woke immediately, and the life that surged through him made her withdraw her hand in apprehension. He was about to

250

touch her hair, to draw her head towards him, when suddenly he checked.

'Lizzy,' he said wonderingly, 'Lizzy. Don't be frightened. I have not forgotten. I will do nothing harmful.' His arm dropped down to his side.

'I'm sorry. I woke you up. I touched your hand.'

'Please touch it again.'

Shyly she did so. They lay side by side, like linked figures on a tomb, and then she leaned over and kissed him. She kissed his cheeks, his eyes, his mouth. And he lay quietly, allowing her to love him the way that pleased her. Then when the dawn came, and he asked if she would undo her camisole, she agreed. He watched her, and held her, and touched her breast. He never startled or disturbed her. She felt cocooned, dreamy, on the perimeter of a journey that would change their lives.

Chapter Seventeen

The next day they fetched her things from the hotel. She agreed there was no urgent hurry to find a room, that she could wait until they saw a really suitable one and in the meantime she would stay at Chatham Place. She had a secure, almost lazy feeling that everything was about to be resolved; that Gabriel was at last in a frame of mind to make her happy. Before they went out, he had insisted on giving her a brief drawing lesson, and under mild protest she had done a quick almost comic, sketch of him standing at the easel.

'But Lizzy, that's better than anything you did in France. You see, you haven't lost your touch.'

'I feel well today, Gabriel. Really well.'

'I bring you inspiration?'

'Perhaps.'

'You love me?'

'I love you.'

'I love you too, Lizzy.' He whirled around. 'Oh just wait until those two see us together. Ned and Top. It'll be perfect.'

She smiled, thinking that she too would enjoy the admiration of these unknown young men. For the first time Gabriel's need to share his life continually with his male friends, to seek constant company, did not threaten or diminish her.

He lolled on the chaise while she unpacked her cases. As the Parisian cream silk dress spilled across her arms, she said, 'I wonder if I will ever wear this again.'

'We'll go to the opera. Then you can wear it.'

'But I'll have to go back to simple dresses for every day?'

'If Ned saw you attired as a fashionable French lady, I think he'd die of disappointment. For them, you're their Lady of Shalott — which they're forever reciting out loud. That should please you.'

She smiled again.

When she opened the box containing all her medicines, he

exclaimed in horror. 'Whatever are all those bottles, Lizzy?'

'They're what the doctor in Nice prescribed for me. He gave me a supply to bring home.'

'But what *are* they?'

'Oh . . . just my usual drops. Only a better compound. And things for the stomach . . . Well, constipation . . . and fatigue . . . He thought the journey might be taxing.'

'You still take those drops?'

'When I need to.'

'The doctor said nothing about them in his letter.'

'Why should he? Everyone takes them.'

'I don't.'

'You don't need to.'

'I've heard Dr Acland talk about them . . . I saw quite a lot of him in Oxford. He says they're pernicious. When they get a hold on people.'

She said nothing.

'Lizzy?'

'Yes.'

'You wanted me to face up to the truth about why you were in Nice. Now . . . will you do the same for me?'

'The same?'

'Face the truth. Will you try?'

She nodded.

'In the past . . . I've noticed those drops seem to make you more weak. Unable to do very much. Listening to Dr Acland talking about some of the young men who take laudanum I realised what harm it could do to someone as delicate as yourself.'

'But —'

'No, please let me finish. I know that sometimes they are necessary. No one wants to endure hours of pain. But they aren't good just for sleeping or taking away mental misery. Their good effect goes after a time and a bad one takes over.'

'That's not what the French doctor said.'

'Not all doctors say the same thing, and I'm afraid it's often in their own interests to prescribe medicines. And you see, I think I realise why the drawings you brought back were so disappointing. You did not concentrate because you were taking too much laudanum.'

'How would you like to be shut up in a foreign hotel all day, with

253

no one —'

'Lizzy, Lizzy, please. I am *not* reproaching you. But, like you, I want there to be truth between us. That little drawing you did of your medicine bottle with the water flask said more than words can about how you depended on it. And I understand why.' He went over to where she was sitting and stood behind her, his hands on her shoulders. 'Now, my darling, please listen. That medicine chest you've brought back with you frightens me. I don't want you enslaved to all those bottles. For you needn't be. We were together all yesterday and last night, and you took no medicine at all. That is true, isn't it?'

Very, very quietly she said, 'Yes.'

'So that proves you don't need it all the time.'

'I suppose so.'

'Then, I would like you to make me a promise. Will you keep your medicine just for real pains — headache, toothache, stomach? And not for everyday? Please? Please say you'll try?'

'I'll try.'

He kissed the top of her head. 'There's a good Guggums. You know, some of the stories I heard from Dr Acland really alarmed me. I suppose he never thought to ask whether you took any form of drops?'

She shook her head.

In the early part of the evening they went to the chop-house they always used to frequent. Lizzy no longer felt any pangs when they passed the doorway of the brighter, noisier restaurant; she was quite content to dine with Gabriel in subdued surroundings. And the waiter remembered that she liked only a small plate of meat and vegetables, followed by some fruit. After the meal Gabriel left her to go to his class at the Working Men's College, and she wandered slowly back to Chatham Place. It was still unseasonably warm, and the bargelights reflected on the calm surface of the river fascinated her with their slowly melding, changing shapes. Perhaps she would try to do a painting of the river at night. She could start by standing on the balcony to make a few sketches. It would please Gabriel, and now that they had been honest with one another, without anger, she felt a confidence welling up that might enable her to experience again the enjoyment she had once had in picture-making.

She searched around the studio for a heavier pencil and larger size paper than she normally used. There was no point in trying to

254

cram the Blackfriars waterfront into a pocket sketchbook.

She moved a pile of Dante and Beatrice drawings to see if there was some clean paper underneath and found instead three head studies, ravishingly drawn, of a woman whose sensuality almost spilled off the edges of the paper.

It was Annie Miller.

She forced herself to keep control. She must stay calm until Gabriel returned. There had got to be an acceptable explanation. She would go out on to the balcony and start her sketch.

But her mind refused to be calm, racing from one angry thought to another. Gabriel had mentioned Hunt's recent return — had that return coincided with his Valentine summoning her home? Had he beckoned her only when Annie Miller was no longer available?

The time he was due home passed. Every minute after that seemed like an eternity, and she paced up and down the studio, her teeth gritted. Once she flung herself on the chaise and started to cry, but then she thought she heard footsteps on the stairs and ran to the door. There was no one there.

She stayed at the top of the dark stone staircase for a full five minutes, all the hope of the past twenty-four hours diminishing in her mind like a hundred-pound note charring and shrivelling against the flame of a match.

Without making a conscious decision she went back into the hall, slammed the door, and walked through the dark corridor to the bedroom and her medicine chest.

She had taken no laudanum for six days, and within minutes it had deadened her misery, leaving her light-headed and angry. When it had taken full effect she waltzed around the studio tearing up the drawings of Annie Miller and then she rushed to the window and threw them in the air so that they floated slowly down onto the surface of the river.

'That damns you for ever,' she called out. 'I'll never paint you now. Never. Not now that harlot's lain on your water. Damn your lights.'

It was midnight when Gabriel finally returned, and she rounded on him like a dervish, screaming accusatory questions that angered him so much he found himself bellowing back answers which a few hours before he would have given anything to conceal from her.

Yes, he had written to her literally the day after Hunt's return.

255

Yes, he had used Annie as a model — Hunt had begged him to, not wanting her to seek work among strangers. And, yes, his drawings of Annie were sensual, just as she was.

'You've touched her! You've touched her! And you have the effrontery, the dirty effrontery to touch me the minute she is no longer available!'

At this he stormed off to the bedroom to look at her medicine chest, and came back with a bottle which he hurled out of the window.

'You've broken your promise! You haven't tried. You're *drugged*. It drugs all your sensibilities. *And* your senses. At least when other girls are touched they respond. Their bodies express their feelings. You're like a nun; your feelings are numbed.'

'They're *not*! They're *not*! My feelings are here in my heart,' she banged the bone between her breasts, 'not on the surface of my body for any man to arouse. You'll never understand. I should have known. You're just like Woolner. I should have heeded the warning of that poem. Even then you were all after women ready to be touched. All of you. Hunt after Annie Miller. Millais chasing someone else's wife. Even Bruno eloped with a country child. There was only Walter ... who understood.' She prostrated herself on the rug by the fireplace, weeping loudly.

Gabriel strode angrily over to her and pulled her to her feet. 'Stop it, Lizzy! Stop! Pull yourself together.' He supported her rather roughly to the chaise where she collapsed in a limp huddle. 'You're going to have to make a choice. Do you want me as I am? Or are you always going to be bound to Walter?'

She looked up at him helplessly.

'Go to bed and sleep on it,' he said. 'I will talk to you in the morning.'

It was hopeless in the morning. They had both barely slept, and each carried the triple burden of fatigue, pride, and misery. All she could say was that she must go away. All he said was that she must do as she wished.

She knew where ladies went in England when they were ailing and she said she would go to Bath.

In utter silence he watched her pack. Towards the end he said: 'Lizzy?'

She made no reply. She had taken another dose of laudanum which by now deadened her responses and gave her the nervous,

256

narrow resolution to follow through her decision.

Gabriel was almost in tears.

The only words she spoke were to ask him to obtain a cab to take her to the station. He obeyed her request, and carried her luggage downstairs.

Bath was almost a repetition of Nice. Lizzy stayed at first in a well-established hotel, and then moved to a small boarding house. Ruskin acknowledged her brief letters equally briefly, but continued to foot the bills. After a month Gabriel had written to her, and when she did not reply, Emma wrote at his instigation saying she realised that Lizzy had had a lot to put up with, but would she not at least let Gabriel come to see her.

One wet afternoon, after spending a boring morning with a loquacious widow who had taken to her, Lizzy sat down and wrote a long, long letter to Emma setting out her version of the story of her relationship with Gabriel. She never mentioned laudanum.

The result of this letter was that Emma sprang wholly to her defence, and the two women wrote regularly to one another bemoaning Lizzy's state and endeavouring to work out a plan of campaign that would salvage something for her future. She herself was not sure that she ever wanted even to see Gabriel again, but Emma kept assuring her that their marriage would be the only rightful conclusion.

The correspondence dragged on for a long time. Lizzy's existence in Bath became one of complete routine. She was liked by a circle of elderly ladies for her apparent combination of modesty and commonsense, and most of her mornings and afternoons were taken up in simple social gatherings and limited outings. Her evenings she spent on her own, usually under the influence of laudanum. She controlled the doses and read romantic novels. In this semi-limbo, where permanent restriction and disappointment were the furniture of everybody's lives, she could almost feel herself becoming inflexible and circumscribed by habit.

In the end Bruno intervened. He wrote to her saying that since Gabriel was contrite and unhappy surely she could consent to see him, and the tone of his honest, worried words, bringing an image of him so clearly to her mind, made her experience some small feeling of liability towards Gabriel. She replied that Bruno might tell him she would see him.

By the time their meeting took place, it was almost exactly a year since she had returned from Nice. As she looked out of the window of the cramped front room of the boarding-house waiting for Gabriel to arrive and watching the cold February rain, she saw the year as a bead off a broken necklace that has rolled away and been lost completely. She had even forgotten that three days ago it had been the third anniversary of Walter's death.

When Gabriel came in, uncertain, damp and chilled, she felt the polite little room would burst at its seams. Suddenly the whole of convalescent Bath became remote and irrelevant, and she found herself running into his embrace.

He had come prepared with a plan, and her welcome made it easier to put forward; but he did not allow it to dissolve his intention to reach a definite agreement.

If she would consent to return to London, he had found a room near Chatham Place where he thought she would be comfortable. Bruno was arranging a free Pre-Raphaelite exhibition in two weeks' time in which he wanted to include several of Lizzy's old drawings. He himself was going to show eight paintings — the first time he had shown in public for several years. There was already much interest in the exhibition and he was sure it would lead to sales and commissions. Then, if Lizzy felt able, they would be in a secure enough position to announce their official engagement, which could be followed very shortly by marriage.

She was completely taken aback. The whole proposal, which she had so often longed for in the past, now sounded so uncharacteristic.

'There's one final thing,' he said. 'Well — two. You seem to have had your say to Emma about Annie Miller. I merely want to state that I have not seen her since you came to Bath, and other than inadvertently will not do so in the future. But I also seek a promise from you. And it is not something I have mentioned to the Browns since I gather you have not written of it. I again ask you to promise not to take laudanum regularly. Then perhaps, with these mutual promises Lizzy, we can patch together our lives. What do you say?'

She thought of her bottles upstairs, and of the pharmacist's shop round the corner with which she was now so familiar. They seemed lifeless props compared to what Gabriel was offering her. She even liked the idea of her pictures being on show, and the thought of another game of whist or day's outing to Weston-super-Mare stifled her. She felt strong.

258

'Yes, Gabriel.'

He took her in his arms again and kissed her for a long time. 'There, Guggums. We will both try to be good.'

When she had been back in London for a few days, installed in a pleasant room in the Strand, Lizzy had the feeling that, rather than the plan actually being performed, they were rehearsing for its fulfilment at some unknown future date. After all that had happened there was something unreal about Gabriel's air of purpose as they prepared their work together for the exhibition, and about the controlled, celebratory dinner they shared with the Browns.

The calm between them was almost disrupted when Gabriel greeted her one morning with the news that Jones and Morris were moving to London. 'They're dying to meet you, Lizzy. And you'll never guess where they've found a studio!'

'Where? Oh — I know, Newman Street.' She remembered the dirty little room and the thud of dancers downstairs.

'No — Red Lion Square. Exactly the same rooms as Walter and I shared. And we're invited to tea any day we choose.'

'Oh . . .' She faltered, unable to find words. She couldn't go. Not to those rooms.

'They're making them so nice. Top has the most elaborate schemes for making and decorating furniture — I'm going to help him. Do you want to choose a day to go?'

'Do you think we can wait until after the exhibition? Only . . . only . . .' Her voice faded away.

His enthusiasm dissolved and he looked at her hard. She knew he realised what had happened, and she felt once again as though they were rehearsing, concealing their real feelings and mouthing innocuous words. 'Oh . . . all right, Lizzy. If you prefer.' He strode to the window, and for a long time gazed down at the street in silence.

They both went to help Bruno with the hanging of the exhibition, which was held in two large rooms in a house in Fitzroy Square. Bruno was particularly careful to see that her drawings — which included her illustration to *We Are Seven* and an old head study of Gabriel — were displayed to their best advantage.

'I'm so glad you've agreed to participate Lizzy. Ever since I saw that self-portrait of yours I've been really curious to know how your work may develop.'

259

'You're very kind. I've done so little beside the rest of you.'

'Quantity isn't everything. Well — good heavens — Gabriel's proved that. And now perhaps you'll both produce more, eh?'

'I hope so.' And she did — she liked to please Bruno.

'Will you come to the next room and see my little display? Before the critics cloud your eye with savageries.'

'I'd love to. And I shan't let them.'

They went through the archway and stood in front of *The Last of England,* the oval emigration painting of which Lizzy had heard a great deal. Bruno had been inspired to do it when Woolner had gone to Australia, and Lizzy stared hard at the sombre young couple who faced into the wind as they sailed away from England for ever surrounded by provisions and belongings. Emma had posed as the wife, and the tiny fist of Nolly peeped out from under her grey woollen cloak.

'It's sad Bruno. And ever so real. It's like looking at two whole life stories.'

'Ruskin won't like it.'

'Well, can you imagine Mr Ruskin coping with the idea of travelling on deck with a baby and enough home-grown vegetables to last him the journey?'

They both laughed — Bruno uproariously, then as he quietened they heard Gabriel's voice followed by Hunt's in the next room.

'Mad, old chap! How splendid to see you. Those Egyptian paintings of yours are quite brilliant. But come and look at this little corner will you? Lizzy's drawings. She and Bruno have just finished hanging them. And I think they're stunning. Don't you agree?'

Lizzy and Bruno waited, embarrassed, until Hunt replied: 'Why, yes. You know if you hadn't told me, I would have taken them for happy designs by Walter Deverell.'

'Deverell!' Gabriel sounded both shocked and put out. 'They're a thousand times better than anything he ever did.'

Lizzy clenched her fingers into her palms. 'They're not,' she muttered. 'They're not.'

Bruno put his arm lightly across her shoulders. 'Don't take on, my dear, please. You know he says it because he loves you.'

She remembered to try, remembered the rehearsal, and showed no immediate signs of 'taking on', and neither did Gabriel.

The day after the exhibition closed, Gabriel and Lizzy helped Bruno with the dismantling of the paintings, and then they all went to a coffee-house. Lizzy had discovered that when there was a third party present, conversation seemed easier; alone with Gabriel she could not cast off a feeling of awkwardness. Once, when he had tried to broach the matter of announcing their engagement, she had deflected him. She did not know why, but something seemed to make her shrink from publicizing their relationship.

There had been a paragraph about her work in the *Saturday Review*. 'More than some people got,' teased Bruno. 'You'll be making us jealous!'

Lizzy smiled.

'Anyway,' Bruno continued, 'It just proves we're right in encouraging you to do more. Even old Ruskin. Which reminds me, Gabriel, have you thought more about my communal college idea?'

'Mm. I've thought of it a lot. But . . .'

'What are your ideas on it?'

'Well . . .' Gabriel looked warningly across the table, but Bruno was busy pouring sugar into his coffee.

'What is this college?' Lizzy enquired, noticing Gabriel's expression.

'Oh,' said Bruno unheedingly, 'hasn't Gabriel mentioned it to you? Well, it occurred to me that we artists live in too much isolation. It's such a trek to get together to talk — and we benefit from exchanging ideas frequently, looking at work-in-progress. So I thought of finding some big, beautiful old building where there would be space for several of us to live and work together. There'd be married quarters, and bachelor studios, and we could all share an occasional meal. What do you say?'

Lizzy paled and glanced urgently at Gabriel, who did not meet her eyes. The scale of the idea, its implications, terrified her. Was Gabriel really thinking that when, if, they married, she was going to share her home with countless others? 'Who . . . who else?' she asked.

'Well Gabriel said he'd have a word with his two new Oxford friends, Ned and William. They seem excellent young fellows. And of course I hoped . . . well . . . if matters . . . that is that yourself and Gabriel . . . Emma likes the idea. She thinks it would benefit the children, and she wouldn't get so lonely when I'm out working. And we thought we should ask Hunt — for old times' sake.'

'Hunt!' Lizzy's shriek startled all the customers in the coffee-house, and there was a rattling of cups and many heads swivelled to stare.

'Ssh, Lizzy. Not now. We'll talk —' Gabriel desperately tried to silence her.

'Hunt!' She was quieter, but only because her anger had grown.

'That means you thought *I* would live in the same building as that . . . that Miller woman.'

Bruno was flabbergasted by her rage. 'Lizzy . . . we never mentioned Annie . . . never really thought . . .'

Turning to Gabriel she hissed, 'You're always at such pains to explain to me that she's Hunt's fiancée. I *presume* that means they will marry. And you think I would live with someone who's . . . who's . . .' She jerked back her chair noisily against the stone floor and ran from the room.

Bruno, following a signal from Gabriel, tore after her while Gabriel settled the bill. He easily caught her up and tried to calm her. But by now she was crying and as soon as Gabriel appeared became even more distraught.

In desperation Bruno said, 'Shall I take you home to Emma? Would you like to talk to Emma?'

'Yes,' she sobbed. 'Yes.'

Patiently he hailed a cab which he could not afford, and they left Gabriel stranded on the pavement looking irresolute and bitter.

The first thing Lizzy begged from Emma was some laudanum for her head, and while Bruno searched at the back of the high shelf in their larder where their few medicines were kept, Emma made up the settee in the parlour into a bed. Then, when Lizzy had taken a dose, she sat down beside her to try to sort matters out.

She attempted to persuade Lizzy that the college idea was really more a figment of Bruno's imagination than anything else, and that no one had seriously looked at it from the point of view of expecting her to live cheek-by-jowl with Annie Miller. Lizzy then expostulated that she would never live near Hunt either, and Emma sympathised, saying that Bruno had told her of the tactless remark which they had overhead him make at the exhibition.

'Why do you think he said that?' Lizzy asked plaintively.

'Well, I admit it crossed my mind that he was trying to get his own back.'

'Own back?'

'Well, I don't suppose Annie will have admitted she got rather too friendly with Gabriel. But he must have heard some of the general rumours.'

'Rumours?'

'About them being seen dancing at Cremorne for nights on end. That sort of thing.'

'*Dancing at Cremorne?*'

'Yes. Surely you knew? I thought that was what you were referring to in your letters. I thought you'd heard the same rumours. Well — they weren't really rumours. Mr Allingham told Bruno he'd seen them several times.'

At this Lizzy started to wail. The thought of Gabriel being seen by their friends at the rather vulgar Cremorne Gardens in the company of the even more vulgar Annie Miller upset her more than anything that had happened so far. Especially as he'd always told *her* he did not care for dancing.

Emma was at her wit's end to know how to calm her, and it was only after another large dose of drops that she finally got her to stop sobbing. Then within a few minutes she was dead asleep.

By the afternoon of the next day Emma had realised that Lizzy was almost probably addicted to laudanum. She did not dare say anything to Bruno, who deplored undue reliance on medicines, but persuaded him to send for Gabriel. The latter came the following morning, and while in no way admitting to Emma that her assumption was true, he did agree that when distressed Lizzy tended to act irrationally.

At first Lizzy refused to see him, shouting out abuse and saying she would climb out of the window and run away if he so much as came into the room. Bruno suggested he and Gabriel take the children for a walk on the Heath, and they stomped gloomily behind Nolly's pushcart, desultorily trying to find some solution. Bruno favoured immediate marriage and he lent Gabriel ten pounds in case it became possible to implement the suggestion. But when later in the day Lizzy at last agreed to see him, and he tentatively suggested a quiet marriage and a long honeymoon abroad, she again became hysterical. Gabriel did not think to return the ten pounds before he went back to Blackfriars.

When, after five days, Lizzy was still undecided what to do, Bruno said very firmly that she must go home to her family. Emma was in the early stages of her third pregnancy, and could not cope with Lizzy as well as her own sickness and the two children.

Lizzy, who was a little in awe of Bruno, agreed, but once inside a cab she instructed the driver to take her to the Strand. Before going to her room she called in at a pharmacist and bought new supplies of all her various medicines.

That night she was racked by bad dreams — both waking and sleeping. Her whole room became the nightmare of her childhood, pulsating and claustrophobic, and gaudily disfigured by a bright red stain. In the morning she knew she could not bear another night alone, and she tentatively made ready to pay a visit to Star Place. She had not been there since just before her journey to France when she and Gabriel had called on Lyddy.

Although she barely realised it, it was a Sunday, so when the cab took her right to the front door of Number Eight there were plenty of people at home to stare — both from the street and from behind their curtains. Self-consciously she chose not to walk round to the back, but went and lifted the knocker.

Harry came to answer, and for a second neither recognised the other — both finding the face in front of them too old and ill-looking to be that of their once-favourite brother and sister.

'Harry.' Lizzy spoke first. 'How tall you are. Is Lyddy home?'

'No. Only mother.'

'Oh . . .' She had not bargained on Lyddy not being there.

'Who is it Harry? Who is it?' Mrs Siddall's voice had not lost its edge.

'It's Lizzy, Mam.'

'Lizzy? Lizzy who?' Mrs Siddall came and peered over Harry's sloping shoulder. 'Good heavens! Lizzy. Half dead to the world by the look of it. We thought you must have come to grief in France.'

'No, mother. May I come in?'

'Yes, yes. Come along. There's just Harry and me in the kitchen. Lyddy and Bill are staying with his folks for a few days.'

'Where is James?'

'James? Why he's been working down Canterbury way for the past twelve months.'

Whereas the last few times Lizzy had visited Star Place she had detected a rise in the family fortunes, this time she sensed that things were not so good. There were only the most simple provisions in the house, and no proper store of candles or fuel.

'And what brings you home? Ill-health, I suppose,' said her mother when the three of them were sitting round the kitchen table.

Lizzy improvised. She said that she and Gabriel would have married long since if it had not been for her health, and that after France she had tried taking a cure in Bath. Now she was unsure what to do.

'And what's supposed to be wrong with you? Still taking too many of those drops, I presume. The idle woman's downfall. Are you frightened of marriage, is that it?'

To her surprise, Lizzy drew some comfort from her mother's abrasiveness, for it prevented there being any possibility that she would have to try to tell her the truth about everything.

'Tump's not frightened of marriage,' Harry said suddenly.

Mrs Siddall laughed. 'That's true enough. Gone and married a schoolmaster she has. Would you believe it?'

'*Tump?*'

'Yes, last year. In Sheffield.'

'And . . . Annie, is she still in Sheffield?'

'Oh, yes. She doesn't write. But Tump gives us the news. Two children she's got now. Reading between the lines, they're pressed to make ends meet. But Madam Clara's fallen on her feet.'

'What is her husband's name?'

'Barratt. Nicholas Barratt. Yes . . . she'll be twenty-one this autumn.'

Lizzy remembered the last time she had seen Tump, and how self-reliant she had seemed.

'You'd do worse than go and stay with her for a stretch,' said Mrs Siddall suddenly. 'She said any of the family would be welcome. And you've not been to Sheffield. A dose of northern air might stiffen you up a bit.'

Lizzy did not reply immediately. The more she thought about the possibility, the more it seemed like the only escape route open to her.

'Do you think I might do that?' she said at last.

'You've only to write and ask,' said her mother. 'And you can have Lyddy and Bill's room here for a few days in the meantime. If you want.'

'Thank you, mother.'

The next morning she wrote a short letter to Tump — remembering to address her as Clara — and in the afternoon she fetched some of her things from the Strand. Her Paris dresses and many other inessentials she left behind, together with an envelope containing the rent. She did not feel able to face the housekeeper and explain she was leaving and no longer wanted her dresses — she did not feel up to explaining anything to anybody.

Clara replied by return of post, and on the Friday Lizzy set off for Sheffield. She had not written to either Gabriel or the Browns.

Chapter Eighteen

Lizzy lay on a bed in a small hotel in Matlock waiting for Gabriel. November mist shrouded the surrounding Derbyshire hills, and a steady rain filled the gutters of the steep cobbled streets. There was a bright fire in the grate, and her bottles and flask were on the bedside table. She felt momentarily very comfortable: untrammelled, and floating above all circumstance. Now she had written to Gabriel, all she had to do was wait.

The months she spent with Clara had ended badly. Nicholas Barratt's positive but undeveloped interest in art had gradually blossomed and had drawn them both into long conversations from which Clara felt excluded. When he had announced he would like to spend Sunday afternoons sketching out in the country under Lizzy's tuition, it had been more than Clara could bear. There had been an argument, and the subsequent hostile atmosphere had driven Lizzy back to the laudanum bottle. Her wretchedness was magnified by the fact that she had felt she was beginning to come to terms with her life. She had at last been able to think quite calmly about the Annie Miller episode, and had made a sustained effort to fulfil her obligation to Ruskin by improving her work.

Before there was time for Lizzy to recover her confidence and try to mend matters, Clara had discovered that she was taking laudanum. With her usual forthrightness and acuteness, she also soon discovered that laudanum had been at the bottom of most of Lizzy's recent ills. She did not in any way attempt to chastize her, but she did make it clear that she was not the person to try to help or look after her.

'Drugs and strong drink both make me impatient, Lizzy—there are too many people without enough food or clothing. And in any case I'm expecting a child.'

Lizzy offered to go back to London immediately, but Clara suggested she try Matlock. The hot springs there were supposed to be a cure for all ills, and if she put herself under a good doctor surely she could break the laudanum habit for ever and then return to Gabriel? Lizzy agreed — it seemed the easiest thing to do since Matlock was only twenty miles away.

Two important matters she had never told Clara were that when she packed up a few of her drawings each month she addressed them to Ruskin and not to Gabriel, and that it was from the former rather than the latter that her regular allowance came. During her last month in Sheffield she had made no drawings, and the day before she left she wrote to John Ruskin saying she was unable to fulfil her obligation to him any longer and therefore would not continue to accept the pension. A little ungraciously she thanked him for all his help in the past. She also sent a note to Gabriel saying that she was moving to Matlock, but not mentioning Ruskin. When she had been in a hotel for a month she ran out of money, and then she wrote to Gabriel saying that she was ill and needed him. She had not bothered to put herself under a doctor, nor had she been near the hot springs. The letter took a little time to reach him for it was addressed to Chatham Place while he was at Oxford painting murals in the new Union debating hall; but as soon as he received it he came.

He seemed in a very strange mood: elated by the mural scheme, which he was sharing with Jones and Morris and any other kindred spirit who cared to join in, yet showing no animosity at being called away. He had already heard from Ruskin that Lizzy had declined her pension, but although short of money himself he did not reprimand her and set about paying the hotel bill. While he indicated no particular inclination to kiss or embrace her, he seemed perfectly happy to sit closely by her in the little bay window in the hall, gazing over the dour wet landscape and talking, talking. Lizzy, as a rule lightly dosed with laudanum, was happy too. Sometimes Gabriel would spend an hour or two sketching — planning more Arthurian pictures for the Oxford murals, he told Lizzy. She glanced at one of them: a strikingly dark and dramatic Guinivere.

One day, near to Christmas, the mists disappeared and it was brilliantly sunny, with views that seemed to extend to infinity. They went out walking, and Gabriel did not take a hat with the result that the following day he had severe neuralgia.

'I'll have some of your drops, Lizzy. I might as well, since you seem to take them most days.'

She had not realised that he knew, but she did not really care.

The next day he asked for some more and then, since the wind had dropped, they wrapped up well and walked to a wooden seat placed in a sheltered recess with a wide view of the valley.

'We're not doing badly are we, Lizzy? Fresh air and exercise.'

'No . . .'

'You shouldn't take too many of those drops. Just because you get upset. But they make one feel very fine.'

She waited.

'Lizzy?'

'Yes.'

'I'm in love.'

In her mind she saw the sketch of the dark and regal Guinivere.

'But it's all right. Top's going to marry her.'

'Poor Gabriel,' she said, looking down at the patterns made by the stone walls and huddled farms. 'But I expect you'll get over it.'

'Do you think so? You may be right.'

That evening they took some more laudanum together and he said he would never leave her. Then he asked, 'Why weren't you angry this afternoon?'

'Because she is chaste.'

'How can you know?'

'You were drawing her the other day. I took a good look at her.'

'Dear Lizzy. Do you know everything about me?'

'What is her name?'

'Jane. Janey Burden. Top worships her.'

'And whom does she worship?'

He shook his head. 'I don't know.'

They stayed in Matlock until Gabriel could no longer afford to pay the hotel bills. The Oxford murals had been abandoned and it was early spring when he took Lizzy back to Chatham Place. One of their first callers was Bruno, desperate for the repayment of the ten pounds he had loaned Gabriel for the marriage that never took place. His and Emma's third child, Arthur, who had been born prematurely, had just died and he had not enough money to pay for the funeral. Gabriel, half asleep, did not have ten pounds. When Lizzy saw the look of despair on Bruno's face as he turned and went away, she wept.

'It won't do any good, Lizzy,' said Gabriel. 'Tears.'

'If I could weep golden sovereigns I would,' she said. 'So that the

269

baby might have a memorial of silver and amethyst.'

'Why do you say such things?'

'It was what I felt as I was speaking.'

'If only Ruskin wasn't abroad. We could have got something from him.'

'We can't rely on him for ever.'

'You know he was very upset when you gave up your allowance. He said he wished you could just have gone on accepting it as you would a glass of water when thirsty.'

'It's easy to equate money with water when you have plenty of it,' she said sharply.

One evening Gabriel came home from taking his class at the Working Men's College and said: 'Do you remember George Boyce?'

'Yes.' She recollected a friendly young painter anxious to please, who had once called round with William Allingham.

'He's commissioned me to do a portrait.'

'Of whom?'

'A lady he likes.'

'Why doesn't he do it himself?'

'Because he's not good enough.'

'Do you want to do it?'

'We need the money.'

She knew from the expression on his face and the spring in his step that he was excited by the lady.

'Will she sit here?'

'No. I'll go to her house in Battersea.'

'What's her name?'

'Fanny Cornforth.'

He started the portrait the following day, and kept up the sittings more assiduously than anything he had done since they returned to London.

Sometimes when he came back from Battersea he would bring George Boyce with him, and occasionally Lizzy emerged from the bedroom to sit with them, for Boyce did not impinge on her mood.

It was not long before she guessed that if there was a contest for Fanny Cornforth's affections, Gabriel probably had the upper hand. She also realised that his attachment was quite different from the emotions he had expressed for Jane Burden. When he had finished the portrait and brought back from Battersea some of his

270

preliminary sketches, she saw just how different. If Annie Miller was sensual, then Fanny Cornforth was downright voluptuous. Yet as she looked at the drawings, Lizzy found herself unable to feel real rage. The woman had such a warm, fair face — motherly as well as beautiful. But the fluency and tenderness of Gabriel's pencil lines gradually spurred her to at least a shadow of her old jealousy and she tore up one of the drawings.

'I'm glad you left the other two,' said Gabriel in the morning, 'for I'll get George to buy them.'

'Don't you care about my feelings at all?'

'I care about them more than anything in the world. But I don't know how to make you happy.'

'Do you love Fanny Cornforth now, instead of Jane?'

'Lizzy — what's the use? I can't explain. I've tried to love you in so many ways.'

'You never come to my bedroom now.'

'You didn't used to want me to.'

'I get lonely.'

That night he came and lay beside her, and started talking about his father: How in Italy he had been a political revolutionary and then had ended his life in exile working out recondite theories about Dante that nobody wanted to read.

'I want to do the opposite, Lizzy. I want to show that the eternal loves and passions of medieval times are as alive today as they were then. I've thought ever since I was a boy that my feelings, *my* feelings, are the richest well I'll ever find.'

'But they don't . . . flower properly. One's feelings.' She was thinking of her early daydreams about princesses and lovers — how they had always ended in perfection, like a rose at dawn.

'You mean you've been disappointed.'

She thought he was referring to Walter. 'I was thinking back to my childhood. My dreams then.'

'You once told me you had nightmares then too.'

'Yes. I still do.'

'The same nightmares?'

'Yes.'

He turned and lightly held her. She could feel her own thinness against his arms. She was like a hollow ivory carving.

'Tell me about them.'

'There was a murderer in our neighbourhood. He carried me

271

home through the snow when I was little. He had a heavy carpet bag in the other hand with a stain on it. Much later I realised the stain was blood and he probably had part of the body of the woman he had murdered in his bag. He touched my cheek when he put me down and left a bloodstain on it.'

'Lizzy! And you dream of him?'

'No, of the stain on the bag. It was shaped like a fiddle. My father played the fiddle. In the nightmare I am always shut in a room. With a great pulsating red stain.' She started to shiver, and he held her more tightly. 'Gabriel?'

'Yes darling.'

'He had murdered the woman because he didn't want to marry her. And . . .'

'Yes?'

'I realised . . . when I so wanted you to marry me . . . what it meant . . . I mean, I could picture that . . . someone might murder . . .'

Her words faded away.

Gabriel jerked his arm away and leapt to his feet. Shouting, he accused, 'You mean you thought *I* was capable of *murder?* Of murdering *you?*'

She was terrified. 'No, no! Just that I could . . . begin to see . . . how dreadful situations arise.'

'Lizzy, how can you even think these things! I adored you. I adored you. And you only looked at Walter. Then you came to me. But you didn't seem to want me. You never . . . adored me.'

'I loved you Gabriel. I love you.'

'But not enough . . . Oh, Lizzy.'

She began to cry.

'Yes . . . weep. Weep. And take your medicine. I cannot stop you. I might as well join you. Or go out. It doesn't really matter which.'

The months that followed this exchange were miserable for both of them. Lizzy sensed that she had done something dreadful to Gabriel, but she did not fully understand what it was. Once or twice she tried to work out a speech which explained, or at least described, her irrational fears stemming from Mr Greenacre, but she could not piece it all together, and could never have brought herself actually to deliver the speech. She took to writing poetry again, and made no attempt to question Gabriel about his activities outside Chatham Place. They were very short of money, and she knew that on at least two occasions his brother had come to their

272

rescue. She vaguely presumed, without really formulating it as a concept, that the reason hardly any friends visited the studio and no mention was ever made of her meeting his family again, was that he now deemed her unreliable. He did not try to stop her taking laudanum, though occasionally censured the size of the dose. If he felt ill or depressed he would sometimes take it too.

She still had not met Jones or Morris, although Gabriel spent quite a lot of time with them, and when the date of Morris's marriage to Jane Burden was announced, they were both invited to attend.

'Perhaps we should go, Lizzy. Find out how it's done, and then if you could recover a little, we could follow suit.'

She just stared at him, and he did not go to the wedding.

Later in the year he told her about the house Topsy was building for his bride. 'It's going to be called Red House — all warm brick, and hand-made furniture. I've promised to go down and paint some panels for him. Would you like to come? It's in the country, with a big orchard.'

'No thank you.' She could not imagine how people would view her now; could not envisage staying with a young married couple rich enough to build and furnish their own house just as they wanted it.

Then, in the spring of the year that she was twenty-eight, Annie Miller again changed her life.

George Boyce came to Chatham Place one afternoon saying it was urgent that he speak to Gabriel privately. They went into the little sitting room, which Gabriel now used as a bedroom, and Lizzy returned to her chair in the studio. It was unlike George to exclude her, and she presumed it must be something to do with Fanny. She knew that Gabriel still saw her from time to time — in order, she supposed, to make love to her.

They were a long time, and after a while she took up the poem she had been writing, completing the final verse:

> A silence falls upon my heart,
> And hushes all its pain.
> I stretch my hands in the long grass,
> And fall to sleep again,
> There to lie empty of all love,
> Like beaten corn of grain.

Then, in her best script, as would have pleased her mother, she wrote 'E.E. Siddall' at the bottom right-hand corner.

She heard Gabriel show George out, and a few minutes later he came into the studio. After glancing at her he went to the window and did not speak.

'What is it?' she asked.

He sighed, and then drew himself up and, still looking out of the window, said, 'Lizzy. Will you please listen very carefully?'

He waited for her reply.

'Yes. Yes, I will.'

'Then I will tell you what it is about. But only on one condition.'

'Yes?'

'Now pay close attention. I will tell you, as long as first you agree to marry me as soon as possible.' He spoke quietly and deliberately.

Fanny Cornforth's expecting his child, she thought.

He turned now and stepped towards her, looking down with troubled, dark-ringed eyes. 'Well?'

'I agree.' She heard herself speaking the words, abandoning them in the air with no knowledge of their real meaning or consequence.

He knelt before her and lifted her left hand, kissing its third finger.

Then he got up and brought a chair so that he could sit beside her.

'George came to see me about Annie,' he said, 'Annie Miller.'

Instantly she stiffened, taken off her guard. Then she remembered her words, 'I agree', which could never now be retrieved, and surrendered her reactions.

'She had gone to him seeking work. Hunt has finally broken off his engagement to her.' He seemed to be searching for words, then blurted out — 'He tried to send her to Australia!'

'*Australia?*'

'Yes. A woman can get a passage there for just a few shillings. He wanted to give her the fares for herself and a companion to go. . . . Almost as though they were criminals.'

'But why?'

'He doesn't want her any more, and he's afraid she'll be a nuisance. He's become very straitlaced.'

Lizzy tried to digest this information. 'And you want us to be married?'

'Yes, Lizzy.'

274

'Trying to show Hunt that you can do the right thing?' There was asperity in her voice.

'His behaviour has shocked me, I'll admit.'

'How did he react when he heard the tales about you and Annie at Cremorne Gardens?'

He turned away. 'That was four years ago.'

'I suppose it was.'

Her writing book slipped from her lap to the floor and he came to pick it up as though glad of a diversion. He glanced at the open page before handing it to her.

'Why have you gone back to putting two 'l's' on Siddal?'

'Did Annie ever learn to write and speak properly, like Hunt wanted her to?'

'No. But what's that got to do with it?'

'You wanted me to change my name so I'd be more acceptable to your family. But it doesn't make any difference how my name is spelt. I don't become different. Clara laughed when she saw I signed my drawings with one 'l'. I'd rather keep the same name as the rest of my family.'

'All right, Lizzy.'

They both agreed they did not want a formal wedding, and Gabriel suggested they slip away to Hastings to marry there, informing their friends and families by letter.

'You liked Hastings, didn't you Lizzy?'

'Yes,' she said unemphatically.

'Than shall we go to Paris for our honeymoon?'

She remembered their walk in the Bois de Boulogne, and the Nice train sliding away from the two men on the platform. Then she lifted her chin, remembering the zestful scent in the Paris air. 'Yes,' she said more enthusiastically.

They spent a month in Hastings, and she continued to take doses of laudanum as she sewed and mended in preparation for Paris, but forgot to take the medicine that prevented constipation. A week before they were due to leave, therefore, she was crippled with pains. Gabriel was just beginning to write the letters announcing their marriage and he told his mother, 'Like all the important things I ever meant to do — to fulfil duty or to secure happiness — this one has been deferred almost beyond possibility.' He sat for hours by Lizzy's bedside in the boarding house, and she had difficulty in seeing their landlady alone in order to ask her to obtain the necessary medicine — for Gabriel was becoming increasingly impatient with all her various bottles, claiming that none of them did her any good. The medicine was smuggled in, and began to take effect on the day before their wedding so that when she and Gabriel arrived at St Clement's Church on the morning of May 23rd, she was able to be cordial to the caretaker and his wife who were to act as witnesses, and to stand erect before the officiating clergyman.

Gabriel's usually sonorous voice was subdued as he said his vows, and for once Lizzy spoke the more clearly, savouring particularly the brevity and finality of the phrase 'Till death us do part'.

As soon as they arrived back at the boarding house, Gabriel wrote to tell his mother that the wedding had taken place. Then they set off for Folkestone.

Chapter Nineteen

The first four days of their honeymoon were spent in a comfortable hotel. The weather was grey and chilly, and Lizzy had difficulty in detecting the singular sweet Parisian smell she remembered. They were shy together in their large room, and she was very tired. Gabriel ordered her favourite foods to be sent up, and encouraged her to rest. He read to her from his translations of Italian love poetry, and brought back from his walks little presents of flowers and sugared fruits. During the evening of the third day he made love to her, and later he sketched her as she lay on the pillows in the lamplight. She looked at the drawing and knew she would never fill the same role in his life as Fanny Cornforth.

Then on the fourth day he made an admission. Just before they had left London he had learned that Ned Jones was to marry his fiancée, Georgiana, early in June, and he had persuaded them to come to Paris for their honeymoon so that, provided Lizzy was well enough, they could all spend some time together.

'I didn't tell you before, in case you were ill, my darling. But you seem so much recovered, and I would never have suggested it if Georgie and Ned were not both the sweetest and gentlest of young people.'

'When are they coming?'

'In a week's time.'

'We cannot afford to stay here for much longer.'

'Would you agree to move to somewhere cheaper — and wait for them?'

'If you wish.'

They took a bedroom and sitting room in a lodging house, and settled down to wait for the Joneses. Although Lizzy did not object to their coming, the prospect of sharing time with a much younger newly-married couple made her nervous. Secretly she took larger doses of laudanum. Gabriel guessed what she was doing and tried to divert her attention — he read poetry to her, and made comic

277

drawings, and one day came back from a walk with two dogs which he had bought in a market hoping they would amuse her. They did indeed take up time, the big one bounding around and the little fat one demanding to sit on Lizzy's lap all the time, but they did not prevent her from taking drops, and after a few days Gabriel reluctantly agreed with the landlady's decree that both dogs must go. Lizzy cried when she kissed them goodbye, not knowing what would happen to them.

When he returned from disposing of them he did not report on their fate, and for two days was moodily immersed in a drawing. When she saw it, she had a shock which she realised was perhaps similar to the shock Walter Deverell had experienced when he had seen the earlier unfinished version all those years before. Now Gabriel's double-ganger image of himself and her was completed — on their honeymoon. Her instinctive reaction was to make a drawing herself; it showed a medieval lady with averted head giving to the knight who had slain her lover the conqueror's prize. She called it *The Woeful Victory*.

When they received an apologetic letter from Georgie Jones saying that Ned had been struck down with an infected throat on the day after their marriage and that they could not come to Paris, both Gabriel and Lizzy agreed they would go back to London the following day.

They lay in bed that night talking about what they would do when they returned. Gabriel was adamant that they could not lead their married life from Chatham Place, and suggested they look for a house to rent in Hampstead. That would be near the Browns, and as soon as possible she was to meet the Joneses — and go down to stay at Red House.

'You've never really mentioned Jane Morris since that time at Matlock,' she said.

'I got carried away that year. There was a spirit of Arthurian romance about.'

'You never finished the murals.'

'Well — we weren't being paid for them. As soon as we get back I must drum up some commissions so that you have a really fine home. Willow pattern china, and Dutch tiles, and velvet curtains — all the things you like.'

She wondered where the two dogs were now.

'Lizzy?'

'Yes.'

'May I talk to you very seriously?'

She did not answer, but moved close to him so that he would hold her.

'Lizzy, when we're back . . . I'm going to try to do everything properly. Give you everything you haven't had. But, please . . .'

She knew what was coming.

'Please try to stop taking laudanum. Because you know half the time you're not really here. Will you let me help you? Not go behind my back?'

'I'll try.'

'Good girl.'

He kissed and fondled her; but the mention of the drug and the suggestion of closer future surveillance, made her numb. Though she made no sign to stop him making love, all she could focus on was the necessity that the bottle should be there whenever she needed it.

By October, Lizzy and Gabriel had decided to settle at Chatham Place after all. They had not been able to find suitable permanent lodgings in Hampstead, and the Blackfriars landlord agreed to put a door through from their rooms to the corresponding floor in the adjacent house so that they could have a much larger flat. For the new sitting room Gabriel designed a wallpaper of trees with black leaves and red and yellow fruit surrounded by stars, and he painted the doors and wainscot a vivid green. He found old Dutch tiles for the fireplace, more peacock feathers for a set of heavy Chinese vases, and hung Lizzy's drawings on every wall. The new rooms also included a kitchen, and every time he saw a bric-à-brac shop he went in search of pieces of willow pattern china. It was in one of these shops that he found some very old, fine, green velvet curtains, which he had trimmed with antique tassels.

When he brought Lizzy to the refurbished apartment he said proudly, 'You remember the day I prophesied you would live in rooms furnished with silks and tapestries?'

But she could not remember at all.

He tried to make light of it. 'Oh well, if you had, you might have remarked that the walls are in fact covered with paper not silk, and that the little cushion you made is all we have in tapestry.'

She smiled, and held his arm. She was very pleased with the rooms, but she was also frightened by the way she now so often

279

could not remember things.

When they had first come back from Paris, Gabriel had taken command of her medicines and only issued very occasional doses. But the apparent result had been that for two weeks she had been very sick and had barely been able to keep down any food at all. She had begged him, weeping, to be allowed to take control over her own regimen.

'That damn French doctor!' he exclaimed. 'If it wasn't for him . . .'

'If it wasn't for him I'd probably be dead by now,' she sobbed. 'And besides I never asked to be sent away.'

Impotently, he threw the key to the sideboard where he had locked away her bottles into her lap. Gradually she got back to her old doseages and the violent sickness stopped. Neither of them felt able to share their knowledge of the root of her disorder with a friend. Indeed Lizzy was always at great pains to behave as normally as possible in company — particularly with her new friends the Joneses.

As Gabriel had predicted, she liked both of them. Ned's detached melancholy and frail appearance often suited her own mood, and Georgie treated her like a beloved elder sister: a sister who was both more beautiful and more talented than she herself, yet also in some mysterious way in need of special sympathy. As Ned had fallen under Gabriel's spell, so Georgie — primed by her young husband's tales of the mysterious, sick Beatrice whom few people saw — fell under Lizzy's. And it was Georgie's sweetness and sensibility that made it easy for Lizzy to join weekend parties at Red House and meet Janey Morris with barely a qualm.

They spent their first Christmas as husband and wife at Red House. Lizzy for the most part lingered on the perimeter of the festivities, watching. Janey was expecting a child — her dark, dramatic beauty even more striking in the full black and gold velvet gown which she wore. She, like Georgie, was only nineteen, and to Lizzy they seemed so blessedly accomplished and young. Gabriel, she suddenly realised, was beginning to look old — plump and balding, with a frenzied need to whip up Ned and Topsy and any other male guests into violent, childish games that wrecked the orderliness of rooms. The rooms themselves were unique. William had indulged his medieval yearnings and had created with his friends panels and frescoes of chivalrous tales, and there were huge pieces of oaken furniture and a minstrels' gallery. Lizzy was wary of his brooding silences followed by loud outbursts, and grew to dislike the way Gabriel made Ned gang up with him in order to tease Topsy and provoke these eruptions. Under one of the frescoes William had painted the motto 'If I can'; and when Gabriel, behind his back, painted 'As I can't' under the neighbouring picture, Lizzy shared William's annoyance. She guessed that the ideas and feelings which seemed to jostle uncomfortably behind his massive brow and honest dark eyes were ones she would have approved, but she never found a way of talking to him.

It was listening to Jane chatting to Georgie on the morning of Christmas Eve about how she had felt before her expected baby was confirmed, that made Lizzy realise that she too was carrying a child. She quietly left the room where they were sewing and went out into the garden.

Everywhere was covered in frost, and she had no cloak, but she was glowing with the warmth of her discovery. She wandered round the gnarled old apple trees in the orchard, then into the formal garden which William had built, and finally to the bowling green where the men amused themselves on summer days. Here she knelt on the grass, which had not been cut since the heavy September rains, and looked at the sparkling encrustation on each blade, and in her mind they became a forest of miniature swords uplifted to salute her.

'Oh I am so happy,' she murmured, her breath visible in the cold air. 'At last I have something which is really mine.'

She did not tell Gabriel her news immediately. They returned to Chatham Place and he resumed a religious painting for which, through Ruskin, he had received a commission. One day she came into the hall to find him speaking angrily at the door to a tough-looking young man who was dirty and clearly very drunk.

'Who was that?' she asked, when the man stumbled off down the stairs.

He gave a short laugh. 'That was supposed to be my model. He's meant to be sitting for David. But he will get drunk and then he just falls asleep.'

'Where ever did you find him?'

'I didn't exactly find him.'

'Who did then?'

'He's Fanny's husband. Timothy Hughes.'

281

'I didn't know she was married.'

'She married shortly after we went to Paris.'

'On the rebound?' she said sharply, and when he did not respond she added, 'So you still see her?'

'George Boyce told me about the marriage. And how she badly needed work. So I compromised by offering sittings to Hughes. He's supposed to be a mechanic, but he can never hold down a job.'

'Poor Fanny,' she said lightly.

That evening he remarked that Lizzy had been seeming much brighter of late, and asked if she would care to meet Algernon Swinburne, the youngest and oddest of the group he had gathered around him at Oxford. 'He's very amusing, and he's just taken rooms in town.'

'If you like,' she said, relishing her secret and its power to give her strength.

The boy Gabriel brought home with him the next day amazed her. He was shorter than her, with flaming red hair and bright green eyes and he never seemed to keep still. The way he darted around reminded her vaguely of something.

She made tea, and Swinburne's passionate exclamations over her drawings and the specialness of their home, together with his daringly acrimonious remarks about the stuffy people he encountered in the literary world, suddenly had her in fits of giggles. Gabriel looked on in astonishment. For the first time for years Lizzy actually seemed to be playful.

After Swinburne had gone, kissing her hand and calling her 'My revered Mrs Rossetti', she remembered that she had first seen similar light-footed, graceful movements in a man when Walter came into Mrs Tozer's shop with his mother.

That night in bed she told Gabriel about the child. It seemed as though at first he could not believe it, though she was unsure whether that was in relation to her health or his fitness as a father.

A doctor was called to examine her and he pronounced her reasonably fit though somewhat undernourished.

'You must take plenty of milk and red meat, Mrs Rossetti, and then you should have a fine baby some time in May.'

'May?' she said.

'Yes — you sound surprised.'

'I thought it would not be until about July.'

'No, no. You are already nearly six months gone.'

To Gabriel in the hall the doctor said, 'Now see she does not exert herself too much, and no strong medicines. She does seem rather small for the stage she is at, I hope she wasn't taking any drugs during the early weeks? That, in my opinion, is the most vulnerable time.' He did not seem to notice Gabriel's lack of an answer, and added breezily, 'It will do her the world of good. Every woman is better for bearing a child.'

Gabriel kept a close watch on Lizzy and soon realised that she was not taking laudanum any more. As she grew larger she became very lethargic, but he put that to good advantage and used her more frequently as a model. At night he could feel the faint flutterings of the infant against his body.

Then one night he woke in stark terror with the thought that he had not felt the child move for almost a week. Very tentatively he put his hand on her belly. He kept it there for an hour and felt nothing.

He asked her in the morning if the baby was still moving, and she replied, 'Oh yes, though not so much.'

She seemed quite unworried — almost disembodied at times as she drifted around the studio touching objects and gazing dreamily out of the window.

Night after night he awaited a flutter, but he never felt one again.

When Lizzy finally went into labour it lasted for a painful and exhausting thirty-six hours and their little girl baby was born dead. The doctor said she had been dead for at least two weeks.

In the days that followed no one could really talk to her. She seemed to exist in a limbo where no one could reach her. Once, when Ned and Georgie came to see her, she had taken the cradle into the sitting room and was rocking it by the empty grate.

'Hush,' she said, looking at them wildly, 'don't make a noise or you'll wake her.'

In desperation Gabriel went round to Star Place thinking that her mother might be able to comfort her. But Lyddy explained that Mrs Siddall had gone for an indefinite stay in Sheffield, leaving her and Bill to care for Harry as well as their own two children. 'And Harry can't work any more — he set about one of the children at the asylum.' Gabriel gave her some money and asked if she would come and visit Lizzy.

Curiously, the tales of her family's new births and minor misfortunes as relayed by Lyddy a few days later seemed to revive

Lizzy. She developed an objective: she would grow well enough to go over and see Harry at least once a week. He was obviously getting on Lyddy's nerves, as well as being a nuisance in the neighbourhood, and she would try to help him into a better frame of mind. Gabriel, who up till then had never shown the slightest interest in Harry, went out of his way to talk about him, waiting for the time she would be well enough to go out and see him.

But that time never seemed to come. The only outings she was able to manage were to the restaurant where they habitually had their main meal of the day, and occasional meetings with Georgie or Swinburne. Gabriel was worried that contact with Georgie might upset her for she too was now expecting a child, yet when it arrived at the end of the year Lizzy calmly agreed that Janey might pick her up in a carriage so they could both visit the new mother and baby together. It was only when she returned from the visit, her tranquil surface now becoming slightly hysterical, that Gabriel realised that for some time she must have been taking laudanum again.

Lizzy knew that he was trying to divert her. He persuaded her to spend time drawing with him in the studio each morning, and he would often ask Swinburne to come and entertain her in the afternoon. But he could never break his own habit of going out into the night to meet friends once they had returned from dining, and then he had no way of knowing how much medicine she took. For she no longer kept just the one set of bottles on which he could observe the levels. There were spare ones hidden in several private corners. She felt no guilt about this. No one would ever understand the black room that had imprisoned her since the death of her baby. In her dreams it was not even any longer broken by a searing red stain, but just black, black, black.

One morning she started doing a drawing of St Cecilia inspired by Tennyson's poem *The Palace of Art* which Gabriel had been reading aloud to her and Swinburne the day before. She showed the young saint kneeling by her 'gilded organ-pipes, her hair / Wound with white roses', asleep. In the poem it simply said 'An angel look'd at her', but Lizzy drew the Angel of Death leaning over her shoulder and kissing her. Gabriel was enraptured by the idea and asked if he might develop it.

'Please do.'

'Will you pose as Cecilia?'

Dramatically she lifted her head and loosened her hair, and then walked to the old chaise. There she knelt on the floor, splayed her fingers on the seat as though it were a keyboard, and flung back her head. Her hair sprang out, unmarred by illness and time, and Gabriel seized a clean sheet of paper and started to draw.

That night he embraced her closely. 'You are still the supreme inspiration of my work. And you always will be.' She clung to him, kissing, and thinking that at last she had felt alive when she knelt in the studio to pose for him that afternoon.

They could not go again to Red House for Christmas because she had another violent fortnight of sickness. She would not allow Gabriel to call a doctor, screaming like a madwoman each time he suggested it, for she knew perfectly well the cause of her illness. She realised that when she had been so sick in Hampstead, before they moved back to Chatham Place, it had been because she was in the very early stages of pregnancy and not because Gabriel had locked away her bottles. And this sickness was of exactly the same nature.

It passed, and she could not bear to think of what the future held.

Once she almost told Swinburne — Mr Swinburne as she always called him since he always addressed her as Mrs Rossetti. But while she felt it would have been possible to explain to him about the laudanum and elicit his sympathy, she knew that talk of childbirth would have disturbed him extremely. So she kept her counsel.

One evening, to cheer her up, Gabriel suggested they join Swinburne for dinner at a French restaurant in Leicester Square. 'It's the only kind of cooking you really like, Lizzy, and you deserve it after being so ill.'

She took a large dose of laudanum to see her through the outing, and it suddenly made her very sleepy while they were taking the short cab ride to the restaurant.

'Shall I take you back home?' Gabriel asked.

'No,' she said, her eyelids drooping. 'Of course not.'

The drowsiness passed when they got to the restaurant, and suddenly she felt in very high spirits. Swinburne was at his most outrageous and she tried to imitate his waspish brand of humour. She could hear that her remarks were spoken rather loudly and were perhaps sometimes beside the point — but it did not seem to matter.

Then suddenly, when they had barely finished the brandy that Swinburne had ordered, Gabriel declared, 'That's enough,' and bundled her out of the restaurant.

She tried to protest in the cab, but he just said resignedly, 'Please be quiet, Lizzy. You were behaving stupidly.'

He saw her to the bedroom, waited until she started to undress, and then went out.

As she heard the front door close, she became rigid with anger. What right had he to criticize her? Why should she not amuse herself? Swinburne understood. He was the only proper friend. . .

She suddenly had an image of Walter, who despite his similar quickness and delicacy had been all the things that Swinburne was not: gentle, conscientious, manly.

'Oh God,' she cried. 'Oh God.'

She finished undressing and put on a clean nightdress.

Stark, incomplete thoughts tumbled through her mind. It was February — eight years exactly since Walter . . . She had murdered her second baby by now — where could she possibly be incarcerated after the black, black, bloodless room? No wonder Saint Cecilia was kissed by Death, that's what involvement with art . . . The linnet, how could she have buried it in the sand, it wasn't stiff, perhaps it might have revived . . . *In the desert a fountain* . . . Gabriel — no, she could not think of Gabriel — his eyes — either everything or nothing. Harry! She had never gone to see him as promised . . . not even kept her promise to . . .

She went to the bottle on the dressing-table — it was full — no need to search for a secret one — and poured it all into half a glass of water. When she had drunk it she looked around for a piece of paper. Seeing none, and too weak to walk to the studio, she took up her pocket book in search of an old bill or letter. The folded note she drew out with shaking fingers was frayed and faded. She flattened it, and saw the ill-written, pencilled handwriting that began 'Dear Mr Rizzetty' and ended 'Your Phoebe'. Phoebe . . . Annie . . . Fanny. . . She turned the paper over and wrote 'Take care of Harry. My life is not worth' — then her will faltered and she dropped the pencil. She pinned the paper to her nightdress, like the price-ticket on a bonnet. Then she lay down.

Postscript

Elizabeth Siddall became legendary not only as a pre-Raphaelite beauty but also because the distraught Dante Gabriel Rossetti cast the manuscript book of his unpublished poems into her coffin shortly before she was buried, and six-and-a-half years later regretted his impulse and arranged for the grave to be opened and the book recovered. He was not present at the exhumation, and it was reported to him that Lizzy's hair was still bright and golden.